NIGHTS OF THE LIVING DEAD

Also by Jonathan Maberry

NOVELS

Dogs of War

Kill Switch

Predator One

Fall of Night

Code Zero

Extinction Machine

Assassin's Code

King of Plagues

The Dragon Factory

Patient Zero

Joe Ledger: Special Ops

Dead of Night

Fall of Night

The Wolfman

The Nightsiders: The Orphan Army

The Nightsiders: Vault of Shadows

Deadlands: Ghostwalkers

X-Files Origins: Devil's Advocate

Mars One

Bits & Pieces

Fire & Ash

Flesh & Bone

Dust & Decay

Rot & Ruin

Bad Moon Rising

Dead Man's Song

Ghost Road Blues

ANTHOLOGIES (as editor)

V-Wars

V-Wars: Blood and Fire

V-Wars: Night Terrors

V-Wars: Shockwaves

Out of Tune

Out of Tune Vol II

The X-Files: Trust No One

The X-Files: The Truth Is Out There

The X-Files: Secret Agendas

Aliens: Bug Hunt

Baker Street Irregulars
(with Michael Ventrall)

NONFICTION

Wanted Undead or Alive

They Bite

Zombie CSU

The Cryptopedia

Vampire Universe

*Vampire Slayer's Field Guide to the
Undead* (as Shane MacDougall)

Ultimate Jujutsu

Also by George A. Romero

AN ANTHOLOGY EDITED BY

JONATHAN MABERRY
AND GEORGE A. ROMERO

NIGHTS OF THE LIVING DEAD

ST. MARTIN'S GRIFFIN NEW YORK

NIGHTS OF THE LIVING DEAD. Copyright © 2017 by Jonathan Maberry and George A. Romero. All rights reserved. Printed in the United States of America. For information, address St. Martin's Press, 175 Fifth Avenue, New York, N.Y. 10010.

www.stmartins.com

The Library of Congress Cataloging-in-Publication Data is available upon request.

ISBN 978-1-250-11224-8 (trade paperback)
ISBN 978-1-250-11225-5 (e-book)

Our books may be purchased in bulk for promotional, educational, or business use. Please contact your local bookseller or the Macmillan Corporate and Premium Sales Department at 1-800-221-7945, extension 5442, or by e-mail at MacmillanSpecialMarkets@macmillan.com.

First Edition: July 2017

10 9 8 7 6 5 4 3 2 1

This book is dedicated to John Skipp,
who made "zombie literature" possible
with his landmark anthology Book of
the Dead *(co-edited by Craig Spector).*
You'll always be our pal, Skipp.

From Jonathan: And, as always,
for Sara Jo

From George:
For Suzanne Desrocher/Romero

CONTENTS

Contents

ACKNOWLEDGMENTS

Special thanks to George Romero and John A. Russo for writing the script for *Night of the Living Dead* and thereby lighting the fuse to something that would blow up bigger than anyone could have foreseen. Thanks to Michael Homler at St. Martin's Griffin for going to bat for this project. Thanks to our agents, Sara Crowe and David Gersh, for guiding this project through the weird and dangerous landscape that is modern publishing. Thanks to Dana Fredsti for being the world's best evil assistant.

NIGHTS OF THE LIVING DEAD

An Introduction

Fifty years ago I was able to convince several friends of mine that we might be able to make a movie . . . a real, honest-to-god motion picture, feature length.

We were in Pittsburgh, Pennsylvania, at the time. No one in Pittsburgh had ever made a movie before. Born and raised in New York City . . . (Parkchester, the Bronx) . . . I was around during those terrible days of gangs like the "Sharks" and the "Jets." In my neighborhood, the "Golden Guineas" ruled the streets. This was an Italian gang. I was thought of as a "Spic." So my ass was frequently kicked around.

My father was the greatest guy in the world. When I was comin' up, he worked three jobs in order to "see me through." (I was an only child.)

This "greatest guy in the world" considered himself to be a Castilian Spaniard. His family was from La Coruna. His mom and dad went to Cuba during its heyday. Finding success, they sent my father and his brothers to New York City. My father met a Lithuanian woman, Ann Dvorsky, and they married. I grew up speaking neither Spanish nor Lithuanian . . . strictly English . . . American English . . . New York English . . . Bronx English.

The Italians in the neighborhood spoke the same . . . Bronx English . . . but because of my name, Romero, they figured me to be a "Spic." (These days, my name is often thought of as being Italian in origin. When I was comin' up Cesar Romero was a big star. No question. I was a Latino.)

But I was only half Latino, right? And, according to my father, I had no Latino blood in me at all! Because, in those days, "Latino" meant "Puerto Rican." To my embarrassment, my father, a Spaniard, refused to associate himself with those "bastard Puerto Ricans" who were turning New York into a "SEWER!"

So, as you might imagine, "labels" never meant very much to me.

When, years later, John Russo and I collaborated on the screenplay for my first film, we never described our principal character as being a man of color. In our minds, when we were writing the character, he was a "white guy." An African American, Duane Jones, auditioned for the role and was, hands down, the best, within reach of our puny budget, to play it.

We didn't change the script. Duane, himself, adjusted some of the dialogue to make the character seem a bit less "truck-driver gruff" than the way John and I had originally written him, but none of the story's intentions were disturbed. The character of Ben met the same tragic end when, in our minds, he was white as he did when he became black. It was an "accident of birth," so to speak.

* * *

When Russ Streiner and I were driving to New York with the very first print of *Night of the Living Dead* (then called *Night of the Flesheaters*) in the trunk of the car, we heard, somewhere along the Pennsylvania Turnpike, that Martin Luther King had been assassinated. After that . . . and forever after . . . our film has come to be viewed as a racial statement. We never intended "race" to be the film's reason for being. We intended it to revolve around a small group of characters who, when caught in an extraordinary circumstance, find it impossible to reconcile their differences and, as a result, bring about their own demise.

To this day, I believe the film's success to be largely a matter of misinterpretation. We got lucky. And our luck continues.

Zombies have earned a place among the "Famous Monsters of Filmland." They've been around for a long time. *I Walked with a Zombie*, *White Zombie*, even Abbott and Costello met a zombie or two. When John and I were writing *Night*, we never thought of our "monsters" as "zombies." We never called them zombies. In our minds, the dead were mysteriously coming back to life and eating the flesh of the living. We called them "ghouls." Only after much had been written about *Night* being a "seminal" piece of cinema, and after hundreds of articles that referred to our creatures as "zombies," did I concede the definition. Ten years after the release of *Night*, I wrote and directed a sequel, *Dawn of the Dead*, in which I first used the word "zombie."

Today the zombie runs rampant through our popular culture. I am honored that I am considered to be the "godfather" of the zombie genre.

I can't appropriately express how proud I am to be considered among so many greats who came before. I have devoted my life to film, and in that way I can feel justified for the kudos I've received over the years, but the title godfather of the zombie genre seems undeserved. It came to me as a stroke of luck.

Nonetheless, I love the genre and I always have. I feel privileged to be a participant. I feel privileged to have been asked to write this introduction to a collection of stories by authors who came to the genre not by accident but by design. I will forever be grateful for the curious circumstances that brought me to this position . . . one that enables me to present the works of all the worthy fiction writers whose names appear in the following pages.

—GEORGE A. ROMERO

REFLECTIONS OF A WEIRD LITTLE KID IN A CONDEMNED MOVIE HOUSE

An Introduction

I have a great deal of affection for our life-impaired fellow citizens.

Zombies. Ghouls. Walkers. Call 'em what you want. I love them with a great and abiding passion.

Really. Nothing but love.

My association with them goes way back, too. When I was ten years old my buddy Jim and I snuck into the old Midway movie theater on a crisp October night in 1968 to see a brand-new horror movie called *Night of the Living Dead*. It was the premiere of the flick and so far all we'd seen was one movie trailer the week before. It looked like it might be scary. But we'd been disappointed too many times to expect much. We were inner-city kids and we'd seen every Universal, RKO, and Hammer Horror flick on offer. The old stuff and the new. We were tough kids, too, because it was a tough neighborhood. Lots of violence, racial intolerance, domestic abuse, gang fights. Very few cinematic horrors actually offered anything more than escapism. Nothing could *really* scare us.

So we thought.

You see, after seeing all of those vampire flicks we realized that vampires were not much of a threat. Let's face it, vamps were dangerous for a while but in the third act they seemed to always trip on their capes and fall chest-first onto inconvenient pieces of sharpened wood. Or they'd get fried by sunlight after having failed to properly sun-proof their castles. Werewolves were only cranky three days out of the month, and I had four sisters, so I felt I was prepared. As far as mummies went, the ones in the flicks back then tended to shuffle along while wearing highly combustible old bandages, and, hell, we liked to play with matches.

On the whole, Jim and I figured we could handle just about anything that came our way. So we snuck in, bringing bottles of Hires root beer and paper bags of Night 'n Day licorice candy. The Midway used to be a vaudeville theater way back when, but most of it was falling down. The balcony had been officially condemned ten years before and was roped off. Which made it a moral imperative for us to spook our way up there and watch movies.

So there we were, two hardened street kids who had the whole thing figured out. We were ready for absolutely anything that could crawl, flap, fly, slither, or shamble across the silver screen.

Except that we weren't.

No one who saw *Night of the Living Dead* without prior warning was ready. Not in 1968. No sir. Anyone who came to zombie flicks later—or to the genre through comics or TV shows—may appreciate and even love the genre, but unless they saw that movie on original release, they just don't know how it felt.

No vampires. No werewolves. No mummies, creatures, demons, radioactive lizards, giant ants, or hideous sun demons.

Throughout most of the film we didn't know exactly *what* these things were. That they were walking corpses we understood. That they ate people was obvious. But the *why* of it wasn't made clear. Vampire and werewolf films carried with them a front-loaded mythology. Mummies were raised by spells and powered by tana leaves. King Kong lived on an island forgotten by time. Ghosts were dead people in danger of being cited for loitering.

But the living dead did not come with prehistory and no one in the film offered a definitive explanation. Scientists and the military speculated and contradicted each other. There was no Gene Barry or Edmund Gwenn to posit theories. Nor was there a Kenneth Tobey or Peter Cushing to dash heroically to the rescue.

The monsters were mysterious. They were enigmatic (a word I didn't know back then). That was part of what made them so damn scary. No one in the story knew what was going on, and they never found out. I couldn't remember seeing a single other movie where the entire cast of characters was clueless and, as a result, helpless because they had no information with which to form a plan.

Sure, there were rules, and I was on the edge of my seat watching as they figured out how to kill the living dead. But they didn't know how the plague spread, and I started to get

mighty darn nervous about the kid in the cellar with an infected bite. Surely that was going to be a bad thing. Right?

Right.

So, how did that film affect two hardened street kids?

It scared the bejeezus out of both of us. Not a joke and probably an understatement.

Jim chickened out and split right at the point where the
young couple gets fried at the gas pump and becomes a hot
buffet for the dead. He had issues with nightmares and bed-
wetting for years. Not joking.

Me?

I stayed to see the movie twice.

And I snuck in the next day. And the next. Jim thought I
was deranged. He thought I was sick in the head. Maybe I
was. Or am. Same planet, different worlds.

I loved that movie. Still do.

That film became the first midnight movie in Philly. By the
time I was fifteen it was the flick they showed at Halloween.
You'd take a girl and she'd scream and bury her face against
your chest and you'd offer comfort and that's the birds and the
bees, campers. At least in the late sixties and early seventies.

Night of the Living Dead became legendary. To be cool you
had to see the movie, ideally at night, ideally at a drive-in or
one of the old theaters. The Midway continued to play it every
October, and then later it was picked up by some of the movie
houses in Center City Philly. Then at drive-ins.

But none of us really knew what the monsters were.

The word "zombie" was never spoken in that movie, and
George Romero was both surprised and annoyed when it was
later attached to his films and then became the name for a new
genre. He hadn't made a zombie film. He'd made a ghoul film.

He'd made a flick about flesh-eating corpses. Zombies were, to him and most of us back then, magically reanimated slaves in old movies from the thirties and forties set in Haiti. *I Walked with a Zombie, White Zombie,* and similar films were not the same genre as *Night of the Living Dead.* Not then and not now. Sure, some writers, historians, and critics have tried to make the connection with Romero and post-Romero living dead and the zombies of voodoo/vodun, but it's a stretch. The Mummy has more in common with Haitian zombies than Romero's ghouls, but that's not a fight you can win.

As far as the entire fucking world is concerned, Romero invented the zombie genre.

What alarms and saddens me is when I meet people at book signings or conventions and they don't know who Romero is. Not many, thank God, but enough to make *me* want to start biting people. Some of them seem to think zombies started with Max Brooks's *The Zombie Survival Guide* or *World War Z.* Others think that the genre started with Marvel's *Marvel Zombies.* And a lot are of the opinion that it started with Robert Kirkman's *The Walking Dead.*

Here's the thing. I'm friends with Max and Robert and I was one of the writers on *Marvel Zombies Return.* We've all talked about the genre and all of *us* agree that George Romero is the godfather. We wouldn't have the careers we have had it not been for *Night of the Living Dead.* Not in any version of reality. That's not to say that Max and Robert and the other top creators in the genre wouldn't have become successful had they written any other kinds of stories, but we're all clear on the debt we owe to George and his landmark film. And that goes for *Shaun of the Dead, Resident Evil, Pride and Prejudice and Zombies, Z Nation, Left 4 Dead, Dead Set, iZombie,* and . . .

well, I could go on and on, because this genre is massive, and there's nowhere on earth you can go where they don't know what a zombie is.

And we owe big thanks to John Russo, who cowrote the script with George, and then went on to create a new generation of zombies in *Return of the Living Dead*. And to the cast and crew of *Night of the Living Dead*. They're all demigods in the pantheon on the living dead.

The zombie (and, yes, we're going to call it that now) was the scariest monster I'd ever seen. At ten years old they were also the most fascinating I'd encountered in books, comics, movie houses, or late-night TV. Walking home (alone) that first night I was already trying to work out how I would survive in that kind of scenario. Even now, I tend to check any building I visit in terms of defensibility, ingress, and egress. Like that. It's a habit, and I'm reasonably sure I have reliable escape and survival plans worked out.

I wanted more of these monsters. There were some truly appalling knockoff movies in the years after *Night* but nothing that really captured the same feel. Then in 1978 George Romero released *Dawn of the Dead*. Not a sequel per se. More like another chapter in the same story. New locations, new characters, same problem. It was a corker of a flick and hits a lot of Best Of lists for enthusiasts of the genre and of horror films in general.

The Midway Theater—which was really crumbling by then—showed it on a double bill with *Night*. Yowzah.

For the record, my buddy Jim did not accept my invitation to go see it. He told me to go pound sand up my ass. Ah well.

In '85, Romero hit us with a third film, *Day of the Dead*. And by now the genre was in full swing, at least in film.

There wasn't much in the way of zombie literature, though. Some comics here and there, a few short stories, but nothing with real punch and not much of enduring quality. So, enter John Skipp. Writer, filmmaker, outside-the-box thinker, Skipp and his colleague Craig Spector were in discussions with Romero about a possible film adaptation of their vampire novel. But Skipp decided to hit Romero with a crazy idea. How about an anthology of original living dead stories? Romero was skeptical that any such project would fly and famously offered to eat his hat if it was a success. Skipp and Spector reached out to the top guns of the horror biz and asked them if they'd like to do stories set in the world of *Night of the Living Dead*. Turns out a lot of the horror crowd had grown up with that flick, too. So in 1989, Skipp and Spector released *Book of the Dead*, with original stories by Stephen King, Richard Laymon, David J. Schow, Ramsey Campbell, Steve Rasnic Tem, Les Daniels, Douglas E. Winter, Joe R. Lansdale, Robert R. McCammon, and other gunslingers.

And that is where zombie literature was born.

The book was a huge hit, and the writers took the subject matter seriously, each bringing their A-game. I read that book until it fell apart and then bought a new copy. I love that book, and its sequel.

Since then I have read a lot of zombie lit.

I even took a few stabs at it myself. First with a nonfiction exploration of how the real world might react if *Night of the Living Dead* actually happened. My book, *Zombie CSU: The Forensics of the Living Dead* (Citadel Press, 2008), included interviews with hundreds of experts in law enforcement, medicine, science, and other fields, and it was no surprise to me that each and every person I talked to, no matter what their field, had already considered zombies and how they would relate to what they do. That was as true of forensic odontologists (bite mark experts) as it was of EMTs, SWAT team members, the clergy, the press, and . . . well . . . everyone.

Mostly, though, I've concentrated on fiction, and about a fifth of everything I've done deals with zombies, including two of my Joe Ledger thrillers (*Patient Zero* and *Code Zero*), a duology of mainstream horror novels (*Dead of Night* and *Fall of Night*), a steampunk novel based on a tabletop role-playing game (*Ghostwalkers*), comics (*Marvel Zombies Return, Marvel Universe vs. the Punisher, Marvel Universe vs. Wolverine*, and *Marvel Universe vs. The Avengers*), teen postapocalyptic adventures (*Rot & Ruin, Dust & Decay, Flesh & Bone, Fire & Ash*, and *Bits & Pieces*), and a slew of short stories and novellas.

Of those, *Dead of Night* and *Fall of Night* are directly connected to *Night of the Living Dead*. I wrote them for George. They're dedicated to him and written because of my love of his movies and his creative vision.

When I cooked up the idea for this anthology and reached out to him, George was immediately receptive and enthused. Having that first conversation was, I admit, a fanboy moment. Luckily I have a pretty well-controlled telephone voice, because in reality I was doing the Snoopy dance. Think about it; the ten-year-old kid who snuck into the movies to see *Night of the Living Dead* was now an adult and a successful writer of weird fiction, and I was talking to Romero about a project we could do together.

So damn much fun.

During that conversation we talked about *Dead of Night* and George invited me to write a short story for our anthology that officially connects my books to his movie. That story, "Lone

Gunman," appears herein. It was an exceptionally satisfying thing to write.

When we were done with our conversation I sent some e-mails and made some calls to see if some of the writers who were at the top of their game these days—and who had particular connections with zombie literature—wanted to come aboard.

I didn't have to ask anyone twice.

George and I gave them the "rules" of the living dead, but we did not impose too strict a set of guidelines. Dates, for example, are sketchy. *Night* was released in 1968, but George's movie *Diary of the Dead*, released in 2007, technically takes place at the same time. So, let's all assume that this happens tomorrow night. Whenever that is.

We also allowed for a little creative freedom in other areas, but you'll see how that plays out. After all, George messed with his own "rules" in each of his films, suggesting that the nature of this catastrophe was misunderstood, misreported, subject to disinformation from authorities, and very likely undergoing a constant process of change.

The stories in *Nights of the Living Dead* are all original and published here for the first time. They're fun, scary, sad, hilarious, moving, thoughtful, weird, and disturbing. Pretty much what you'd expect for stories set in the world George Romero and John Russo created nearly fifty years ago.

If you're like me—a longtime fan of the genre—or a newbie, or if you followed one of your favorite writers here to see what all the fuss is about, then welcome to the apocalypse.

It's about to get weird in here.

—JONATHAN MABERRY

NIGHTS OF THE LIVING DEAD

Joe R. Lansdale is the author of forty-five novels and more than four hundred short works, screenplays, teleplays, comics, and graphic novels. He has received numerous recognitions for his work, including the Edgar, the Spur, ten Bram Stokers (eleven counting the Lifetime Achievement Award), and others. He lives in Nacogdoches, Texas, with his wife, Karen, and a pit bull named Nicky.

DEAD MAN'S CURVE

by Joe R. Lansdale

I can't build them and I can't fix them. That's what my brother Tommy does, and he does it well. He could make a lawn mower outrun a flathead Ford, but if I'm short in the mechanic department, I sure can drive them. No brag, just fact.

That's what Tommy was trying to explain to Matt.

"She may be a girl," Tommy said, "but she can drive."

"May be a girl?" I said. "What the hell is that?"

"You know what I mean," Tommy said, glancing back at me. I knew what he meant all right.

Matt leaned on the hood of his Pontiac GTO and studied me, his hands thrust into his blue jean pockets. I thought he was taking a bit long for the evaluation. His friend Duane stood nearby. He looked amused.

"She looks all right, and she'll make someone a good wife, but drive?" he said.

"Goddamn you," I said.

"Okay," Matt said, "she might not make someone a good wife either."

"You scared a girl will beat you?" I said.

Duane snickered. Matt didn't say anything, but even in the dying light, I could tell he didn't like that. Duane wasn't quite the asshole Matt was, but my rule of thumb is simple. You're an asshole until you prove otherwise. It's just that right then I took Matt to be the bigger asshole of the two.

Matt studied me again. Now I was doing the leaning, my blue-jeaned butt against the apple-red Dodge Charger. I cocked a foot against the bumper so that my knee was up high, in what I thought was a cool-looking position. I stuck a finger into the pocket of my blue jeans like I might have money in it. And I did.

I gave Matt what I thought was my movie star smile and tried to look as smug as a duck with a june bug. The Charger I was leaning on was Tommy's, being bought and paid for by part-time work. It might as well have been mine. It liked me best. Tommy drove it, shifted gears, it sounded like someone was trying to beat a cat to death with a logging chain, but when I drove it, it purred like a tiger cub and ran like a cheetah with its ass on fire.

"Are all the girls from Texas like this one?" Matt said.

"Well, they got their similarities," Tommy said, "but Janey is a little bit special."

"You Yankees afraid I might blow your asses in the trees?" I said.

Matt turned and looked down the road. The sun was dropping down at the end of it, seeming to melt into the earth like a heated snow cone. It looked like a northern sun to me, not a Texas one. The one in Texas was a whole hell of a lot brighter and warmer. The air here, even on the edge of summer, was nippy.

"All right," Matt said. "She can race me."

"Why thank you, Mister Matt," I said. "You're quite the sport."

"Don't push it," Matt said.

"You don't race me, who else you going to race?" I said. "No one else is here."

"I thought I was going to take money from Tommy, not some cute girl who likes to hang on to a stick shift."

"Oh, you'll never know what I like to hang on to, Matthew," I said.

He gave me a sour look.

"What I got is this," and I reached in my jean pocket and pulled out a wad of bills that would have choked a horse and made its stablemate cough.

"This here, Matthew, is two hundred dollars. You ever ran for two hundred dollars?"

"I've ran for more than twice that much. And I won."

"Then you can sure run for two hundred."

"Hate to take your makeup money, baby."

"Just show your dough," I said.

Matt turned to Duane, said, "Hey, I'm short about a hundred and forty."

3

"Damn," Duane said. "Might as well ask for the whole enchilada."

"Come on, man. Help me out."

Duane removed his billfold from his hip pocket and peeled some bills out of it with all the enthusiasm of a man removing layers of skin from his forehead with a pair of tweezers.

"You lose, you owe me double," Duane said, and gave it to him.

"Man," Matt said, "double?"

"You're the one so all-fired certain," Duane said.

"All right," Matt said. "All right. Let's fire 'em up. See who makes those hard left turns."

"What hard left turns?" Tommy asked.

"Couple of them," Duane said.

"First one, it's not so bad," Matt said, "but then the road gets so narrow another coat of paint and you're rubbing the bark off the trees. Got a ways to go then, but there's another curve, down by the old quarry. Dead Man's Curve. Take that one too quick you'll find yourself airborne, sailing over the rim. Drop don't kill you, you drown."

"It's like a lake," Duane said.

"After that, if you make that curve, because I know I will, we'll end it at the hospital parking lot," Matt said.

"Hospital?" Tommy said.

"What are you, a fucking parrot?" Matt said. "Yeah, the hospital. Just beyond it is the city morgue. We can end it there if you prefer."

"Hospital is fine," Tommy said.

"Bunch of dead old folks in the morgue right now," Duane said, "some kind of convention, they all got sick at the hotel. Bet twenty of them died. Hospital has a bunch of sick ones

4

packed in, some in bad shape, probably buying a ticket for the morgue right now."

"Read about it," I said. "Some kind of mold in the ventilation system, I think."

"Who knows?" Duane said. "All that's certain is that stuff is killing them and packing them in the dead house."

"Let's talk about racing," Matt said. "That's what we're here for."

"Cops?" Tommy said.

"No worries there," Matt said. "Law rarely comes out here."

"What if you're wrong, and they're sitting around the corner?" I said.

"Well, girly, we get a ticket. You up for it, or are you just going to stand there trying to look good?"

"Oh, Matt, honey," I said, "I have no need to try."

As I settled in behind the wheel, and Tommy sat beside me, I had a small faint feeling that I might have mouthed myself out of some money. I had enough confidence to loan some of it out, but I was uncertain about those sharp curves. If I had driven them once before, that would be different. But when we agreed to meet Matt and Duane on the road, we didn't know the route. That was a bit of a mistake, and it was too late now. Matt was revving his engine.

"You sure about this?" Tommy said.

I lied a little. "I was born sure."

"I was there," Tommy said. "I don't know how certain you were then."

"You were at Grandma's house playing with building blocks or some such shit," I said.

"That's true," he said.

He was the older sibling by three years, but most of the time it seemed the other way around.

Matthew revved his engine some more, then pulled his Pontiac to the right side of the road. I was on the left, of course. We hadn't seen a car yet, and we'd been there talking and wheedling about who drove against who for half an hour. I think Matt was afraid of me and wanted Tommy to be his opponent. I had a bit of a reputation.

"You know he's got more under the hood than came with it," Tommy said.

"So does this one," I said.

"But I don't know if he's got more or less."

"You wanted me to race him," I said. "That's how you find out who's got more or less, who's the best driver. Have I ever let you down?"

"Twice."

"Blew a tire once, bad carburetor the time after. Tonight, everything under the hood is as fresh as a baby's first fart."

"You know, half that money in your pocket is mine."

"The die is cast, brother mine. Grab your ass and grit your teeth."

Matt rolled down his window, and Tommy rolled down his.

"What we do," said Matt, "is I count to three, or you can do it, no matter, but count to three, and on three we go for it. And watch those curves. Something happens to you, we just go home and have a hot chocolate like it never happened."

"Quit talking, and start counting," I said.

"One," said Matt, and when he got to three you could hear those motors roar, hear those tires scream for mercy. We both blew out of there like rockets to Mars.

Let me tell you, there's nothing like it. The car leaps, and then it grabs the road, and then it doesn't feel like there is a road, just you and the machine floating on air.

Glanced to my right, saw that Matt and I were neck and neck. He had his teeth clenched, his window still down. That was a mistake. It gathered up air that way, pushed it to the back insides of the car, lay there like a weight. Tommy knew that, and he had rolled up his window to streamline us.

Let me tell you, that first curve came up fast, and we had to make it together, and the road, just as you made the curve, grew narrow, and then there was another problem.

The road was full of people.

There were at least twenty, men and women, and one of the men wasn't wearing any drawers. He had it all flapping out. The rest wore hospital gowns. They stretched across the road in a thin line, seemed drunk the way they staggered, and that was all I could tell in that moment when they suddenly appeared, dipped in moonlight as pale as Communion wafers. Even the one black lady seemed pale.

I fought the wheel and tried to avoid them, but they were straight across the road and there really wasn't anywhere to go. On the left were trees, on the right was Matt's car. I veered as far left as I could, and fortunately, two of them on the left wandered right, and I missed them, but I'm sure I made enough breeze to blow up their gowns. My car threw up gravel, a bit of forest dirt, and then I spun beyond them like a top, turned the wheel in the direction of the skid and righted myself onto the road again. In my rearview mirror I saw Matt hit a couple of them staggering in front of his car. It was a hard, loud smack. They went flying like Mighty Mouse.

Matt was braking, and it made his car scream like a panther.

It slid sideways, almost up to where we sat in the road, and then it stopped, rocking like it had palsy.

Duane rushed out of the car on his side, started running toward the people lying in the road, the ones wandering about.

"You okay?" he said.

Me and Tommy were out of our car too, wandering back to Matt, who opened his door and jumped out, stumbled a little.

"I didn't see them," he said. "They were just there."

That's when the two lying in the road tried to get up. One of them, a woman, managed it, but stood with her head dangling to the side, like it was held there by a thin string. Something like that, that kind of injury, you don't expect people to be walking around. The other, an old man, his legs smashed, pulled himself forward with his hands, his fingernails scratching along on the blacktop. His legs as useless as mop strands.

The others closed around Duane, and then, as if he had been lowered into a pool of piranha, they swarmed him. They could move pretty fast when they wanted to. They grabbed Duane.

I could understand they were angry, and had reason. We were irresponsible jerks driving too fast on a narrow road—

And then they began to eat Duane.

The one crawling had him by the ankle and was biting through his pants legs, gnawing at his high-top boots, and the others were all over him, biting and pulling at him. I saw the black woman bite his ear and rip it off.

Duane screamed. I started toward him, but Tommy, who had come around on my side of the car, grabbed me and pulled me back.

I could see more clearly now, but somehow, what I was seeing was too strange to be real. Yet, there I was, standing next to Tommy on a moonlit road, far from where we grew up, watching a mass of people bite and gnaw at Duane.

Duane screamed. Blood flew. Teeth snapped. They took him down. I could see naked asses through the hospital gown slits as the crazed crowd bent over him and began to rip at him with their hands and pull guts from his belly, lifting them to their mouths as if they were huge strands of spaghetti coated in marinara sauce.

I could see too that some of those people had awful bite marks on them, like they had just escaped a pack of wild dogs. And the other thing was, well, they all looked dead. There was no spark in their eyes and they moved like puppets. And those two Matt had hit with his car, there was no way they should have survived, but they were going at poor Duane like he was a buffet.

I ran around to the trunk, stuck the key in there, popped it, and pulled out the tire iron.

"No," Tommy said, but it was too late. I was weighing in. Those people were murderers, and they were killing . . . well, had killed, Duane. His body steamed in the cool air where he had been ripped open. One of those things was pounding Duane's head with its fists, cracking it apart like a giant walnut. Brains oozed and hands tore at the break in his skull. Brain matter was snatched and eaten.

My hits were good ones. I turned my tire iron blows to their heads. If I hit their heads hard enough, they went down and didn't get up. Otherwise, I didn't hit the head, they just kept coming. None of it made any sense, but I knew I hated those things, and I was proving it. I knew too, without having to really think about it, they were all dead and I was making some of them deader.

There were a lot of them, and then there were more. Tommy grabbed me, was pulling me back toward the car. Matt climbed into his GTO, woke the engine, and roared around us, nearly clipping us in the process.

"Look," Tommy said.

I was no longer swinging the tire iron or struggling, so I looked. There were more of them coming down the hill, out of the woods. Some of them looked to be little more than skeletal structure with a thin parchment of skin stretched over them. Many were naked.

"In the car," Tommy said.

The ones who had been snacking on Duane were close to us now, and I had no more than closed the car door, Tommy slipping in on the other side, when those things began to beat on the door glass. I fired up the engine, gunned it, hit one in front of the hood and sent it flying backwards into the road, and then I ran over it.

We drove on, had to stop once and pull a small tree out of the road. It had taken that moment in time to fall and block our path. It took some work, but thank goodness it wasn't too big a tree and those things weren't around.

Some time later we saw Matt's car. He had skidded out and hit a tree. Driver's side door was open, but he wasn't in view.

Eventually we came to Dead Man's Curve, and since we had outdistanced those things by quite a bit, we were going slow and made the curve easy, but I was glad I hadn't been racing. That curve, let me tell you, it was a bitch. I saw off to our right that the earth fell off into a man-made cut about the size of the largest moon crater, and it was full of still water. The old rock quarry. It stretched for a great distance, and across the way I could see the straight-up wall on the other side, slick and snot-shiny in the moonlight.

That's when we came to more of those things, wandering across the road, and there was a driveway on the left, and I took it. I thought about smashing through those things, whatever the hell they were, but they were too thick, and if I wrecked the car we'd be out here with them, just me and Tommy fighting for our lives with a tire iron and wishful thinking.

Still, didn't mean the driveway was a good idea. It was a reflex move. It was a long straight shot on concrete, and in the rearview mirror I could see those things lumbering after us. The drive ended at a nice farmhouse. Out beside it was a large barn. Behind a long white-board fence on the left was a lot of pasture.

As we drove onto the looping driveway in front of the house, I saw the front door to the place was open, and wandering out of it were two of those things. The yard was full of them. Not all of them were wearing hospital gowns or were naked. Some were fully dressed. Young and old. No doubt they were like the others, way their bodies jerked, way their heads rolled from side to side and their eyes seemed to look off in one direction or another, not latching right on you. Some of them were bloody, fresher.

"Damn," said Tommy.

"Double damn," I said. It was something we almost always said when one said damn, or hell. Double damn. Double hell. This time it was not pure fun and hyperbole. It was accurate.

I glanced toward the barn, saw a woman there. She had pushed one of the two wide doors open, probably hearing us roar up, and was waving for us to come that way. Then I saw Matt appear, grab her by the arm and jerk her back.

I gunned it. There was a gravel drive from house to barn, and I went that way fast as a bullet. When we got in front of the barn, Matt was struggling with the woman, had her bent back and was flinging a fist into her face, time and again, until she fell down.

The tire iron was in the seat beside me. I got out of the car with it. Matt tried to grab the open door and close it. I leapt forward, swung the tire iron, hit his arm through the crack in the doors, made him scream and stumble back. Tommy had slipped to the driver's seat, and he tooled the car inside as I pushed both doors wide. Up at the house I could see dead people wandering around in the yard, starting to trudge toward the barn.

When Tommy had our ride inside, I closed the doors. Tommy got out and helped me put a large and heavy wooden slat between two metal supports, barring the doors soundly.

That was done, I took a moment to kick Matt in the head. Within seconds the barn doors began to rattle, and you could hear those things moaning on the other side of it. The noise they made caused me to feel like my panties were crawling up my ass like a spider.

Tommy was helping the woman up, and he sat her on a bale of hay. A boy came out of the dark, ran over to her. She hugged him to her. Three more children, a couple of boys and a girl, eased out of the shadows too. The girl looked to be the oldest, but she wasn't more than twelve, if she was that old. They didn't go far. The boys were wandering about more than moving forward, and the girl seemed frozen, as if her feet had been stuck down in a tub filled with cold water and held there until the water turned to ice.

"You damn near broke my arm," Matt said. "And that kick cracked my jaw. I can feel it."

"Why thank you," I said.

"Bitch," Matt said.

"My middle name," I said.

"He was trying to force us out," said the lady, who held a hand to her battered eye.

"It's survival of the fittest," Matt said.

"You're not that fit," Tommy said. "A girl whipped your ass."

"You say that like it's a bad thing," I said.

"You sons of bitches," Matt said. "A woman, some brats, and one of them a retard, what the hell?"

"And you such a sterling member of society," Tommy said.

There were electric lights burning inside the barn. It was a class thing with front and back double doors, lots of hay. A tractor with a trailer fastened to it was parked near the back door. Two of the horse stalls had horses in them. A sorrel and a paint. I liked horses. Me and Tommy used to ride all the time at summer camp. That was before our parents split up.

I went over and took a look at the lady's eye. She was pretty bedraggled. She looked to be in her sixties, solid and sun-coated, time-worn. There was a toughness about her. The boy she had her arm around was obviously disabled. Must have been thirteen or fourteen, oldest of the children. I could tell he was disabled because of the way he looked. He had a sweet and innocent appearance that most of us lose about the time we realize the shit in our diapers stinks.

"My grandchildren," the lady said.

"What's happened?" I said.

She shook her head, tears streamed down her face. All of the children had come over now and were sitting on the bale of hay with her, close to her like a cluster of grapes.

"I don't know exactly," she said. "But those people, they're dead. You can tell."

"I'll say," I said. "But again, why?"

She shook her head. "Can't say. No idea. I have my daughter's kids with me. One of them left the front door open. I went to close it, and the yard was full of them. Kids were playing outside in the moonlight, and I saw those things coming up on them. I yelled at them and then, for whatever reason, we all broke toward the barn. We got here just as that asshole," she pointed at Matt, "showed up. He was trying to barricade himself in the barn. I struggled with him so the kids could get inside. I saw you pull up, and I wanted to help you, but he started fighting with me. He wanted to leave you out there, with those things. He wanted us out there too, to keep them busy I guess. So they'd forget about him."

As if to emphasize that, the barn doors on both ends rattled like giant dice.

"I can't believe it," she said. "I keep trying to figure it. What brings people back from the dead? Old Man Turner was with them, and he died yesterday. He was in the morgue. I knew him well. He was ninety years old if he was a day."

"Did you recognize others?" Tommy said.

"I did. Friends. Neighbors."

"How far is the town from here?" I said.

"We're practically in it. Town's not far from the hospital and the morgue. Couple miles maybe."

Tommy looked at me, said, "They could be all over town as well."

I said to the woman, "People out there, recognize any from town?"

"Don't know everyone in town, of course," the lady said. "But it's not that big. Everyone I recognized was from out here, houses nearby, but there were plenty I didn't know one way or another. They could have been from town, I suppose."

"Or the morgue and the hospital," Tommy said.

"Way some of them are dressed, sure," said the woman.

Matt started to get up.

"Lie down," I said, and lifted the tire iron.

He stayed where he was, said, "What we do is we stick the woman and the kids out there, get those things busy on them, and then we make a break for it. Drive out of here."

"So now you and me and Tommy are a team," I said.

"Please don't," the lady said.

"Of course not," Tommy said. "Don't you worry about that."

"You can't think the old way," Matt said. "You got to think about how it is now. This could be happening all over."

"Just stay there and shut up," I said.

"You need to think of yourself," Matt said. "You don't even know these people."

"Can't say I actually know you," I said. "And what little I do know of you, I don't like."

"We're racers. We go fast and live fast, and we survive. We know how to take a curve."

"You don't," Tommy said. "You smacked your car into a tree. Hell, it was a straightaway. Unfortunately, you survived. My guess is you're part cockroach, and the rest of you is all asshole."

"They are our way out," Matt said, nodding toward the woman and her grandchildren.

"I said shut up." I slapped the tire iron in my open palm and Matt went silent.

I turned to the woman. "Does the tractor run?"

"Yes. But it doesn't have a lot of speed, more if you drop the trailer."

"We want to keep the trailer," I said.

Tommy said, "What are we talking about here?"

I turned and looked at Matt lying there on the ground. He had abandoned us back on the road, and then he had tried to lock us out, and now he wanted us to take him and leave these people to their fate.

The barn doors rattled.

"Ma'am," I said, "would you and the children go to the back of the barn, over behind the horse stalls? Stay there for a bit. And you might want to cover your ears."

They didn't stir.

"Now," I said.

They moved then, quickly. When I saw they were behind the back stall, out of sight, I walked over to Matt. He saw it in my eyes. He tried to get up and make a break for it. But it was too late. I think the first swing of the tire iron killed him. I can't be sure. It knocked him down and out, that's for sure. And if it didn't kill him, the other blows did.

I hit him a lot.

Me and Tommy fastened Matt to the back bumper of the Charger with baling wire, several strands. I felt like Achilles tying Hector to the back of his chariot.

The woman and her grandchildren came back into view. I was covered in blood and I was shaking. But there was nothing for it. They would see what they saw. Therapy was in their future. If they had a future.

"What's going to happen," I said, "is Tommy is going to open the door, and I'm driving out. I could try and stuff you all in the car, but if they're thick on the road, well, you can only get so far, even in a car. But Tommy here, once I'm out there, once they get after Matt's body, which I think they will, you guys will go out the back with the tractor and trailer. Head toward town. Maybe it's safe there. Just sit quietly and ready to go until I can give them a whiff of this guy, let them smell the blood."

"I can't let you do that," Tommy said.

"Yes you can. You have to. I'm going to be the Pied Piper, but it's going to be my car engine and the smell of this dead bastard that're going to lead the rats away. You and the family go out the back."

The woman came up closer, stared down at what was left of Matt's head. I had hit so many times you could have slipped his head through a mail slot.

"You're going to go the opposite way I go," I said. "You might come across some of those things, so you'll need to take something to fight with. I see farm tools on the wall, that pitchfork, the hoe, things like that. It's not a perfect plan, but we can't wait here in the barn until we eat the horses. Two horses might last a while, but not forever."

"Grandma," said the granddaughter, who had started to cry. "We can't eat the horses."

"Of course not," the woman said, but the look in her eyes made it clear to me she knew they would have to if they stayed, and probably raw.

"You let the horses out of their stalls, let them run. What

you do is you drive that tractor to town, pulling Tommy here and the kids on the trailer. He can help you fight if you run into more of those things. It's the only choice."

Tommy helped me lift off the door barrier. When we dropped it, I ran and got in the car. Tommy pulled one of the barn doors open slightly, then darted back to the tractor. The lady had already started it. The kids were on the trailer. Everyone had a farm implement. That was a little like giving everyone switches to fight a bear, but it was all they had.

I could hear the things outside not only the front door, but the back door as well. This was going to be tricky.

When that unlatched front door was shoved wide open by those monsters, I turned on the headlights, startling them, put my foot on the gas and made the engine roar. I popped the clutch and jerked the car into gear. It leapt, knocking several of those things back. I let the car bunny hop a little, and die. They were smelling Matt back there, and they all went for him. It was like someone had rung the dinner bell. They had started crawling over the car too, pounding on the window glass, as if I was a pie on display and they wanted it.

I started up the car again, eased forward, but not too fast. Enough I was able to break free of them, and yet keep them interested in Matt, the hot lunch.

I drove around the barn. There was a well-worn path, and the car went smoothly. When I had driven around a couple of times, the car was covered in those things. I could hardly see out the windshield, they were gathered on it so thick. The back way was open.

I didn't want them to eat all my bait, so I drove faster, onto the drive. I reached the road, and they were still with me. I heard the back glass crack from the pounding the clingers were giving it with their fists. I glanced in the rearview mirror. The back window still held, but it was starred and lined with breaks.

If Tommy was lucky, they would have the tractor going now, following slightly behind, turning the opposite direction toward town. Maybe all the things were following me. Maybe Tommy, that woman and her grandkids, would do all right.

The moon had brightened up the road as the night had worn on. It was like having your own night-light. I decided it was time to pick it up a little, make it hard for the things to keep clinging to the car. As I increased speed, they peeled off the Charger like dead skin.

I sped up enough to get ahead of them, but not so much they couldn't see me. They kept following.

I wondered how much was left of Matt. Way I had him fastened on back there, I couldn't see him in the rearview. That was probably best. I had killed him in cold blood, and now I was feeding him to those things. Was I any better than him, choosing to do such a thing?

I thought on that for a short time, came to a conclusion.

Yeah. I was.

I kept teasing those things with the body, speeding and slowing. I checked the gas. Low. When I glanced up from the gauge I checked the rearview mirror. The road behind me was a wall of those things.

And then I saw him. He was on horseback. He was carrying

something shiny and swinging it as he rode through the mass, surprising them, smashing heads, sending them sprawling.

It was Tommy playing cowboy. He had saddled up one of the horses and was riding it through the drooling crowd toward me. When he burst out in front of that bunch, I slowed to a stop.

Tommy rode up to the passenger door, swung off the horse. I leaned across the seat and opened the door. Tommy dropped what he had been carrying into the seat—a lawn mower blade. He unsaddled the horse, dropped the saddle in the road, peeled off the bridle, and slapped the horse on the ass. It went off the road and up through the trees and out of sight, a flock of ghouls pursuing at a considerably slower pace.

"Good luck, noble steed," Tommy said.

He jerked the door open and climbed onto the seat, placing the lawn mower blade in his lap.

I turned and looked back. Those things were almost to us. I clutched and geared and we started rolling.

"What the hell?" I said.

"What the double hell, you mean. The lady is driving the tractor, taking the kids into town. I saddled a horse and rode along with them. When I figured they were doing good, because we didn't see any of those things, I turned around and came after you. I always had that in my head."

"You're a good brother, Tommy. I never thought you were before."

Tommy laughed.

As we came around a patch of trees we saw the road had quite a few of those things in it. I put the pedal to the metal and knocked a couple aside, crunched one under the wheel. Now I was gaining speed. I glanced at the gas gauge. Before long we'd be walking, and that wouldn't be good. I only had one headlight now, the left one. The other one had been broken in my collision with those things. Bless the moonlight.

I was picking up speed.

"Buckle up. We're going to straighten out the curve."

"Damn, girl."

"Double damn," I said.

Tommy reached across me, got my seat belt and strapped it over my lap, and then he buckled his own.

I was hot on the straightaway now, and Dead Man's Curve was coming up, but I wasn't slowing. I could see those things in the faint light from the left head-beam. They were coming down the wooded hill on our right. A better-dressed group than before. Probably from farmhouses that had been attacked, survivors who had not been consumed. It was clear that being bitten made you like the others. You died and came back. Hungry.

"We're going to overshoot the curve, out into the quarry," I said.

"Big drop, Sis. Full of water. You know that, right?"

"You can swim."

"Only if the fall doesn't kill us, and then, swim where?"

"To the other side."

"Walls are slick."

"Maybe there's a way up."

"Maybe?"

"We're short on options. Roll down your window. Water pressure may not let you later."

Tommy frantically rolled down his window, and I did the same.

Now the curve was ahead, and when I made it those things

were in the road. I clipped a few of them, and long past when I should have turned the wheel, I kept going, wearing a few of those monsters on the windshield. I put my foot through the floor, and we went sailing off the edge of Dead Man's Curve.

There were bits of tree limbs and brush growing out of the side of the quarry, and we shot out over it. Limbs and brush scratched the bottom of the Charger like a pissed-off cat. Out of instinct I looked in the rearview and saw what was left of Matt floating up in the air on that baling wire, coming apart in pieces that were sailing backwards in the draft like wet confetti.

Way, way out that car sailed, and in the moonlight I saw the wall of the quarry on the other side. It looked slick and straight up. The Charger dipped and the car was an angular shadow shooting toward where the moon floated in the water like a target. The water looked as firm as a giant piece of sheet metal.

The air whistled in the windows. The back glass of the car, already cracked and pressured by the wind, shattered into a mass of moon-colored stars and was gone.

We smacked the water.

I don't know exactly what happened after that. I guess the impact knocked me out. My head may have bounced off the steering wheel. The water eventually brought me around. I didn't know where I was right away, but the water went in my mouth and nose and I finally realized I was drowning. I felt out for Tommy, but he wasn't there. I reached for my seat belt. There wasn't any. I came to understand I had somehow gotten out of the car, that I was free and floating, twisting around underwater like a strand of weed. I couldn't remember how I got out.

Then something had me. I was pulled up and out of the water, gasping for breath, sputtering and spitting. Tommy was holding on to me. We were moving our feet to stay afloat.

"You all right, Sis?"

"You saved me," I said.

"Yep. Started to leave you, but then I remembered you win all the races. That's too good a money to throw away."

I thought about that fine Dodge Charger, down below in the deep dark wet. What a waste.

Those things, maybe half a dozen were in the water, having grabbed at the car, or having run off the cliff after us. They weren't close and they weren't swimming. They bobbed a little and sank like anvils.

I was coming back to myself by then.

"What now?" Tommy said. "So far, I'm not crazy about your plan."

"We swim together," I said, "then we take turns with one swimming, the other hanging on. Then we go back to swimming separate. We take our time, do that until we get to the other side."

"It's a long ways," Tommy said. "I already feel like I was eaten by a wolf and shit off a cliff."

I looked at the far quarry wall. It was a lot more distant than it had seemed from above.

"And the walls are high and slick as glass," he said. "What do we do if we get there? Levitate?"

"If we have to."

We started seriously swimming, first side by side, and then I put an arm around Tommy's neck and he swam. Then we switched and he held my neck. I was the stronger swimmer by far. When I looked around after what had seemed like forever,

23

I couldn't tell that we had covered much distance at all. But I thought I saw a trail going up the far wall, and then the moon was shadowed by clouds and the shadows lay on the quarry wall like a curtain. I couldn't be sure if I had seen a trail or not.

Maybe the moon would break the clouds apart and I would see the trail again. If it was there, and I hoped like hell it was, I thought we might just make it.

Craig E. Engler is the co-creator/writer/co–executive producer for Syfy's hit zombie series *Z Nation*, and co-writer of the *Z Nation* comic book. He also co-wrote *Zombie Apocalypse*, starring Ving Rhames, one of Syfy's highest-rated original films. As a journalist he's written for *The New York Times*, Wired, and many other publications. He also created the comic *Lovecraft* and a how-to guide for geeks who want to lose weight called *Weight Hacking*.

A DEAD GIRL NAMED SUE

by Craig E. Engler

You're fucking arresting me for killing a dead person?"

Cliven Ridgeway sat in the back of the sheriff's cruiser, unsuccessfully trying to wrestle free from his handcuffs.

"It's open season on them. Says it on the news even."

Sheriff Evan Foster didn't turn around to address Cliven. Didn't even look at him in the rearview.

"Last time I saw Etta, she was as alive as you and me," the sheriff said. "Until I know different, that means it's a homicide, and that puts you back behind bars."

Cliven spat on the floor of the car. "So that's what this is, huh?

Railroad job. And you taking me to jail in the back of the car my family bought for the department. It's a disgrace."

The sheriff turned down Harrison Lane. The streetlights were out, the houses dark. The power had gone off eight hours ago and he didn't figure it to come back on anytime soon. The word the electric company had used was "indefinitely." That was when the phones worked and you could still get through to someone.

"It's not the first time you been in the back of my car," the sheriff said. "And I thanked your folks at the ribbon cutting ceremony. That don't excuse you of murder."

"Only it's not Etta Winnerson's murder you're arresting me for, is it?"

The sheriff didn't say anything. He came up to Schaefer Road and hooked around the turnabout where the Ladies Petunia Club had planted an array of their namesake flowers, dominated by an impressive spread of "wild white," if he remembered last Thursday's lecture at the library correctly. He frowned at the body lying in a patch of multifloras. Made a mental note to come back and check whose it was after he was done at the jail. Clearly not one of the reanimated dead. And probably someone the sheriff knew.

Just a few hours back he'd had to put down three of his friends, including Deputy Sheriff Jackson Hayes. He couldn't say for sure how they'd died, but he suspected two of them had been in a car accident and Hayes had tried to perform CPR on one of them. That seemed to be how a lot of the early victims of the outbreak died, trying to help what they thought were living people.

Cliven was still messing around in the back with his cuffs.

A satisfying *click* followed by a curse told the sheriff that Cliven's efforts were only succeeding in making them tighter.

"Only two ways this goes, sheriff," Cliven said. "Either tomorrow the courthouse is open and the judge hands me a get out of jail free card, or the courts never open again and you got to let me out on account of there ain't no courts anymore. Anyways I can help clean up this mess. I'm a better shot than most of your deputies."

"Maybe so. We'll see how it goes either way. But I wouldn't count on Judge Henderson letting you out again."

"He'll let me out or my sister will kill him." Cliven smiled. "Or worse, divorce him. But you and me both know I'll walk. How many times you have to try and frame me for this or that crime before you realize, they ain't never going to put me in jail? Hell, you're only sheriff because my daddy said a good word for you at election time. Maybe next time I'll run for sheriff so's I can arrest you for made-up shit you never done."

Cliven gave up on the handcuffs and switched to kicking the reinforced panel that sat between the rear and front seats. Every kick coinciding with a word: "They." Kick. "Ain't." Kick. "Never." Kick. "Going." Kick. "To." Kick. "Put." Kick. "Me." Kick. "In." Kick. "Jail." Kick.

"I've never arrested you for something you didn't do, Cliven. Not being convicted of a crime isn't the same as never having committed it. That's a lesson I don't think you've learned."

Two more kicks: "Fuck. You."

"Take old Etta," the sheriff went on. He'd still not so much as glanced back at Cliven. "She might have died of natural causes, or maybe unnatural ones. And yeah, you might have come across her and been attacked."

27

"I told you she come after me! Thought she was drunk, her housecoat open and her not even wearing granny panties or nothing. Disgusting is what it was. She come at me and tried to bite my face off!"

"That could be true, Cliven. But it could also be true that you figured you could pretty much kill anyone during a thing like this and no one would question it. Especially an old lady who can't remember her own name most days."

"Fuck." Kick. "You." Kick. "Twice." He ended the sentence with two kicks, maybe trying to be clever.

"Is that what you did? Murder an old lady in the street because you thought it'd be fun? They call that a 'thrill kill,' Cliven, did you know that?"

Cliven looked out the window at nothing in particular. "I ain't no thriller killer. It was self-defense. And even if it wasn't, no way for you to know different."

The sheriff saw the lights of an oncoming car. He slowed down as it got closer, recognized Chris Miller driving the Municipal Road Works van. He pulled to a stop and the van pulled up opposite him.

"You boys okay?" the sheriff called out his window. He could see young Billy O'Connell in the van alongside Chris.

"We got delayed some but we're all right," Chris said. He looked in the back of the cruiser, spotted Cliven.

"Guess things are still on track then?"

"Still on track," the sheriff said. "I'm just taking this suspect to the jail."

"All right," Chris said. "It shouldn't take us too long, though it's not the kind of thing I've ever done before."

"You don't have to do it if you don't want to. I can find some other volunteers."

Chris let out a short laugh. "It might be wrong to say it, sheriff, but I never wanted to do something more in my life. Me and him"—he nodded at Cliven—"go back a long way. Most people in town could say the same."

"Most could."

"We'll see you at the jail then."

"See you there. And you two take care you don't get yourselves hurt."

Chris waved as he pulled off down the road.

Cliven had followed the exchange closely.

"What the fuck is going on, sheriff? Why'd he look at me like that?"

"I suppose he don't like you much."

"Why's he even allowed to drive around? Thought we was all under martial law?"

The sheriff watched until the taillights of the van disappeared down the road, then he continued on.

"I deputized those boys to help me out during the crisis. I got them running some errands."

"Them, deputies?" Cliven scoffed. "You'd have done better to make me a deputy than them two. They couldn't find their asses in a dark room even if you was to give 'em flashlights."

"Oh, I think they're the right boys for the job I need doing."

Cliven looked like he wasn't sure what to make of that comment.

The sheriff continued on to the municipal building, which is where the three-(now two-) person sheriff's department was housed. It also contained the holding cells, the courthouse, the mayor's office, and the town clerk's office. The double-wide front doors had both been left open by someone, and the glow of the interior emergency lights spilled into the night.

He pulled up right in front by the stairs to minimize the distance he and Cliven would have to walk in the open, then got out and surveyed the quiet street. All dark as midnight except for a few stores that had their own emergency lights. The pharmacy. Hardware store. June's Café.

Someone had tried to pry open the security gate of the pharmacy to little success other than busting the window. The sheriff added a note to his mental to-do list to try to figure out who'd attempted to break in, though he was pretty sure no one was going to file a complaint about it.

As he turned to retrieve Cliven from the car he glimpsed, or thought he glimpsed, a figure in the distance. He put his hand to his gun but took it away a moment later. If it was one of the walking corpses he thought he would have seen its herky-jerky movements again. So it was either a real person or nothing at all, and neither was enough to distract him away from his current business.

He pulled Cliven out of the back of the car and marched him up the stairs into the mostly dark building, Cliven protesting the whole way.

"You can't put me in here if the power's out. I got my rights. I won't be able to see nothing."

"Emergency lights are on. Good for forty-eight hours."

"Yeah, and what then?"

"According to you, the judge will have you out come morning. So nothing to worry yourself about."

"And what if it's like you said?"

The sheriff didn't answer for a moment. "I'm just taking things one step at a time, Cliven. It's fair enough to say the night has been full of surprises and I expect things to continue that way."

As they walked down a hallway and past the sheriff's personal office, a figure suddenly loomed out of the dark at them.

Cliven stiffened and tried to pull away, but the sheriff had him by the cuffs and held him steady. The figure stepped into the halo of an emergency light and revealed itself to be Joe Donovan, owner of Donovan's Tree & Lawn Service and father to Sue Donovan, who'd recently been found murdered.

Cliven recoiled from Joe more fiercely than if it'd been one of the walking corpses.

"What's he doing here?" he demanded from the sheriff.

Joe's eyes were rimmed with red and his face was pale as death. His skin had a clammy look to it and you could just about feel a wave of heat coming from him. Joe stared at Cliven like the prisoner was some kind of demon who'd just erupted from hell. Then he turned to the sheriff.

"I can't do it, Evan."

"Do what?" Cliven asked.

The other men ignored him.

"That's okay," the sheriff said. "We'll handle it from here. In fact, I think it'd be better if you left before the boys get back. No need for you to see that."

"I thought I could, but I can't," Joe said.

"Do what?" Cliven demanded again.

The sheriff put a hand on Donovan's shoulder. "Go home. Be safe. See your wife."

"I don't know if I can look her in the eye after . . ."

"You can look her in the eye. You haven't done anything. Something's been done to you. Now you got to try to heal from it."

"What in the fuck are you two talking about?"

"The others are downstairs," Donovan told the sheriff. Then

he turned to face Cliven. Without warning he struck the captive man across the face, an open-handed slap that rocked Cliven's head to the side.

Joe raised his finger to Cliven's face like he was going to say something, but then lowered it and shoved past him.

"I'm going to go see my wife like you said," he told the sheriff, and hurried out of the building.

"Jesus Christ!" Cliven said. "He can't just hit me like that! Ain't you going to arrest him?"

"I must have been looking away, Cliven. I didn't see anyone hit you."

Cliven kicked at the floor in frustration.

"Goddamn it, sheriff, this ain't right. You arresting me for no reason, then letting crazy Donovan use me like a punching bag. This ain't right at all."

"If he did hit you, you might consider how lucky you are that's all he did. Another father in his situation, you in front of him cuffed and all, things might have turned out worse for you."

"I fucking told you I ain't had nothing to do with his daughter! Nothing. I got eyewitnesses back up my alibi. You all don't even have a single piece of evidence."

The sheriff stood in silence, as if pondering some weighty question.

"Funny how things work out, isn't it?" he finally said. "The only forensic tech we got access to decides to go on a European vacation, of all things. First class tickets. Staying at the Four Seasons no less. Would've been a hell of a trip I imagine if it wasn't ruined by the ongoing situation."

"I ain't had nothing to do with that," Cliven said. "I can't control when someone decides to take a vacation for fuck's sake."

"Never said you did," the sheriff said. "I expect that was your daddy." He guided Cliven toward the stairs in the back that led to the cells.

Downstairs there were two small jail cells off an equally small kitchen where the deputies liked to make coffee and bullshit. Fiona Hapsburg, the town clerk, would come down for a cup anytime she smelled a fresh pot, but never made it herself because she's "not drinking coffee no more 'cause of her blood pressure." No one minded too much.

Today Fiona wasn't there but Jeremy Potter and Cindy Kerr were at the table, sitting around an electric Coleman lantern and eating granola bars. Both armed. Him with a Colt .45 that was his daddy's during the war, and her with a hunting rifle she'd gotten on her fifteenth birthday.

"Hey, sheriff," she said.

The sheriff nodded at them.

"What the hell are they doing here?" Cliven asked. "More of your new deputies?"

Jeremy gave Cliven an icy look. Cindy smirked at him, like she knew a secret he didn't.

"More like interested parties," the sheriff said.

He tried to guide Cliven toward the cell but now the prisoner started resisting in earnest.

"I see what you got here," Cliven said. "You're rounding up everyone ever held a grudge to me, is that it?"

The sheriff said nothing, tried again to urge Cliven toward the cell, but Cliven was having none of it.

"Is this some kind of execution, sheriff? You gonna take me in there and put a bullet in my head while these watch?"

"Why would I do that for?" the sheriff asked.

"'Cause you believe all the shit they talk about me. What Jeremy said I done to his brother, what she says happened on prom night, what Donovan thinks happened to his daughter. And you got a bee up your ass about old Etta who attacked me tonight."

"Them other things you got off for. And like I said, your story checks out about Etta, we'll let you go."

"We ain't talking about Etta and you know it."

"If you got things weighing on your conscience, Cliven, that's not my fault."

The sheriff stopped him and looked straight into his prisoner's eyes for the first time all night. Cliven was taken aback by what he saw in the sheriff's gaze. The rest of his face was unreadable as stone, but the sheriff's eyes practically burned with hatred.

"You got something you want to confess to me, boy?"

Cliven looked around for help, but only met Jeremy's cold stare. When he looked to Cindy she let out a small giggle but said nothing.

"You got maybe one chance to say something decent here," the sheriff said. "I'm asking you again, you got something you want to confess to me?"

Cliven turned away from the sheriff. "No," he said weakly. He didn't protest any more when the sheriff led him to the cell.

The cell was ten feet long and five feet wide, with the obligatory bare metal toilet and sink, and a bench inset along one wall that could double as a cot. It wasn't meant to house prisoners for more than a night or two before they were moved up to county jail.

There was a small, rectangular opening about waist height in the cell door where prisoners put their hands to be cuffed or uncuffed as needed. As soon as the sheriff put him in the cell, Cliven backed up to the opening and held out his hands to be released, like it was something he'd done before. The sheriff ignored him.

"Ain't you going to uncuff me?" Cliven asked.

"No, I don't believe I will tonight," the sheriff said.

An hour passed with Cliven loudly moving around the cell trying to get as comfortable as possible and the other three chatting in semi-hushed tones around the table.

"Maybe we should go look for them," Jeremy said after a while.

"They'll be all right," the sheriff said. He idly went through his notebook, going over the events of the night. It was his habit to jot some unofficial thoughts here in addition to the formal notes and paperwork the job required of him. Just little bullet points to keep things straight in his own mind. The current day's entry was filled with more notes to himself than almost all the preceding pages combined. One stood out, scrawled larger than the rest: "Shot Hayes in the head."

The only time before tonight that he'd discharged his firearm in the four years since he'd been elected sheriff was to put a deer out of its misery. It'd been hit by a car and half crippled.

Tonight he'd fired seventeen shots and "killed" eleven people, or at least former people who'd died and somehow been reanimated. Tonight was also the only time he'd had to go into the trunk of the cruiser and get extra ammunition.

People often say it felt like "living a nightmare" when bad things happened to them, but this was the first time the sheriff could recall experiencing the sensation himself. Even more shocking was how routine it had become, shooting at another person. Once someone figured out you needed to hit them in the head to keep them down, it'd gone a little easier. Whatever made them like that also made them slow and uncoordinated. Long as you didn't get too close or run out of ammo, and you didn't panic, it wasn't too hard to keep safe.

In a small town like this with everyone owning guns and knowing how to shoot them, they'd eventually been able to clear most of the dead they could find. The sheriff thought the worst of things might even be over for now. When it got light they'd take the municipal van out and start collecting the bodies and try to figure out how the rest of the world was doing. He was pretty sure things would be bad in the big cities.

His thoughts were interrupted by a loud bang from upstairs, and the sound of people struggling. Cindy and Jeremy readied their guns straight off, but the sheriff left his in the holster. He figured it was just Billy and Chris returning with their package.

"The thing of it is," he told Cliven through the bars, "that because the forensic tech was in Europe, we had to send Sue Donovan's body to Summerton County for the autopsy. At least we were supposed to, but they're backed up on cases so she's just been sitting in the morgue."

There were more sounds of struggling upstairs and a crash as some of the photos that lined the main hallway were knocked down. Then there was the loud, meaty *thunk* of something falling and Chris called out, "Hold her steady, damn it."

The sheriff didn't pay it any attention, but Cliven's eyes were riveted on the stairway.

"You see what I'm getting at?" he asked Cliven.

More noises from upstairs. The rustle of thick plastic, bumps and thuds. You could hear Billy and Chris breathing heavy from all the way down here.

"I'll go give them a hand," Jeremy said, more loudly than he'd intended. He bolted up the stairs as more noises drifted down to them. *Bump, bump. Thud. Bump.*

"I don't know why you're going on about an autopsy on some dead girl," Cliven said.

"Because if they'd performed the autopsy in the normal course of events, they would have taken out her brain to weigh it," the sheriff explained. "But in this case we didn't touch her other than some basic measurements and to put her in the drawer."

Cliven was pressed up against the bars, eyes wide as he waited to see what Billy and Chris were going to bring down the stairs.

"What, you mean she's . . . she's one of them?"

The sheriff nodded.

"Strangulation doesn't affect them, Cliven. I guess because they don't breathe although I don't really know."

Bump, bump, bump.

"You gonna tell me what that noise is, for Christ's sake?" Cliven said.

The sheriff stared at him, as if deciding whether he was going to respond. Finally he said, "I think you already know what it is."

Cliven made a noise that was probably supposed to be a "no" but that sounded like the last breath a man dying of tuberculosis might take. He cleared his throat, tried again. "No, I . . ."

Just then Chris came down the stairs, walking backward with his arms wrapped around the bottom end of a long black bag that was twisting and bucking. A body bag. Then Billy came into view holding up the top part, with Jeremy following ineffectually behind him.

The bag gave a shudder and the end of it hit the railing, hard, almost knocking Chris off balance and making the metal rail ring with a deep *bong*.

It finally dawned on Cliven what was happening.

"Don't you bring that thing down here!" he shouted up at them.

The sheriff gave him a puzzled look.

"I thought you wanted to get closer to her, Cliven? Her best friend, Jenny Jacobs, told me you wouldn't leave her alone that night. Followed her like a dog in heat, she said."

"None of that's true!" Cliven screamed. "None of it! You got the wrong guy!"

Chris and Billy wrestled the slowly writhing body bag down the last of the stairs and dragged it in front of the cell. It slowly flopped back and forth, an obscene sight, and Chris had to step on one edge to keep it in place. Both he and Billy were sweating from their efforts. Jeremy was sweating too, but not from any hard labor.

"A thirteen-year-old girl, Cliven," the sheriff said. "What's a man like you doing chasing around a thirteen-year-old girl?"

Cliven backed into the far corner of the cell, putting as much distance between him and the body bag as possible.

"Fuck you, fuck you, fuck you!"

Cindy let out another giggle. "I don't think we're the ones getting fucked tonight," she said.

Jeremy looked like he might throw up.

"I'm . . . I'm going upstairs for some air."

Before he left he turned to Cliven.

"I hope it takes a long time, you son of a bitch. A long time, you hear?"

Chris was having a hard time keeping the bag in place.

"We going to do this, sheriff?"

The sheriff nodded, took out his gun and the keys to the cell.

He unlocked the door with one hand and held the gun on Cliven with the other.

"I'm opening the door, Cliven. You try to come out of there and I'll shoot you for attempted escape."

The fight had gone out of Cliven, though. He remained cowering in the corner.

"This ain't right," he said, mostly to himself. "It ain't right."

"Like you ever done anything right in your life," Cindy said. "I'm going to enjoy this, you piece of shit. I'm going to enjoy every minute of it."

The sheriff motioned to Chris and Billy.

"Put her in."

The two men dragged the body bag into the cell, snagging it on the doorframe for a second before wresting it free. The whole time the bag shifted around like it was full of huge, drunk bumblebees trying to get out. Finally, they got it all the way in and Chris stood straddling it.

"Now what?" he asked.

"Open the zipper a little, then step out. Billy, you back out of there now."

The sheriff kept his gun ready, to use on Cliven or the dead girl as the need might arise.

Chris pulled at the zipper tentatively, like he was trying to snatch hot food off the grill. The zipper only moved an inch. He tried again. Four more inches, then a hand pushed its way out, grabbing for him. The hand had painted red nails that contrasted unpleasantly with its dark blue-gray skin.

Chris yelped and leapt for the cell door, catching his foot on the top of the bag. The hand scrabbled for him and he heaved himself out of the cell to avoid it, landing on his ass.

"You clear?" the sheriff calmly asked. When Chris nodded he closed the cell and locked it.

"You know what I found out?" the sheriff asked Cliven.

Billy and Chris had gone upstairs as the dead girl started to emerge from the body bag like a broken butterfly coming out of a cocoon. Billy said he didn't have the stomach to watch what was coming next, and Chris had wordlessly tagged along. Cindy, however, watched the whole time, munching on a granola bar.

"They'll eat anything that lives. A man, a horse, a dog. And if you leave them at it long enough, they'll eat right down to the bone."

The dead girl named Sue managed to stand upright, her jaws working silently as if already biting into flesh.

Cliven pressed up against the concrete wall in the back of the cell as tightly as possible, turning his shoulder as if he could somehow block the girl with it. He was talking continuously to himself now, like a scared child might.

"No, no, no, no, no, no, no, no . . ."

Sue seemed to get her bearings and spot Cliven at the same time. She let out a sort of hissing sound and reached for him.

Cliven panicked, kicked wildly at her, an awkward movement with his hands cuffed behind his back. He missed her entirely and she clutched at one of his legs, getting a momentary grip on it. As soon as her hand touched him he thrashed like he'd been burned, managed to get his leg free and aimed a kick at her head. This time the blow connected, catching her across the jaw. It was a hard hit, but she reacted as if she didn't feel it at all. She grabbed at his leg again, catching it, and tried to bite through his jeans into his calf.

Cliven's mumbling turned into a screaming, gasping howl of terror. He pulled his leg back from her and kicked at her head again, but she got his foot, pulling him off balance and sending the two of them to the floor. He twisted around, trying to get back up as she lay on top of him.

The sheriff turned to leave.

"You coming?" he asked Cindy. He had to raise his voice to be heard over Cliven's yelling.

She shook her head, never taking her eyes off the cell.

The sheriff nodded. He went up to his office on the main floor as Cliven continued to howl and scream below. He pulled out his notebook and flipped to the page about the Sue Donovan case. He crossed off Cliven Ridgeway's name under the heading "Suspect." Farther down the page, under the heading "Aid and abet," was another name, Abel Ridgeway. Cliven's father.

The sheriff figured they'd have enough time to get to Abel before dawn.

Jay Bonansinga is the *New York Times* bestselling author of twenty-four books, including the Bram Stoker finalist *The Black Mariah* (1994), the International Thriller Writers Award finalist *Shattered* (2007), and the wildly popular *Walking Dead* novels. Jay's work has been translated into sixteen languages, and he has been called "one of the most imaginative writers of thrillers" by the *Chicago Tribune*. In the world of film, Jay has worked with the Great George Romero, Dennis Haysbert (*24*), and Will Smith's Overbrook Productions. Jay lives in the Chicago area with his wife, the photographer Jill Norton, and his two teenage boys, and is currently hard at work on the next *Walking Dead* book in the Woodbury quartet. You can find Jay online at www .jaybonansinga.com and www.magnetikink.com.

FAST ENTRY

by Jay Bonansinga

– 1 –
Thinking About Not Thinking

She arrives at Fort Denning that day, death and mayhem the furthest things from her mind. Parking her shit-kicker Chevy S-10 a block from the entrance, according to proper protocol, she pauses to clear her mind. It's a beautiful day on the Atlantic seaboard, the sky a clear and wide expanse of robin's egg blue over the tide pools and estuaries of eastern Maryland. The sun filters down through palisades of white oaks, dappling the hood of her rust-pocked pickup. The air smells of magnolia and clover. She turns the truck off and then studies her face in the rearview.

She lets out a long breath, clearing her mind in the mode of Zen masters—*thinking about not thinking*—pushing the ubiquitous white noise from her brain. The constant drone is the occupational hazard of all psychics, and it plagues *her* on a daily basis. But today, she has no reason to believe that she's about to encounter a waking nightmare. The message delivered to her this morning at dawn on the secure line gave her no cause to be nervous.

"Command control here," the flat, officious, blandly pleasant female voice informed her at a few minutes after 6:00 a.m. Eastern Standard Time that morning. "Identify yourself, please."

"What?—what time is it?—*wait*," she stammered at first, trying to wake up and fake her way out of an obvious hangover. She had tied another one on last night, drinking herself blind and doing two eight-balls at the club. Feeding the beast. Staggering home like a common derelict. Now she was struggling to sound like a self-respecting Sleeper for the Defense Intelligence Agency. "Oh, sorry, my bad . . . um, yeah . . . you got four-three-two-whiskey-zebra here. Go ahead, Command."

"Four-three-two, we have a red level event in progress, initiated at three hundred hours Greenwich Mean Time."

"Copy that."

She waited for the time and place designated for her inser-
tion, finding little to worry about. The last red level event was
a colossal waste of time, a scan of some naughty diplomat's
memories. The man had been suspected of being an asset
for the Iranians, but the only thing she found in his head was
masturbatory fantasies involving some ambassador's daughter.
Now she waited for the details to another piece of government
drudgery.

"You will need to provide fast entry at Black Candlestick
today at twelve hundred thirty hours. Highest priority, security code blue in effect."

The call disconnected itself at that point, which seems now
like weeks ago even though it was only this morning. She stares
at her round caramel face in the rearview, her flat nose with its
gold ring in one nostril, and her huge chocolate eyes as blood-
shot as tiny scarlet road maps of some tangled interstate system. She takes one last, deep, girding breath and pops the
glove box.

A pint bottle of Tito's vodka rests in there under her registration wallet and holstered .45 caliber DoubleTap ACP pistol.
Vodka is her chosen hair of the dog—odorless, colorless, and
effective at momentarily satisfying her gargantuan Need. The
Need is with her constantly, a salve on the cross she bears as
a government mind-reader and dancing monkey, wallowing in
the filthy chambers of people's innermost thoughts.

She takes the pint out, unscrews the cap, and knocks back
a third of the bottle.

"Another day, another fucking dollar," Jasmine Maywell
mutters, putting the pint back.

She takes the gun with her.

– 2 –
Remote Viewing

The codger at the guard shack gives her a funny look when she flashes her visitor's lanyard.

"That's an old one," he says, pursing his lips, looking her up and down, pretending to inspect the badge. An old, droopy, graying veteran, obviously regular army from a long time ago, maybe the Napoleonic Wars, he lets his eyes linger just one millisecond too long in the general direction of her chest. She doesn't have to enter his head to know what's oozing through *his* stream of consciousness.

All of which she's used to, of course, a woman of her shape and size, but that doesn't make it any less enervating to her. She sometimes gets off on flirting with guys, but not now, not today.

The old man ogles her with a lascivious little twinkle in his eye, lowering his voice, Mister Big Shot, the man in-the-know. "You here 'cause of that ruckus up north?"

She cocks her head at him. "What ruckus is that?"

"Shit that went down at that cemetery outside Pittsburgh? Evans City?"

She gives him her best demure smile. "I wouldn't know anything about that."

"Something's going down inside," he says, jerking a thumb toward the complex of stone-brick buildings behind them.

"Duly noted," she says.

He sniffs and nods at her lanyard. "Ought to replace that someday soon, or mark my words, somebody out here's gonna stop ya."

"I'll keep that in mind, Dad," she says with that flirty little smile, fighting the urge to get him to buy her a drink later. "I'll get it updated soon as I see the CO." She winks at him. "Promise."

She walks onto the base, hyperaware of the old guard eye-balling her booty for the entire trek across the lot. She gives him plenty to look at. A big girl of mixed race with spacious hips and fulsome breasts, decked out today in spandex and knee-highs, Master Sergeant Jasmine Maywell walks with the studied, rhythmic sashay of a fashion model, as though she were balancing a book on her head. She cooked up the walk during her tour of service in Iraq, when her fellow soldiers told her she walked like a grunt.

She heads for the main processing center, which sits on the southern edge of the grounds.

Located in the leafy, middle-class suburb of Frederick, Maryland, Fort Denning is laid out over twelve hundred acres like a big L-shaped college campus, its ostensible purpose to serve as the United States Army Medical Command. At first glance, the place looks so innocuous, so bland, so slate gray and redbrick featureless, it seems to hardly exist. Or at most, it seems to blend in with the strip malls and insipid office building architecture of the DC government corridor with chameleon-like proficiency.

In fact, the mundane, landscaped, motel-building design is a thousand times more sinister when one considers the history of the place. During the Cold War years, Denning was the heart of the military's biological weapons research program. Everything from mustard gas to weaponized ocean tides were toyed with and implemented. Denning personnel also experimented in the 1950s in the potential use of insects as disease vectors, including ticks, fleas, ants, and lice—but mostly mosquitoes carrying yellow fever virus over international borders. Human subjects were used in the development of biological weapons. It has been rumored over the years that Denning is the place where the United States government "invented" HIV.

Fort Denning also produced Jasmine Maywell's abusive father. Captain Bertrand Maywell was one of the most gifted subjects in the highly classified Project Sun Streak. As a "remote viewer," Bert Maywell would sit in Denning's isolation tank and psychically project himself into the eyes and ears of enemy pilots and soldiers, gleaning incredible amounts of intel and also a slow-growing tumor that nobody knew about until it was too late.

The last years of the old man's life were a living hell for Jasmine. As his only caretaker, she was treated worse than shit—regularly spat upon, slapped, yelled at, scourged with profanity-laced tirades, and ultimately turned into a ravenous addict. But perhaps the worst thing that Captain Bert Maywell had inflicted upon his daughter was the psychic skill that had ruined his own life, a recessive gene handed down from his mother's mother, a Santerian witch who was lynched in 1955 in Mississippi. It became a dominant trait in the captain, handed down unceremoniously—like flat feet or seasonal allergies—to his daughter.

All of which had turned Jasmine Maywell's life into a lonely succession of one-night stands and wasted, narcotic days of not-so-quiet desperation.

Of course, not a single one of these ominous, classified pieces of Fort Denning's secret history occurs to Jasmine Maywell until she makes her way through the preliminary security checkpoints, showing her ID tag and her tiny two-shot pistol to a succession of nervous MPs. Nobody uses phrases such as "high alert" or "scrambled" until she gets to the final vestibule at the bank of elevators leading down into the innards of the earth.

"I'm sorry, but you can't go down there today, ma'am," the guard with the starched uniform buttoned up to his Adam's apple tells her in a nervous monotone. He stands between Jasmine and the elevators with his M4 up high across his chest, his boyish face as grim and sullen as a golem.

She looks at him. "I got orders."

"They're on lockdown, ma'am. Some kinda shit going on down there. It's under quarantine now. Alarm is sounding. You go down there, I can't let you back out."

She sighs, thinking of all the paperwork she'll have to fill out if she leaves without completing her task. "Maybe I can help." She digs her orders out of her handbag. "They gave me these at the first checkpoint." She hands the single typed sheet over to the guard. "I think they might need me down there."

The truth is, she had only skimmed the classified document. Hadn't yet studied it closely. It said something about "*scanning the memories of a patient zero to ascertain any information on the origins or spread of an outbreak discovered less than forty-eight hours ago in western Pennsylvania.*" But Jasmine also knew that in the case of a code black outbreak with unknown origins, the CDC often handed the mystery over to the DIA, who usually threw everything they could think of, including the kitchen sink, at the investigation—SEAL teams, NSA, Interpol, even black ops units such as the Natural Anomalies Group and government-trained psychics. Hence the need for a fast entry specialist such as the illustrious commissioned officer and high-functioning drunk Master Sergeant Jasmine Meredeth Maywell.

She waits for the guard to read the order, dying for a drink.

"Suit yourself," he says finally, handing the document back to her, and stepping away from the elevator.

"Appreciate it," she says, pressing the down button. The door clatters open. She enters the enclosure, and the door rattles shut.

The elevator seems to take an eternity to descend into the sublevels.

– 3 –
The Black Oblivion

She doesn't encounter the first body until she has made her way off the elevator, has moved down an empty corridor with an alarm screaming in her ears, has pulled her pistol, and has passed an unattended guard desk splattered with blood. The atmosphere is charged with static electricity and the coppery odor of gore. She turns a corner and sees the security door to the medical wing hanging wide open and a body lying in a fetal position on the parquet floor just inside it, marinating in a puddle of its own blood. The victim, an older, balding man—whom she's assuming has expired recently—still wears a white lab coat and security tag. His eyes are closed in the endless sleep of death. Jasmine approaches cautiously and kneels by the body.

Chills rash her arms as the extent of the man's injuries make themselves known to her in the bright fluorescent light of the hallway and the shrieking buzz-saw din of the alarm. His neck and half his torso are gone, spilling entrails across the tile, chewed away by what looks like a wild animal. She takes a deep breath and against her better judgment decides to do a quick entry.

It's a process that she discovered early on in her life, sometime around age sixteen, when a boy got a little too cozy with her under the bleachers in the high school gymnasium. What started as a little heavy petting had deteriorated quickly into what can only be called rape. But in the moments before the kid entered her, she grabbed his face, a hand on each temple, fingers pressing in on his skull, and all at once the boy's innermost secret thoughts flooded her brain—unbidden, inexorable, in Technicolor and high definition. She saw through *his* point of view not *her*, but the *past*, an older boy molesting *him*, and her cry exploded out of her almost involuntarily. "You can't *excuse* this . . . just because *it happened to you*!"

She barely remembers what happened after that, the boy skulking away, thunderstruck by her eerie cognition, but the memory will always be with her. Even after years of harnessing the gift for the government, she still thinks of that primal incident.

Now she lowers herself to both knees in front of the dead scientist, the blood soaking into her leggings. She positions his head for better access, and she gently but firmly grasps the man's skull, cradling it just so, fingertips electrodes on a cardiogram.

She flinches at the violent stream of thoughts and imagery crashing down on her:

> *(. . . 7 June, three hundred twenty-two hours, Eastern Standard Time, DOA from Evans City . . . disposition of*

remains, pathologist's notes . . . the decedent, female, Caucasian, mid-thirties, delivered to Fort Denning restrained in body bag . . . cause of death unknown . . . digits on left hand twitching . . . initial thoughts, postmortem spasms due to residual electrical energy . . . gases built up within the esophageal walls . . . anomalous, unexplained . . . eyelids retracting spontaneously, the corneas exhibiting some kind of patina, vestigial cataracts, milky, iridescent . . . I see the hands clenching, clenching . . . rigor mortis? Wait . . . wait!)

Jasmine winces, sympathetic adrenaline coursing through her, a kind of narcotic, which years ago she dreaded but later started to crave, not at all unlike the acquired taste for a really good whiskey. Nowadays, she could not get enough of that nectar of the gods, that inimitable smoky burn repellant at first, but later in life a salve on her soul. All of which is now overridden in lieu of the heroin-like blast of terrified recall streaming into her:

(. . . The corpse convulsing, straining against the straps, discoloration around the nose, mouth, and teeth . . . incisors grinding against rubber guard . . . swallowed the tongue?)

Jasmine's hands tighten on the scientist's mandibles, her knuckles whitening as the dead man's mind-screen downloads the horrors into her:

(. . . Straps breaking . . . decedent slipping off table . . . now I'm kneeling to administer 100 milligrams ketamine . . . oh God! Fuck! Pain . . . searing pain shooting

up my rib cage! . . . The thing has latched on to me! . . .
Dear Lord I've been bitten! . . . Tearing into me! . . .
Mortified teeth like black needles!)

All at once, the screen in Jasmine's mind contracts into a black void, a single white dot remaining at its center, a TV at the end of the broadcasting day. She loosens her hold and lets out a sigh of exhaustion—memory-scanning can take its toll, a real bitch on the upper vertebrae and joints—when something starts to vibrate in the center of that luminous pinprick emanating from that black oblivion.

Something like a wasp in a jar buzzes in the heart of that white spot.

Jasmine tries to pull her hands away from the scientist's blood-sticky temples but they won't cooperate. In her mind she sees the strange alabaster dot swelling, expanding, blazing brighter and brighter, the droning white noise inside it intensifying, a wave breaking on a beach, a tsunami coming straight out of the dead scientist's mind and heading straight into Jasmine.

She blinks, then looks directly into the face of burgeoning apocalypse.

The eyelids open, revealing orbs of milkglass.

– 4 –
Postmortem

The labyrinth of hallways in the lowest sublevel of Fort Denning glows with a uniform kind of fluorescent light, which gives the place an air of the operating room, walls and tile floors virtually radiating sterile, antiseptic containment. Nothing enters, nothing escapes. Everything is opaque, immutable, air-tight, regulated, and scoured clean. All of which is why the blood streaks registering now in Master Sergeant Jasmine Maywell's peripheral vision on the walls and glass doors as she rises to her feet and begins to slowly back away from the inex-plicably animate corpse on the floor strike her as anachronistic, wrong.

The creature that used to be a government scientist named Hanrahan—Jasmine caught a glimpse of the man's nametag—now sits up with the flaccid, twitchy movements of a rag doll or a puppet. Jasmine keeps backing away as the thing reaches for her stupidly from its spot on the floor, its liver-colored lips peeling back from its teeth with canine ferocity. It makes a sound like rusty hinges creaking inside its mortified throat as it claws its way up the side of the wall to a standing position.

If asked later, Jasmine would not even remember pulling the DoubleTap pistol from its hip sheath. She would not recall raising the gun, aiming it at the creature shuffling toward her now with inebriated purpose—a baby taking its first steps—clawing at the air, drooling black foamy bile. If she were asked to fill out a report the next day, she would have absolutely no memory of firing off a single round at that menacing, lumber-ing corpse.

The blast hits the former scientist in the chest, between the nipples, sending a plume of blood mist and pink matter out the back of the lab coat.

In her imaginary report—a document that she would, sadly, never get an opportunity to draft—this would be the moment she described as *time standing still*. All the cryptic information that streamed into her only moments earlier now chimes and flashes in one-hundred-point marquee type font. Words such as "postmortem" and "anomalous" and "unexplained" now spontaneously blaze in her midbrain, exclaiming their portents in fiery revelations as she sees the thing that used to be a scientist unfazed by the catastrophic ballistics of the gun blast.

The creature barely slows down, barely recoils from the bullet's impact, its pale shoe-button eyes still fixed on Jasmine.

She turns and runs.

– 5 –
The Smell of Gasoline

Her memory of Fort Denning's lower levels is sketchy and vague at best. She has been down here once before to locate a missing person—a diplomat's wife—whose single white glove conjured an image of a body-dump, a woman raped, wrapped in Visqueen, sunk into the silt at the bottom of the Potomac. Most of the classified missing-person cases that Jasmine has worked in her career have ended in tragedy. Which seems to be exactly how this day will end for *her* if she fails to find a way out.

She does remember the place being lousy with dead ends. Everywhere you turn, another airtight, sealed security door with triple-pane, bulletproof, mesh-reinforced safety glass. She turns a corner now, and she runs directly into just such an impediment.

She sees through the impermeable window into another corridor, which leads to another dead end. She can hear the dragging noises behind her, the relentless drunken gait of a dead scientist coming to—what? Sink its mortified teeth into her as some other cadaver had done to him?

Head spinning with dizziness, flesh crawling, blood vibrating in her veins with adrenaline, Jasmine turns and heads down a side corridor.

This hallway leads to the pathology lab. Jasmine remembers the tiled walls lined with metal doors, each one numbered cryptically. The smell of gasoline? Is it disinfectant? One of the burned-out fluorescent tubes overhead flickers back on as though the very current running through the sublevel is nervously reanimating. Something rumbles beneath her. Emergency generators?

She reaches another dead end—a blank tile wall with evidence of black mold in the seams of the grout—her heart hammering. Incredible how quickly all the complicated tasks are reduced to simple survival—fight or flight. She hears the foreboding sounds of dragging behind her, coming around the corner of the side hall, closing in on her, heavy, thick, feral, perhaps additional sets of shuffling footsteps coming.

Glancing over her shoulder, she sees three, maybe four skeletal humanoid shadows appearing at the mouth of the narrow corridor, seeping across the tiles as long and distended as oil spills.

If asked to recount the next few minutes in her nonexistent written testimony of the day's events, she would now, for the first time this morning, for some unknown reason, have total recall of every minute detail. She would be able to describe her instantaneous decision to kick open the last door on the right—a space she would later learn is the main examination room of the pathology lab—and would have no problem expounding on the single, forceful impact of her right boot-heel on the door. The noise of that bolt snapping is punctuated by the sudden pain shooting up her leg from the impact.

She would be able to give precise descriptions of the odor that greets her in that dark, stainless steel, tomb-like room with the high ceilings, powerless halogen lights hanging down, and banks of body drawers embedded in the walls: The air reeks of gas with a darker accent beneath it, something protein rich and spoiled like old raw meat in a refrigerator that has long ago lost power.

In her report that will never exist, she would make crystalline clear—at this point in the time line—how she madly slams the door, wedges a chair underneath the knob, and searches in vain for the light switch.

Now, at this very moment, as her options run out, she spins and scans the room with eyes still adjusting to the darkness. She grips the DoubleTap pistol in her right hand, a single round left in the chamber. Something moves to her left. She jerks toward a shadow that she may or may not be imagining in her heightened state. With her inherited skills, she is not unlike a psychic medium entering a haunted domicile or a place of historical upheaval, assaulted by the noise of the residual trauma. Now her senses overload with voices and images coursing through her brain all at once, a fractured mosaic of blood, infection, misery, and hate—a great, heaving tidal wave of emotion seizing her.

Something to her left pounces at her in a whirlwind of death-stench.

At first, Jasmine registers only a blur slamming into her as she raises her gun with both hands and involuntarily squeezes off the second round, the barrel pressed against something soft. The creature going for her jugular whiplashes backward—hit dead center in the neck—the point-blank blast sending pink aerosol out the back of its nape. In eyewitness testimony that will never be written, Jasmine would probably describe the moment as instinctual, transpiring so quickly it's difficult to parse every action and reaction that follows.

One thing is certain: The impact of the bullet passing through its mortified flesh does very little to impede or discourage the thing, as Jasmine learns almost immediately. Instead of falling down, the creature staggers for just an instant, then lurches a second time for Jasmine's throat. This time, the impact of the creature ramming into Jasmine sends her stumbling.

She trips over her own feet, dropping the gun and collapsing to the floor.

The thing lands on top of her, its jaws already dilating, gaping, its bloodless lips peeling back, exposing wormy gray teeth, some as sharp as X-Acto blades. Jasmine once again reacts reflexively, with involuntary speed, grabbing the thing by its wounded neck one nanosecond before it sinks its incisors into Jasmine's arm. The jaws snap and clack like castanets. The ratcheting teeth gnash and grind, seeking live flesh, the head attempting to oscillate back and forth, going for the inner parts of Jasmine's wrists as she strangles the scrawny creature with little or no effect.

The stalemate that ensues practically mesmerizes Jasmine. She stares into the frosted portals of the creature's eyes, seeing nothing but urgent hunger. There is nothing else there. No life, no blood flowing through its veins, no blush of vitality in the flesh—only pallid dead skin and hunger. Jasmine remembers then what smells like gasoline: embalming fluid.

All at once, the identity of the creature becomes clear to Jasmine—the high cheekbones, the stringy long hair, the emaciated limbs of a former middle-aged rural housewife, maybe a matriarch of a farm. Jasmine realizes on a wave of nausea that this is the *decedent*. This is the fatality from Evans City, the Caucasian, mid-thirties female delivered to Fort Denning restrained in a body bag . . . cause of death unknown. This is patient zero.

In the wake of this revelation, a circuit of empathy opens inside Jasmine Maywell—a current crackling through the contact of her fingertips—which erupts inside her like two catalysts crashing into each other.

– 6 –
Eating Disorder

It's never just booze. It's sex, weed, food, porn, blow, poppers, tobacco, pulling your hair out, eight balls, masturbating, caffeine, smack, cutting yourself, crystal meth, forcing yourself to vomit after every meal, sleeping pills, huffing, oxy, and playing endless video games.

Jasmine Maywell grew up consuming all manner of substances in compulsive ways. She was a restless child, nervous, bit her fingernails, suffered from eating disorders, overweight by the time she hit puberty, diagnosed early with ADD. Her special talents had been fully formed from birth, but they had caused her only agitation and night terrors until she was well into her teens. Kissing a boy with whom you're desperately in love and discovering that he just wants to feel your tits was heartbreaking for a sensitive teenage girl of color in the 1980s.

Now, lying on her back in a dark, malodorous lab, in the thrall of patient zero's cellular memory, she convulses on the floor. Back arching, jaws locking, mind imploding with the force of an epileptic seizure, Jasmine digs her hands into the ex-woman's putrid, skinny neck as the poisonous narrative flows into her:

> *(. . . Daniel! Daniel, where are you?! . . . Screams coming from the barn . . . horses shrieking . . . me running across the back lawn, plunging into the stench of the stable . . . Daniel crouched on the floor of the barn, awful smell, blood coating his face . . . horses dead, torn open, guts spilled . . . Daniel eating . . . eating the entrails?)*

Jasmine shudders, her hands welded now around the collapsed windpipe of the former farm wife. Jasmine's fingertips adhere to the moldy, decomposing flesh as though super-glued to it as the jaws work and the teeth grate.

> *(. . . Losing track of time, Daniel feasting on my blood, my insides . . . Why, God? . . . Blackness drawing down over me . . . Why, Lord? Why have you forsaken us? Why?)*

Darkness encloses Jasmine. All the sound and odors and echoes in the underground lab cease. The connection falters, flickering in the back of Jasmine's mind, a weakening signal . . .

*(. . . Wandering . . . aimless . . . so hungry . . . hungry
for warm flesh . . . never enough . . . never satiated . . .
always, always hungry . . .)*

The third eye inside Jasmine contracts into itself, her inner mind-screen reaching the end of its programming block, the images in her head shrinking into a single, luminous, cold white pinpoint.

For a moment, the dot hangs in space, the black void around it deepening, sucking every last iota of humanity into its vacuum. In some distant chamber of Jasmine's soul, she feels an emptying, a leeching of her humanity, the eradication of her ability to love, to laugh, to cry, to reason, to communicate, to appreciate, to empathize, to remember, to be *alive*, to be human. She senses the seismic shift inside her as the wasp in the jar buzzes in the heart of that icy white spot.

Jasmine increases the pressure on the mangled, turkey-like neck of the former country wife. The creature writhes and wriggles in her grasp like a fish on a hook. The need to fill the void—to put a salve on the hunger, to chase away the emptiness, to self-medicate, to forget—all of it begins to rise up within Jasmine's wounded soul. In her mind, that ivory-bright spot swells, expands, blazes brighter and brighter. The hunger, the addictions, the need to consume thunders within her, resonating like a massive chord harmonizing with the diseased alpha waves of a dead woman flooding Jasmine's brain.

The singularity—the big bang of Jasmine's condition—now ignites, forcing her eyes to pop open, focus, and fix on what exactly is wriggling in her grip.

Food.

– 7 –
Solitary Exit

Jasmine doesn't hear the far door burst open, the chair skidding across the floor, the barrel of a Beretta M9 poking into the dark lab, gleaming in the shadows like the tip of a divining rod. Jasmine is preoccupied. She's too busy eating to notice anything else.

The lower part of the farm wife's face is the most tender. In a gluttonous, mad frenzy, Jasmine bites off the creature's lips with the hasty flourish of a famished gourmand slurping tendrils of fresh squid. The creature shudders and quivers in Jasmine's grasp. The soft palate and sinus cavity are next. She spits out a rotten tooth as though it's a seed. The truth is, Jasmine has always been addicted to, among other things, shellfish, so the process of greedily burrowing her teeth into the former farm wife's mouth and hungrily chewing through the tongue, the facial and lingual arteries, and the soft tissues of the nose comes naturally.

The fluids and juices, seeping slowly due to the farm wife's lack of circulatory functions, ooze all over Jasmine.

Within seconds, the creature's face has been reduced to pulp. But Jasmine keeps gorging on the dead flesh, gobbling her way up into the orbital sockets. She slurps the eyeballs with the intensity of a Cajun sucking the heads of crawfish, oblivious to the two military police behind her, taking their first steps into the room with guns raised, muzzle sites at eye level, weaver positions, safeties off. Jasmine is too absorbed in her binge to notice, the hunger persisting like an ache, an itch that cannot be scratched.

Covered now in black, oily spoor, she starts in on the neck, gobbling through the creature's slender, gristly cords, chewing through carotid down to the windpipe, hardly pausing to take lusty breaths. The former rural matriarch continues trembling and quivering beneath Jasmine, an engine that just keeps on dieseling even as it's being dismantled. Jasmine has no idea that she is now in the front site of a nine-millimeter pistol.

The gun roars.

The single blast strikes Master Sergeant Jasmine Maywell two inches above her left ear, silencing her world forever and bringing an end to her own hunger that she was never quite able to slake.

– 8 –
Into the Dark

The second blast penetrates the farm wife's mutilated head, sending a putrescent cloud of brain matter and skull fragments out the back of her ruined skull. The farm woman—restored in her gruesome death to her mortal self— collapses next to Jasmine.

The two military cops stand motionless in the cloud of cordite fumes for a moment, staring at the remains. The younger one holsters his weapon, then looks at the older one. "What the fuck."

It's not exactly a question as much as a commentary on the whole mess that has dropped in their laps over the last forty-eight hours.

The older one—heavier, grayer, his uniform stained in bloody blowback—shakes his head. "What the fuck indeed. I'm going home."

"Good luck with that," the younger MP says. "You see the reports? Nobody's getting in or out of Frederick, it's a goddamn shit storm out there."

"We'll figure it out." The older one holsters his piece and walks to the door. "Send for cleanup, will ya? Bag and tag these stiffs."

He walks out, leaving the younger MP standing there, scratching his chin nervously, pondering the connection between the two females lying in a spreading pool of blood on the parquet floor.

With no answers forthcoming, he turns and walks out, shutting the door behind him, leaving the human remains—as well as the world as a whole—in the dark.

Mike Carey is a British novelist, poet, comic book writer, and screenwriter whose many works include the *New York Times* bestselling series The Unwritten and the celebrated comics *Carver Hale, Lucifer, Hellblazer, X-Men: Legacy,* and *Ultimate Fantastic Four.* His novels include the enormously popular *Felix Castor* series and *The Girl with All the Gifts,* which has been adapted for film.

IN THAT QUIET EARTH

by Mike Carey

I lingered round them, under that benign sky: watched the moths fluttering among the heath and harebells, listened to the soft wind breathing through the grass, and wondered how any one could ever imagine unquiet slumbers for the sleepers in that quiet earth.

—Emily Bronte, *Wuthering Heights*

Later, when the risen dead were at high tide and the world as it used to be was scarcely even visible any more, Richard Cadbury came to see his wife Lorraine's demise as the first domino, which in toppling had brought down everything else.

Though that made no logical sense, on an emotional level it was compelling.

In her passing, Lorraine had tilted the world.

Cadbury rolled with it, to the furthermost edge of existence. In the months following his bereavement he seemed to retreat into a smaller and smaller space, excluding in succession all of the people he knew—friends, family, work colleagues, neighbors—from his interior life. It was not that he ceased to feel affection for them. It was rather the opposite, that he wished to spare them the utter anomie, the lack of meaning and sense and direction that now defined and delineated his life.

These changes in him were profound, but they were hard to see from the outside. Cadbury continued to drive to the lab every day and put in a full day's work. He took a single day off for the funeral and then returned to his bench, politely declining the offer of compassionate leave and the equally well-intentioned, equally misguided offer of counseling. What he felt he could not utter. Even within his own mind it remained entirely unarticulated. There was, simply, a hole where his heart had been. The rest of him was falling into it in a slow-motion cascade that would probably last until his death.

In a sense, then, death became his vector. Perhaps that was why—despite his profound isolation—he became aware of the risen dead very quickly. He was unable to remember later on where and when he picked up the first hint. It was most probably through a radio item, but he turned on the TV shortly afterward and watched the longer and longer segments devoted to the crisis on the TV news.

He made the journey from skepticism to belief quickly and smoothly.

It was easy to be dismissive at first, when all anyone had to go on were the verbal accounts of inarticulate witnesses re-mastered into media-speak by bored TV anchors who didn't believe or care what they were saying. Easier still with those preposterous fragments of found footage, so ineptly framed and focused they screamed amateurishness and implausibil-ity. The men and women lurching around streets and parks looked as though the night before had instantaneously turned into the morning after. No worse than that. No hint of a new ontology, a turning point in the history of life on Earth.

But when Cadbury opened his door the next morning to go to work he saw the lurchers out in the street. Saw them see-ing him, and switching their attention to him. Converging on him, even while he got into his car and drove away. Quite an extraordinary length to go to, for a hoax. Some of them had wounds on their bodies that looked very convincing.

He didn't get into the lab. The receptionist, Sheila, was on the other side of the double doors, throwing herself repeatedly against their shatterproof glass. Her face was a pulped mess in which bloodied teeth worked constantly, as though she could gnaw her way through the glass to get to him.

In the ninety seconds or so that Cadbury stared at her, ir-resolute, almost a dozen lurchers appeared around the corner of the building or from the alley behind the storage sheds, all stumbling and staggering toward him. The smell of decay came with them on the light breeze, mild but unmistakable.

So then he knew. Knew what everybody else knew, anyway. Death had become a reversible condition, but something was lost in that brief crossing of the threshold. Something pro-found, evidently. The returned seemed to be neither blessed nor burdened with sentience. They enjoyed a more rudimen-tary existence, governed by a single impulse.

What that impulse was he saw for himself on his journey home. A number of lurchers had trapped a dog and were devouring it messily even as it struggled to get free of them. Cadbury was distressed by the creature's suffering but could see no way of alleviating it. Within a few seconds it was borne down, the teeth of a middle-aged woman fastening in its throat. The woman's handbag still hung from her left shoulder, vestigial and grotesque.

When Cadbury got back home he had to run the short distance from the curbside to the house, keys at the ready. Even so the lurchers scattered around his lawn and his driveway almost got to him before he was able to get the door open and get inside. He slammed it shut on clutching fingers, severing two that seemed from their appearance to come from different hands.

The phone was ringing. He hurried across the room and picked it up.

"Hello?" he said.

"Dr. Cadbury? Richard? Is that you?" It was the senior supervisor at the lab, Graham Theaker, but his voice was so high-pitched and his diction so broken that it took Cadbury a moment to identify who was speaking.

"Hello, Theaker," he said. "The most astonishing thing is happening. I wonder if you're aware of it?"

"Aware of it? Dear God, Richard, it's—it's the end of the world! It's the apocalypse! The—the dead! The dead are coming back to life to devour the living!"

"I know that, Theaker. They've been talking about it on the news. And when I tried to get into the lab half an hour ago I saw what had happened to Sheila."

"Sheila." Theaker sounded close to tears. "She has three children. Sweet Jesus, if she's spread the infection to them . . ."

"Is it an infection?" Cadbury inquired. "I wasn't aware that any explanation had been generally accepted yet."

Theaker didn't seem to have heard him. "But it's not just Sheila, Richard, it's everyone. Almost. Almost everyone. Dr. Herod. Lowther. Alan . . ."

"Alan?"

"The intern. He went into Dr. Herod's office to deliver her mail. She bit him in the throat! He was able to get out of the room and lock her inside, but he died soon after from loss of blood. Or he . . . he *seemed* to die. We called for an ambulance, but nobody came. And then an hour or so later he stirred, and got back up again. Harrison had to strike his head off with a fire axe. It was horrible. Horrible!"

"Yes, no doubt, no doubt," Cadbury agreed. The bulk of his attention was already elsewhere, parsing the meaning of this strange apocalypse. That is, its meaning for himself, and for his dead wife. He tried to offer Theaker some solace, but really he just wanted the call to be over so he could pursue his thoughts to where they seemed to be leading. "You should turn on the TV," he suggested, "or the radio. The government is coordinating local task forces to deal with the situation. It might be a few days before they get a handle on it, but they're coming. I would imagine that the best way to survive is to remain in complete isolation until they arrive."

"Isolation?" Theaker repeated.

"Absolutely. Stay at the lab. It's more easily defended than your house. Go out once to secure some food and water, if you must, but then barricade yourself in and wait for the all-clear.

Use the security shutters, so long as you can fit them without exposing yourself to risk."

"Of course!" Theaker sounded energized now, and even hopeful. "And you'll join me, Richard? If you drive your car right up to the doors—"

"I will be working from home," Cadbury said. "Goodbye, Theaker, and good luck."

He hung up the phone. When it started to ring again he first ignored it and then unplugged it at the wall. He had work to do.

Obtaining a specimen was the first order of business, and it wasn't hard. The lurchers converged on the living without hesitation, and every such encounter left casualties. There was a window of time, some few hours, before these casualties underwent the same metamorphosis as their killers. Cadbury cruised around the neighborhood until he found a dead man lying at the curbside. He quickly bound the man's hands with kitchen twine and muzzled him—after a fashion—with wire mesh taken from a garden center, the loose ends twisted together with pliers.

He drove home with the dead man in the trunk of his car. He didn't open the trunk until the car was in the garage with the roll-over door drawn down and locked. By that time the dead man was no longer dead. He was squirming and writhing in the trunk, trying to break free of his bonds. Cadbury considered trying to remove him and secure him to a workbench, but thought the risk too great. He got out his circular saw instead and removed the man's head directly. There was less mess than he expected, possibly because of postmortem changes to the viscosity of the man's blood. It had not coagulated completely but it had thickened to the consistency of molasses.

Cadbury took the head into his basement, which he had long ago converted into a laboratory both for his own pet projects and for unofficial overtime. He excised the brain and examined its structures on a microscopic level with growing fascination.

They were, for the most part, no longer viable. The brain had already begun to decay, but it seemed that with the quickening back to life that process had been arrested. Even within a head that had been severed from its body, the brain was inexplicably drawing—from the syrupy blood, or the ambient air, or some storehouse as yet unidentified—the nourishment it needed to keep itself alive.

But that word seemed tendentious, in Cadbury's opinion. Like its opposite, *dead*, it assumed a binary system in which all things that were not in group (a) must be in group (b). But the risen dead were anomalous. They had a tithe, a fraction of what might be called life, rather than the whole complex extravaganza of thought and feeling, selfhood and sentience. The minds of these revenants should have shut down entirely: instead they were open just a crack, like the door of a child's room at night before the child has accustomed himself to the dark.

For his second sample he did not remove the head. He searched for a small and manageable corpse, and found one at last after two hours of driving around. She was a woman of very slight build. She began to stir to life while Cadbury was binding her, which was alarming but fortunately not fatal. He was able to keep her pinioned with one knee on her chest while he tied her arms, and then to wrap the mesh around her mouth from behind. She bit him in the hand despite all his precautions, but he was wearing thick gardening gloves and the bite did not break the skin.

With the woman bound in a chair in his basement he measured the electrical flow through her brain using a device of his own manufacture—an encephalometer. He found that most aspects of brain function were no longer present. Instead of the rich three-dimensional ebb and flow of charge, the endlessly rewoven tapestry of neural connectivity, there was a single cyclical pulse. A powerful stimulus endlessly repeated, like the radio signals sent out by pulsars.

Cadbury remembered the old saw: the fox knows many things, the hedgehog knows one big thing. The risen dead were not cunning. They were not versatile. The panoply of human response had been pared down in them to one impulse, one behavior. It was a minimal, utilitarian sort of resurrection.

Was it, though, in any sense, elective? Could a man enter that state of his own volition, and control his immersion into it?

He thought of Lorraine, awake in the earth, alone. Of his own life, in the free air but still no less entombed. This situation, he felt, was not supportable. He had to go to her. But there was no point in embracing her if she saw no more in him than a warm meal.

Five cadavers later, Cadbury took his research from the universal to the personal. He constructed a machine whose business end was a plastic bucket with layers of padded latex covering most of its open end. He could thrust his head into the bucket and then seal it by means of an adjustable metal collar into which the overlapping pleats of latex were gathered. Oxygen could then be extracted from the air within the bucket by means of a Jessom-Simmonds filter and an electrically operated pump.

The hardest part was the timer. Cadbury needed to be able to calibrate it very finely, but also to adjust it in use without being able to see the numbers on the dial (because his head would be inside the bucket). He taught himself the rudiments of braille and labeled the dial with carefully placed dots of hardened resin.

Over the next two days he subjected himself to 182 near-death experiences. Each was unique, minutely different from the others either in the percentage of oxygen depleted from the air or in the duration of the ensuing suffocation.

His head began to throb after only a dozen of these self-inflicted ordeals, but he did not falter. He made notes, at first in his usual meticulous hand but then in an increasingly messy and uncoordinated scrawl. Orthography was the least of his worries. After the blood vessels in his eyes began to burst it became harder and harder to see what he was writing.

You can't make an omelette, he reminded himself stoically, without breaking a few eggs. He was the egg, in this scenario. He broke himself time after time, and charted the damage with precision. The encephalometer became his map, and his holy writ. He squinted at its endless printouts with his head tilted back almost to the horizontal, the angle that seemed optimal for what was left of his erratic vision.

The dividing line, he finally decided, was three minutes and fifteen seconds at an eight percent oxygen saturation. The encephalometer's readout showed a progressive simplification of neuronal activity from two minutes and forty seconds onward. He had ventured as far as three minutes and five seconds and come back—but only just.

He had actually *felt* the change. The replacement of his brain's complex staging of past, present, and future, real and counterfactual, felt and believed, with a single bellowing hunger. But he had still been himself. The bellowing was a din through which he could still hear, a splash of hypersaturated red through which he could see. And think. And be.

Ten more seconds, then, to take him up onto that knife-edge, but not over it.

The lab had a van with a portable generator. Cadbury ventured out and requisitioned it. He saw Theaker watching from one of the upstairs windows. The man did not look well. He waved frantically at Cadbury and tried to get the window open to shout down to him, but by the time he had done so Cadbury was inside the van and driving away. He had nothing to say to Theaker, and no interest in hearing what Theaker had to say to him.

The generator was not at maximum charge, but it would be more than adequate for his purposes. Cadbury loaded the van with his suffocation device, as well as a shovel, a screwdriver, a crowbar, and a double-barreled shotgun. He hoped he would not have to use either of these last two, but it was as well to be prepared.

He drove to the cemetery. There was a parking area just inside the open gates but he ignored it, taking the van up over the cement shoulder and in among the graves. It was difficult to navigate here, the way very narrow, but he needed to have the generator close at hand for what came next.

The lurchers were an additional hazard. They were very numerous here, for whatever reason, and they did not move as the van bore down on them. He felt their bodies crunching under the wheels, the van rising and falling as it rode on over them.

He pulled in at last, right beside the familiar headstone. LOR-RAINE MARGARET CADBURY, it read, followed by two dates and a platitude. SHE IS BUT SLEEPING. He hoped with all his heart that was a lie. That Lorraine was wide awake, and waiting for him.

He opened the door and stepped out. All the lurchers in the vicinity immediately swiveled and headed in his direction. He took out as many as he could. A head shot was required to dispatch them, and a head shot could not always be managed. Before the vanguard got close enough to be a threat he got back into the van and decamped to another spot, a hundred yards away.

The lurchers followed, and Cadbury saw off another half dozen as they lumbered toward him. Again he got back into the van before any of them were close enough to be a danger, and again he relocated. He repeated the maneuver seven more times before he had finally cleared the area.

He returned to Lorraine's grave and set himself to dig.

This physical labor was the hardest part of the whole procedure. He was unused to using his hands to manipulate anything heavier than a pipette, and the effort told on him. Before long he was panting and sweating, his hands trembling and his shoulders aching from the unaccustomed effort.

Did the lurchers hunt by scent? He did not believe so, but it was an unnerving thought. He might be taken as he toiled in the deepening hole, unable to escape to the van before he was overrun.

But his luck held. By five in the afternoon or so he had completely uncovered the coffin. Moreover, he discovered to his intense relief that the screws were largely pristine. If they had rusted he would have been forced to resort to the crowbar, prizing the casket open by main strength and damaging it in the process.

As it was, a few minutes sufficed to remove all six screws.

Long before he had finished he could hear the faint scrabbling from inside the coffin. He threw open the lid and beheld her, his lost love.

Cadbury was a realist when it came to physical processes, and he was not squeamish. He had prepared himself mentally for what he was about to see. There was therefore no moment of shock or resistance. If anything he was amazed at how recognizable Lorraine still was. Wasted, of course, and decayed, with her face sunken in and more of her hair lying on the white silk behind her head than on her scalp. A gray fungal growth on the left side of her chin made her look, strangely, as though she had decided in death to sport a beard but had trimmed it too recklessly.

Her upper body squirmed as she tried unsuccessfully to raise herself. Nine months dead, her muscles were too atrophied and eaten away to support and animate her frame, meager and hollowed out though it was. Her eyelids fluttered but could not close over the dry, sunken pits of her eyes.

"Lorraine," he said. "It's me, Richard." He did not know if she could understand him. He presumed not. But he did not wish to intrude on her privacy without announcing himself.

He set the dials. Eight percent. Three minutes and fifteen seconds. He slid the bucket over his head and pressed the switch. The van's generator chugged and the pump hummed, industriously extracting oxygen from the air circulating around his mouth.

The descent seemed to take much longer than it had the other times. Perhaps, though, that was merely because this time he had an actual destination. His head began to pound around the end of the second minute. His lungs sucked helplessly for sustenance that would not come. A wave of dizziness compelled him to sit down, and then to lie full length on the ground.

The third minute was an eternity; the final fifteen seconds longer still. His last, failed breath was drawn out unfeasibly, his chest taut and quivering, until the muffled ding of the bell announced that his time was up.

He struggled out of the helmet. It took a long time: he could barely remember where the fastenings were, or how they worked. His thoughts passed through his brain like flotsam bobbing on a sluggish tide.

But Cadbury had measured the time and the saturation to a nicety. He had dosed himself with death, as a man might dose himself with penicillin. He was one of the reanimated now, yes, but he was still himself. His descent into death had been a series of progressively longer immersions, all of them under his own control. His resurrection was the same.

Piecemeal.

Fragmented.

Mediated.

He felt the stirrings of the all-consuming hunger that defined the rest of the risen, but it did not overwhelm him. He could think through it, though it took a vast effort and a vast time. He remembered himself, and his purpose.

Slowly he stood. He advanced to the lip of the grave and lowered himself into it, taking care not to step on Lorraine in the narrow, confined space.

He squeezed in beside her, gradually and gently.

As he had hoped, she did not respond to him as food now. He was of the dead, as she was—at least to the point where his proximity did not stir her appetites.

He tried to speak to her, to tell her not to be afraid, but

speech was no longer available to him. Though he could form the words, he had no breath to push them out into the world. They lay on his tongue, which vibrated with stillborn syllables.

He lowered the lid of the casket.

He settled himself into as commodious a position as he could find, on his side so that he took up less space and did not press against Lorraine in a way that might be constraining. Her body stirred softly against his. Perhaps she was still trying to raise herself up, but he thought not. The movement had nothing of urgency about it. Rather it seemed that, like him, she was making herself comfortable.

Goodnight, my love, he said. There was no sound, only the flexing of his throat and the rise and fall of his tongue against his palate.

He found her hand, and held it. He closed his eyes.

Eternity passed, on the whole, very pleasantly.

John Skipp is a Rondo Award–winning filmmaker (*Tales of Halloween*), Bram Stoker Award–winning anthologist (*Demons, Mondo Zombie*), and *New York Times* bestselling author (*The Light at the End, The Scream*) whose books have sold millions of copies in a dozen languages worldwide. His first anthology, *Book of the Dead*, laid the foundation in 1989 for modern zombie literature. He's also editor in chief of Fungasm Press, championing genre-melting authors like Laura Lee Bahr, Violet LeVoit, Autumn Christian, Danger Slater, Cody Goodfellow, and Devora Gray. From splatterpunk founding father to bizarro elder statesman, Skipp has influenced a generation of horror and counterculture artists around the world. His latest book is *The Art of Horrible People*.

JIMMY JAY BAXTER'S LAST, BEST DAY ON EARTH

by John Skipp

I just gotta say: the end of the world is what you make it. It all depends on your attitude and perspective.

For me? Once I figured out what was what, it was all hog heaven.

Right up till the very end, at least.

* * *

The first one was rough, I will grant you that. Was just washing my truck, minding my own business. Saw Wendell wandering up the street in a T-shirt and shabby pajama bottoms, looking drunk and disheveled as usual. Was surprised to see him without Rascal yanking on the leash at this time in the morning, but didn't think much of it.

"Where's your dog?" I said, and he didn't say. His hearing ain't great, so I gave it a pass, went back to scrubbing birdshit off my windshield, big old sponge in one hand, hose nozzle in the other.

When he came straight up to me, I was like, "What the *fuck*?" And began to tell him so, when he straight-armed me back into the driver's side door, bringing his face right up at mine, growling and making like he wanted to bite.

Call it impulse, but I shoved the sponge square in his face with my left, pushing back, soap suds gushing down my wrist and his neck. I thought it would chill him out, make him choke, bring him back to his senses. But he just kept pushing, and I swear to God I could feel his mouth trying to chew his way through it.

"*Wendell! Jesus Christ!*" I hollered, but he didn't seem to care. Just kept pushing forward, and chomping at the sponge.

So I whacked him upside the head with the hard plastic nozzle, once, twice, till he staggered back a bit. It didn't stop him like it should. So I did it again, till he dropped to his knees, scraps of shattered plastic hitting the pavement between us.

Then he tried to take a bite at *my* knees, and I kicked him hard. Knocked him back on his ass. Kicked him again, for good measure.

When he grabbed my leg on the way back, tugging forward, I gotta admit to a moment of panic. I dropped the sponge and the busted-up nozzle, grabbed him by the scalp, and yanked his head back.

It was right then, staring eye to eye, when I realized he wasn't Wendell no more.

Lemme be clear. I never much cottoned to Wendell. He was queer as a three-dollar bill. But friendly enough, in a neighborly way. Not all faggy about it. Could pass for normal. And I always liked his dog. Since he never ever tried to get all grab-ass on me, I was just kinda live and let live, you know? Like, "Oh, there's old Wendell. What a character. Takes all kinds, I guess."

But once I saw the lights were off in his eyes, a terrible truth rolled through me.

No, make that a *beautiful* truth.

I no longer had to even pretend like I cared.

He still had ahold of my leg, so I dragged him toward the back door of my truck, threw it open with my free hand. I knew where my bat was without looking. The vintage Mickey Mantle Louisville Slugger my grandpa gave me when I was a kid was right where I always kept it, just in case. Strapped in a sling on the back of my driver's seat, ready for action.

In the second it took me to grab hold of the handle, he got close enough to nip at my thigh. Not enough to draw blood, but enough to freak me out. I said, *"Whoa!"* and fell back on the seat, letting loose of his hair, kicking him hard in the face with my free sneaker. His teeth tugged at my jeans as he fell back. I kicked him again. He flew back and let go.

I heave-hoed off the backseat, bat in tow. He lurched toward me. I popped him in the forehead with the butt end, brought the pay end up as he began to rise again.

Then I beat his fucking head in. Beat it till it cracked and caved in, squirted brain all over the pavement. Till he finally stopped twitching.

"*You done?*" I yelled. And yes, he was.

Right about that time, a car screeched to a halt in front of us, yanking me out of my buzz. I felt a moment of embarrassment and fear, like your old lady walking in on you banging the waitress.

But it wasn't my old lady. And I didn't feel guilty. So instead of apologies and shame, I just stared through the windshield at the nigger behind the wheel and yelled, "*You want some of this?*"

She backed right the hell off, screeching into reverse fast as she could. And God help me, I could not stop laughing.

She knew in a second what I had just realized.

As of that moment, all bets were off.

I left Wendell where he lay, like a sloppy speed bump in the middle of the road. Let somebody else clean him up. Wasn't my job. I'd done enough here. With a whole lot more to do.

It was time to make use of my God-given Open Carry privileges.

And finally do what was right.

Didn't take but ten minutes to load up the cream of my armory. That's what trucks are for. I had more weapons and ammo in my basement alone than Venezuela and Vermont combined. More than I could probably ever personally deploy. But damned if we wasn't about to find out.

Sent a couple text messages to buds that might heed the

call. Had a couple dozen extra semiautomatics handy for the under-gunned.

Meet me at the mosque downtown, I said. *Let's make this happen.*

Then off I went, rolling over Wendell twice just for kicks before heading into the greatest fucking day of my life.

Halfway down Creston to El Dorado Boulevard, I saw a skinny *chingado* stagger into my path. The only other car on the road swerved around him, but he didn't even seem to notice. Doing the same sleepwalker shuffle as Wendell. Didn't need to see his eyes to strongly suspect he was part of whatever the hell was happening.

I always wanted to hit somebody with this truck. Thought about it all the time. Some asshole just wanders into your right-of-way, and you're supposed to stop? How about they just wait, or speed their lazy ass up a trifle?

I didn't speed up, but I didn't slow down, neither. Even at 37 mph, he came up quick.

At the very last second, he looked at me.

And there was nobody home.

So I stomped on the gas, and *bam!* He took the hit and disappeared under my hood. I saw it just before the impact shot my forehead half an inch from the dashboard. (I don't give a shit about the law, but *thank you, seat belt!*)

My tires missed him to either side. But as I passed over and past him, he didn't look like he was getting back up. I screeched to a halt. Yelled, "*Wooooo!*" real loud. Took a second to rejoice in this Bucket List moment.

Then jumped out of the cab. Unhooked my vintage '45 authenticated World War II German Luger from its holster on my hip. Strode up to the Mexican mess on Creston Drive. And confirmed all of my suspicions.

The fact that he was still *trying* to twitch, with his spine snapped in half, was one thing. The fact that he wasn't screaming in pain was another. He didn't look like he was in shock. He didn't look sad. He didn't look scared. He barely even looked like a human being.

By some trick of fate, his head was twisted half around and toward me. And all I saw in his eyes was the same thing I saw in Wendell's. A naked hunger, with nothing behind it. Busted to fuck. Way past dead. But not done yet.

Even now, all he wanted to do was eat me.

"That's all you ever wanted, *cabron*," I said. "Am I right? Eat my job. Eat my life. Take me down. Take the whole sovereign white race down."

He tried to bite me from ten feet and closing.

"Straight down to the bottom is where you want us," I said. "Till America's not ours no more. Till it's all mud races, and we're *your* slaves. You'd like that, wouldn't you?"

I shot him in one of his broken legs. He didn't even seem to notice.

"You think it's payback. You think we owe you. But, fucker, we don't owe you shit. You're taking more from me right now than I *ever* took from you."

He didn't understand a word I said. And I could not have cared less. Blowing a hole in his shoulder, then another in his heart, made about as much difference to him as it did to me.

"Right?" I said, aiming the barrel at his braincase, just above them empty eyes. "You want me. But you know what I want?

"I just want you gone."

I pulled the trigger. And he was.

Next, I checked my front bumper. It took a little ding; but once I wiped the blood off, you'd barely even notice. I might be able to do this a couple more times before taking on serious damage. Something to think about, on the way downtown.

Round the corner at El Dorado was my local liquor store. And right away, I saw how shit was escalating.

As I pulled up to the curb, a little Mexican girl was being eaten by some homeless piece of trash. A degraded white man, I'm ashamed to say. Three other people were on the sidewalk, screaming. And one black dude—I gotta give him credit—was trying to peel that fucker off, pull him back off the chunk of cheek he'd just ripped from that pretty little dead girl's face.

I came out locked and loaded, right up on the derelict with the mouth full of meat. At close range, I don't miss. His shit-for-brains chased the bullet that raced toward the brick of the twenty-dollar Thai massage parlor wall behind him. The bullet won. And over he went.

Next thing I knew, a big-tittied *mamacita* was hugging me from behind, saying, *"Gracias! Gracias!"* and weeping as that white trash hit the concrete and stayed there. The black dude turned to look at me.

We locked eyes together.

And jigaboo or not, the one thing for certain was that he was one hundred percent alive. Brave, angry, and scared. Looking at me, and my gun, still aimed in the neighborhood of his skull.

And the question in his eyes was, *are you gonna kill me, too?*

Then I thought about that little girl, who didn't do nothing but get born the wrong color. Gave the black dude a nod of respect for his courage. Put the gun back in my holster. Saw him sigh with relief. Shook the *mamacita* loose as she kissed me on the chin.

Then walked into the liquor store, nonchalant as you please. Grabbed two pints of Jack and a carton of Marlboro Red, just in case. Smiled at Gus, the cheap-ass Filipino motherfucker behind the counter, as I gave him exact change.

And walked out, feeling like the king of the world.

Next thing I knew, I was barreling down El Dorado at sixty per, daring the red lights to stop me. Made it all the way to Standard Ave., where there was a scene out front of the Sacred Revenant Church of the Almighty that made me slow down hard.

Sacred Revenant was one of them wackjob outfits that believed Christ was gonna come back any second now. They kept setting the time. It kept not happening. So they'd set it again. Like, for forty years and counting.

Me, I didn't believe none of that crap. I knew Christ wouldn't be back till shit hit the fan for real. He didn't show up for football games, no matter how much you loved your team. He didn't show up just because the new Pope had a thing for losers and pussies and faggots. He didn't even show up if you poured every speck of your righteous prayer into the most righteous causes of all. That wasn't his job.

His job was to inspire us to do *His* work, so that when we finally fulfilled His prophecy, and all the groundwork had been laid, the real deal could go down. The battle lines were not just to be drawn, but to be executed with ruthless precision.

Only then—*only* then—would Christ return to smite the unholy, only hopefully more like Thor or Odin than that sad sack hippie on the cross. And whether we survived the ultimate conflagration or not, we would glory forever in Heaven. Or Valhalla. Or wherever. Past there, the details weren't exactly clear.

That being said: in the Sacred Revenant parking lot, there was maybe fifty screaming people in their Sunday best. And they was backing up toward the street in a slow-moving wave.

I couldn't see what they was backing away from. But I had a pretty good idea.

So I whipped past the right lane, tore ass into the parking lot, slammed into park about ten yards behind the wave, and jumped out, engine still running. This time, I brought my favorite AK with me, name of Ursula, on account of her Russian design.

The women were almost all dressed in black, and they shrieked as I pushed through the crowd. The men didn't put up much resistance, neither. Didn't take but twenty seconds to cut all the way through.

And then, oh lordy, there he was.

I recognized Pastor Luke at once, although the first thing I thought was *don't he look like himself?* With his funeral makeup caked on, and fresh blood and meat smeared across his maw like chocolate cake on a two-year-old, he mostly resembled a nightmare mannequin from some old monster movie, all spastic herky-jerky in motion. And his eyes as dead as night.

I'd almost forgot that he died last week. Heard about it in passing. My joke was, "Well, looks like he got to Jesus before Jesus got to him!"

But here he was, and it didn't look like Jesus had nothing to do with it. The blood on his hands was as thick as the blood on his mouth. It was my guess he wasn't the only dead person at his funeral anymore.

There were a couple of terrified guys behind him, pacing him but afraid to jump in. The second I brought up Ursula, their eyes went even wider. And the second I waved her barrel at his face, they wisely ducked to either side.

Pastor Luke didn't give a shit. All he saw was walking meat, as he set his dead eyes upon me.

"Listen up!" I hollered loud enough for all to hear, then fired a couple shots over Pastor Luke's head. I spun around to make sure no one was sneaking up on me. One was. He backed the fuck off quick.

"Just so you know: he ain't the only one back from the grave. I took down three in the last forty minutes. Whatever this is, it's all over town. Maybe all over the world, for all I know."

Pastor Luke was getting a little too close. I knew that. It was part of the excitation, the crazy thrill I was feeling at that moment.

So I turned back to him, brought Ursula to bear, and shot him straight through the heart. Everyone shrieked, then gasped and whimpered when he didn't go down. Staggered on impact. Then just kept coming.

"This is not God!" I howled. "This is the Devil! You tell me if I'm wrong!"

I put three more holes through his chest and out the back. It jitterbugged him around some, but only made his focus clearer.

"Are you seeing this?" I turned to clock their faces, streaming tears and blank with shock. He was less than three feet away now. I could feel his closeness in my bones.

I turned around, smiling, switched to full auto, and made a hasty vapor pudding of his skull. Even then, it took a full three seconds for Pastor Luke's body to give up the demon ghost.

The crowd went silent as he hit the ground.

"This is what we're dealing with, people," I said. "This is how it's gonna be from now on. Satan don't care if we're good or evil. Except the better we are, the more he wants us. Which means we gotta fight harder, if we're going to win.

"So I'm going downtown, to that mosque full of Muslims,

and wage me some holy war. Because if there's anyone who's anti-Christian, it's them fucking jihadis. And anti-Christian equals *Antichrist*, last time I checked!"

The first True Believers snapped out of shock, gave me my first hallelujah.

"You want Christ to come back? Then let's give him a reason! Let's *show* Him we mean business!"

That brought a howl. The crowd was catching on quick. You could see their eyes light up with the holy power of belief.

"So how many of you people are packing?"

"I got a hunting rifle in my truck!" yelled a sixty-year-old hardass.

"Shit, I got *three*!" yelled a kid toward the back. "In my rack!"

"*All right!*" I whooped. "*So are we down?*"

And that's when I became a king with an army.

On the way back to my truck, this hot little number came trotting up behind me, and I was like, *damn*. Milky-white just-this-side-of-jailbait redhead in a black funeral dress that didn't leave a whole lot left to imagine. From what I gather, it's hard to run in high heels, but she was making some serious haste.

"I'm riding with you," she said. It wasn't a suggestion. It was a challenge.

"Yeah, okay," I said. "Just don't slow me down."

She cackled. "Oh, dude. I don't slow down for nothing."

"Well, all right, then." Opening the door for her, like a gentleman should. Suddenly hard enough to cut glass.

"You got some firepower for me, right, Jack?"

"It's Jimmy Jay," I said. "You know how to shoot?"

"I bet I blow your little mind, old Jimmy Jay."

"Oh, it's like that, is it? And what's your name, sweetheart?"

"Wouldn't *you* like to know!"

I laughed. She cackled some more, and the challenge was on. I shut the door behind her, circled around my dinged-up fender, felt her bright eyes upon me through the windshield glass.

It had been months since the last time I fucked—since Jeanine caught me with that waitress, left me high and dry—and it felt like Jesus and the Good Luck Fairy just decided this was "National Jimmy Jay Baxter Day."

The second I hopped in, she held up a pint of Jack and said, "May I?" I nodded my head, strapped in, hit reverse, pulled a tight half-donut, and was peeling out and then left onto Standard before she had the screw top off.

"Well, all right then!" she howled, swigging hard, then offered it to me. I waved it away, running a red light at sixty. Traffic was sparse. Another blessing. At this rate, we were five minutes away, tops.

She took another swig, then punched my stereo on. Oldschool Nordic Thunder, baby. *Born to Hate*. I couldn't believe I hadn't thought to crank the music before. So up in my own head.

But the music was our soundtrack, as we whipped down the miles, not stopping for nothing. And it was perfect. Savage, ragged, and righteous. A punk rock White Power triumph of the sonic will. It felt exactly the way I was feeling, said everything I had to say.

She head-banged in her seat beside me, revving up to the groove. Whipping me up, as well.

The next time she offered me the bottle, I chugged that fucker hard, right through a red light, barely dodging a Charger that honked and veered at the very last second.

It was clear sailing till two blocks from our destination. We saw the bottleneck on Main a block away, and I screeched left on a side street, took it down to the next intersection. That one was blocked, too.

She turned down the music as I looked for parking. The only curb left was marked fire hydrant red.

"Let it burn," I said, pulling in.

And she was looking at me. I could feel her gaze, and it burned with meaning. Like maybe I had some sort of answer. Or *was* some sort of answer, to a question she'd been asking herself a long time.

I cut the engine, took a very deep breath that filled the silence where Nordic Thunder just rang. In the time it took to pull the key out, she had one hand on my thigh and the other on my cheek, turning my face toward her.

"Jimmy Jay," she purred, as I popped a bone that could crack Fort Knox. "I would like some guns now, please."

I always wondered what it would be like to fuck for what you knew was the very last time: be it a meteor coming in, or an invading army, or a nuclear bomb, or what have you. Would that last fuck be the ultimate summation and culmination of every fuck you ever had, or hoped to? Would all of your life's long-squandered sexual energy wind up focused in that moment, like a laser beam, resulting in the biggest bang of all?

We went into the back. And there, surrounded by my Armageddon stockpile, I am here to tell you that it was *all that and more*. We went at it like there was no tomorrow, mostly because there probably wasn't; and if her eyes-rolled-back screams and convulsive shudders were any indication, she erupted roughly as volcanic as me.

Fifteen minutes later, we staggered weak-kneed out and back into the world. She looked amazing with straps of ammo crisscrossing her funeral dress, popping her boobs out, M-15 in her hands. Black heels, red hair, and semiautomatics, dude. All she needed was an SS hat and a swastika on her panties, and I'd be hers for life.

"You ever gonna tell me your name?" I asked her.

"When the time comes, you'll know it," she said, popping in a fresh clip. "Now let's take out some assholes."

Couldn't argue with that.

The reason for the traffic congestion came clear as we rounded the corner, and the turrets of the mosque loomed into view. Not only were cars gridlocked far as the eye could see, but the sidewalks were packed with flipped-out pedestrians, radiating panic.

I headed straight toward the middle of the gridlocked traffic, roving between the cars. It was the straightest way in, and she followed me. An Open Carry Parade of two. The handful of gawkers we ran into moved out of our way, the second they saw what we were packing.

The crowd at the end of the cars in the road was sparser. Just a handful of people blocking traffic. All white. All of them armed. All the ones who beat us to it, knew today was the day. None of them facing our way.

All of them aimed at the mosque.

That's when I saw the ring of infidels with machine guns, all pointing them straight back at us.

I guess I didn't realize how many white-hating, heavily

armed Black Panthers already lived right here in town, pissed off and ready to defend all the Middle East sand nigger refugees we let in when Uncle Sam invited the whole world's terrorist population straight up his liberal candy ass. Was used to the protests of the latter camp, bleating *"But you don't understand us!"* as they tirelessly worked to undermine and destroy us from within.

It was another to see forty loaded gun barrels aimed straight back at you. Forty sets of enemy eyes, staring you down. It made me wish I'd plugged that nigger at the liquor store. Cuz his eyes were just like that. If he'd been armed, I'd be a corpse back on El Dorado. No doubt about it in my mind.

"Holy fuck. *It's on now!*" she laughed, over my shoulder. I could barely hear her over the din.

There was a good thirty yards of space between the front line of white Christians and the heathen horde, all of them yelling back and forth. The cars caught between were well past the horn-honking phase: mostly empty, their drivers and passengers having bailed from the firing line. Thinking about their bullet hole insurance coverage. While everybody took up sides.

People flashed me White Power symbols. Flipped me off. Hurled curses. Started chanting eight different things at once, only some in English. All turning to mush in my head.

That was when the crowd parted off to my left.

And the dead transsexual what-the-fuck staggered into the breach between us.

I couldn't say if it was black or white, because the only color I could see was red, splashed all over it from ankle to skull. It had a long beard and a short dress, great tits and broad shoulders. It dragged a picket sign behind it, with the words SHARE

HAPPINESS scrawled in rainbow letters freshly spackled with blood.

But the second it looked at me, I knew it was gone.

It turned its back to me, aimed its blank gaze at the Islamist horde, looked back again. Like it couldn't remember which side it belonged to anymore. Which, frankly, was neither.

If there was one thing we had in common with the fucking Muslims, it was that none of us were real big on the fags. They were the loneliest ones of all. Because there wasn't a god or religion worth mentioning that wanted to admit having anything to do with them.

When it finally staggered toward us, I pushed to the front of the line, Ursula up and ready. The second I stepped forward, it came for me, like I was the only person in its world.

And when I took aim, it was like taking out every last worthless speck of the whole human race that I wanted no part of, in one single shot.

It was the greatest single feeling that I have ever known.

I squeezed the trigger, and the world erupted in gunfire even before he/she/it collapsed from view, forehead gone forever. Felt a bullet whistle past my ear and laughed, firing back with a withering spray. Focusing on the Panthers right in front of the door. Watching one of them cave in, sawed in half. And a dozen others scrambling, barrels blazing.

That was when my lungs blew eight holes through my chest.

Not from in front. But from behind.

The pavement came up fast, with no seat belt this time. I hit face-first. The world shattered to black.

Next thing I knew, I was staring up at a clear blue sky, laced with fluffy white. But big dark ominous clouds were closing in from all sides, crawling across the heavens. The pain was unbelievable, the shock like a drug that only barely helped halfway.

That's when my D-Day Fetish Queen leaned over me, M-15 still smoking. Used the red-hot barrel to turn my other cheek toward her. Made sure she had my full attention.

"Thanks for the guns, you stupid fascist sack of shit," she said. "And no, you *don't* get to know my name."

Then she pulled the trigger.

And I was gone.

Sending me straight back to Jesus, or Odin, or whoever will finally hand over my well-earned and just rewards. Although it seems to be taking forever.

Like I said: the end of the world is what you make it. But frankly speaking, I'm feeling a little ripped off by the end game.

No Heaven. No nothing.

And lord almighty, is it hot.

George A. Romero is the co-writer and director of *Night of the Living Dead*, and the writer-director of *Dawn of the Dead*, *Day of the Dead*, *Land of the Dead*, *Diary of the Dead*, and *Survival of the Dead*. His other works—as writer, director, or both—include *The Crazies*, *Season of the Witch*, *Martin*, *Knightriders*, *Creepshow*, *Monkey Shines*, *Tales from the Darkside: The Movie*, *Bruiser*, and more. He is credited with creating the zombie genre (though he still hates that word!).

JOHN DOE

by George A. Romero

Within the early months of the twenty-first century, even before the terrorist attacks of 9/11, most hospitals, nursing homes, and police departments in the United States—those sophisticated enough to be computer-equipped—were mandated to join the VSDC (Vital Statistics Data Collection) network, a cyber-system that received and instantly downloaded information to a division of the Census Bureau known as AMLD (American Model of Lineage and Demographics). Jokingly referred to as "A Matter of Life and Death." Whenever a birth or a death was recorded anywhere in the country, the doctor, nurse, registrar—whoever was doing the local filing—simply had to click on a link that copied the statistic directly to the VSDC.

John Doe's VSDC case number, 129-46-9875, was recognized by the system twice on the night he died. It was initially forwarded by St. Michael the Archangel, a Catholic hospital in San Diego, California. The second entry, the one that made the case notable, came in almost three and a half hours later from the Medical Examiner's Office in San Diego County. It reached the VSDC at 10:36 p.m. but went unnoticed for another forty-eight hours, until statisticians at the department started to search for abnormalities in recently entered files.

Thousands of similar files were received over those forty-eight hours. Statisticians only began to focus on John Doe's case when they finally tried to determine when the phenomenon actually began. As sophisticated as the VSDC system was, it was unable to automatically organize entries by date and time. Statisticians had to search manually. John Doe's dossier—temporarily catalogued in a file labeled *Beginners*—predated any of the others that were found. There may have been earlier cases, but they went undiscovered because the statisticians simply stopped looking.

After only four nights—four nights after John Doe's death, when the whole thing seemed to have started—there were only two men and one woman left at the VSDC. They remained there, alone, working around the clock, clinging heroically—or perhaps stubbornly—to the idea that their work was in some way essential.

After another forty-eight hours nothing seemed essential. One of the men, John Campbell, shut down his computer, went home, and shot himself in the head. At the end of the seventh night, the remaining man, Terry McAllister, made one final entry in his log. It read, *Merry Christmas to all, and to all a good night.* Appropriate, as Christmas was in two weeks. He and the woman, Elizabeth O'Toole, left their computers running when they walked out of the bureau for the last time. They went to the man's apartment in Georgetown, shared two bottles of Don Julio, and fucked with abandon until the sun rose on the eighth day.

On that day, at 6:20 a.m., Elizabeth O'Toole e-mailed her cousin, a priest, to confess her sins and to say that she and her male companion were going to try to get out of Washington. The message ended with *We might not make it very far. I probably won't ever see you again. I don't even know if you are still there to read this. I hope that you are, and I hope that God will accept a confession that comes via cyberspace. I have tried to make an Act of Contrition, but I can't remember all the words. Absolve me if you are able.*

I think this is the end of the world. Goodbye. Your loving cousin, Beth.

John Doe's case file was forwarded to the VSDC by Luis Acocella, an assistant medical examiner in San Diego. The subject carried no ID. No one knew his real name. Sixtysomething and homeless, he was panhandling on Mission Bay Drive when he was startled by what sounded like firecracker pops. An old panel truck with S.O.B ("South of the Border") plates came careening around a corner with an SDPD cruiser in hot pursuit. A coyote sitting in the truck's passenger side had his door open and was leaning out firing an Uzi at the black-and-white. The truck swerved out of control. Rounds from the automatic whizzed wildly. Seven of those rounds took out the window at a taco joint. Four of them hit John Doe: one high on a thigh, one high on the belly, one low on the left shoulder, and the fourth low on the neck. The homeless man dropped to the pavement and tried to scream. The wound in his neck turned those screams into sounds that resembled the wheeze of escaping steam.

The truck crashed into a telephone pole. Two more black-and-whites arrived and a gun battle ensued. Two police officers were wounded, one critically. As it turned out, there were six Mexicans in the truck, two coyotes and four illegals, all of them male. Four of them were killed, each taking more than two dozen angry rounds from police sidearms. In the end, two were captured alive.

Purely by coincidence, Luis Acocella had been enjoying a caldo gallego at the taco joint when the window was shot out. Once the gunfire had stopped, he rushed out onto the street. When he reached John Doe's side, the man was still wheezing. Acocella ran to his car to get his medical bag. By the time he returned, the first of three ambulances had arrived and the wounded man's wheezing had stopped.

Acocella glanced at his watch. It showed the time was 6:05 p.m. If John Doe was dead, it happened sometime in the last three minutes. If Acocella had agreed to fill out the standard paperwork, he would probably have approximated the "Time of Death" as 6:04 p.m. But he never wrote anything on the forms. None of the man's bullet wounds seemed like killshots. Acocella believed there might be a chance of resuscitation if they could get the victim to a qualified hospital ASAP.

The chief detective got in the doctor's face, saying, "This man is dead, you hear me? And it was your kind that killed him!"

"My kind?" Acocella tried to look innocently puzzled, though he knew exactly what the man meant.

"Fuckin'-A, Jose," the detective came back, not trying at all to disguise what he was thinking. "They killed him. Not us. Them! The coyotes. And we're countin' on you to prove it! Got that? If you don't prove it, your ass is grass. That worthless kind of grass that comes pukin' up from where your daddy fucked his first *chicken*!"

Acocella wanted to kill the guy, wanted to strangle him, but he never so much as let annoyance show on his face. There wasn't time. He quickly said, "I believe this man can still be saved. If we move quickly."

There was an audience, people had gathered, so the detective was forced to call another ambulance, though he did so reluctantly. One finally arrived, no siren, no lights. Paramedics scooped up John Doe and took him to nearby St. Michael's. Acocella knew it was already too late.

He forced himself to be civil with the detectives, but as he walked with his old medical bag toward his car, he kicked a bottle of Corona lying in the street and said, "Fuckin' gringos!" He knew there would have to be an autopsy. So he knew that he would be seeing John Doe at least one more time.

At 8:22 Acocella was in his office at the county morgue. He had just finished some overdue paperwork and was staring with some bitterness at a sign on the wall which was written in Latin; HIC LOCUS EST UBI MORS GAUDET SUCCURRERE VITAE— THIS IS THE PLACE WHERE DEATH REJOICES TO HELP THOSE WHO LIVE—when the phone rang.

An intern informed him that the homeless man had been pronounced dead at 7:18 p.m. in the hospital's ER.

"An intern." Acocella spit this out angrily as he slammed down the receiver on his fifty-year-old, rotary dial telephone. He knew that John Doe died at 6:04. He picked up the heavy receiver and dialed a familiar number.

"Complainer!" Charlene Rutkowski—friends called her Charlie—tossed this barb over the phone at her boss.

"I complain because you're not ever here."

"Gimme a break, I'm always here. What, are you kiddin' me?"

Charlie was a total Bronx bombshell. From Parkchester near the Whitestone, she had Marilyn's body and Judy Holliday's brain. Not that Judy Holliday was ever quite as dumb as she was able to make herself look.

"You complain all the time," Charlie went on. "You enjoy complaining."

"Because nothing—*nothing*—satisfies. Not often enough. If you have a taste for, say, caviar, foie gras, Château Latour, you get enjoyment one, two, maybe three times in a great while. A Cuban cigar hand-rolled on a woman's thigh . . . sex itself . . . maybe once a year! The secret to a satisfying life is to take enjoyment from something that you can have as many times as possible. Once a day. Several times a day. Now, what might that be?"

"I dunno." She paused. "I have to pee several times a day."

"Well, urination is, for the most part, quite a pleasant experience, involving, as it does, our most intimate parts. But more than that, each and every day—each and every day—there are a hundred moments that are, to say the least, irritating. So if we want to get the most out of life, we must learn to enjoy the act of *not* enjoying!"

"Okay, so what are you not enjoying right now?"

"An intern. A fuckin' intern! Who logged in a TOD over an hour after the stiff bit the crang!"

"How d'ya know, over an hour?"

" 'Cuz I was there when the poor guy was *shot*!"

"Get out."

"No bullshit, I was *there*!"

"So . . . what, they brought him in too late?"

"Yeah. Too late." He thought back, remembering the crime scene. "They outranked me. Do you believe that some asshole detective outranks a medical examiner?"

Acocella was, to some extent, playing a role. Playing to Charlie. In his heart, he didn't blame the detectives for what happened. He blamed his own weakness. But he wasn't ready to admit that to Charlie.

He pulled open a drawer and rooted around until he found an old pack of Marlboros. He pulled out a stale cigarette, then did more rooting around looking for a light.

"You're smoking again?" Charlie heard the sounds.

"No. I'm not 'smoking' again. I'm just going to have a cigarette! *One* cigarette. If I can figure out how to light the fuckin' thing!"

He finally came up with an old pack of matches. Tried to strike one.

It snapped in two. He tried to strike another.

Its tip came off.

A third left a residue on the striker but never ignited.

"Jesus Christ," he complained, "you used to be able to rely on these things! A pack of matches! They used to make them differently. Used to make them better! They must be cheaping out or something. They—"

His rant was interrupted when his fourth match produced a flame. Acocella quickly, needily, lit his Marlboro and took a deep puff. It made him dizzy.

Without taking a second puff, he dipped the lit end of the cigarette into yesterday's coffee and pitched it into a garbage can.

"Fuck!" he said.

Then repeated, more loudly, more angrily, "Fuck!"

Then, calming himself a bit, he circled back to what was most bothering him. "I'm telling you, I don't think this guy was dead tonight. Not when I first got to him, anyway. They weren't killshots. I really think I might have been able to save the guy!"

Charlene was Acocella's diener. She had always liked the sound of the word. "Diener." She thought it sounded French. When she pronounced it, improperly, it came out like "DNA," which, in her not-so-analytical mind, took on a certain importance. Acocella never told her that the origin of the word was not French, but German, and that it meant "servant." He knew that being called a servant would not please Charlie one little bit.

Luis told his diener what had happened outside the taco joint, how authorities had insisted on an autopsy, and how he was stuck having to perform one. She empathized, as any Bronx bombshell is expected to do, especially if she has a heart of gold . . . and Charlene's heart was twenty-four carat.

"Okay, so what are you gonna do?" she asked. "You don't wanna be in this mess. I for sure don't wanna be here with you, which I automatically am. But, hey, what's either one of us gonna *do*? Am I right?"

It was 9:42 when a bell went off indicating a delivery. Within three minutes, two gum-chewing paramedics had wheeled John Doe into the autopsy room, plopped his body onto an insulting steel slab, taken their gurney, and left.

"Charlie?" the doctor called.

His diener appeared from out of the washroom.

"He, er . . . he's here," the doctor said.

"So I see," said Charlene, fresh and ready for work. She started to collect sharp tools from hard metal drawers.

The corpse would normally have first been photographed wearing the clothes in which it had died. But it had been sent over from St. Mike's unclothed, so it was naked when Charlie maneuvered an overhead arm that enabled a digital Pentax to shoot angles front, right, and left. The body had to be turned onto its belly for the camera to photograph its back. Acocella helped with the turning, but Charlene performed all other tasks.

The table on which the body rested was also a scale. John Doe weighed 186 pounds.

Other measurements were taken.

X-rays were zapped.

Charlie had done similar duties for more than six years. Seen and handled hundreds of corpses, yet she still found it disturbing, frightening, to be in a closed room with a dead body.

She had a recurring nightmare. At the outset, she would always be in a different place, an office building, a supermarket, a friend's house. At some point, she would walk through a door. After that the dream would always be the same. Exactly the same, but for two small details which were to change in time.

She would step into an autopsy room. It would always be very dark, except for a point at the center of the room where a dead man lay on the examination table. It would always be the same dead man, always formally dressed in a tuxedo. His face would always seem vaguely familiar, but Charlene, the dreamer, could never identify it, not at first. Above the table there would always be a high-intensity surgeon's lamp that called to mind some sort of show-biz spotlight. It made the corpse shine like a misshapen sun in the darkness of space.

It would take a moment or two for the dreamer to realize

that the place was sealed. There were no windows, or doors, not even the one she had just used to enter the room. There was no escape. (After having experienced the dream a dozen times, she no longer bothered to look for a way out; she knew from past experiences that there wasn't one. This was the first of the small details that changed over time.)

The corpse would always speak before it moved. "Hello, Charlene," it would say in a soft, pleasant-sounding voice. "Wanna dance?"

Then it would sit up.

The dreaming Charlene would instantly start to race around the room, slapping at walls, looking for something, anything—a hidden seam that she might be able to tear open. As she searched frantically, fruitlessly, she would glance back over her shoulder and see the corpse swing its feet down onto the floor. She would see it stand. See it beginning to shamble toward her with the slow, uncertain movements of a body whose limbs had atrophied.

Charlene would always, in the end, find herself trapped in a corner. She would think to herself, "How stupid! Next time I have to remember. I have to get out into the middle of the room. If I'm in a corner, it gets me every time. If I'm out in the middle, I can run away so it can't get me!"

She would try to escape . . .

Always a moment too late.

The corpse would be there, inches away. "Wanna dance?" it would say, as it reached out for her with a smile.

No. It wasn't a smile. Well, it was for a moment. Then it would morph into a snarl. Then, a moment later, become a smile again.

That morphing business . . . smile, snarl, back to smile . . .

was the most frightening aspect of the dream for Charlene. Once the corpse was on its feet, once it had started to come after her, she knew that the moment would come soon, the terrible moment when the corpse would say "Wanna dance?"

After having the nightmare at least once a month for more than a year, Charlene, while visiting her mother one day, focused on a picture of Jesus hanging on a wall in the dining room. Charlene moved her head slightly to the left, then slightly to the right. The picture changed. Slender strands of tubular plastic allowed a benign, almost smiling Jesus to appear from one angle, while from three inches to the left or right Jesus was seen to be bleeding and in agony.

The same picture had been hanging in the same spot since Charlene was born. She had walked past it a thousand—a hundred thousand—times as a little girl. Fascination with it had worn off before Charlene was three years old. The picture itself had been forgotten long before adulthood, long before Charlene became a dinier. But it had obviously made enough of an impression to earn a starring role in her most popular nightmare.

Once she had made the connection, once she had realized that the shifting in the corpse's face was basically a replay of that old Jesus picture, that part of the dream became less intimidating. This was the second detail that changed over time. The rest of the dream, however, remained trapped in a sealed space inside her mind, where a corpse that was coming after her never changed, and never became any less terrifying.

At the end of the nightmare, just before Charlene would snap awake, when the corpse was inches away from her, she would finally recognize its familiar-looking face.

It was Fred Astaire.

"Wanna dance?"

Charlene's mother, Mae Rutkowski, still lived on the Grand Concourse, that old Jesus picture still on the wall when Charlene told her about the dream. Her mother asked, "Why do you stick? Doin' what yer doin', formatics."

"Forensics."

"Why do you stick if it's givin' you nightmares?"

"Good money," Charlene replied, pouring herself another green crème de menthe—the only booze in her mother's house. "Hey, it's a job, right? Remember Carol Springer? Became a flight attendant, right? Told me she has bad dreams every night. Her plane goes down! Every freakin' *night*! The worst that happens to me is that Fred Astaire invites me to dance."

"I always loved Fred Astaire," said Mae a bit dreamily.

"I never did," said Charlene. "By me, he always looked a little bit like a—" She stopped, sipping syrupy green. "—a bit like a dead man."

By 10:17 p.m. John Doe's corpse was in the process of being dissected. Charlie dutifully made the necessary Y-shaped incision, shoulders to mid-chest and down to the pubic region. There was virtually no blood, not on the surface.

A dead heart doesn't pump it. The Bronx bombshell, looking entirely out of place, reflected back the soft tissues on the front of John Doe's chest. It was as if saloon doors were swinging open. Inside, the man's bones resembled sauce-covered racks of pork at Damon's, "The Place for Ribs."

John Doe was old enough that his cartilage had begun to morph into bone. Charlie used a serrated knife, essentially a small saw, to cut through cartilage that had fused to the breastplates. This enabled her to enter the corpse's chest and begin to explore. Very shortly she discovered something that the man wasn't born with.

"Bogie," she said as she used forceps to remove . . . "a bullet."

"Vital?" asked the doctor.

"Nyet. Stopped by a rib. A week and some Darvon, this dude goes home. What're we lookin' for here anyway?"

"For whatever killed the guy."

"Wrong place, wrong time. Bad luck. City living."

"Mmmmm." Acocella made handwritten notes in a loose-leaf binder. Certain that it wasn't a bullet that ended John Doe's life, he was content to let his diener be the "prosecutor." The written notes were for his own files. Occasionally he reached up to press a button on a small microphone that depended from a plastic mounting he wore on his head and spoke essential bits of information out loud. His words were wirelessly transmitted to a computer that sat on a dry table at the side of the room. A voice-recognition system translated those words into readable text. That text was then forwarded to a prescribed list of city and county agencies. It became the ME's official autopsy report.

The voice-recognition processor was meant to make the pathologist's job easier, but the system was, to say the least, imperfect. Acocella knew that once the autopsy was finished, when the corpse had been rebuilt and rolled into the freezer, he would have to check the text for errors. It wasn't an entirely fruitless process. Most of the resulting texts were eighty percent correct. So on this night, while Charlene did the wet-work, Acocella, a rules-follower if nothing else, dutifully wore his microphone and occasionally spoke into it.

"White male," were the first words he eventually dictated. Then he took his finger off the microphone button and said privately to Charlene, "Let's see how that gets fucked up. How's it gonna come back? 'Why,' 'wire,' 'write'? 'Mail,' 'mole,' 'mule'? Computers, I'm telling you."

"You have an accent, what d'ya want?"

"I do not."

"Sure ya do, come on. Say 'No fuckin' way.'"

"What?"

"Don't gimme an argument, just say those words, 'No fuckin' way.'"

"All right, 'No fuckin' way.'"

"There, ya see?"

She was right. He did have an accent. Latino. Ever so slight. He couldn't hear it at all himself. "You're the one with an accent!" he said. "You say it. Say 'No fucking way.'"

Charlie did. She had an accent, too. "New York." The doctor pointed an accusing finger at her as if having caught her in a lie. "You are New York all the way!" His "You" sounded a bit like "Djoo," "York" a bit like "Djork."

"So we both got accents," said Charlene. "So machines can't figure out what we're sayin'. Fuck machines. Did you ever have a problem figurin' out what I was sayin'?"

"Never." He looked at her directly, with warmth in his eyes. "Everyone else, almost everyone I've ever known, it seems that I'm always trying to figure out what they're saying. You? Never."

Charlene found herself hoping that this was some sort of a compliment. Maybe even more than a compliment.

That's when the doctor pressed the button on his microphone and said, for publication, "White male." Before he went on, he let go of the button and spoke to Charlene. "Let's see how that gets fucked up. How's it gonna come back?"

The electronic brain recorded "write meal." When Acocella later dictated the word "occlusion," what registered was "confusion."

The doctor never knew any of this. After 10:36 on the night of John Doe, he never got a free moment to check the text. He never got a free moment to do much of anything.

Except try to survive.

Forty-eight hours later, when an electronically translated text of what Acocella ended up babbling into his microphone reached the computers at the VSDC, Terry McAllister, Elizabeth O'Toole, and John Campbell, who hadn't left to go shoot himself yet, were hard pressed to make heads or tails of it.

They were able to tell, with certainty, that the frenzied message from San Diego was an eyewitness account of the same sort of phenomenon that had been reported, by computer count, 300,642 times in the last two days. They couldn't be sure that San Diego was the first incident, so they kept digging. Two of them did, anyway, for four more days after Campbell bailed out, until Elizabeth O'Toole looked at Terry McAllister, shuddered, and said, "I really think this might be the end of the world."

"If it is . . . then what the fuck are we hangin' around here for? I got some good tequila over at my place."

Within forty minutes of John Doe's arrival in the autopsy room, Charlene Rutkowski, Bronx bombshell, had effortlessly extracted two more bullets and several vital organs from inside the corpse. Her moves were so efficient, her manner so offhanded, that one might have mistaken her for a waitress at Manhattan's Carnegie Deli. Lung. ("Here's your sandwich, sir.") Kidney. ("Here's your side order.") Liver, spleen. ("Here are your complimentary relishes.")

She plunked the bullets into a piss-pan, used scalpels to slice off organ samples, which she submerged in preservatives while pitching the bulk of each organ into its own biohazard bag. There were a dozen such bags standing open on wire skeletons. Finally she came to the heart.

"Wait!" Acocella looked up from his binder. "Not yet."

"Why not?" asked the diener.

"He was hit four times. We have to find the last bullet. Or find where it exited. We need to prove that the gunshot wounds were survivable, that it wasn't a GSW that shut this guy down." "GSW" was autopsy-room shorthand for "gunshot wound."

"The reason we're here is because PD wants it to be a GSW."

"I am out to prove they're wrong."

"Why?"

"Because I want to embarrass them. Annoy them. Because they're assholes. What difference does it make?"

"Come on. The truth."

Acocella looked up from his binder.

"Because they never thought twice about this," he said, his anger showing. "Fucking detectives see Mexicans with guns, figure they can blame it all on them! So they want me to prove they were right! I don't know who shot the guy. All I know is . . . I might have been able to save him!"

Acocella stepped away from his binder, walked over to the exam table, picked up a scalpel and a probe, and began to dig at John Doe's flesh. It wasn't very long before he shouted,

"Ah!" and used forceps to pull a bloody lump of lead from the tissue beneath John Doe's left shoulder blade.

"Sorry," Charlie apologized. "I shoulda found that."

"The point is we did find it." Acocella examined the damage caused by the missile. "Non-lethal."

Using the forceps to hold the bullet up into brighter light, he smiled. "This puppy never killed the poor bastard."

"So, what d'ya figure," asked Charlene. "Heart attack?"

"Likely," said Acocella.

"Couldn't hardly be anything else, right? Nothin' hit this guy's vitals. He's old. Out of shape. A kid in a Halloween costume could have scared this guy to death. Four bumps from an Uzi? Forget about it. Heart attack. Gotta be."

"If you're right, then I was right. Maybe he could have been resuscitated!"

They both worked on the corpse for another fifteen minutes or so until Acocella was satisfied, from examining all the insults, that none of the Uzi's bullets had dealt anything close to a fatal blow. He gave Charlene permission to extract the corpse's heart and he went back to his binder.

As she set to work with a long-bladed knife, the doctor pushed the button on his microphone and, for publication, said, "Cause of death not . . . repeat, not . . . ballistic insult. Proceeding with examination of the heart. Check for occlusion. Cardiomyopathy." He released the button and spoke more softly, not for publication, partly to himself, partly to Charlene. "Not just on the left. Could have been an arrythmogenic right ventricle. Or it could have been purely electrical. An inherited condition. IQTS. Brugada."

Within minutes, Charlie had carefully lifted the heart out of John Doe's chest cavity. Before she could transfer it to an examination basin it slipped out of her hands and dropped heavily to the floor. She had lost her grip on it. She nearly lost her grip on sanity when the eviscerated corpse on the autopsy table began to move.

Entirely on its own.

Acocella saw the movement. "Jesus," he uttered in a barely audible whisper before—by reflex more than religious faith— he made the sign of the cross and said, a bit more loudly, "*Madre de Dios.*"

"How long . . ." asked Charlie with a tremor in her voice. "How long after a man dies can the body still have muscle contractions?"

"There have been cases—"

The corpse interrupted by opening its eyes. It turned its head, drawn by Acocella's voice, and looked directly at the doctor. Beneath sagging lids, the corpse's eyes were clouded with mucous. The irises, once the color of black coffee, had been turned mocha by some deathly internal milk.

Acocella was seven feet away from the corpse. Those dead eyes were focused on a point much farther away. They seemed to be looking right through the doctor, at something way out on the horizon. Rather than actually seeing the man, the corpse seemed to be sensing his presence. Acocella felt something far worse than a chill. It was as if all the blood in his veins was suddenly replaced with ice water.

"Is . . . is this really happening?" asked Charlie, that tremor in her voice worsening. Acocella never answered her. John Doe did, in a way. The corpse turned its head again, drawn by her voice now, and cast its blank gaze in her direction.

"Wanna dance?" The corpse never said this, but Charlene heard it.

Ryan Brown is the author of the acclaimed novels *Play Dead* and *Thawed Out and Fed Up*. Raised in Texas, he now lives in New York City with his wife and son.

MERCY KILL

by Ryan Brown

I wanna get this down while it's still fresh, especially as I'm not quite sure what the future holds . . . or if there'll even be one.

My name's Marvin Whatley, and I figure I'll begin at the juicy part, when I finally reached Pam's double-wide at dusk and stormed inside to save her life, to take her away from all this, to make her my own once and for all.

My platoon sergeant would've called it my *objective* or my *mission*. Either word fits, seeing as how in the past twenty-four hours the whole world had gone bat-shit crazy.

Good news, Pam was there. Bad news, her face had been completely chewed off. As had all her limbs, save for one arm.

I hope you'll forgive me for not going into much more detail. Not an easy thing to see, your childhood sweetheart reduced to a writhing, faceless torso on the floor of her tore-up trailer house, the only recognizable part of her being the bloodied-up Lynyrd Skynyrd concert T-shirt you'd bought her on a date, sophomore year.

Here I'm back from Nam only one day, and already I'm fightin' another war. And this one I sure as hell didn't sign on for. Saw a lot of blood and guts over there along the Mekong, but nothing like this. This is a whole other deal.

Did I mention the dead started rising yesterday? Started eating people, too, which made other dead people rise, like some kind of bass-ackwards epidemic. They're saying the cause might be radiation from a Venus probe or some damn thing.

Doesn't matter.

All I knew at that moment was that Pam had been half eaten; she'd turned into one of those undead things, and would probably be making a run at eating me if she'd still had the limbs to get herself up off the linoleum. As it was, about all she could do was wiggle around in her own pulp.

My heart was broke clean in two. I wanted to tear my hair out, break a lot of shit, cry until I was cried out.

But I'm a soldier.

I'd seen buddies get blown to bits. Learned real quick in that goddamn jungle to survive first, cry later.

I'd heard you could kill one of those ghoulish things only by destroying their brain. If I'd had a gun I'd've shot Pam in the head right then and there rather than let her go on wallowing in her own entrails. But I didn't have a gun, and there wasn't time to think up another way to put her out of her misery because through the open door I could see some thirty or more ghouls approaching the front of the trailer in that slow, drunken walk of theirs.

Survival instinct took over.

Stepping over Pam, I moved to the small window above the turntable and saw they were approaching from the back, too. The trailer was surrounded.

I returned to the kitchenette, and as I was rifling through the drawers in search of anything that might be lethal, something clamped down on my ankle.

Pam. She'd managed to schooch across the floor and take hold of me with her one remaining arm.

Jerking my knee up, I kicked free of her grasp before she could get her teeth sunk in. I snatched a butcher knife from outta one of the drawers, backed into the corner of the trailer, and took a moment to consider my situation and what I should do about it.

I was horrified by the sight of what had become of Pam, but also fearful I might wind up just like her—undead.

Been there, thank you. A year spent slogging through that godforsaken Delta, tired, hungry, wet, too damn far from home, sometimes not caring if the next booby trap had my name on it. That's as close to being undead as I ever wanna get. I for sure as hell didn't wanna become a bloodied-up goddamn ghoul craving human flesh.

While such a fate certainly didn't appeal, I had an even better reason to survive: I aimed to get the fucker responsible for me not making it to my girl in time to save her life. But more on that later.

I figured I could take out one or two ghouls with the butcher knife, maybe break off a chair leg and use it to clobber a few more. Trouble was, that still left too damn many.

The odds of success sucked.

Seeing as how they'd honed in on the trailer, they clearly smelled blood. Living blood. *My blood*.

Desperate for ideas, I looked down at Pam and damned if that sweet girl didn't present a possible solution—camo. Here I'd been dreading the notion of winding up just like her when it suddenly occurred to me that becoming like her might be my only way out of this. What if I could mask my appearance, my smell, so I'd be just like one of them?

With no time to think it over I stepped over Pam again and toppled to the narrow floor space just beyond her, where a good deal of her innards still lay in a glistening heap. Fighting not to puke, I rolled around in it, covering myself head to foot with gore, even taking fistfuls of the stuff and slathering it across my face the way I'd once smeared on jungle mud for camouflage.

About the time I got back to my feet, the first flesh eater to make it up the steps was standing on the threshold. His face was caked with blood and his spleen was dangling from his midsection.

It was Tidwell Sweeny, who rotated tires over at the Conoco. I knew him right off from his greasy coveralls and cauliflower ears.

As he lumbered into the trailer, I froze, held my breath, and let my jaw hang slack just like his was, trying to look dead.

Or undead.

Through gray lifeless eyes, he seemed to study me with no visible hostility. It looked as though my ruse had worked, that my life force—or whatever you wanna call it—was undetectable beneath all the blood and entrails.

Then he lunged for me.

Jaws chomping, the sumbitch went straight for my jugular. I managed to dodge him and in the same motion, acting on a soldier's instinct, drove the butcher knife all the way to the hilt into the base of his skull. The fat bastard toppled like a stack of retreads.

My rush of victory didn't last long, 'cause the rest of the ghouls were still steadily approaching. I could hear 'em now. Christ, I could smell 'em.

If Tidwell Sweeny's actions had been any indication, appearance alone wasn't enough for them to mistake me for one of their kind. I needed . . .

Goddamn, I needed to *become* one of them.

I recalled meeting a guy at a bar in Da Nang. Davie something-or-other. A sniper. Special Forces. He'd been about to ship out, headed home after two tours.

When I asked him the secret to going home alive, he told me he'd served both tours on a strict diet of raw fish, rice, and green tea. Gook food. Claimed that in the jungle the enemy could smell a stomach full of good ol' American pancakes and hot dogs from a mile off. Said it was a body chemistry thing, as if the smell seeped right out of our pores. So he put gook food into his bloodstream, and swore up and down it'd saved his life.

I'd forgotten to ask him how long it took for this body chemistry thing to kick in, but I was pretty sure I was about to find out.

Just as another ghoul stumbled into the trailer, I tore off my first bite of Tidwell Sweeny's spleen. I'd like to say it tasted like chicken. Truth is, it tasted like shit. Warm, salty, chewy. Godawful.

But the flesh-eating version of Shelly Cleaver—night manager over at the roller rink—paid me absolutely no mind. Neither did the next ghoul to wander in, or the next. Maybe it was a bloodstream thing after all.

For good measure, I choked down a few more hunks of spleen and, just like that, I'd become just another face in the undead crowd. Soon a good fifty of us at least were shambling around outside the trailer. By now it was full dark, which I hoped would help me get hell and gone from there.

I started drag-stepping my way toward the edge of the group, planning to sprint free as soon as I was clear of the park's main gate.

But before I reached it, a gunshot rang out and the skull of the ghoul beside me burst open, sprayin' brains and hair. The man fell to the ground with a thud.

My army grunt impulse was to hit the deck, but somehow I managed to remain standing, ghoul-like, as I turned toward the source of the gunfire.

Soon as I did, some half a dozen pairs of headlights flashed on and more rifles than I could count began firing. Bodies dropped all around me as the headshots hit their marks.

I stood rigid, watching the shooters move closer as they reloaded. They were uniformed lawmen—all Stetsons and swagger. By the time they'd split the distance between us, I could hear their laughter.

And I'll be damned if leading the pack wasn't the same sumbitch I'd vowed not five minutes before to seek and destroy—Assistant Under-Deputy Shane Garrett.

He was the one that kept me from saving Pam in time. He was the reason I'd never kiss my girl again, hold her tight, make sweet love to her.

Garrett may not have killed Pam, but it was because of him that she'd wound up a flesh eater, which is a much worse fate than death.

'Least in death, Pam would still have her soul.

I wanted to charge him then and there, but I'd have been brained before getting anywhere near him. No way was I going to break character now. The sumbitch would have shot me regardless, but I'd rather let him think I was already dead than give him the satisfaction of knowing he'd taken my life hisself.

As the lawmen approached, they kept their rifles shouldered. Every couple seconds another few shots rang out and more bodies around me fell. In no time the gunmen were upon those of us few ghouls still standing, close enough for me to smell the menthol in their snuff. They were all smiles as they lowered their rifles. Clearly, ghoul shooting had become sport for these assholes.

I let my eyes glaze over and dropped my jaw to allow a red rope of drool to stretch from my bottom lip. Garrett spat chaw through a sinister grin as he scanned our pale, blood-smeared faces. When his eyes fell on me I made a point not to blink, to literally look straight through him, even as I watched his grin widen.

"Well, I'll be a sonofabitch," he said.

No shit, I thought.

"What?" asked one of the deputies.

Garrett pointed at me. "It's that fucker, Whatley."

"The soldier boy you dragged into the station house last e'ning? The one who threatened to separate you from your privates first chance he got?"

When a few of the others chuckled, Garrett swung his rifle their way. "Any o' you still think that's funny?"

None did, apparently. The snickering stopped.

Garrett lowered his rifle. His gaze shifted to Pam's trailer. Giving us ghouls a wide berth, he approached it, climbed the cinder block steps, and looked inside. He remained there for a moment, muttering something under his breath I couldn't make out. As he turned and came back down the steps his grin returned.

"Shitass sure wouldn't have wanted the bitch now," he said with a shrug.

The bastard. For him it wasn't even about having Pam anymore. It was just about making sure I couldn't have her either.

He looked my way again. Lord knows how, but I kept my cool, staring into space, drooling. The other ghouls who were still upright were getting restless and beginning to close in around the deputies.

One of them said to Garrett, "The paddy wagon's already full, boss. It won't hold all these here."

"Finish 'em off," Garrett ordered.

When I heard the click of cocking triggers all around, my gut clenched. But before anyone fired, Garrett pointed me out.

"All except for him. We're taking him along with us."

"Why bother?" asked the deputy.

Beneath his hat brim, Garrett's smirk stretched into a wide smile. "'Cause I want my trophy."

It wasn't an actual paddy wagon, only an old Chevy flatbed with a high steel railing. There were already a good thirty ghouls squirming around in there when two of the deputies grabbed me by the seat of my Levis and tossed me onto the pile.

The ghouls stunk something fierce. Most were pretty docile, but a few—Mayor Felder and Reverend Pruitt in particular—were downright ornery, snapping their jaws at anything that moved. Hunger pangs, I figured.

Blaring out of the truck's radio was a recorded message running on a loop, ordering anyone seeking refuge to report to the Slocum spread. We were headed west on Route 6, so I figured that's where Garrett and his cronies were taking us.

Garrett was riding shotgun in the truck's cab along with three deputies. Three more sat on the roof, rifles across their laps, spittin' into their dip cups, keeping an eye on us ghouls.

About all I could do was stare blankly into space and work at holding down Tidwell Sweeny's spleen. One of the ghouls had discarded a severed foot, which I claimed, occasionally gnawing on the pinky toe to look busy.

I guess I should fill you in on what happened last night and how I came to be in this fix.

I was only a few hours back on U.S. soil. The sun was just going down as I sped across the county line, heading for Pam's place, a bottle of Boone's Farm and a bunch of flowers in the passenger seat. I couldn't get to her fast enough.

But about a mile shy of the trailer park, a squad car roared up behind me, lights flashing.

It was Garrett. Like he'd been on the lookout for me. Probably paid the guy at the garage where I'd stored my Ford dually to notify him as soon I got back in town, 'cause he knew that as soon as I'd reunited with Pam, I'd be coming for his ass.

This deal with me and Pam and Garrett started back in high school. Bottom line, Pam chose me over him, and Garrett never got over it.

After graduation, I got drafted; Garrett, rather conveniently, got a 4F deferment.

Fallen arches, my ass.

Anyway, no sooner had I gone to war, Garrett moved in on Pam. Or tried to. She fought off his advances. Then when he started knocking her around, she fought for real. She'd always been a fighter; it was one of the reasons I loved her.

But sometimes, he got in a good pop. She mailed me pictures of bruises and black eyes. Made my blood boil, but being stuck in Nam there was nothing I could do.

Let's just say it was a long-ass tour of duty for me, and that's before you factor in little details like killing the enemy and surviving.

So, last night at dusk, Garrett's stopped me for speeding, which I wasn't. Then he pulls a half dozen unpaid parking tickets out of his ass, all of them trumped up. A quick swing of his billy club into my rear taillight, and boom, he's got me for driving an unsafe vehicle.

Looking back, I reckon I was already on my way to jail by this point . . . even before I told him to go fuck himself.

When we got to the sheriff's office, he didn't even allow me my one phone call, which would have been to Pam to tell her to hold off putting the corn bread in.

Turned out I never actually made it to a jail cell. Garrett was still writing me up and I was still cussing him from the chair beside his desk when all of a sudden Tina Gladwell's Dodge Dart came crashing through the south wall of the building, plowing through cubicles in an explosion of shattered wood and glass.

That alone was enough to shift attention away from the future I had planned for Garrett's manhood, but when Tina's pigtailed four-year-old daughter Milly came tumbling out of the broken windshield gnawing hungrily at her mother's severed arm, well, all hell broke loose inside the station house.

In the confusion, I managed to escape, but then spent the next twenty-four hours dodging ghouls, fires, car wrecks, panicked citizens, and police roadblocks, still with only one thing on my mind: getting to Pam.

But, thanks to Garrett, I'd got there too late. I couldn't save Pam, but I sure as hell was gonna avenge her. As that makeshift paddy wagon was steered off pavement and onto dirt, I made a vow to see him dead. He needed killin' and needed it bad.

The Slocum property was a scene of total chaos. Emergency vehicles, triage tents, frantic citizens searching for loved ones, public officials with bullhorns, shouting for calm and control when . . . Who the fuck were they kiddin'?

But, nearer to where they stopped the paddy wagon, it was practically a carnival.

Failed cattlemen and failed pool hustlers, Lenny and Delroy Slocum were half brothers (same mama) who now ran a deer lease and taxidermy outfit on the family's four hundred acres of cracked dirt and scrub brush. To my knowledge no one had ever actually killed a deer on the lease—or seen one for that matter—but from what I eventually gathered, it was open season on the lease and business was booming . . . because tonight it wasn't deer in crosshairs; it was ghouls.

Leave it to the sorry Slocum brothers to turn a profit out of an apocalypse.

Floodlights run by coughing portable generators shone down on a dump truck that was tipping some fifty flesh eaters into a corral where twice again that many were shuffling around.

One of them was Flint Hatfield, a tight-fisted loan officer at the First National who always wore a silk hanky in the pocket of his sport coat, which now had a blood-drenched clavicle poking out of it. 'Bout the time I recognized him, a shot rang out and his bald head split open like an overripe pumpkin.

Rousing applause rose from the crowd that surrounded the corral—your basic bikers, truckers, and burnouts, standing three-deep against the split rail, drinking beer and placing bets.

From the deer blind above the corral came the amplified voice of Delroy Slocum. "Hell of a shot, there, Bobby Ray, hell of a shot. Would've liked to plug ole Flint Hatfield myself," he added. "After all, the limp-dick did work in foreclosures!"

Laughter all around.

"We appreciate yer bidness, Bobby Ray," added Lenny Slocum, taking the bullhorn from his brother. "And remember, that single-shot kill wins you ten percent off the optional taxidermy package."

Delroy reclaimed the bullhorn. "All right, who's next? Step right up! Three shots, fifty dollars! Bag the ghoul of your choice, then have it stuffed to put in your den."

Above the whoops and hollers, I heard Garrett say to his deputies, "Corral's too crowded. We'll dump this last bunch here soon as the herd's been thinned out some."

The deputies nodded and lit smokes. One of them asked, "Them Slocums *are* gonna give us our cut, right?"

"Bet your ass they're gonna." Garrett smiled. "And I'm gonna get that discount on my trophy."

As he turned my way, I went back to gnawing on the foot, hoping my eyes still looked vacant and empty, and weren't revealing my disbelief.

Suddenly my ears caught the thump of running footfalls approaching the truck. And then a voice that nearly jolted me clean outta my Tony Lamas.

"Where is Marvin?"

Pam! My *Pam! Alive!*

"I know you've seen him, Garrett. Where is he?"

Crying. Desperate. Panicked, even. But it was definitely Pam, and she was very much alive.

Both my heartbeat and my breathing went into overdrive. I risked blowing my cover to cut my eyes as far to the left as they would go. There she was, intact, standing face-to-face with Garrett.

She wore tight frayed jeans, sneakers, and an old flannel button-down, untucked. Her long brown hair was pulled up off her neck with a clip. She looked frantic and scared and beautiful.

Garrett was as shocked to see her as I was. "Wha—what the hell are—"

Pam cut off his stammering. "Answer my question, damn you. *Where is Marvin?*"

He blinked a few times. "I went to your house. You were . . . *dead.*"

Pam just looked at him, shaking her head, confused. Then, in realization, she covered her face with her hands. When her head came back up, tears were streaming.

"Oh, Becky Lynn . . ." she said.

Suddenly it made sense. Becky Lynn did manicures with Pam over at the CUTEicle. They're best friends. They're also the same age and shape, both brunettes. Chew off three limbs and the face of one, and it'd be pretty easy to mistake her for the other. And they've always shared clothes, which explained the Skynyrd T-shirt.

It seemed that Garrett was still trying to sort it all out when Pam wiped her tears with the back of her hand, and pulled herself together. "Somebody said you hauled Marvin off to jail. Where is he, Garrett? What'd you do to him?"

Garrett finally snapped to. "Nothing he didn't have comin'."

"What'd you do, you bastard?" She started beating on his barrel chest with her small fists.

I could have married her right there.

Her name-calling—not to mention the drubbing—pissed Garrett off. He roughly took hold of her wrists.

I became a coil, prepared to spring.

Garrett sneered. "Your boyfriend's dead."

"You're a liar!"

"Am not!"

"Liar!"

"I'm not lying, you crazy bitch, the worthless fucker's dead!"

I'd have jumped him right there had Pam not beat me to the punch. Literally. Her left hook landed square on Garrett's jaw. I'm sure Garrett would have hit her back if by now the commotion hadn't drawn a crowd.

He looked around at all those gawkers. The sumbitch was gutless enough to beat up a woman, but not fool enough to do it in public. He turned back to Pam.

"All right, you don't believe me?" The crowd gasped as he whipped out his Glock. He marched around to the flatbed's tailgate and swung it open. Five or six ghouls separated me from him. He fired a bullet through each of their skulls, one right after the other. Then he climbed onto the flatbed and stepped over the fallen bodies to get to me.

Yanking me up by the hair, he spun me around so Pam could have a good look at my undead self.

"No!" she screamed. "Oh, god, please no!"

I don't know how I managed to stay limp and not reveal the pain I felt over causing her such anguish.

But Garrett was so lathered, if he'd known I was alive, he'd have killed me instantly. By playing dead, at least I had a slim chance of living. Or so I hoped.

He chucked me off the flatbed. I hit the dirt like a rag doll. I got to my feet on my own, but made a slow show of it, keeping my movements labored and uncoordinated. Ghoul-like.

Pam was sobbing and reaching out for me. It took a couple of bull-necked deputies to hold her back.

The crowd had grown but become quieter. Even the Slocum brothers had stopped their hawking and made their way over.

Head cocked sideways, one arm dropped, and the other bent awkwardly across my stomach, I pretended to be unaware of all these goings-on. Truth was, I never let Pam out of my sight.

Garrett jumped off the flatbed and bore down on her. "Look at your precious Marvin now. You wanna snuggle up with that?"

Through all this, I'd managed to keep a grip on the severed foot. For effect, I now brought it to my mouth and bit a good chunk out of the arch.

When I did that I noticed a sudden change in Pam, as though a switch had flipped. It was like she had suddenly accepted what she didn't want to believe.

In a voice filled with more resolve than sadness, she said to Garrett, "He was ten times the man you'll ever be."

With that, she pulled the pistol from the nearest deputy's holster and cocked it.

Holy shit, she's gonna kill the sumbitch! I thought.

Till she pointed the goddamn bore straight at my face.

This deal was about to get mortal.

Pam can shoot good. Real good. I oughta know; I taught her how. Once saw her shoot a thimble off a fence post from four hundred yards in a high wind. That's how good she is. So I doubted she'd miss me from twelve feet, give or take.

Things happened quick then. The bystanders panicked and scattered out of her line of fire. Garrett leaned over Pam and growled, "Go ahead . . . finish him."

Her intention was clear: the mercy kill. The same thing I'd wanted for the ghoul I'd mistaken for her back in the trailer house.

But at the moment, it wasn't mercy I was needin'.

Desperate, I opened my mouth to holler out, but before I could even make a sound, Pam shot me in the head.

I have no recollection of blacking out, but I reckon it's just as well I did, because when I woke up, I was at the bottom of a pile of mostly headless torsos and severed appendages, all dripping red and reeking to high heaven. I must've been assumed dead and lumped in with the rest.

I had a mouthful of jellified blood. My face hurt like holy hell. A tentative probe of my tongue revealed that Pam's shot had passed straight through my left cheek without killing me or even nicking a single tooth. A goddamn miracle if ever there was one.

It was dark beneath that mass of gore, but there was just enough hazy moonlight coming through the window for me to make out all the glassy eyes looking down on me—the lifeless gazes of stuffed bucks, birds, badgers, and bass. The poor suckers were mounted on every inch of wall space.

I was inside the Slocums' taxidermy shack. Before I had time to chew over what that might mean to my immediate future, the door creaked open.

"Marvin?"

It was Pam's voice, whispering my name.

"Marvin? Where're you at?"

I tried to speak, but all that came out were gurgly sounds.

"Oh, baby!" Pam rushed to the heap of decaying flesh pinning me down and furiously began tossing aside the spare parts.

When I was free and she managed to pull me upright, I took her in my arms and squeezed her tight. For a few sweet moments all I could do was hold her face between my hands and look at her to insure that she was real . . . that we were together at last and still alive.

"I'm sorry," she said. "Got here as quick as I could. Had to wait till things quieted down, you know."

I swallowed some of that congealed crud in my mouth. "How . . . how long was I out? What time is it?"

"A little after midnight."

I smiled as best I could with a hole in one cheek. "I'm just glad your shot was off, honey."

"Off, hell! I had plenty of time to aim 'cause you took so damn long to open your mouth. Thought you never would."

Smart girl. She'd waited for me to try and call out before she fired, creating a clear target into my gaping mouth. To the witnesses, it had looked like a prize-worthy kill shot. For me, it had meant deliverance.

Of course, it was much later that I pieced all this together. At that moment, my mind was still in a swirling fog.

"But how did you know I was still . . . *me*?"

She rolled her eyes. "Because, sweetie, you bite into a human foot the same girlie way you eat corn on the cob . . . pinkies raised."

She'd been ribbing me about that for years. Never imagined that one day it would be the giveaway that saved my life.

"We have to go." She pushed me toward the door. "My car's outside, gassed up, with the engine running."

We slipped out and headed toward the rear of the shack. The floodlights had been turned off, so we had darkness on our side.

But it didn't matter anyhow, 'cause the ranch was deserted now. Those seeking safety from the ghouls had retreated to the tent city that had sprung up on the other side of the main road.

We were only steps away from Pam's idling Corvair when headlight beams drew my attention. Another paddy wagon was pulling onto the Slocums' place, crammed axle-to-axle with a fresh crop of flesh eaters. Even from that distance, I could hear their hungry growling.

Pam must've heard 'em, too. She tugged me toward that gassed-up Corvair. "Come on, darlin', we gotta go while we got the chance."

She was right. 'Course she was. We needed to get gone. But damn my hide if I didn't stop short.

"Hold up, baby. I got an idea."

It was close to 2:00 a.m. when I busted down the door of Garrett's one-room shithole just east of the lake, catching him reclined in his La-Z-Boy, where he'd passed out drunk, still in uniform, a twelve-gauge across his lap, a *Penthouse* splayed over his chest.

Once his eyes focused on me, I said, "Time for you to die."

He fumbled for the shotgun, but I drove the toe of my boot up hard under his chin. He was still spitting out teeth as I cuffed his wrists behind the recliner with his own handcuffs.

When I came around to face him, he looked equal parts shocked, scared, and pissed.

"Whatha hell's zis?" he mumbled through bloody gums. "You were dead, sure's shit!"

"No, Garrett, I'm not dead. Not *undead*, neither. I'm alive and well." I brought myself eye level and smiled wide enough to stretch the bullet hole in my cheek. "But you're fucked."

He struggled against the handcuffs as I headed for the door. Soon as I cleared it, I gave a sharp whistle.

An engine thundered. Tires spun. A truck roared out of the darkness, coming on fast . . . in reverse. I leaped off the porch to get clear.

The truck had built up a good head of steam by the time its back end plowed through the front wall of the house, tailgate open.

When the dust settled, I could see Pam through the truck's rear window, grinning at me from behind the wheel. She kicked open the passenger door. I climbed in, shouting, "Gun it, baby!"

She jammed the stick into first, popped the clutch, and floored the gas. The flatbed lurched, sending its cargo of flesh eaters tumbling out the lowered tailgate.

The last we heard from Garrett were strangled screams coming from beneath the horde of feasting ghouls.

He was begging me for a mercy kill.

I'd run plumb out of mercy.

That was four hours and two hundred miles ago. The last report we heard on the radio was that the undead had been largely contained in the area . . . but that there was still no word from across the state line.

As I sit here writing this, in a ransacked room in an abandoned motel, listening to the sounds of Pam's fitful breathing while she sleeps, watching the candlelight dance across her pretty face, I can't rightly say what's in store for us. I only know we'll find a way to survive . . . together.

And I'll tell you one more thing I know from experience. Being undead ain't anywhere near the same thing as being alive. I'm pretty sure there's a lesson in that somewhere.

David Wellington is the author of twenty novels, which have appeared around the world in eight languages. His horror novels include *Monster Island*, *13 Bullets*, *Frostbite*, and *Positive*. His thriller series starring Afghanistan war veteran Jim Chapel includes *Chimera*, *The Hydra Protocol*, and *The Cyclops Initiative*. He also writes fantasy under the pseudonym David Chandler, and science fiction, including the hit Silence trilogy, as D. Nolan Clark. He lives and works in New York City.

ORBITAL DECAY

by David Wellington

[The following is the final radio transcript of the International Space Station, discovered on a backup drive at the Lyndon B. Johnson Space Center in Houston, Texas. That night three astronauts and one cosmonaut were aboard the station, identified by their initials in the transcript:

JH: Jackson Hartzfeld, "Hartz," Mission Commander
SF: Sergei Favorov, Russian Mission Coordinator
KR: Karl Guernsey, Science Mission Specialist
MJ: Marcia Jernigan, Flight Engineer

Throughout, all mission control personnel are identified as MCC.

Given the events of that night on Earth, it is little surprise that the video feed of the following events is lost to history. However, we can piece together a partial account of what happened from the words of these final space travelers. Those of a sensitive nature, or who suffer from post-traumatic stress disorder resulting from the events of that night, are advised to stop reading now.]

> MCC: Go ahead, Hartz. Feeling nervous?
>
> JH: A little.
>
> MCC: It'll be fine. Just remember to smile. You're on in five. In position okay?
>
> JH: I'm okay, just—
>
> MCC: Two. One. Go ahead.
>
> JH: Hello, Baker Elementary! My name is Jack Hartzfeld, and I'm talking to you from space! I'm on the International Space Station. Look, I'm floating! That's because there's no gravity in space. I'm in orbit around the Earth—you can ask your teacher what an orbit is. Right now I'm almost directly over Pittsburgh, about two hundred and fifty miles overhead. When it gets dark tonight, you might actually be able to see me. I'll be a bright dot moving across the sky pretty fast . . .

[Portions of JH's presentation to Baker Elementary School have been omitted from this transcript due to lack of relevance. Simultaneous to the presentation, MJ was overseeing the final approach of a Soyuz spacecraft, which was due to rendezvous with the ISS and deliver three new crewmembers, allowing JH to rotate home.]

> MJ: Mission Control, I have visual on Soyuz TMA-21M. These numbers are a little—
>
> MCC: Confirmed, Jernigan. We have a radio fault with Soyuz.

Not getting any voice, and our telemetry looks a little off. Can you confirm Soyuz velocity?

MJ: About ten mps over nominal. Do we need to go to manual docking?

MCC: Negative, Jernigan. We can't raise the crew. We'll have the fault fixed soon, promise. In the meantime we're going to scrub the rendezvous. Just to be safe.

MJ: Hartz isn't going to like that. His stress level . . . man. I'm looking forward to him getting off of this tin can, I tell ya . . .

MCC: We'll reschedule for tomorrow. He'll be fine.

JH: . . . station is built from modules, kind of like Lego bricks. In fact, we built the station up piece by piece, from what we call modules. The first parts were called Zvezda and Zarya, which are Russian names, because those modules were built by Russians like Sergei here. Sergei is running on the tread-mill, because in space you have to exercise constantly or your muscles get weak. Sergei, say hello to—

SF: Hello, Amerikanski children!

JH: Ha ha, Sergei's a pretty funny guy. He speaks English as well as you or me, don't let him fool you.

SF: Da, is true, this thing he say.

JH: Oh, Sergei! Anyway, mostly we live and work in the Zvezda module, but I'm talking to you from an American-built labora-tory module called Destiny. There are also labs called Colum-bus and Quest. Next we have the BEAM module, which is like a balloon you can float around in, it's kind of like a bouncy house; and there's the Cupola, which is a whole module that's pretty much all windows, so we can see outside. We call it our observatory module. Hey, would you look at this pen—see how it floats in the air? It can't fall down, because without gravity there is no . . .

MJ: Houston, I need a range check on Soyuz.

MCC: Looks good down here. What are you seeing?

MJ: Getting a little close for comfort. You aborted the docking sequence?

MCC: That's affirmative, ISS. Soyuz should swing past you with plenty of room to spare.

MJ: Range check, Houston, this is—this is too close, we have—

MCC: Still showing fifty meters clearance, somebody— somebody get that radio fault fixed now. Now! ISS, we are not anticipating any issues. Soyuz is still five minutes out, plenty of time to fix the fault and adjust course if necessary.

MJ: Holding my breath up here, Control.

JH: . . . what everybody wants to see, right? Our bathroom! This is the question every astronaut gets asked. How do you go to the bathroom in space. Well. I don't want to be too gross about it. Everything in space is different, though. In fact—in fact—let me tell you the truth, kids. Space . . . space fucking sucks.

MCC: Hartz? Did you just—

JH: I've been up here three months. I am sick and fucking tired of floating pens and clamping a vacuum to my ass every time I take a shit.

MCC: Hartz, please respond, you are—

JH: There's nobody there, Control.

MCC: Say again.

JH: Houston, I'm telling you. I'm looking at video of an empty classroom. No kids, no teacher. What the hell is going on here?

MCC: Checking now. Okay, okay. Yeah . . . hold on, Hartz.

JH: Jesus, can we get it together down there? I rehearsed this stupid presentation for hours, and—

MCC: Okay, we have . . . we have an explanation, there was

some kind of evacuation at the school. They're all out in the parking lot right now and police are—

JH: Holy shit. Are the kids okay? Tell me they're—

MCC: Sure they're fine. This is probably nothing. Just an Active Shooter Drill or something, those happen all the time.

JH: They have . . . what did you call it? Active Shooter Drills now? Like they have to teach the kids what to do if a crazy guy comes into the school shooting?

MCC: In my day we had Duck and Cover. Maybe you want to stay up there, Hartz? Maybe it's not safe down here.

JH: Hardy-har-har. No, Control. I am coming home tonight. I'm going to kiss my girlfriend and pet my dog and drink about fifty beers. Okay, what do we do now? No point in continuing my presentation without any kids, so—

MCC: Stand by, Hartz.

JH: What?

MCC: Just stand by. We have a . . . let's not call it a problem, yet.

MJ: Soyuz is still approaching—Control, you need to tell this thing that you aborted the rendezvous. Or I need to move the whole damned ISS out of its way.

MCC: Jernigan, negative, we've figured out the problem, or rather—

MJ: I can see it. I can see Soyuz right outside, it's moving too fast.

MCC: There is no radio fault, that's the problem, we just can't raise the crew.

MJ: Say again?

MCC: Crew is not responding. There may have been a depressurization event during liftoff—

MJ: Oh, shit. You're telling me the crew is dead in there? They're dead in there and—

MCC: ISS, do not panic, we're going to move the station, okay? We'll just move the station, and—

MJ: It's right outside! It's right here and it's moving too fast, it's moving too—

[Seventeen seconds are missing from the transcript, presumably due to a failure in ISS's main communication antenna. The transcript remains garbled for another thirty-nine seconds, with only sporadic voice data remaining legible.]

KR: Control, it took off—

MJ:—depressurization in the Kibo lab module, in Columbus module, in Destiny, in—

KR:—lost, port photovoltaic arrays all gone, we have lost some heat radiators, checking which ones, we have lost the Canadarm-2, we have holes, actual punctures in—

JH: Sergei! Sergei, get out of—Sergei!

MJ: Control, please come in, Control! Control, please please please . . .

JH: Sergei! I have to—I can't stay, I have to—

KR:—feel funny, my ears are, shit, that's blood, there's blood coming from my—

MJ: Columbus is *gone*. Truss P1 is *gone*. Truss P2, Truss P3, the Pirs airlock is *gone*.

KR:—a little . . . can't . . . my vision is restricted and blurry, my nose, my nose is bleeding . . .

MJ: Control! Come in, Control, we are—

JH: Sergei—I'm so sorry, man, I—I'm so sorry . . .

[Radio contact between ISS and MCC was not fully reestablished until 23:04 UTC. Several lines of the transcript were illegible and have been omitted here. It is believed they represent KR moaning in pain, and nothing more.]

MJ: . . . bus four is reporting yellow. Bus five is reporting yellow.

JH: I could have . . .

MJ: Bus six is, well, that's new. It's not reporting at all. Bus seven is—

MCC: ISS, are you receiving? ISS, come in please.

MJ:—red. Shit. Bus seven is reporting red. That's . . . that's not good, Hartz, are you—

JH: I could have saved him, Marcia. I could have. I could have.

MCC: ISS, please reply. Are you receiving?

MJ: Houston? Oh, God—Houston, is that you? We thought—we—

MCC: Took us a while to get the secondary antenna up, there's—

MJ:—alone up here, thought we—

MCC:—not a lot of power, and we lost most of the camera feeds. Can you tell us what happened?

MJ: What happened? You want to know what happened? You ought to have a better idea than we do, Control. We're half blind up here.

MCC: Situation's not much better down here. I've got video of you and Hartz, but can't seem to find Karl or Sergei anywhere, can you—

JH: Sergei's dead. I killed him.

MCC: . . . say again, Hartz?

MJ: He's being dramatic! Hartz, shut up for a second, okay? Control, we . . . we're kind of screwed right now. Soyuz smacked into us at a pretty good clip. Tore right through the labs, and debris knocked out all the solar panels. We're running on batteries, and those won't last long. We need immediate rescue.

MCC: Sergei's dead?

MJ: Yeah. Yeah, he. Yes, Control. Crewmember Sergei Favorov is deceased, time of death . . . it doesn't matter. Hartz and Sergei were in the Destiny laboratory module when Soyuz crashed into it. Hartz was able to make it back here, to Zvezda, before he could succumb to decompression. Sergei wasn't as lucky, he was—

JH: He was still strapped into the treadmill, he couldn't get loose. Control, I could have helped him, I could have gotten him out of there. I take full responsibility, both as mission commander and because I could have fucking helped him, but I was . . . I was terrified, I just wanted to escape, to get away before—

MJ: Hartz! Shut the hell up! Let me tell them our situation, or we're all dead!

MCC: What about Karl? Is Karl alive?

MJ: Affirmative, Control. Though he's in bad shape. He was in the BEAM inflatable habitat module when Soyuz hit. The BEAM didn't take immediate damage and I guess he thought he was going to be okay. He was monitoring the damage, seeing what we could salvage immediately after the impact, and I guess he just didn't notice that the BEAM was losing air. That thing is just a big balloon, it must have been punctured . . . he started reporting signs of decompression sickness but by the time I dragged him out of there he was unconscious. I brought him in here and stuffed him in a sleepsac, I didn't know what else to do. He lost some blood, and his eyes are pretty red. I don't know. I'm not a flight surgeon, Control. I just don't know.

MCC: Is BEAM sealed off, now? Zvezda is airtight?

MJ: Yeah.

MCC: How is your life support situation, ISS?

MJ: Not great. We're down to bottled oxygen, all the oxygen
generators are gone or down. Water and food supplies are
good, I guess. Temperature is a little high, but not uncomfortable
yet. We can hold on a couple days, should be long enough
until the rescue boat gets here. If we're careful. The real problem is going to be power. I've switched off everything that isn't
directly keeping us alive, everything but a couple of lights, and
those'll have to go, soon enough. We can ration battery use,
but—it's going to be close. It's going to be close but we are
going to live through this. Right, Hartz?

JH: I . . .

MJ: I said we're going to live through this. Hartz, say yes.

JH: Yes.

MJ: Say fuck yes, we're going to live. Say it!

JH: Fuck yes. We're going to . . . live.

MJ: Jesus. Control, tell me something. Tell me something, just, just
anything—tell me why this happened, why your range estimate
on Soyuz was off, why we couldn't move the station in time.
Tell me why this is happening to us. I don't want to hear that it
needs further study. I don't want to hear you don't know. I need
to understand what happened.

MCC: Well . . .

MJ: Please, Control. Come on.

MCC: I . . . look. This isn't an excuse. What happened, yeah, it
was our fault.

MJ: Huh.

MCC: Again, not an excuse, but—but only about half of the crew
down here showed up for work today. There's something going

around, some kind of flu or something, and we didn't have enough people, we didn't have the *right* people—

MJ: You hear that, Hartz? It wasn't your fault. Look at me, you fucker!

JH: Ow! Jesus, you didn't have to slap me, Marcia, you—

MJ: You didn't kill Sergei. Control did. They just admitted it, okay? They just told us that. So you didn't do it. Okay? Okay?

JH: . . . okay.

MJ: But if you don't help me right now, if you don't work with me, then you *will* be killing me. And Karl. You understand that?

JH: Sure, Marcia. Sure.

MJ: Control—I'm going to switch off the radio to conserve power. I'll report in every half hour. You make sure there's somebody listening when I do.

MCC: Understood, ISS.

[The following transmission was received at 23:37 UTC.]

MJ: Control? I'm in the Cupola, looking at you. Looking at Earth. We're over California, and I can see a forest fire down there, and it's just beautiful. I know it's terrible, I know it's a disaster, but up here it's just flickering lights, red in the green. It's kind of beautiful. I guess. There's never enough time for this, you know? To just take in the view.

MCC: You sound like you're in a little better spirits, Marcia.

MJ: Do I? I must have been a wreck before. I've been crying . . . I can't seem to stop. Damn. Big tough astronaut ladies aren't supposed to . . . hell. Maybe I sound better because I'm away from Hartz for a second. He's working, but he's slow, dragging. Helping, I guess, but damn. Being around him . . . never mind,

Control. Talk to me about rescue. What's the ETA on our rescue ship?

MCC: We're working on it. The second I have actual numbers I'll let you know.

MJ: Sure. Sure. Okay. Shit, I'm getting tears everywhere. They're just floating away from me, kind of drifting toward the air vents. I'll catch them before they short anything out, don't worry.

MCC: We've got a lot of faith in you, Marcia.

MJ: Thanks.

MCC: Listen, there's something . . . maybe it's better if Hartz doesn't hear this.

MJ: . . . go ahead.

MCC: We've seen a kind of weird reading. It's got to be anomalous, I don't want you taking any action on this. It can't mean anything.

MJ: Go ahead.

MCC: It's the treadmill. In Destiny. It's moving.

MJ: What?

MCC: The treadmill, the one Sergei was using. It's reading out as still being in motion, as if he was still using it. Which is, of course, impossible.

MJ: Yeah.

MCC: It can't mean anything. But you need to know about it. Because it's draining your batteries.

MJ: Understood, Control.

[23:46 UTC.]

JH: . . . have to. We have to! If he's—

MJ: Control, Hartz is going to—

JH: If Sergei is still alive, somehow, I mean, maybe there's still some air trapped in there, or, or something—

MJ: Houston, are you receiving?

MCC: We're here, Marcia. Please report?

MJ: I'm helping Hartz get into one of the old Russian Orlan
spacesuits. I'm helping him because he's still mission commander and he gave me an order. I'm calling you to register the
fact that I disagree with his decision.

JH: We can't just leave him in there! He could die at any minute!

MCC: Please confirm, here. Hartz is suiting up so—why? So he
can—

MJ: He's going into Destiny. To see if Sergei is still alive.

JH: Help me with this, Marcia. Help me get the gloves—there.
And the helmet.

MJ: Sir, yes sir.

MCC: Hartz, this is a waste of mission resources. If you open
that airlock you're going to lose a lot of air. We cannot advise
an EVA at this time.

JH: Understood. Marcia, get the hatch open.

[The following transmission was received directly from JH's suit radio, a
low-power signal at the threshold of what MCC was able to receive on
Earth. As a result, some words were illegible. These sections are repre-
sented by four asterisks (****).]

JH: Okay. I'm through. I . . . wow. The module is just a mess, stuff
everywhere, exposed wires. Oh, Jesus. The ****—**** hamsters
we were raising to see how they developed in microgravity.
They're, uh, well, there's some fur floating around in ****. Not
going to think about what happened.

JH: Dark—my suit lights aren't **** me much, with all this floating
crap, but—yes, I can see Sergei, he's—shit! He's **** he's
moving! He's . . . he's walking on the treadmill!

JH: No, Marcia. No! Fuck you, he's alive somehow, I don't—I

don't care, I'm—yes, I see it too. Yes, I can see open space through that hole in the wall, **** **** **** yes, I know that means **** no air in here. No. No, Marcia . . . No. Fuck you. Fuck you. Fuck that.

JH: Sergei—can **** **** **** you hear me, buddy? No, no, of course not. Marcia, his eyes are open. He's looking at me . . . he wants something **** **** ****.

JH: Sergei, are you **** **** **** **** ****?

JH: Going to just . . . release the straps holding him into this **** thing. Going to . . . gah. Okay, Sergei, just **** me a chance here, just **** hey, come on, just **** **** **** hey! Hey, get off, get **** **** **** Jesus! Jesus! Marcia!

JH: **** **** **** **** **** **** **** ****!

JH: **** bit my sleeve he **** **** **** teeth, just **** fuck! Fuck! I'm leaking, I'm **** Marcia, open the fucking **** leaking air, he just bit right through six layers of **** **** oh God, oh God, oh ****.

JH: Marcia! Open the ****!

[00:07 UTC.]

MJ: Control? Control, are you there? What the hell? Where are—

MCC: Sorry! Sorry, had to run to the bathroom, I'm not feeling great. Go ahead, ISS. Go . . . go ahead.

MJ: Jesus, Control. Are you okay?

MCC: Just, just tell us what happened, in there. In, ugh, in Destiny. With Sergei.

MJ: He attacked Hartz. Tried to bite him.

MCC: Oh.

MJ: It's not . . . I mean, he can't be alive, but he just, just attacked Hartz and bit through his suit's sleeve. With his teeth, goddamnit.

MCC: Where is he now?

MJ: Hartz? He's right here, trying to get out of the suit. He's pretty shaken up but—

MCC: No, damn it. I meant Sergei. Where is Sergei?

MJ: . . . he. Uh. Well.

MCC: Where is he? Please be specific.

MJ: He's, uh, still in Destiny. Hartz came through the hatch, in, you know, a hurry. He was pretty scared. And he kicked the hatch closed behind him, he . . . he sealed it before Sergei could come through. We decided together that . . . um . . .

MCC: Marcia, this . . . this is important, we need to know. Did Sergei break Hartz's skin? Did he bite Hartz directly, or just his suit?

MJ: Not sure, just a second—

MCC: We have to know, Marcia. A lot depends on it.

MJ: Hold on . . . no, he's—Hartz, would you sit fucking still? No, Control, no, he's intact, he—Control?

JH: I'm fine, damn it. Fine.

MJ: Control? Control? Are you there?

MCC: Sorry, your previous controller had to use the bathroom again. It was an emergency. There's a bad stomach thing going around down here. I'll be taking over for now. So it sounds like everything is fine, Sergei is quarantined, there was no direct fluid contact, and—

JH: Fine? Things are fine? Oh, hell, you don't even—

MJ: Control? What's going on? What's . . . I mean—what's going on down there?

MCC: Nothing you need to worry about.

MJ: When I switched on the radio I heard . . . there were just . . . all over the radio, there were distress calls and may-days and even a couple SOS signals, from ships out at sea, from police stations and army bases and—

MCC: Nothing you need to worry about. You just focus on staying alive up there, okay? We'll focus on getting you home. Deal?

MJ: I . . . guess. Deal.

[00:37 UTC.]

MJ: Control? Come in, Control.

MCC: Right here.

MJ: Not as many distress calls, this time. Maybe things are getting better down there?

MCC: Maybe. Listen, we've been talking to Russia, talking about getting a rescue mission together. It's moving along. Can you hang in there a little longer?

MJ: Karl's not going to make it. His breathing is . . . really bad, and his pulse is weak.

MCC: Okay.

MJ: It's not, it's not okay, but I guess—

MCC: We need to be realistic.

MJ: Yeah. I guess that's what I was going to say.

MCC: Marcia. I need to give you some new instructions. You're not going to like this. It's important, though. If Karl dies, you'll need to take . . . certain actions.

JH: Karl's going to live. I know CPR.

MCC: Negative, Hartz. Do not touch him. Not now, especially not if he—if he dies.

JH: I won't let anyone else die. Not on my watch. Not after Sergei—

MCC: Marcia, can you get to the Cupola?

MJ: . . . okay, I'm . . . I'm alone, that's what you wanted, right? You wanted me to get to where Hartz couldn't hear us.

MCC: Yes. Marcia, listen to me very carefully. The second Karl dies, the second you even think he's dead. You're going to have to bash his head in.

MJ: . . . hold on. I don't—can you repeat that?

MCC: This is crucial. The second you even think he's dead.

MJ: I don't know if I can do that, Control.

MCC: It's not optional. This is a direct order from your Flight Lead.

MJ: Control, you understand how crazy that sounds? Do you—
do you understand—

[The transcript records that at this time, MJ's conversation with Control was interrupted by a loud, repetitive clanging noise. No transmission was recorded for another five minutes. The clanging noise continues throughout.]

MJ: Control, it's—

JH: It's Sergei! He's banging on the hatch, he's banging on the hatch and he wants to get in, he wants—

MJ: Control, I know how it sounds, but Hartz is right, Hartz is—

MCC: Marcia, we have instructions for that, we have—

JH: I'm going to let him in, we can restrain him. It's going to—

MJ: Don't you dare!

JH:—going to be okay, we'll be ready, we'll pin him down, and—

MJ: Get away from that hatch! Hartz, you bastard, don't you dare—

JH: I'm opening the hatch, Control. If he's alive in there, then there must be air on the other side, it's fine, it's going to be—

MJ: Control, I'm trying to stop him, I'm trying to stop Hartz but he—but he—ugh!

MCC: Marcia, come in. Marcia?

MJ: Bastard just punched me in the face and now he—

[A loud, roaring noise is heard, presumably a rush of air leaving the Zvezda module. A scream can be heard, but its source is unclear. For a period of six minutes, only MCC's side of the transmission is audible.]

MCC: Marcia. Marcia, if you can hear me. You know what you
have to do.

MCC: Marcia? Are you receiving? You need to close that hatch.
You need to get that hatch closed, and you need to make sure
Sergei stays on the other side.

MCC: Marcia, you do what's necessary.

MCC: Marcia, are you receiving?

MCC: Marcia?

[Normal, two-way transmission is restored at 00:48 UTC.]

MJ: I hear you, Control. I hear you. He . . .

MCC: You did what you had to do. You know what's going on,
don't you?

MJ: No. Damn it, no, I don't know anything. I . . .

MCC: You're a smart woman. You're figuring it out. If I say it
out loud then you won't believe me. If you hear it out loud it'll
sound ridiculous. But you saw Sergei's face, didn't you? You
saw the look on his face. I saw it down here. You must have
seen it.

MJ: I did.

MCC: Yes.

MJ: You . . . you're not the same controller I was speaking to
before.

MCC: No. No, they're all gone now. I'm all that's left. And
I'm . . . well, I won't be here a lot longer, let's just say that.

MJ: Oh, no. No, don't . . .

MCC: Tell me what happened. Just say it, for me.

MJ: He . . . Hartz, I mean. He opened the hatch. There was no
air, so . . . so our air just rushed out into space, and I couldn't
breathe. I couldn't think. Hartz, he, he was there, inside the

hatch and then Sergei . . . Sergei grabbed him. Bit him, bit his throat out, Control. There was blood but it all got . . . got sucked out through the open hatch. Sergei pulled Hartz through the . . . through . . .

MCC: No. No, he didn't. He bit Hartz, yes. But he didn't pull him through.

MJ: . . . he . . .

MCC: We're past the point of lying to each other, Marcia. Let's promise not to bullshit each other now. I saw it on the video.

MJ: Okay.

MCC: Tell me what you did.

MJ: I . . . I pushed Hartz through. I pushed Hartz into Destiny and then I closed the hatch. Sealed it up.

MCC: You did the right thing.

[00:53 UTC.]

MJ: Now they're both out there. They're both . . .

[Repetitive clanging noises can be heard.]

[01:39 UTC.]

MJ: It's . . . bad? It's really bad down there?

MCC: Yes.

MJ: There's no, there's not going to be a rescue ship . . . is there?

MCC: No.

MJ: I, uh, I have something I have to do. Right? I have to, um, check on Karl.

MCC: Yes.

MJ: He. He's. Well. He's not breathing. No pulse. He. Oh shit!

MCC: Marcia?

MJ: Oh shit, oh shit! Jesus! Shit, his eyes, his eyes, they're open but—but—but—

MCC: Do it.

MJ: Yeah, I mean, I mean yes, he's stuck, he's stuck in the sleep-sac but he's trying to get out, he, he—there's a fire extinguisher.

MCC: Do it.

MJ: Oh God! Oh, God! What did I . . . Control, Control, there's . . . there's . . .

MCC: Go ahead.

MJ: There's blood and, and bits of brain, everywhere, just everywhere, and it's getting in the air vents, oh, God, I'm going to be sick, I just watched part of his brain get sucked into the, into the air filter, he's—he's—

MCC: Breathe.

MJ: *And they're still over there*, in Destiny, they're still pounding on the hatch, and—

[Transmission was lost, for unknown reasons, until 02:19 UTC. In the following, what appeared at first to be noise in the signal has since been identified as the sound of MJ, weeping.]

MJ: Control? **** Control?

MCC: Still . . . here.

MJ: **** **** **** **** ****.

MCC: Hey. Hey, now.

MJ: You sound **** **** ****. Were you . . . you know? Oh, God. **** **** ****.

MCC: Yes. I was attacked. I'm . . . I'm going to die, Marcia. And then . . .

MJ: No. Don't say it. We both know it's true, just don't . . . don't say it.

MCC: Okay.

MJ: Jesus. Jesus. **** **** ****. Shut up! Shut the fuck up! Shut the fuck up! Shut the fuck up! They're still, they're still beating their fists on the, on the **** **** ****.

MCC: You're safe in there, Marcia. They can't get to you.

MJ: Shut the fuck up you fucking bastards! Stop it! Just stop it, stop it, stop—****.

MCC: I'll stay with you as long as I can.

MJ: Karl . . . and Hartz . . . I killed them.

MCC: You did what you had to do. Didn't they teach you that in astronaut training? To survive, no matter what it takes? Didn't they teach you that?

MJ: They . . . they did. But if there's no rescue ship . . .

MCC: No.

MJ: I need to conserve power, but . . . when you feel it happening. When you know it's almost time. Call me. Please.

MCC: You really want to hear it?

MJ: You're all I have, now, Control.

[03:58 UTC.]

MJ: Control?

MJ: Come in, Control. Please.

MJ: Please come in.

MJ: Please.

[04:21 UTC.]

MJ: You bastard. You promised me . . .

MJ: They're . . . they're still pounding on the hatch. They don't ever give up, if anyone's hearing this . . . fuck. I'm still doing science, aren't I? They sent me up here to do experiments on hamsters.

MJ: Now I'm doing experiments on . . . whatever these things are.

MJ: Test subject responds positively to acute cranial trauma.

MJ: Test subject does not require oxygen to sustain metabolic processes.

MJ: Test subject . . . oh, fuck this.

MJ: Shut the fuck up shut the fuck up just stop just shut the fuck up **** **** ****!

[06:46 UTC.]

MJ: Batteries all but gone. This is probably my last . . .

MJ: Jesus. The air in here. I'm, uh, seeing spots. Feeling a little . . . a little light-headed.

MJ: Please. Shut up . . . shut up . . . please.

MJ: Control? You aren't . . . I mean, you might actually still be listening. I just . . . just thought of that. You might still be hearing me.

MJ: Maybe you're thinking I sound like I would taste pretty good right now.

MJ: Maybe you're thinking something else. Something . . . more human.

MJ: I . . . just wanted to say thank you. You stuck with me, I—

MJ: Control—what was that? That sound?

[06:48 UTC.]

MJ: It's the crew of Soyuz. It's the crew from Soyuz, and they're . . . they're missing pieces, and one of them, his face-plate is cracked, but I can see him, looking in at me, looking in through the windows of the Cupola and they're beating on the glass, beating on the glass with their fists . . .

Max Brallier is the *New York Times* bestselling author of more than thirty books, including the middle-grade monster-zombie series The Last Kids on Earth. Under the pen name Jack Chabert, he is the author and creator of the Eerie Elementary series for Scholastic Books and authored the *New York Times* bestselling *Poptropica: Vol 1: Mystery of the Map.* Max also writes for adults, including the bestselling series Can YOU Survive the Zombie Apocalypse? When not at home in New York City, Max enjoys his favorite bar, Joe's, in western Pennsylvania, where he's surrounded by the trophies of a hunter far better than he. Follow Max on Twitter @MaxBrallier or visit www.maxbrallier.com.

SNAGGLETOOTH

by Max Brallier

Beau Lynn had a rotted gray snaggletooth that bugged me half-mad and that's why I blew his Adam's apple through the nape of his neck.

Beau Lynn was the town dentist, and it was a goddamned dead decayed-to-the-center fang jutting from his face, long as I knew him. Believe that?

But it wasn't the tooth that got it started.

What got it started was me and Deb Lynn on the porch out back of her house, sticky with July sweat, working our way through a case of Iron City.

Beau, her husband, the man with the rotted tooth, was in Pittsburgh for two days. For me and Deb, that meant no need for sneaking around that night—no quick, hard pawing, mauling in my rusted Impala. No wasted money at the ABC Motel.

We could sit on the back porch, civilized, and take our time easing into the fun part.

That back porch.

See, that back porch—it was like a damned deer blind. A field of tall grass ran nearly two hundred yards from the house to the woods, which backed up to the Allegheny Forest.

If that back porch was mine, I'd rest my Savage 99 on the railing, Bucs game on the radio, pick off whitetail bucks, no need to check them, no limit, the house too far out for anyone to be nosy.

Sure, it was that rotted snaggletooth that brought me to murder, but it was the thought of that back porch that had me listening when Deb leaned across the patio table, a spark in her eyes I'd never seen before as she said, "It's a foolproof plan, Jack," and I was shaking my head, drinking my beer, saying, "The only type of person calls a plan foolproof is a fool."

Deb leaned back, arm like a twig resting on the flower print seat cushion.

I told her, "I'm not sure if you watch too many movies or you don't watch enough, but killing the husband of the lady you're seeing, chasing after the insurance money? That tends to not go well."

"But this is different," Deb said, "because I took out the plan last month, and you won't be doing the thing for half a year. Sure, you take out life insurance on your old man and he dies ugly two days later, yeah, people will be curious."

I finished my beer and opened another, and that was enough for her to think I was half-interested.

She said, "You'll do it while hunting, in December. White-tail season."

"What's he even want to go hunting with me for anyway?"

"You went to war, he didn't. He's all tight about it, half the town going off, but him staying back."

I drank, thinking, running my tongue over my teeth—feeling that sharp canine dagger.

Deb's nails tapped the cloudy glass tabletop. "Beau's got a fancy, loop-de-loop signature, but I spent time practicing, and I got it just right. Paperwork's already on file with the insurance man. Two hundred and fifty thousand dollars, Jack. *Two hundred and fifty thousand*."

"And we split it?"

"If you want."

"Why else?"

"Because after, it'll just be you and me, together. And what's it matter whose is what, then? Would you like that?"

"I might."

She slipped her foot out of her sandal, ran it up my leg—kept going until she got to the parts that started a man thinking less than straight.

"I certainly might," I said, and stood, telling her I had to piss.

Inside the man's house, then. Passing a table—knickknacks, wedding photos. There was Beau, holding some dental award—a big, goofy bronze tooth. No, not bronze. Plastic, painted like bronze, I bet.

Beau was grinning, looking out at me.

I had left for the war when I was nineteen. Drinks at Bull's Tavern the night before I shipped, and Beau was there and he shook my hand and said good luck and his smiling lips revealed, as always, that rotted snaggletooth.

After my tour, the mood at the welcome home drinks was very different, but the rotted snaggletooth was the same.

It was foul.

Inconsiderate.

I had gone and done and watched friends get exploded to nothing and this man—*the goddamned town dentist!*—wouldn't remove that hideous thing from his *fucking mouth.*

So coming back out, I told Deb I'd think about it.

Deb shrugged, fine.

And I told her if I did decide, I wanted to do it up close. World falling apart, like my old man says. Men with hair like ladies. Ladies working jobs supposed to be for men. Tattoos. Athletes dancing in the end zone. So if I was going to do it— I'd do it real close, like a man ought to.

Deb shrugged, again, fine.

And that was it.

That one evening.

A short conversation—with a break to piss—on the back porch, and then we were inside, to the bed, tossing on Beau's sheets, but the whole time we were tossing I could scarcely stay hard because I was imagining that rotted snaggletooth, and by the end I'd made up my mind on the thing, and there wasn't nothing else to think about.

* * *

The whole of summer and fall, it was like climbing the rungs of the high-dive ladder.

Each day, another rung. And the higher I climbed, the harder it'd be to turn back—'cause that's darned embarrassing, you got someone behind you, nine rungs down, and you both have to go back, rung by rung, everyone watching.

No, once you start climbing—no matter what you're feeling—you need to just keep on.

And the pool. The jump. That thing you have to do. That was Beau. That was the dentist with the rotted snaggletooth and the wasted porch that'd make for a fine backyard deer blind.

There's a sort of person, I guess, that once an idea gets in their head—it can't be stopped or rerouted. Only thing that can stop it is the introduction of some new, better idea or some hard force coming the opposite way.

And unfortunately for Beau, I didn't get any new, better ideas all summer and fall, and no hard force came the opposite way, either.

We went out on day four of rifle hunting season, December 9, coffee with a splash of whiskey not doing much to fight the cold sting in the air. Beau got me in his shiny red Chevy pickup and we were parked by five thirty, stepping into the woods before the first light of morning.

Beau brought a flashlight, and he flicked it on—but I threw my hand over it. "Dark's nice. Enjoy it. Sun'll be up soon. This hour, the quiet, it's right."

"I can't see where I'm walking."

"I know the way."

We trekked across the Derry Ridge, thick with spruce and white pines, walking more than an hour—following the old logging path at first, then veering off, deep, where you get twisted and lost if you aren't careful.

Beau wore a bright orange vest and his hunting gear was all fresh—got it at that new Ace Hardware. He had all variety of gadgets and devices dangling off him, clanging with each step.

We came to the blind, and the first thing he said was, "We should have brought stools."

The blind was simple: a wide, overturned spruce, one gnarled branch making for a natural rifle rest. Sitting on stumps, we had a view of a stream fifty feet out and a wide clearing beyond it.

It was fine, but it was nothing like Beau's back porch.

I smiled, knowing soon, I'd be shooting off that back porch.

We opened our first beers just after five thirty, the sun up but not fully at 'em, casting light through the trees in spotlight arrays—yellow-orange shafts, slicing down.

Beau wanted to clank beers, toasting to a good day, and I did it but I had to swallow a lot of words. I hate that, drinking with a guy who always wanted to hit your beer.

Clank. Clank. Clank.

Like you had to keep reminding each other you were having a decent enough time.

But I wanted the booze doing backstrokes through his bloodstream, wanted him loose and cocky and rubbery, so every time he raised, I clanked. And every time he slowed down on his drinking, I'd crack another, and that'd cause him to quickly finish his and fish for a new one.

"Safety off," I said, tapping his rifle. "That 'safety on, until you're ready to shoot,' stuff? That's for kids and women. I discovered that overseas, first time it got hot."

That was a lie, the stuff about learning that in battle, but I knew it'd pull at him right.

Beau reached out, *click*.

He drank and he talked about the Steelers, then about his dental practice, saying it'd be a life of free checkups for me if we bagged something more'n five years old.

Then there was a silence, and I could feel him wanting to say something, and I hated that sort of holding pattern quiet, so I out and said, "What?"

"I heard, over there—that some of our guys, they go around, slicing off people's ears."

He smiled timidly, like he was nervous he'd offended me. "Did you ever see that? Guys slicing off ears? Wearing them around their neck like trophies?"

"No."

"Well, I guess that's a good thing—we can't have our boys in uniform cuttin' off ears, wearing them around," he said, and then he raised his beer, and we clanked to that.

You believe it?

We really did—we clanked to not cuttin' off ears.

And he smiled as we clanked, and the dead snaggletooth showed itself again, and I decided *damnit, I can't stand to wait much longer*.

So I finished the beer in my hand while I let the feeling build in me—an anticipation I hadn't felt since the war. This sort of shaky hand, tooth-clenching exhilaration, knowing what was to come.

It'd been just under two hours when I stood and said, "It's going right through me."

"Drinking beer is like trout fishing."

"How's that?"

"Catch and release," he said, and he laughed too loud, and then said something about how I'd barely even drank the amount he had and *he* hadn't had to piss yet.

I left my rifle propped against the limb, then walked twenty feet through the brush, slipping behind a wide oak. The piss came in short, hard spurts that stung a bit, splashing the oak and the forest floor. A sour smell, pooling around my boots.

I zipped, shut my eyes, breathed in and out slow and long, then called out in a half-whisper—

"Beau. I got a view. Come on, it's yours."

I heard Beau stand, all his devices dangling and clanking, then him stomping through the grass, slowing, moving half-gentle as he crept up.

"Where are you?" Beau said, and I could imagine him now, eyes narrow, searching, anxious, probably imagining it like *this* was his war.

I pressed my back to the oak. Heard him trudging, eager.

So eager, he'd be running his tongue over that tooth.

I watched the ground, seeing Beau's shadow fall, hearing the footsteps like kindling popping, one final step, and then my breath was held.

"I don't see it," Beau said, and then he didn't say anything again, ever, 'cause I was spinning out from around the oak, grabbing his .270 by the barrel, his eyes popping, a quick hiccup of a laugh, not believing for a moment, thinking something like, "well this is a strange joke"—and then I was jerking the gun down, bringing Beau with it, my finger finding the trigger and pulling as I continued yanking down, safety off, firing, the blast muffled just slightly because the barrel was so tight against the flesh of the man's chin, and his whole jaw blew open like he'd been chomping on an M-80. The base of his skull blew out the back of his head, a whirling, spinning plate of flesh and bone and greasy hair.

The butt of the rifle hit the dirt, pushing up into Beau's mouth, so he flopped onto his back.

His jaw, his throat, the ground—just dripping, sopping red flesh, everywhere. His breath was coming only in small, spitty bits—like trying to drink pop through a straw with a split in it.

Beau's eyes found me. His upper lip—his only lip, now pulled back, and I saw the rotted gray snaggletooth.

And his tongue running over it.

It felt like he watched me a long time—longer than he should have. His tongue running over the tooth for minutes.

Die.

Go on.

His tongue licking that tooth twice more, and then, for a final moment, his eyes focused on me—and I only then realized I hadn't breathed, not once the whole time.

I breathed then, and at the same instant, Beau finally stopped licking.

He was dead.

I ran my handkerchief along the end of the barrel, where I had grabbed it.

I walked back to the blind, drank two thirds of a beer. I checked my watch. It was a quarter past eight.

It should have been done.

But that rotted snaggletooth.

That hooked, nasty thing—protruding, everyone having to look at it. That tooth that chewed meat, chomped cod each Sunday at the Methodist fish fry—he left it there, for everyone to see.

Suddenly, Beau's voice: *"You ever see that? Guys slicing off ears? Wearing them around their neck like trophies?"*

I admit, my heart jumped, thinking it came from the man. But it was just my brain making noises.

Go on, Jack, I said. *You're on the final rung, just pull yourself up and over and march to the end of the high dive.*

But I didn't.

Beau's hunting pack was in the blind. I removed a curved, freshly sharpened blade and walked to the body.

His tongue was hanging out and his face was pale.

Would anyone know?

No.

His lower jaw was blown apart, everything pulpy and wet.

So I crouched down and pulled back his upper lip. I dug the knife in to the gum, gentle, rocking it back and forth, loosening that rotted snaggletooth.

And his eyes stared up, still open, watching me.

Beau's voice, again, in my head: *"You ever see that? Guys slicing off ears? Wearing them around their neck like trophies?"*

"Yes," I answered, and I twisted the blade until the tooth popped into my hand.

I walked to the water, held the tooth in, let the blood stream off it. The rotted snaggletooth—still wet—went into my watch pocket.

Then I pulled the truck keys from Beau's coat, took a final glance at his body, and began jogging back through the woods.

It was nearly nine thirty that morning when I got to the Chevy, and that's when the first thing went wrong. Beau's CB was busted. Beau was a volunteer fireman, and his CB was shot—and even though it was a wrench in the plan, it made me feel less bad about the whole thing. Not that I felt bad to start with, but if you're a volunteer fireman your CB had to work, and if it don't, you're asking for it.

So I sped toward town, tires screeching as I hauled past the Five & Dime, feeling folks' eyes on me, but knowing that was fine—that was part of it.

The police chief's name was Tharp, and he was at his desk when I came in, me waving past the deputy, saying it was an emergency. I was proud of myself, the way I did it, panting a bit, adding just a little struggle to my voice as I said, "Chief, there's been an accident. Beau Lynn shot hisself. He's dead, I'm certain, and hell—ah hell, just shit—I saw the whole thing, the way he fell and—shit, Chief, it's an awful mess."

Fire ants had begun to eat at Beau's body, parading down his exploded throat, funneling in and out of his nostrils, picking at his open eyes—a few drowned in the red pool where he lay.

Tharp looked at the body for a long moment, then lit one of his long cigarettes. "Tell me again, how you saw it?"

"I was right here. I saw a buck, but I didn't have my rifle—I was taking a leak—so I whispered to Beau. He walked out, and then I see his foot catch the root, and he starts to fall. It happens sort of slow, the way he goes down, and I open my mouth to heckle him a little, but then I hear the shot. He smacks the ground or the gun or both, I guess, but then he sort of trampolined back up, only when he came back up the blood was like a fountain."

And as I said it to Tharp, I was thinking, that *is* what it looked like.

"Did you try to revive him?"

"Revive? He didn't have a throat."

"You check for a pulse on the wrist?"

"He didn't have a throat, Tharp."

Chief Tharp glanced at me. "You got blood on you," he said, stating it, but also saying it like a question.

I looked at my finger, where I'd pried the rotted snaggletooth free. Blood on the tips, under the nail, dried.

"Right, well, sure. I had to fish the keys from his coat. I didn't say I didn't touch the body, just that I didn't check for any pulse 'cause the man's face had been blown to nothing. Also, some got on me when he fell, I'm sure, I wasn't but five feet away."

Quiet for a bit, Tharp looking the body over.

"See, he had the keys 'cause he drove us out," I went on, smiling inside as I said it, because I had the answers. "Insisted on driving, with the new Chevy. Wanted to show off the leather."

Tharp nodded slowly. "That does sound like Beau."

Tharp said a bunch more, about an incident report, about calling Fish & Game, about Deb, about me sitting for a taped conversation, about what a shame it was. He didn't want to leave the body, but wouldn't anyone be able to find us here. Reluctant, he decided we'd both walk back, and he'd lead the state troopers back in. He lifted Beau's rifle, said he'd bring it out. Last, he took my rifle, said he had to check it, and I said of course, sure, I understood.

Back out through the trees, one state trooper waiting there, leaning against his cruiser, along with an ambulance and two paramedics.

I packed a lip and stepped away, letting them talk, no point in listening.

There was this feeling like the tooth was squirming in my pocket—yet when I stuck my finger inside and felt that rotted snaggletooth, it was perfectly still. I was rubbing it when I heard Tharp calling, like he'd been calling for a long while.

"Jack! You hearing me?"

"Sure," I said, quickly slipping my finger out, turning. "Little shaken. Just didn't realize at first, I suppose."

"You can head back to town."

"You want me to tell Debbie?" I asked.

"Ah, shit. Needs to come from my office. Soon, before the poor woman hears. I'll radio the station, have Leonard head over."

And so I pulled out, in Beau's Chevy. As I left, I saw Tharp and the troopers and the paramedics heading in.

I split off before town, pulling into Ruthie's Roadside. I ordered the open-faced meatloaf sandwich but I skipped the potatoes, got the coleslaw. Soon, I saw Deputy Leonard's car speed past, toward Deb and Beau's house, off to deliver the news of Beau's accidental passing.

It was just past two o'clock when Leonard came back up the road. I paid, stopped at Bull's Tavern, picked up a case of Rolling Rock, and got back into the dead man's truck.

* * *

"So you really did it," Deb said.

We were on the back porch, same place where the idea got started six months earlier.

The sun was low—that depressed winter sunset, always coming before you're ready for it. As it went down, a strange fog rose up.

Living in the valley, sometimes the morning fog—you could barely see your hand in front of your face. But this was night fog, and as the moon rose—a silver dollar spotlight being lifted in the sky—a green haze built.

We were five beers into the case of Rolling Rock.

"How'd the deputy tell it to you?" I asked.

"Plain. Straightforward."

"You do a lot of fake crying n'at?"

"Some crying came for real."

"Sure, sure," I said, and then after a moment, "He mention me?"

Deb shook her head. "Only to say you were there. Not like anyone was suspecting or suspicious."

Inside, the radio was on—music at first, but they had cut in with news. Something happening in Pittsburgh, at a hospital. Something else at a cemetery.

"You shouldn't be here tonight," Deb said. "But Christ, Jack, I need you to be."

She got up, sliding into my lap. Her hands along my skin, nails scratching in that good way.

She was reaching for the button on my jeans, face close to mine, and I saw she had these green earrings, dangling. I heard

Beau: *"You ever see that? Guys slicing off ears? Wearing them around their neck like trophies?"*

I ignored it—mind playing tricks—and let Deb make me feel good.

Her hand ran up my chest, brushing against the dog tags that I still wore. And as she flicked the metal, I heard Beau again, barking, *"You ever see that? Guys slicing off ears? Wearing them around their neck like trophies?"*

I pushed her off, saying I need the bathroom. Soon as the screen banged, my finger was stabbing into the watch pocket, clawing, bringing the snaggletooth out, nearly dropping it.

I held it in my palm, the dead thing.

Again, Beau's voice in my head—and that sound, bouncing around, got me stomping through the house.

Beau had a tiny office in the basement, where he did his billing, balanced the checkbook. An old dental chair in the corner, and a few supplies.

It didn't take me long to find what I was looking for: a small drill. Not the dental kind, but the bit was thin, and it would do.

I gripped the snaggletooth between my fingers—saw Beau's blood, and I began to drill through the side.

It started slow, and then a rush as the bit pushed through, and I nearly dropped my trophy.

But I didn't.

I unclasped my dog-tag chain, held it out.

I fiddled with the tooth, struggling to pull the chain through, and it began to feel like I couldn't breathe, and then the chain finally slipped through, and I drew it, and the feeling in my chest was relief.

Back upstairs. Another beer from the fridge. Each step was

more solid now, confident—the tooth bouncing against my chest.

Chief Tharp was outside.

Stepping out, I saw him on the porch, his back to the field and the tree line. The air was raw and his breath was thick in the moonlight.

Deb glanced at me, and I saw her mouth was drawn tight. I smiled, cool—as cool as the metal and the rotted snaggletooth against my skin.

"Jack," he said, with that policeman-like nod. I wondered if he practiced a nod like that.

"Jack was returning Beau's truck," Deb said, as a way of explaining my being here. But there was no need to explain, the whole day was a triumph, done perfect, and I greeted Chief Tharp with a wide grin. "I get you a beer, Chief?"

Tharp shook his head. "Deb, you mind if I take a seat?"

Deb said 'course not, and Chief Tharp tugged at his big coat and settled in. "I'll just out and say it. Beau's body—it's not there anymore."

Deb, after a moment: "What do you mean?"

"Not there," he said, then looked up to me. "I took the others in after you left, Jack. When we got to the site, Beau's body was gone. Simply not there."

I felt the tooth against my skin and I said, "Black bear, maybe?"

Tharp half nodded, half shrugged. "There was a path of blood leading away, but it didn't appear as if the body had been dragged. Some bits of skin. Deb, you don't need to hear any of this if—"

Deb said, "It's fine."

"We lost the trail at the stream—"

Tharp kept talking but I didn't hear the words anymore.

Inside, I started laughing.

More than that—I was screaming hysterically, overcome with this pure, childlike, new-day joy.

Could it be any better?

Like winning the lottery twice in the same day. Kill the man, police chief confirms it, sees how it happened, then the body up and disappears. Nothing to investigate.

Chief Tharp and Deb talked, but I only heard bits and pieces: the state police might find more, Tharp said, or maybe someone else was out hunting and found him, Deb said.

I was looking out from the porch—*my blind*—and began wondering if and why I even needed Deb. She was fun, but her voice was the slightest bit shrill and her hair was always dry, sort of like straw.

It's a good thing she didn't have a rotted snaggletooth, I thought, or I'd have blown her away right there. And that made me really laugh, out loud, and Tharp and Deb both sort of gawked at me, but I just laughed again.

Maybe I'd arrange something for Deb. And then the blind, with that damn majestic view of the high-grown grass running straight up to the forest—I'd make it mine.

And then I stopped daydreaming, and I started falling apart.

There was movement along the tree line, where the oaks thinned out.

Something coming out of the woods.

A whitetail?

No.

It was two hundred yards from the porch to the trees, and even squinting, it was hard to see much. Then the clouds shifted and that swirling, swamp gas sky shone green light on the field and I saw it was a man.

The man exited the trees, moving through the field in a staggered gait—like a buck, shot through but not killed, feet stabbing for balance.

Only I saw it. Chief Tharp was across the patio table, facing the house, and Deb beside him—only me with a view of the field.

I didn't know what I saw, didn't know what to say, so I said nothing.

But my heart, it was picking up speed, sliding into second and then third, gears grinding as my breath became ragged.

"Jack?" Tharp was watching me. "Jack, I said, it's too dark now, but first thing tomorrow, I'll get together a search party. You should join."

"Sure," I said.

"You joining, helping, that'd go a long way to soothing any suspicions."

"Suspicions?" I asked, but I didn't hear the response. The clouds moved through the sky, and the yellow moon made my view clear, for a moment.

One hundred and fifty yards from the house, and I saw that neon orange vest. Couldn't make out features, but I could see those damned toys—fresh from the Ace Hardware—bouncing off the man's chest, reflecting in the moonlight.

It was Beau.

And I sucked in air, and I glanced from Tharp to Deb, waiting for I don't know what—waiting to discover I was a victim of some elaborate, maddening scheme.

But they only kept on talking.

My mind, my sanity—it was suddenly a rock, skipping along a lake—Beau had flung it, one moment my rationality all there, the next it was slicing away.

But I was *not* mad. I knew that, for sure—but then—goddamnit, answers!—if I was *not* mad how was the man I had killed now lumbering through the field toward me?

Had I been wrong? Had I not killed him?

No! *No!* Chief Tharp had seen Beau, too, the body bled out.

I had stood over Beau and I had dug that blade into his gums and sliced out that damned snaggletooth, hadn't I?

I ran my finger around my collar, feeling the dog-chain, tugging it slightly, causing the tooth to tap against my chest.

The snaggletooth was there, so it had all happened—not some lunatic's dream.

But still, Beau drew closer.

I wanted to leave. I wanted to get up, go to the dead man's truck, get in it—and drive. I'd drive until I hit the Ohio, and I'd cross, and I'd keep going—no need to ever know *what* in hell had happened.

Or Tharp. Could he leave. Get out. What was he still doing here?

But the chief and Deb talked more—only their voices sounded so far away. I opened my mouth again, hoping to say something that might bring the night to a quick close, but I couldn't speak, words stuck in my throat.

Leave, Tharp, damn it. Leave. Get in your fucking car.

The night was quiet—miles from town, no houses nearby—and in the moments when Tharp and Deb would just *shut up for one fucking second* I could hear Beau moving through the overgrown grass.

Did they not *hear* his footsteps? If they could just *turn*, they'd see the man.

But they did not.

And he kept on coming.

Sixty yards.

Less.

I could see his mouth. Open. And there was no glimmer of that rotted snaggletooth.

A slap on my arm, bringing me back. It was Tharp. "I said, Jack, you always pick up beer when you're visiting a widow?"

"Uh?" I said. "No. These were Deb's. From the fridge."

Tharp's head, back and forth. "No. I stopped by Bull's Tavern. Mike said you were in earlier, picking up a case."

"Right. Sorry, my mind's a little not right."

Tharp's eyes narrowed, watching, then hitting me again, "Hey, when Nancy passes, you just get me scotch, all right?" and he laughed—loud and short.

On the radio, the voices drifting out—I could only make out a bit, but one word kept popping up: *Dead. Dead. Dead.*

And I heard those words, and I saw the man, and my sanity was an avalanche, tumbling down, going to nothing.

But still *no* I was not mad, this was goddamned real!

Beau.

Shambling forward, body jerking like it had when he died. Only thirty yards now. His clothing was darker. Damp, I realized, from the stream.

I glanced to Tharp and then to Deb. They were still talking, discussing the details of what would happen next, the search, if she'd be right to make the funeral arrangements now or wait.

Looking at the pair, my brain shrieking, *There! There! I murdered him! Tharp, turn and look!*

A sound.

I heard Beau moan for the first time, then.

Arms were raised, out, stiff. Like he was coming for something.

The rotted snaggletooth?

Did he want it back?

Was that it?

Maybe he did, because it seemed to burn against my chest. And it all built, spinning inside me:

This awful husk staggering closer.

The radio, *dead, dead, dead*.

Tharp, on and on, ass glued, not leaving.

And *that goddamned gray, putrefied, hideous snaggletooth against my skin*.

I watched Beau, watched what was left of his mouth open up, and he moaned and I couldn't hold it anymore, I shrieked, curdling blood, a scream from somewhere deep.

Erupting then, chair tumbling back, beer spilling, my hands clawing at my chest, cursing, goddamning it all, ripping the dog tags off, smacking them down onto the table like a bad beat at the card table.

The chain just sat there.

The tooth.

"You ever see that!" I barked at Tharp, hearing my voice sounding a bit like Beau's. "Guys cutting out rotted teeth? Wearing them around their neck like a trophy?"

Silence.

Tharp's eyes tight, Deb's mouth a small O.

And then them both realizing—seeing that discolored thing on the table—Tharp putting up a hand to calm me while his other hand reached for his revolver.

But it was too late for that, I was snatching up the spilled bottle and swinging it, cracking it against Tharp's face, rolling his head, and then smacking again, the bottle smashing this time, knocking him from the chair, and then jamming the bottle into his throat.

Deb screaming.

Me, diving, pawing at Tharp's holster, pulling the revolver, then stepping to the edge of the porch.

A huge smile stretching across my face then, knowing I'd finally get that moment—hunting from that back porch blind. A grin so wide, like it was carved from my lips with a bowie knife, sawed ear to ear.

Hunt to kill a man I'd already killed once that day. This lurching, possessed thing, just twenty yards from the house.

The gun bucked in my hand as I fired, the bullet punching Beau's chest.

He staggered but continued.

I fired twice more, but he kept coming, and my brain was on fire then, erupting, volcanic, nightmarish thoughts sluicing through my skull. I stomped out, down the steps, across the grass, to meet the man, to see how he could still live.

Or not live.

Flies buzzed about him. He moved like a drunk struggling to make it home. His face and skin all melting plastic.

Dead.

Dead as he was when I left him.

He had no throat. The fire ants had taken much of his skin, and they were there still, picking at the flesh of his face, covering it, so I saw more crawling red than anything else.

Beau moaned and his lip pulled back and I saw the purple-red hole, where I had ripped out the snaggletooth.

I raised the revolver and trained it on his chest and I fired, blowing open a dangling compass, putting a fist-sized hole through his heart, but he only moaned louder and shuffled closer.

Footsteps on the patio, Deb running. A car door opening, her escaping, I guessed.

I put the final two rounds into his chest, but he kept on, and his hands were on me, cold and clammy and waxy, and I saw his remaining teeth bearing down on me.

I hit the grass, Beau on top of me, saliva and blood dripping onto my face. Clawing. This inhuman, unholy thing trying to gnaw into me.

And then, suddenly, a reverberating *boom* and his face shattering, skull exploding.

Shrieking, sobbing, I pushed the thing off. I rolled and gasped and got to my feet.

Head still spinning, wondering, sincerely, if this was a dream and I'd soon be slapped awake.

Turning, I saw Deb there, on the porch, Tharp's cruiser beyond, door open. Deb holding Beau's rifle, the barrel and stock still gore-splattered from the morning's hunt.

And I started to say thank god, started to ask what madness had overcome us, when the gun leapt in Deb's hand and a shot ripped through me and I was knocked back, falling beside Beau's diseased husk.

Deb coming down the steps, striding through the grass, then standing over us both. Her sort of smirking, curious, like she was catching some insanity herself, asking out loud, "Christ almighty, I wonder just what in hell will the insurance man have to say about this?"

Carrie Ryan is the *New York Times* bestselling author of the Forest of Hands and Teeth series, *Daughter of Deep Silence*, and *Infinity Ring: Divide and Conquer* as well as the editor of *Foretold: 14 Stories of Prophecy and Prediction*. Currently she's working on *The Map to Everywhere*, a four-book magical adventure series cowritten with her husband, John Parke Davis, and a new young adult novel. Her books have sold in more than twenty-two territories and her first book, *The Forest of Hands and Teeth*, is in development as a major motion picture. A former litigator, Carrie lives in Charlotte, North Carolina, with her husband and various pets. Visit her online at www.CarrieRyan.com or follow her on Twitter at @CarrieRyan.

THE BURNING DAYS

by Carrie Ryan

We all know the fire will burn out eventually. There's only so much fuel left and the rain that's been threatening for days has to fall at some point. It's just a matter of when.

But not a question of what'll happen after that. We'll be dead—all of us. If we're lucky, it'll happen quick. If we're unlucky . . . I swallow the bile eating its way up my throat.

If we're unlucky we'll end up like *them*. Broken. Shambling.

Dead.

At night they're nothing more than shadows lurching in the darkness beyond the flickering flames. In the day, though—in the day we can see them. Their wounds glisten in the heat of the sun, gaping red and raw.

When Henry's car blew early on we figured out they were afraid of fire. We realized all we had to do was keep the perimeter around the cabin burning. We started with the easy stuff: dusty drapes, tattered blankets, clothes long stored in mildewed drawers. We piled it on, forcing the flames higher until we realized we were burning through our fuel too fast.

After that we took a more measured approach. Breaking the furniture into kindling and spreading it out. Since then it's just been about keeping things steady. We take turns, an ever constant rotation. When there were six of us, it was enough that a couple of us could get sleep, even if a few hours at a time. But now that there are only four of us, we're spread thinner.

I've slept maybe five hours in the past three and a half days. But I can't really blame the work. It's impossible to sleep with them out there. The dead.

The inevitability that we all have only so much time left before we join their ranks.

And with each room we burn, the closer we come to that inevitability. We've already cannibalized most of the first floor and as much of the second floor as we can without compromising the integrity of the structure. We've torn it all out—the drywall, the floors, the subfloors, the framing—and fed it to the flames.

It's nauseating how fast it goes. How little is left.

How quickly our options have dwindled.

"We should have gone with Ruth and Andy." Lainey sits on

the porch with her back against the stairs, a shotgun cradled loosely in her lap. She's staring at a patch of red dirt, her eyes unfocused and tear tracks cutting through the soot staining her cheeks. "They've probably already made it to the guard station."

I look up and catch Robert's eye. He's standing on the ladder I'm bracing, prying siding from the house. Neither of us has told her that we saw Ruth early this morning. Half of her face was stripped away and her arm was missing, but I still knew it was her.

She'd borrowed my jacket before leaving. In case it got cold at night down the mountain. "You won't need it up here. You'll have the fire to keep you warm," she'd reminded me.

I'd let her take it and that's how I'd recognized her. She still wore it, though it hung on tatters from her shoulders. It was the kind of detail Lainey would never notice—that Ruth had left wearing my jacket.

Not that Lainey would have remembered what my jacket looks like in the first place.

I keep waiting for her to spot Ruth, shuffling along the edge of the crowd with the others, but she never looks at them that closely.

To her they aren't people.

Maybe that's the smart approach. Maybe that's why she's able to actually sleep during her off shift. Because so far as she's concerned, her best friend and her best friend's boyfriend are still alive—are probably even safe.

According to Lainey, they were the smart ones.

And we're to blame for arguing against going with them.

I wait to see if Robert's going to say anything to her, but he just clenches his teeth and shoves the claw end of the hammer underneath another nail to pry it free. He's already stripped away most of the siding along the porch. It burns fast, sending up great clouds of billowing black smoke that catches in the wind and tangles in the branches of nearby trees.

He and Lainey had had a massive blowup late the night before that had ended with her screaming that he didn't love her and him finally snapping and announcing in front of everyone that he was done with her and would have broken up with her at the start of the trip if the whole world hadn't fallen apart first. Ever since then, they've been treading warily around each other, the tension between them thick.

"We can still go, you know," Lainey continues from her perch on the steps. "Try to make it to the guard station tonight. I think they're slower in the darkness."

"No they're not." Henry punctuates the statement by throwing a piece of siding on the fire along the right of the house. Sweat glistens across his forehead and he swipes at it with a bare arm, leaving a trail of ash in its wake.

"Then let's just go now," Lainey proposes. When no one says anything she adds, "I'm serious. The longer we wait, the more of them there are going to be."

"It's already too late, Lainey." Robert rips free the hunk of siding and drops it toward me. I carry it out to the waiting pile in the yard.

"You said that yesterday," she shouts. "And the day before!" She throws up a hand in frustration. "We're not going to have a choice pretty soon, you know. If you haven't noticed, we're running low on fuel."

"Thanks for pointing out the obvious," Robert grumbles.

"That's the problem," Lainey says through clenched teeth. "If it really was that obvious you'd agree with me that we have to leave."

"There's still half of the upstairs and then the attic," Henry points out.

"And how long's that going to last us?" she demands. "Another two days? Three at the most?"

Her question hangs in the air.

"At least we're safe here," I offer, still thinking about Ruth and her torn face.

Lainey usually ignores me, but she pins me with a crooked eyebrow. "Really? You call this safe?"

I glance out at the line of fire and the shambling bodies beyond. I remember that first night when they came for us. There were only a few—enough that we could knock them back as we struggled to understand what was happening. This was before we'd found the emergency radio and cranked it up.

Before we knew they were risen dead. And that they were everywhere.

The cities were the worst, we learned. Most people hadn't survived that first night. The only reason we'd made it was because the population this far in the country was low.

But the dead were still able to find us, even out here. And every day more and more of them find their way through the trees to crowd the clearing beyond the fire.

Could things be better? Of course. But they could also be so much worse. At least we've figured out a way to keep them at a distance. At least the cabin's safe. Even now, when I try to sleep, I can't forget that long first night: the scratch of their fingers against the glass. Their moans as they pounded at the doors for us.

As the memories well inside, I feel my chest collapsing in on itself, the familiar fear beginning to choke me. My knuckles burn white I grip the ladder so hard. Robert must notice because he brushes his hand across mine as he drops down to the porch.

"Look," he tells Lainey. "We agreed that our best move was to stay here."

A look of desperation crosses her face. "But that was before," she argues. "When we still thought there was a chance we'd be rescued."

"We still could be," Henry offers.

Lainey shakes her head, spinning to face him. "Don't you think they'd have sent help if they could? It's not like they wouldn't be able to find us with all this smoke we're sending up."

Once again her question hangs in the air. "You're acting like we have some sort of choice here," she adds, almost in a plea. "Well, we don't. We're running out of fuel and that means we're running out of time." She chokes back a sob, tears already spilling freely. "I'm tired of being the only one who cares if we live or die." She drops the shotgun and flees into the house.

Robert shoves his hands into his hair in frustration, clasping his fingers behind his head as he leans his forehead against what's left of the porch wall. More than anything I want to reach out and place a hand against his back. Let my palm rest between his shoulder blades and my fingertips press into him, measuring the rhythm of his heart.

But instead I stand there, looking between him and Henry. Feeling helpless and scared. "She's right, isn't she?" I ask them. "We're screwed."

"Not yet." Robert says it so softly that I wonder if he even intends me to hear it.

It's the "yet" that causes my chest to squeeze. I step toward him, thinking that I should just do it. Just reach for him the way I've imagined doing a hundred times. Push him back against what's left of the wall and let instinct take over.

Who cares about consequences when it's the end of the world?

But then he turns and I'm standing awkwardly close and I wish he'd grab me. Hold me. Kiss me. *Anything.*

My cheeks flame and I drop my eyes, unable to look at him with thoughts of our bodies twisting together flooding my mind. I grab the easiest excuse to escape: "I'll go talk to her."

Because if there's one thing I know for sure, it's that the only way we have a chance of surviving is if we work together. Which is why I'd been the one to pick up the pieces after Robert and Lainey's breakup the day before. She'd sobbed on my shoulder in the guest room while railing about what an asshole Robert was for breaking up with her with everything else that was going on.

When I find her upstairs today, she's more angry than upset. She paces the room, hands clenched into fists. As soon as she sees me, she starts in. "I can't believe I let him talk me into staying," she complains. "I'd already decided to go with Ruth. She begged me but I didn't because of Robert."

Technically it's my shift to sleep and hers to keep lookout but she doesn't seem to care about details like that. So as she continues her diatribe I keep an eye out the window and start mentally counting. For most of yesterday the number of dead crowding through the woods was pretty constant. But now there seem to be more. I have no idea where they're coming from or what it means, except that the sight of them all makes my lungs go tight and I have to focus on breathing so I don't hyperventilate.

Then I realize that Lainey's been silent and I look up to

find her staring at me, as though truly noticing me for the first time. She's waiting for something and I realize she's just asked me a question. "Why didn't you go with Ruth and Andy?" she repeats.

I shuffle my feet, uncomfortable. I'm the fifth wheel of the group—the tagalong added to the trip at the last minute when Henry's little brother dropped out. When I don't answer fast enough, Lainey narrows her eyes at me and I swallow, wondering if she's finally put the pieces together.

Apparently, she has. She smiles, but it's not friendly. "You stayed for Robert, too."

My eyes go wide as my heart thumps harder against my ribs. She has my full attention.

She laughs. "I'd say your secret's safe with me, but it's not much of a secret."

I wince, and she waves a hand in the air dismissively. "If I had a dollar for every frosh who fell for my boyfriend, we'd have rented a much sweeter cabin than this one."

"You mean ex-boyfriend," I correct, hating the way my voice cracks.

She doesn't miss a beat. "This breakup will be as temporary as all the others." Her smile is indulgent when she adds, "It's the end of the world. No one wants to die alone. Including Robert."

It feels like I've been sucker punched even though she hasn't laid a hand on me. Her calm assurance that Robert will always choose her and they'll be together while I'm the one dying alone.

And I forget that the most important thing is for us all to work together. I just want her to hurt the way I do. Before I know what I'm doing I blurt, "Ruth didn't make it out."

Her eyes go wide, and for a moment it's obvious she doesn't understand.

It's too late for me to take it back so I barrel forward instead, trying to convince myself that I'm doing the right thing by telling her. "I saw her this morning." I point to the window. "On the other side of the fire with the others." And then, because I'm still not sure she understands, I add, "Ruth's dead."

Lainey opens her mouth but the only sound that comes out is a strangled, "What?" She stares at me, waiting for me to take it back or tell her I was kidding and when I don't she curls in on herself, as though shattering in slow motion.

I hate myself for doing this to her. But before I can tell her I'm sorry or try to comfort her, I hear screaming from outside.

There's a split second when my eyes meet Lainey's. For the barest moment, she lets the fear shine through and everything broken between us clears away. I know the terror stinging her heart just then because I feel it, too. And we're both desperately wondering if the screaming is Robert or Henry and what it means.

I bolt for the bedroom door, but she's closer and beats me to it. Together we thunder down the stairs and out onto the porch. The screams are coming from the side of the house and I jump the railing, ignoring the twinge of pain in my ankle at the landing. I round the corner and pull up short, my entire body freezing.

Instead of fire, there's just smoke. Great black billowing clouds of it. It chokes the air, turning it thick and hazy. In the midst of it eddies dance and swirl, curling in patterns that would be mesmerizingly beautiful if it weren't for the awful realization of what's causing them: the dead have broken through.

The fire wall's collapsed.

My brain locks, too many thoughts vying for dominance. I should add more wood to the fire; fix the perimeter. But there's hardly anything left, certainly not enough to keep the flames high enough. I should grab a torch to beat back the dead, but what good will that do if there's no fire wall to keep them at bay?

I should retreat into the cabin and barricade myself inside but there aren't any walls left downstairs. There's nothing to barricade.

This is it, I realize. This is all that's left.

But I'm not ready.

Frantically I search for Robert, but I can't see him. The smoke is too thick, it turns the shambling bodies into nothing but outlines, streaks of solid amidst the swirling blackness.

It's impossible to tell the living from the dead.

Except for the screaming. Because the only sound the dead make is a grating, constant groan.

"Robert!" I cry. "Henry!"

I hear a moan, a wet sickly thudding sound that ends with a crack, like bone snapping. A body falls at my feet, spilling free of the smoke, and I stare at it. At the way the head is crushed, bowed inward like a deflated ball. Then I recognize the jacket. My jacket. And I realize that the body is Ruth's.

Looming behind her stands Robert, a length of two-by-four clutched in his hands like a club, the end of it bathed in blood. He glances my way but I don't even think he sees me. There's something feral in his expression—in the way he bares his teeth and the intensity of his focus. He steps over Ruth's body, feet on either side of her hips, and he swings the length of wood, muscles in his arms straining as he brings it down on Ruth's head as hard as he can. Again. And then again.

What's left of her face implodes, scattering bits of blood and bone and other stuff I don't even want to think about. I feel the wet heat of it slapping against my bare shins. I thought I was immune to the violence by that point. Immune to the dead. But I was wrong.

Because intellectually I know that Ruth was one of them. I know she was dead. She was a monster who would stop at nothing to destroy us. And I know that Robert had no choice. That the only way to stop them is to destroy the head.

He was protecting us. Protecting me.

And yet watching it—watching this person I've daydreamed about for months so viciously attack a creature who has no realistic way of defending herself. Of fighting back. It causes something inside me to revolt and I heave.

When I look up, Robert still hovers over Ruth's body, staring down at her with eyes like hardened glass. Then he blinks. And all it takes is that split-second hesitation. Because behind him I watch as another body looms. This one a middle-aged man with a receding hairline and a gaping hole in his neck.

"Robert!" In my head it's a scream but it comes out as a choked gurgle.

He looks up, right at me. And so I see the helpless horror that passes across his features when he feels the man's fingers grab at his shoulder. When he realizes what's about to happen.

Everything about Robert is laid bare in that moment.

The instinct that eluded me earlier kicks in, overriding any sense of self-preservation. I lunge forward, no weapons but my bare hands and my white-hot rage. Robert's already twisting against the man's grip when I reach them. I throw myself at the man, shoving him as hard as I can.

Even as he stumbles backward, the man reaches for me. Grabs me. I feel his fingers slip down my arms. The dig of his nails scraping against my flesh. I try to yank away, but his momentum is too great. His grip strangely strong. He falls to the ground, dragging me down on top of him.

And then we're a tangle of limbs. He's ravenous, uncontrollable, every bit of him straining to consume me. He claws at my hair, at my shirt. Mouth open, groaning with his teeth bared.

Scratching at him is useless. As is punching and kicking. There's no amount of pain I can inflict that will deter his onslaught. I wedge my forearm against his throat, pinning his head to the ground to keep his teeth from my flesh. But that leaves his hands free to drag me dangerously close and I don't know how long I'll be able to keep any distance between us.

At that point I'm nothing but pure panic. I look around, desperate for help. But in the choking smoke, everything is confusion and shadow. The others are engaged in their own battles: Robert fighting off a young woman in a nightgown while Henry struggles against two figures in firefighter uniforms.

And then Lainey is there, running toward us with the gun raised. She pulls the trigger again and again. Almost wildly. One of the firefighters collapses and Lainey swings the gun on the other.

Below me, the man writhes and I feel the strength in my arms weakening. We're only a few feet from the edge of the fire-line and I don't think. I just act. There's a length of burning chair leg within reach and I grab it. Not caring that I have to plunge my hand into the fire to do so.

I roll from the man, swinging the torch toward his face, slamming it against his skull. I'm not strong enough to break bone, but it's enough to get me free of him. I scramble back and strike him again. And again.

The flames catch his hair first, then lick at his clothes, swooping along the formerly fine lines of his suit. But it doesn't stop him. Even on fire, he rolls and pushes to his feet, flailing.

He staggers a step toward me, his desire unrelenting. That, more than anything else, causes the dread in my chest to solidify into something solid and heavy and yet somehow empty.

Because it is then that I truly understand. There is nothing human left in these creatures. There will be no stopping them. No reasoning or bargaining. Only delay. We shall push them off again and again until our strength or our will fails, and we succumb to the inevitability.

There is no if, but when.

The realization causes something so black and fathomless to open inside me that I just sit there, watching the flaming man stagger toward me. Wondering, suddenly, about the life he lived before. He had a name, once. A family. A job. He had dreams and nightmares and aspirations and struggles. And he will never be known for any of that.

He will be known only for this.

And someday the same will be true for me.

All the things I've left undone. All the things I've left unsaid. All the wants I've swallowed back. All the times I've been afraid. Or embarrassed. Or hesitant. None of that will matter.

It makes me realize just how wasteful I've been with all those days and hours and minutes leading to this moment. I want them back.

So I fight.

I push to my feet and kick at the man, sending him sprawling. The flames have eaten away enough of him that his muscles begin to fail, and though he struggles to stand, it's impossible. He collapses in a burning heap.

I start toward him, flaming chair leg clutched above my head, but something grabs at me, holding me back. I spin without thinking, swinging wildly. Somehow I miss and arms wrap around me from behind, forcing the chair leg free and pinning my wrists across my chest.

I buck wildly when I feel a mouth at my ear, teeth skimming the tender edge of my flesh. But then I hear words and I realize that whoever's holding me is also talking to me, which means they aren't dead.

"Shhhh, Carson, it's okay," the voice tells me again and again, until the meaning of the words penetrates deep enough for me to understand. I stop struggling, but still the arms hold me tight.

I don't ever want him to let me go and not because it's Robert, but because I can feel the way his chest jerks as he tries to breathe and I know he's experiencing the same terror as me. And that reminds me that I'm not alone.

I blink, taking in our surroundings. Bodies of the dead litter the ground, most of them with their heads crushed or beaten. Henry stands among them, a bloody length of wood still clutched in his hand. Behind him Lainey leans against the side of the house, body trembling as she lowers the gun to her side.

But the flow of dead has stopped. The man I'd set fire to collapsed across the break in our fire-line, completing it. His body continues to burn, buying us more time.

"Fuel," I murmur.

Behind me, Robert nods. "An unending supply of it."

And I can't believe it, but I laugh. Because it seems so absurd that the very thing that's been threatening us is now what might save us. So long as the dead keep coming, we'll be safe.

"It's okay," Robert tells me again, voice soft as a breath against my ear. And I realize that I'm not so much laughing as crying. At the horror of it. And the relief.

With his arms still wrapped around me, he gently turns my wrist so he can look at my hand. He sucks in a breath and I wince at the sight of it. The chair leg I grabbed to fend off the undead man had still been burning and the flesh along my palm and fingers bubbles an angry red. I don't feel the pain yet, but I know it will come.

And that's okay because at least I'm alive to feel the pain.

Henry moves to one of the bodies and grabs its feet, dragging it toward the fire. My instinct is to look away—to think of them as nothing more than fuel. It would be so much easier that way. But it would also be unfair. Because I feel like I owe it to them to remember that they were once people, too, with names and wishes and hopes.

Just like me. But I still have time to act on mine.

Robert's arms begin to loosen, but before he lets go I turn. I'm still cocooned by his embrace, the entire front of my body pressing against his. His heartbeat shudders through me and I feel his sharp intake of breath as I push up onto my toes, using my good hand to pull his head toward mine. Without pausing or hesitating, I draw my lips across his.

There's fear in the kiss. And longing.

I pull back to find surprise and a bit of confusion in his eyes as he looks down at me. I feel the heat, then, infusing my cheeks. But I don't let myself look away. At least not for a few more seconds.

The sound of Lainey's voice cuts through the moment. She stands with her arms crossed, an eyebrow raised as she glares at us. "Seriously?"

I hold my breath, waiting for Robert's response. Because he didn't exactly kiss me back, nor did he push me away. I didn't really give him the time for either.

He looks at me a moment longer and there's a small tug at the corner of his mouth that slowly blooms into a smile. He shrugs a bit self-consciously.

Henry rolls his eyes as Lainey tosses a hand in the air with a clearly annoyed "Whatever," and moves to help with the fire. Already the flames have risen higher, sending waves of heat wafting across the clearing. The dead have fallen back once more, keeping their distance.

"You know this changes nothing, right?" I realize Lainey's talking to me. She kicks a body onto the fire. "Everything I said earlier is still true."

I think about her telling me that Robert will always come back to her in the end. That this breakup will be no different. I struggle to keep the brightness of my earlier excitement from dulling, but it's difficult.

Lainey smiles, clearly triumphant at cutting the grin from my face. And I realize that this is how things are going to go from here on out. That we've found a way to stay safe, but in doing so we've trapped ourselves in this roaring inferno indefinitely, our only company the moaning dead and the sickly sweet scent of their burning bodies.

John A. Russo, with twenty books published internationally and nineteen feature movies in worldwide distribution, has been called a "Living Legend." He has earned legions of zombie fans by co-authoring the screenplay for *Night of the Living Dead*, writing the novelization of *Return of the Living Dead*, and co-producing the 1990 *Night of the Living Dead* remake. Plus he's currently starring in his own zombie comedy, *My Uncle John Is a Zombie!* But he wants everybody to know he's "just a nice guy who likes to scare people." He's had a long, rewarding career and doesn't intend to slow down. This story is abridged from the second half of a screenplay by John A. Russo and George A. Romero, entitled *Night of the Living Dead and the Day After*.

THE DAY AFTER

by John A. Russo

Sheriff McClelland lit his gasoline-soaked torch and touched it to the pyre, which had already been soaked in gasoline. The pile of zombie corpses went up with a *whoosh*, the flames licking high into the morning sky. The sheriff and his posse had gunned down more than two dozen of the flesh-eating ghouls that had been lurking around the Miller farmhouse.

He said to Deputy Vince Daniels, "You think we got 'em all, Vince?"

Vince said, "We rooted 'em out best we could and shot 'em in the head. But I couldn't swear none of 'em managed to sneak into the woods. Gunshots scare 'em just like fire does. They coulda hid from us when they heard us shootin'."

"Chopper's still circlin'," said McClelland. "If they spot any they'll let us know. Let's head back toward Willard the other way round the valley in case folks're holed up in some other farmhouse."

Rasping, drooling zombies moved through a patch of woods, some of them carrying partially devoured body parts from the people who were overrun at the Miller place. One zombie was sitting under a tree gnawing on a hand and forearm. On the wrist dangled a charm bracelet, burnt and discolored, a trinket once worn by a girl who had been blown up in a truck, along with her boyfriend.

The zombie drooled, then used his big yellowish teeth to pull off one more string of flesh. Then he dropped the picked-clean bones onto the ground and slowly trailed after some other zombies who were already shambling out of the woods.

An undead woman's mangled hand reached down and picked up the remains of the hand and wrist that were dropped. She growled, lusting after the slim pickings. In life she went by the name Barbara, and she had a brother, Johnny. He had helped others like him to drag her out of the Miller farmhouse. But then, after they killed her, he stopped them from completely devouring her. Pieces of her were now gone. She bore big bloody bite marks and gaping wounds on her body. Parts of her lips, nose, and ears were missing.

A beastly little girl, known as Karen while she was living, sneaked up on Barbara and made a grab for the stringy remnant of wrist bone and hand. Barbara tried to keep it, but it fell onto the ground. Both of the female zombies gave up on the morsel and hastened to keep up with the rest of their kind.

Just off a two-lane blacktop, a gas company right-of-way curved through some woods. Telephone poles laden with cables stretched one after another through the wide, grassy lane.

Lineman Jed Harris, a tall, lanky thirty-year-old, dark-haired with a full beard and mustache, shinnied up a pole wearing hobnailed boots, a safety harness, and a wide leather belt with a pouch full of tools. He wore a plaid shirt, blue jeans, and a cap bearing the logo of the Willard Power Company. A company van bearing the same logo was parked near the foot of the pole. Finding a frayed break in one of the power lines, he muttered, "No wonder," then set to work with wire cutters, pliers, and electrician's tape.

Meanwhile, three zombies came out of the woods and approached his van. For a long moment they stared up at him, drooling, but he was preoccupied. Jed's dog, Barney, was sleeping in the passenger seat. His ears pricked up and he awakened when he smelled the ghouls. He started barking and jumping all around on the front seat. And the zombies picked up rocks and started smashing the van's windows.

Barney howled, and Jed started rappelling down the pole. He saw that the side windows of the van were pulverized and zombie hands were reaching in for the dog. Barney bit one of the grasping hands and hung on, snarling viciously. Refusing to let go, when the ghoul pulled away he was yanked out of the van through a shattered window. Both Barney and the ghoul tumbled to the ground.

Jed yelled, "Barney!"

One of the ghouls smashed a rock at the dog's head. Barney howled. The ghoul smashed at him again and again, till he lay still.

Jed was down off the pole now, his harness strap dangling from his waist. He pulled a big screwdriver and a claw hammer from his tool pouch. Consumed with rage over the death of his dog, he advanced toward the three flesh-hungry zombies. He tried to bash one of them in the head with his hammer, but he missed, dealing only a glancing blow to the dead creature's shoulder. The other two were closing in, and Jed was in big trouble, kind of like a gazelle being circled by hungry coyotes.

He jabbed his screwdriver at one of the zombies' eyes, and it backed away. But the other two, drooling and slavering, were unfazed. They were in front of the driver's side of the van, blocking the door. Jed came at them, swinging his hammer and jabbing with his screwdriver.

The nearest zombie dove and tackled him. He fell, dropping his screwdriver but managing to hang on to his claw hammer. He thrashed and struggled, trying to get back up, but the zombie that tackled him was lying heavily across his legs. He tried to crawl away, dragging the zombie clutching at his ankles. He managed to get partway up and smashed his hammer down upon the zombie's head. He smashed again and again till the zombie was done for, its yellowish dead eyes staring straight up into the sky, its cracked skull oozing dark blood.

When Jed looked up he saw five more zombies coming out of the woods. He scrambled to his feet and ran, with the zombies in pursuit. Then three more zombies emerged, blocking his escape. He stopped in his tracks, brandishing his hammer but not knowing if it would do him much good.

Suddenly he heard a loud roaring engine. A Jeep appeared, humping off the edge of the two-lane blacktop and onto the right-of-way, heading straight for three of the menacing ghouls. To his amazement, the glimpse he got of the driver showed her to be a blonde young woman. She plowed her Jeep right into the three ghouls, sending two of them flying through the air and crushing the third one against the telephone pole. Then she backed the Jeep up, careening it in a sharp turn, and screeched it to a halt, just a few feet from Jed.

She yelled, "Quick! Get in!"

Jed didn't hesitate. He ripped open the passenger door, dived onto the seat, and the Jeep peeled out, getting away from the advancing ghouls. As they made it out onto the blacktop, Jed eyed his rescuer. She was not only good-looking, but obviously brave. Her low-cut blouse and hiked-up skirt revealed a terrific figure. "Thanks, you saved my life!" he yelled above the roar of the engine.

"What in the world are you doing out here by yourself?" she yelled back. "Don't you know what's been happening?"

He shot her a bewildered look. "I got attacked. Who *are* they? They killed my dog. They look crazy or wasted or something."

"They're not *crazy*—they're dead!"

"That's impossible!"

"That's what *everyone* thought—but now the whole world's been turned upside down. The dead are coming back to life. Don't you watch TV or listen to the radio?"

"I've been out here in the boondocks on my own, checking and repairing telephone lines. The job got harder and stranger, 'cause all of a sudden there was no communication from my home office. I kept on trying to do my job, trying to figure out the problems. Power lines seem to be out of whack everywhere—malfunctioning at best."

The woman said, "Our whole society is malfunctioning, coming apart at the seams! And nobody knows why. It's a strange new epidemic, an insane outbreak that no one understands."

Jed told her, "I tuned everything out, just me and my dog, Barney. We sleep in my tent, or just under the stars. But now . . . now Barney is dead."

"What's your name?"

"Jed Harris. What's yours?"

"Danielle Greer. I sell cosmetics and stuff door-to-door. I have lots of rural customers. I live in Willard, but when I work my route out here I stay in my cabin by myself. I didn't know this plague, or whatever you want to call it, was happening till I found a woman chewed up and dead in her living room. All the power was out, her phone wouldn't work. I decided to head for Willard to make a police report. Meantime, my radio in the Jeep came back on. They're running emergency broadcasts now and then. That's the only reason I have any kind of clue as to what's going on."

Jed said, "I work for Willard Power. They sent me out because the pastor of St. Willard's church called the main office and said they had no electricity for the church or school. Before I even got on the road, more calls came in, all from this same part of the county."

"I hate to tell you," Danielle said, "but we had better check out the school. By now they could be surrounded."

"Surrounded by what? What would you call them? Nutcases? Mentally diseased?"

"I don't know what to call them, except *ghouls*. They have to be killed, that's what the authorities say. It's us or them."

At St. Willard's Catholic Church and School, the church itself, a hulking stone structure with stained glass windows, remained intact, but the one-room school had been under assault for several hours, and its tall windows of ordinary glass were boarded up. But some of the glass behind the boards had already been smashed. Almost two dozen ghouls were surrounding the place, hungry to get inside and devour the living.

Father Ed, the bespectacled middle-aged pastor in a clerical suit and Roman collar, was trying to make the place more secure. The church was on the other side of the parish cemetery, too far away for the kids to make a run for it, especially the littlest kids, who were only five or six years old. So Father Ed had made a decision to wait for rescuers, after he heard that kind of advice on the intermittent radio broadcasts. He had a hammer and some large nails, and he was trying to hold a heavy piece of a desk in place and pound a nail in at the same time. He called out, "Annie, will you give me a hand, please?"

Annie Kimble, a bright, winsome twelve-year-old, jumped up and helped hold the board up while Father Ed drove his nails.

A radio on the teacher's desk emitted a burst of static, and

Sister Hillary said, "It's picking up a signal again! Listen! There's going to be another broadcast."

She and Father Ed and Annie gathered close to the radio, and most of the other children did likewise. The broadcast told them that armed policemen and volunteers were combing rural areas, but help might be slow getting to everyone in need. It advised them that if they were in temporarily safe surroundings, they should stay put, unless they were in imminent danger of being overrun.

Sister Hillary said, "You see, children, we're doing the right thing. We'll be safe here, and our prayers will be answered. The rescue teams will come. We must trust in Almighty God."

But a sandy-haired little boy named Bertie Samuels, precociously bright, but terribly spoiled, whined, "That's not what the radio said! We're *doomed*! They don't have enough rescue workers! I want my daddy!"

Sister Hillary tried to calm him, saying, "You'll be seeing your father soon enough, Bertie. He can't come to you right now. It's too dangerous out there."

Bertie wailed louder. "I want my daddy!"

Father Ed said, "Shush! They can hear you! You might make them move in closer."

Annie and her mother, Janice, moved to a window on the far side of the building and saw zombies doing just what Father Ed feared, milling around, looking more alert than before, sniffing for the scent of fresh young human flesh. Annie gasped, "Oh my God, Mom, there are more than before!"

Her mother said, "She's right! We'll never get out of here alive."

She made the Sign of the Cross over herself, and some of the kids started to cry again. Little Bertie cried the hardest.

"Calm down, Janice," Father Ed pleaded. "You're scaring the kids worse."

Janice joined her daughter at the window again and now even more zombies were arriving. And, though she did not know it, three of the new arrivals were Barbara, Johnny, and Karen, who had become undead during the previous twenty-four hours.

Sister Hillary said, "Come, children, let me lead you in prayer. Pray along with me, Janice. You, too, Annie."

Annie said, "What happened to the broadcast? It cut out."

"No, it ended," said her mother.

Annie picked up the radio and shook it, hard. "I think it must've died."

Bertie wailed louder than ever. "Just like us! We're *all* gonna be dead! I want my daddy . . . I want my daddy . . . I want my daddy . . ."

Pete Gilley, the janitor, came into the room with a toolbox in his hand and eyed Bertie with a sour grimace. He put the toolbox down with a heavy thud on top of one of the intact school desks and said, "I can't take that brat anymore. I gotta get outta here."

"He can't help it," Janice told him. "He's just a little boy, and he's scared."

"Jesus said, 'Suffer the little children to come unto me,'" Sister Hillary reminded them.

"Yeah, well, he's sure makin' *me* suffer!" Pete snapped. He sneaked over to a cabinet that held cleaning supplies, rummaged behind paper towels and rolls of toilet paper, pulled out a half-pint of whiskey and furtively uncapped it with his back to the wall. He chugged a gulp or two, then wiped his mouth and hid the flask by tucking it into a side pocket of his coveralls. Then he went over to his toolbox, took out a sharp chisel, and tucked it into one of his back pockets. "Wish I had a shotgun," he said, "but all I got is a box of tools. I guess one of them critters might back off if I stab his eye out with my chisel. I got my motor scooter out back in the shed. If I could get to it I could make a break. And I think I can do it. Them dead critters is slow moving."

Father Ed warned, "There are too many of them. You couldn't crash through them on a motor scooter. The machine's too light to run one of them down."

"Mebbe I could zigzag right through 'em like I used to when I played halfback for Willard High. One of your puny barricades give way, we're all gonna be zombie feed."

Defiantly he took out his flask with no pretenses and gulped down some whiskey right in front of the kids. Then he lit up a cigarette and blew out smoke rings. Father Ed eyed him with disapproval but said nothing. Sister Hillary, however, said, "Pete! Shame on you!"

Pete said, "I'm sick and tired of all your rules, Sister! If I have to die, I'm goin' out drunk and full of nicotine!"

Two six-year-olds giggled. They were both in short pants and short-sleeved shirts with neat little neckties.

Eyeing Pete angrily, Father Ed said, "Put that cigarette out or I'll fire you."

Pete snapped, "You don't have to, I quit! I'm gettin' the hell outta here. Don't try to stop me."

"I'll follow you to the back door and make sure it's locked after you go out. And may the Lord have mercy on your soul."

They both went to the gray steel door, and Father Ed opened it a crack. Garbage cans were stacked near it on a slab of concrete. They both peered out, casing the back lawn and the aluminum garden shed, and it appeared that no zombies were close by. Pete took a swig of whiskey, then tucked the flask back in his coveralls.

Father Ed said, "Good luck, Pete. I wish you'd change your mind."

But he went out, and the priest closed and bolted the door.

Wielding his chisel, Pete crept stealthily across the backyard toward the shed. From one of his pockets he pulled out a ring of keys attached to a belt loop by a long chain. With shaking hands he managed to insert a key into a Master lock and undo the hasp. He glanced all around, and now he spied the Johnny, Barbara, and Karen zombies coming toward him, starting to rasp and drool. In a panic, he pulled open the door to the shed, got in there, and wheeled out his motor scooter as fast as he could. He jumped on and tried to kick-start it. But the engine didn't catch. He tried again. And again.

The three ghouls were getting closer.

Johnny stooped and picked up a thick piece of kindling from the log pile.

Finally the motor scooter came to life with a loud sputter and a cloud of dark smoke. In drunken triumph, Pete tossed his chisel away and yelled, "*Now* try to stop me, motherfuckers!"

He gunned the scooter right for an opening between Barbara and Johnny. If he could get through the gap he could speed to relative safety. But his front tire kicked up a partially devoured arm bone, and it flipped into the spokes of Pete's wheels, and with a loud clatter the scooter went flying and tumbling—and so did Pete! He hit headfirst against the trunk of a tree and fell, arms and legs akimbo, his neck twisted and broken, a horrid death grimace distorting his face.

Father Ed saw all this from a shattered boarded-up window. He pulled away, a sick look on his face, and told the others, "They got him. It's awful. Don't none of you look."

They all knew without looking that Pete was being devoured.

Punching button after button on her Jeep's radio, Danielle Greer said, "I wish another news bulletin would come on. Even if we get to the school, I don't think we can rescue them all by ourselves. We don't even have any guns."

"I had one in my van, but couldn't get to it," Jed told her.

She said, "There's a general store at a crossroads we're coming to. They sell shotguns and rifles, maybe a few handguns. We might have to bust our way in if the store's locked up."

"That's if the zombies didn't bust in ahead of us," Jed said.

Under a short, narrow bridge, seven zombies waded into a creek polluted with greenish foam, black crud, old tires, and debris. Spotting them wading into the poisonous-looking water, Sheriff McClelland and a squad of his vigilantes opened fire on them from up on the bridge. When the fusillade ended, the zombie corpses were left floating in the creek.

The front door of the general store was hanging half off its hinges, wide open. The remains of three chewed-up bodies lay strewn on the gravel.

"Holy hell!" Danielle said. "A horde of those things must've torn them apart!"

Jed said, "I don't want to go in there unarmed. You have a tire iron?"

"How about an aluminum bat? I keep one under the seat."

"Stay here," Jed said. "Honk the horn if anything comes at you."

He cautiously entered the general store, which was a mess. Not only were windows smashed, but also glass display cases. Canned goods, produce, all kinds of things were all over the floor, bloodied and trampled. Jed swung the aluminum bat as hard as he could and smashed the glass front of a gun cabinet. He grabbed two rifles, rummaged till he found the ammunition, and loaded the weapons.

At St. Willard's School, some of the kids were crying and others were too scared to cry or even move, except for Bertie the whiner. Janice Kimble was patting him and cooing to him, trying to get him to be quiet. Sister Hillary was kneeling in a corner, praying.

Father Ed and Annie Kimble were looking out two different windows, trying to monitor the ghoul activity outside, through shattered glass and nailed-up boards, when suddenly they heard a car honking loudly and insistently. Annie spotted it and shouted, "Someone's coming! Look, Father Ed! Maybe we're gonna be rescued!"

He darted to her window, peered through it, and said, "That looks like Kyle Samuels's car!"

Bertie jumped up and said, "*Yay!* It's my daddy!"

He ran to where Annie was, anxious to catch sight of his father.

But zombies were already closing in on Kyle Samuels, and

he didn't dare get out of his car. He was frozen in fear. The zombies, led by Johnny, Barbara, and Karen, started pounding on his car with rocks and sticks and pulling at the convertible top, their ghoulish hands poking through the weak glassine rear window.

Bertie was utterly horrified, his face a mask of fright and despair as Father Ed yelled, "Bertie! Don't look!"

Bertie wailed, "My daddy . . . my daddy . . ."

The six-year-old boy broke for the door and tried to get it open, but twelve-year-old Annie was much stronger and was able to pull him back, though her eyes were filled with bottomless pain.

Outside, flying glass shattered by a rock showered into Kyle's face, and he covered his eyes with his hands. The convertible ripped open and now zombie hands were clawing at him from all sides. He desperately thought of starting the car up again and twisted the key in the ignition and slammed it into gear. He gunned it out, trying to make it closer to where he could perhaps make a run for the hoped-for safety of the school. But the Karen and Barbara zombies were hanging across the hood, blocking his view through the windshield. Then a third zombie flopped through the ripped-apart glassine rear window onto the backseat—and began choking Kyle from behind, pulling his head back and making him let go of the steering wheel.

The car went out of control and rammed into the log pile with a loud clatter. The impact tossed the Johnny and Barbara zombies clear and almost flipped the car over, but instead it careened it right toward the one-room school, where it crashed and exploded in a ball of fire. A huge hole was ripped in the wall as flaming shrapnel flew everywhere and Janice Kimble was struck in the back and went down, her clothing on fire. Her daughter Annie ran to her to try to smother the flames with her own body, but luckily she saw it was no use—Janice wasn't moving one bit as the fire consumed her.

Father Ed yelled, "Quick, everybody! We've gotta get out! The back door!"

Bertie screamed, "No! My daddy!" and tried to bolt toward the flaming car.

Sister Hillary grabbed him and held him back, saying, "We can't help him now except with our prayers."

Bertie continued to wail, and the ten other kids of various ages cried and panicked, too.

The exit used disastrously by Pete Gilley was the only hope of escape, and Father Ed led the way. There were few zombies in the backyard right now because they had been diverted by the smell of Janice Kimble's flesh smoldering inside the building. Father Ed ran toward the log pile and snatched up a thick piece of kindling, yelling, "Grab something to bash them with!" The others hastened to do what he said—but two zombies were almost upon him, and he bashed one of them in the face. It fell, then kicked and writhed on the ground like a badly wounded animal.

But now there were more zombies in the backyard, and three of the children never got a chance to pick up sticks from the log pile. The ghouls swarmed them, pulled them down, and started feasting on them as they screamed and struggled.

The rest of the people, led by Father Ed and Sister Hillary, ran toward the woods. But on the way, two more children got pounced on by zombies who leapt at them from behind trees and bushes. The survivors kept running, hoping to find some semblance of safety, however temporary, as a half dozen zombies pursued them, shambling in their slow rigor-mortis-inhibited gait, drooling and hissing hungrily.

Danielle drove dangerously, almost too fast for the sharp bend in the blacktop.

Jed said, "I'm scared of what we're gonna find. That sounded like one hell of an explosion."

"Yeah," she said, "look at the smoke above those trees. That's where St. Willard's is."

A couple of minutes later, she braked at the edge of the gravel lot. She and Jed were struck dumb by what they saw. The school building was being consumed by fire. A car plowed into the black flaming timbers was nothing but a skeleton of twisted metal. Zombies backed away from the flames, carrying pieces of human flesh. Some of them hovered over remnants of the children who were killed when they tried to escape after the explosion. The undead creatures fought over scraps of meat like a pack of starving wolves.

Jed said, "There's nothing we can do here. Obviously they were overrun."

"There would've been more of them," said Danielle. "Where do you think they could have gone?"

He saw something dangling from a bush at the edge of the clearing, and went over to have a closer look. "A scapular," he said. "Look at the trampled-down weeds. Some people must've escaped."

She thought about it, then said, "We should try to find them. They're probably not armed, and we are. They could probably use our help. Especially any of the kids who might still be living."

* * *

Father Ed and his group of survivors were at the edge of a small clearing and staring at a cave they had spotted in a rocky cliff. It looked like a safe place to hide if they could get up there, but not only was it a steep, hazardous climb, but four ghouls hunkered at the base of the cliff, munching on the remains of recent victims.

The children whimpered and stared, anxiously waiting for the adults to think of something that might save them.

Father Ed said, "Look at that cave. If we could drive the ghouls away and climb up there and barricade it, it'd be almost impregnable."

Sister Hillary said, "We could drive them away with fire, but we don't have any. I never thought I would say this, but I wish we had guns."

Annie, being a bright little girl, mused that they could have made torches from their sticks and the fire at the school, but they never had time to do it—they had to get away or else be devoured.

"If we could circle around and get up on top of the cliff, we could lower ourselves down into the cave," Father Ed speculated.

Annie said, "How?"

He said, "We'd need a bull rope or something."

Sister Hillary said, "We have nothing. We're poorly equipped for survival, Father. Our lifetime of prayer has put us in good shape for the next world, but not this one."

"Don't despair," said Father Ed. "God is on our side."

Just then shots rang out—a sudden vicious volley—and the four feasting ghouls at the base of the cliff were blasted down.

Two rough-looking men with AR-15s and sidearms emerged from the woods into the clearing.

Sister Hillary gasped and said, "Oh, thank the Lord!"

She blessed herself, immediately viewing the men as saviors. But Father Ed was more cautious, and he just stared at them. They wore boots, jeans, flannel shirts, and leather vests, and were laden with bandoliers of ammunition. Father Ed jerked his head around as a blue van motored out of the trees across the way. It pulled up and braked and another rough-looking man got out. "Well, well, what've we got *here*?" he said gruffly. He eyed the kids as if he wanted to smack them—or do worse. The kids cowered closer to the priest and the nun.

One of the men who had gunned down the ghouls said, "More hostages. More zombie feed, Blaze."

His buddy said, "I don't wanna deal with any more adults, Butch."

Butch said, "Yeah, Stan, we're on the same page."

Father Ed pleaded, "Whatever you've done, we can't tell on you. We have no cell phones, we have nothing."

Sister Hillary said, "Please . . . don't harm the children."

The men sneered. The one called Blaze said, "Maybe God'll protect them from us—and from the ghouls."

He and Butch aimed their sidearms at Father Ed and Sister Hillary and he barked, "Down on your knees! *Now!*"

The kids were wailing and crying.

Father Ed and Sister Hillary both knelt and started saying Acts of Contrition. But they didn't get very far into the prayer before Butch and Blaze shot them in their heads.

Jed Harris and Danielle Greer were working their way along a path when they heard the gunshots. They started running, but they were at least a hundred yards from the gunfire. When they burst out into the clearing, they were almost too late. The last of the kids had their hands tied with rope and were being herded toward the open rear door of the van.

Jed and Danielle reflexively aimed their rifles in the direction of the would-be abductors but momentarily held their fire for fear of hitting the kids. Then they glanced at each other and knew what to do. They aimed higher and blasted a volley of shots just over the men's heads.

"Run, kids! Run!" Jed yelled.

Blaze jumped in behind the steering wheel, and Stan slammed the rear door shut. Butch dived into the front passenger seat, but Stan didn't make it. With the kids out of the way now, Jed squeezed off a round that struck Stan in the chest. The van peeled out. Jed and Danielle blasted away at it. But it kept going.

As the blue van made it out onto the blacktop, Butch said, "Shit! I thought we'd have lots of kids to ransom! Now we'll have to collect more."

"But we've got a shithouse full of loot in the back," Blaze said. "And with Stan gone, it's only a two-way split."

But their gloating didn't last long. All of a sudden they heard a police siren. A county patrol car was coming up on them from behind, with its lights flashing.

Blaze hit the gas harder. In the rearview mirror he saw that the driver of the police car was in uniform. But the passenger was wearing the same sweaty, rumpled suit he had been wearing for three days. "Oh, fuck!" Blaze said when he recognized Sheriff McClelland.

"That's the van we been lookin' for," the sheriff said to the cop who was driving. "Don't lose it."

Behind the patrol car were two military trucks full of National

Guard troops. Slower than the patrol car, they had to struggle to keep up.

In the clearing at the base of the rocky cliff, Jed patiently looked down at Stan. He was going to transform, and that's what Jed had to wait for.

A distance away, Danielle huddled with the kids. She tried her best to soothe and comfort them. And brave young Annie Kimble was helping.

Jed watched over Stan as he groaned and sweated, in severe pain from his chest wound, till he finally died. Then, in a little while, he "revived." He sat up, moving stiffly. But instead of giving him a chance to stand up all the way, Jed shot him in the head.

"Good for him!" Danielle called out.

"Amen!" said Annie.

Then the sheriff's patrol car pulled into the clearing, followed by one of the National Guard trucks full of soldiers.

Sheriff McClelland got out of the car and listened to the fusillade of gunfire in the distance. He knew that the soldiers in the other truck were taking care of business. This was a severe emergency, and they were giving no quarter to the bad guys. The ones they had chased down and cornered were done raping, killing, and robbing.

There was a look of gratitude and relief on the faces of the ones they had saved. Now the sheriff would find out what their story was.

Isaac Marion is the author of the *New York Times* bestselling Warm Bodies series, which has been adapted into a major film and translated into twenty-five languages. He lives in Seattle with his cat and a few plants.

THE GIRL ON THE TABLE

by Isaac Marion

A girl lies on a table in the basement of a stranger's home and wonders why she feels so wrong. She's hurt. She's sick. But there's something else. A hush inside her body, like all her cells are an audience awaiting some terrible show.

She searches for answers in her parents' faces. They're supposed to have them all. All her life, they've insisted they do. But the girl finds no clues in the sweaty furrows of their sagging flesh. Her mother looks sad and helpless. Her father looks angry and scared. But they always do.

The girl's arm is missing a chunk of flesh. Under its thin layer of pale skin, her meat is bright red, like the roast her mother was preparing just a few hours ago. Her mother needed wine. Her father needed cigarettes. A quick trip to the store while the roast soaked in dark marinade.

"I'll get your cigarettes, dear," her mother says. "No need for us all to go."

Her father stands up without looking away from the news broadcast on television. "I don't like you out there alone," he says, and snatches the keys from his wife. "The world's gone crazy."

This man. Da-da, Daddy, Dad. Barely forty but already ruined. Bald, stooped, crushed by his scowl, crumpled inward as if hiding from the air itself, an omnidirectional retreat. He says the same thing every time he watches the news. It doesn't matter what it's about—the war, the protests, the latest outrage in music or fashion—it's always the same. *The world's gone crazy.*

"Get your shoes on, baby," the girl's mother says.

"Can't I stay here?"

"You're not staying home by yourself," her father says. "You're only fourteen."

The girl sighs and follows them to the car. The sun is almost down. It's Friday night. She closes her eyes and imagines she's going dancing.

She doesn't know how long she's been on the table. Time is taffy; it stretches and bends and dangles as she drifts in and out of dreams.

Last year's school trip to New York, the bus like a scuba tank full of compressed excitement, seventy young people getting their first glimpse of the city. The girl pressing her face to the glass: the gleaming towers, the infinity of the place, the endless possibility. Movie star, stockbroker, dancer, singer, senator—she'll need to live to three hundred to fit in all these lives.

"It'll chew you up and spit you in the gutter," her father says when she gets home. "You want to live in a leaky roach nest next to a bunch of thugs and perverts?"

"It's boring here. It's too small. I want to be out in the world."

"Baby," her mother says before her father can start yelling, "you don't need to be thinking about all that yet. You're just a little girl."

She drifts out of memories and into shapeless fever dreams. Orange and black, hot and sticky, a gnawing hollowness in her belly, her mouth, her fingers and teeth—

"Take the boards off that door!"

"We are staying down here!"

The girl wakes up. They're shouting again. All the old arguments amplified by terror. At home, it was just the sneering and sniping of a restrained but obvious loathing, a rich broth of unhappiness in which they seemed to enjoy simmering. Now, here in this basement, their misery has risen to a boil. Every time the girl surfaces, their voices scald her.

"I know what I'm doing!"

"How are we going to know what's going on if we lock ourselves in this dungeon?"

The girl's arm twitches. Her stomach knots. How long ago

was dinnertime? Was it days ago? Years? Are the maggots and flies enjoying her mother's roast?

They drive in silence to the grocery store. That long, straight stretch of Pennsylvania road, the daily commute to school, to church, to anywhere. The big rock, the broken tree, the same scenery over and over like the background of a cheap cartoon. Her father clicks on the radio. Something about exploding satellites, radiation from space, a string of murders; he opens his mouth to say it again, *the world's gone crazy*, and his wife changes the station with a violent twist of the knob.

It lands on static. But the static is strange. Not the usual oceanic rush but a rhythmic pulse of low, abrasive noise, like a monstrous heart pounding in the dark.

"What is this?" the girl's father says. He glances at her in the rearview mirror. "Is this what you kids are calling music?"

The girl does not know what this is. It is not what she calls music. It rises to a high, sour shriek and her mother clicks it off.

"It's probably that radiation they were talking about." Her tone is dismissive, but the girl sees the hairs on the back of her neck standing up. She feels her own doing the same. No one speaks until they arrive at the store and pull into the nearly empty parking lot. An overturned cart near the entrance. Groceries scattered and smashed. Red wine soaking the pavement.

The bite itself no longer hurts. Its searing heat has dissipated throughout her body and she feels the same thing all over.

When she locks herself in the bathroom to read *Rolling Stone* and *Cosmopolitan* and other forbidden texts and her legs fall asleep on the edge of the toilet seat, she feels this. A black-and-white crackling like TV static in her nerves, a confused noise of numbness and pain. But not just in her legs now. Everywhere.

What is happening to her? She knows she's sick, but there's more. She feels something coming. Rising up from black caverns in the cores of her bones. She's afraid. She's excited. She doesn't know why.

"It's Friday night," her mother says, glancing around the parking lot. "Where is everybody?"

"Good riddance," her father says. "Checkout will be quick."

The girl watches the rivulets of wine creep across the pavement. "Maybe the store's closed," she says.

"They're not closed, the lights are on."

The girl looks through the windows. Pale fluorescent bulbs flickering faintly. Amorphous figures behind the dirty glass. "Can I stay in the car?" she asks.

"Of course not," her father says.

"Come on, baby," her mother says. "I'll buy you a treat."

The girl gets out and follows them to the entrance. She watches the shapes moving behind the windows. She sees heads and shoulders, blurry silhouettes in the pale light. The way they move is wrong . . .

"What a dump," her father says, stepping over the mess of the overturned cart. "Cleanup!" he shouts as the doors slide open. And then he stops talking.

Hinzman's Grocery is a clean, quiet store in a clean, quiet

town, and the girl hates coming here. Everything is always the same. The same music on the speaker. The same boy mopping the floors. The same man running the register and making the same small talk to every customer, as if the ones next in line can't hear his robotic repetition. *How are you today? How are you today? How are you today?* The store carries no books, no magazines, not even newspapers—nothing that changes. The store is static.

So maybe it's just surprise that triggers the girl's laughter when she sees the bodies. A giddy yelp like someone has goosed her. Harder to explain is the thrill that rushes down her spine, not fear but exhilaration, almost arousal. Like she's stumbled through a secret door and discovered a secret world.

The bodies are like the cart outside, flabby arms sprawled on the gleaming white tiles, organs spread out like ruined groceries—smashed tomatoes and sausage links and of course the wine, the wine everywhere. But she spares only a glance for these gruesome heaps. She is more interested in the gray people hunched over them, tearing at their meat, gnawing at their bones. They look up at her. Their eyes are empty in a way she's never seen before: no tight politeness, no stern purpose, no pained restraint or bitter resignation. Just pure, effortless, unapologetic existence, like lukewarm water flowing freely.

They stand up and move toward her and she has a wild urge to greet them. Hello, who are you? Where did you come from? What are you here to show us?

Then she feels pain in her arm. Her father's big fingers digging into her flesh, dragging her back to the car. She hears her mother screaming. She hears her father cursing as he fumbles with the keys. The gray people are shuffling out of the store and spreading through the parking lot. Her father shoves her into the car and starts it and the tires squeal. She rolls around and bounces off the windows as the car swerves left and right—how strange, to be in motion without being belted tight!—and then her father utters a curse he rarely uses and there's a crunching sound and the girl slams against the front seats.

She hears the engine hissing. The car is rocking back and forth. Gray faces peer in at her through the windows, expressionless, a rioting mob with the serenity of a church congregation, and then the girl is upside down, and hands are reaching through the shattered windows, big fingers clamping onto her arm, the wetness of lips—

The voices are muffled now, drifting down to her from somewhere overhead. She wonders how deep underground this basement is. She feels the weight of earth around her, cool and thick, alive with crawling things. She feels herself sinking.

A burst of static jabs her ears, startling her back to the surface—her eyes snap open wide, terrified, then sag shut again. She can't hold them. The static pulses with a few hideous heartbeats, then fades into voices. Not her parents' acrid whining but big, booming television voices. Voices that have the answers. The girl tries to listen, but she finds them hard to understand. They seem to be speaking a foreign language, one she's studied a little but never mastered. The words blur and drift out of sequence as they filter down through the earth.

Rising. Killing. No time for funerals. Burn your family.

The girl writhes on the table. She clenches her fists, trying to squeeze this dream out of her head.

Outer space. Venus. Burn your family.

A spasm of pain rattles through her body. She's so hungry. Dinnertime was so long ago. That thick hunk of raw meat dripping in its marinade, ripping in her fingers, her teeth—

"Baby. It's Mommy."

The girl opens her eyes to escape what's in her head. She sees her mother's face hovering over her like a vast planet. That cloying, cradling smile, like she's just given birth to her, like the girl still fits in her hands. "She's all I have," the woman tells someone somewhere in this dim basement, a truth more grotesque than she seems to realize—it's a surrender, a suicide, and she will suck the breath out of her daughter as she dies. The girl hates her mother, the girl hates this woman, the girl wants to hurt her, she wants to—

No.

No she doesn't.

Tears trickle into her eyelashes. Why are these thoughts in her head? How long have they been there?

She wants to warn her mother that she wants to hurt her. She wants to make her get away, but all her words are melting, concepts crumbling, memories blackening. With a final flicker of will, she drags her voice up from the silent pit inside her and she whispers, "I hurt."

When the girl was a baby, she touched an electric fence. It is her only memory from those years, a jolt that cut through the fog of her prehistory and burned itself into permanence. It hurt. She has felt worse pain in the years since—bloody knees from biking too fast, broken limbs from falling out of trees— but at the time she touched the fence the pain shot right off her scale. She had never felt anything like that crackling in her nerves. Her infant brain hadn't known such pain was possible.

As she lies on her back in the upside-down car, covered in glass like a blanket of diamonds, a gray-faced man bites her arm, and she experiences this transcendence again.

The pain is impossible. Absurd. Vastly disproportionate to the severity of the wound. The man's teeth pierce barely an inch but they are electrified and poisoned and searing white hot. The pain burrows through her body, cracks her bones and splits open her muscles, yanks her nerves taut and strums them hard, a hideous chord jangling in her brain.

She screams so high no sound comes out. For maybe five seconds she screams, eyes bulging, throat straining—and then the pain stops. It rushes out from the wound and dissipates throughout her body, fading to a dull ache as her parents drag her away from the gray-faced mob.

They don't notice she's hurt until she collapses on a stranger's lawn, facedown in the grass. She feels dirt in her mouth. A worm wriggles on her tongue. Her stomach rumbles.

Time is taffy. It sticks in her teeth and dangles down her throat, past and present twisting all through her, but it is not sweet. She hears shouts and screams up there on the surface, a man who isn't her father shouting to a woman who isn't her mother. She tries to imagine their faces, lit first by daylight, then by moonlight, then lost in darkness. She hears shattering glass and rushing fire, and a spike of terror stabs into her brain, but she doesn't cry out. She doesn't ask for her mother. Such soft filial instincts are charring in the heat.

Another crack of glass. Another burst of flame. She shudders on the table.

Why should fire terrify her? She has never been burned. It's one of the few common injuries she hasn't experienced. But while she feels these rational thoughts buzzing near the surface of her brain, she feels the fear somewhere deeper. Down in that dark, wordless place where the urge to run bumps into the urge to fight and the urge to eat and fuck and have babies, those primal marrow caverns where she feels that other thing. Reaching up. Rising.

A loud noise outside. An explosion—*fire*. That terrible bright god that kills flesh and forests and worlds. Her fear surges to a shriek, but beneath it she hears something soft. A small, sad voice. The voice of a young girl, alone in the seething jungle that's creeping into her head:

Am I dying?

She hears shouting and scuffling upstairs, snarled curses and hammers against wood.

Is this all I get?

She hears a gunshot. A scream. A nightmare of disjointed noise as she writhes on the table.

Is this all they let me have?

She hears groans from outside. Not her parents. Not the handful of frightened strangers who joined them. Dozens of people. Perhaps hundreds. Their groans drown out the fire and her fear. She stops writhing. She goes still. A profound calm washes over her body like a cool bath for a fever.

She lies there for a while. She hears nothing. Thinks nothing. As the gray gloaming in her mind fades to full black, she watches the stars come out. Bright, hungry pinpricks fill her head by the billions. There's no moon, but she sees Mars. She sees Venus. She feels their strange music humming in her limbs, filling her empty body with power and purpose.

She hears footsteps on the stairs, and she imagines that they're hers. But she's climbing up, not down. She's rising, carried aloft by that thing that rises with her.

She sits up.

There's a man on the floor, a heaping portion of life just lying there unused. She takes it. She feels it slide into her growling belly and spread through her thrumming bones. She feels strength. She feels clarity. She feels hunger—not just in her belly but in her feet and hands and teeth, in her chest and groin and in every organ, a relentless desire free of doubt and fear.

A woman wanders down the stairs. She moves toward the girl, tilting her head from side to side, simpering, whimpering—"baby, poor baby," over and over—and some distant part of the girl throbs with loathing. What is this quivering mass of confusion and conflict? Why did she do whatever she did to get here? Why did she make choices she didn't want and slacken at the thought of undoing them? Why does she stagger toward the girl with her arms outstretched, begging to be consumed?

Something is wrong with this woman. The life in her meat is tainted. The girl's hunger twists into rage and disgust.

She kills the woman. She has to. But she doesn't eat her. She leaves her intact, and somewhere in the jungle that has filled every crease of her mind, that tiny voice calls this a kindness. A chance to become something else. To finally become strong.

The girl climbs the stairs.

There is a man she's never seen before waiting at the top. She approaches him and he runs from her. He hides in the basement. But there are others. So many others. She can sense

227

them out there—smell them, hear them, feel them, that thing lurking in everyone's bones, waiting for its chance to rise.

She stops pounding on the basement door and slowly turns around. She is surrounded by strangers. She is a girl in a crowd, unsupervised, unprotected, unafraid. She listens to their groans and hears her own among them. The whole universe is groaning: the atonal choir of the planets, the rumbling bass of the blackness behind them, the howling of the jungle in her head. She looks into the eyes of these people and sees what she saw before: pure, honest, unbridled existence. A primal truth older than life. And now she knows what it is.

The girl and her new family wander out of the house. Into the streets. Into the world.

David J. Schow is an award-winning writer who lives in Los Angeles. The latest of his nine novels is a hard-boiled extravaganza called *The Big Crush* (2017). The newest of his nine short-story collections is a monster-fest titled *DJSturbia* (2016). He has written extensively for film (*The Crow*, *Leatherface: The Texas Chainsaw Massacre III*, *The Hills Run Red*) and television (*Masters of Horror*, *Mob City*). His nonfiction works include *The Art of Drew Struzan* (2010) and *The Outer Limits at 50* (2014). He can be seen on various DVDs as an expert witness or documentarian on everything from *Creature from the Black Lagoon* to *Psycho* to *I, Robot*. Thanks to him, the word "splatterpunk" has been in the *Oxford English Dictionary* since 2002. He was one of the original contributors to *Book of the Dead* in 1989 (with the splatterfesto classic "Jerry's Kids Meet Wormboy") and had more stories in the original two volumes than any other writer, courtesy of his pseudonym, Chan McConnell.

WILLIAMSON'S FOLLY

by David J. Schow

The thing from outer space did not come by night.

It did not sizzle Earthward from the troposphere like a sulfur match scratching against starry blackness, to land in some farmer's remote field and disgorge a blob. Instead, it punched a hole in a cloudbank like a huge, blunt bullet, just after lunchtime. It came down with the scream of a buzz-bomb to tear through the roof of Handelmeyer's Hardware, destroying most of Aisle Four (all your gardening needs) and splitting the brick wall of the First Federal Credit Union. It put a big ding in the east face of the vault but did not breach the sandwich of layered steel and reinforced concrete. The contents of the two-room safe and the fiscal hoardings of approximately thirty percent of the population of Williamson, Nebraska, remained inviolate. Luckily, there were no casualties apart from Alma Teetle's claim that she had turned her ankle while dropping a fifteen-pound bag of birdseed in Handelmeyer's Aisle Three (pet supplies). She was swiftly quoted by Olnee Strats of the Williamson *Star-Ledger*: "Then the roof came apart and it sounded like the end of the world." It was the seventh time Alma's picture would appear in the modest local paper. She organized nature hikes and pamphleteered a lot about missing pets and animal rights. Her old frame house on Siddons Street was mildly notorious as an unlicensed menagerie for ferals. She usually smelled of cat pee and was somewhat of a fidget-pickle.

The duly appointed law enforcement officers of Williamson deployed—all five of them. Olnee Strats took a lot of pictures of the "devastation" (his word) on what was shaping up to be one of those rare days that merited a special edition. Since the *Star-Ledger* was the only surviving newspaper in a town of twenty-five thousand citizens (the *Bugle* had folded in 1965, and good riddance to it, as far as Olnee was concerned), the story was an exclusive that Olnee's wife, Emmalene, would happily vend to the wire services. Olnee's Linotype operator and chief printer, sixty-seven-year-old John "Blackjack" McCormick, would earn himself a shot of overtime. Before now, the headline for the next edition was to have been a bracing piece on the acquisition of new, clearly labeled litter receptacles for the intersection of Main Street and Grand Avenue, the heart of Williamson's business district since it featured the most traffic lights—four.

As a benefit of being surrounded by farmland, Williamson was a minor Union Pacific rail hub. Its principal commodities were cattle and calves, soybeans, dairy products, and wheat, all of which required processing. Most of the beef was rawhided directly to the big Kendrick Meats slaughterhouse five miles southwest of the center of town. Academics from Nebraska College of Technical Agriculture often conducted field research in Williamson, and a good proportion of the eastern suburbs were occupied by retired military, many of whom were former missile silo workers. The next nearest town, Humbridge, was twenty-five miles away. The Chamber of Commerce (Lyle Witwer) liked to pitch Williamson as a "more nature, less noise" type of environment for those seeking a "neck of the woods" without the urban cacophony of, say, Lincoln, the state capital. The Williamson economy was vibrant enough for Joselle Turner to actually turn a buck by running a bed-and-breakfast place.

But there was not a preponderance of what might be called "local scientists," and was therefore a scenario in which Dr. Manny Steckler's phone was fated to ring sooner or later.

Dr. Steckler had moved to Williamson ten years ago, in 1958. He quickly grouped local physicians into a sort of co-op—one of the first of its kind for this neck of the country—and founded the Williamson General Clinic two years later. The populace seemed to like the arrangement, and Steckler's then-innovative model had been copied in other towns of similar size, especially those communities that could not support a full-blown hospital. So it seemed like the most obvious thing in the world that once Sheriff Joseph Delaney had gone on the record for Olnee's tape recorder ("It's a miracle nobody got hurt, except of course for Missus Teetle; everybody should stay calm; we're looking into it"), he would ring up Dr. Steckler—who by broad taxonomy was close enough to Delaney's brand-new need for an "expert"—double-quick.

Delaney said, "Doc, I'm gonna need your professional input on something like this, if you don't mind. Shouldn't take too much time. I'll buy you a coffee." This was no casual largesse. Delaney always mentioned the coffee as a homey, small-town inducement; a just-between-you-and-me familial ritual. He favored two cafes on Grand Street, where he usually got the coffee for free, with a wink and a smile and a refill and all. Later, he deducted this cost of doing business at a set rate on his tax returns, with a name from his notebook to go along with each transaction or consultation.

What the hell, the coffee at Diane Crispen's diner was always great, anyway.

At the time of Delaney's call, there were exactly nine recently deceased people in Williamson. (For a comparison figure, it should be noted that there were only 360 students matriculating at Williamson High School.) Six of these were in the basement morgue of the Williamson General Clinic.

The six dead bodies cooling off at the clinic, in order of age, were:

Eleanor "Hattie" Brainard, ninety-two, natural causes (myocardial infarction), a grandmother eight times over who had outlived her husband, Kenneth, by a decade and change, their union constituting one of the area's three silently condoned biracial marriages. Since they had come from out of state, already hitched, there was nothing much anybody cared to do about it. But there was always talk.

Charles Lee "Chuck" (also "Champion") Greene, eighty-one, natural causes (died in his sleep from chronic obstructive pulmonary disease), Loving Husband, Devoted Father, all the usual eulogistic stats, a litter of descendants, a raft of vague compliments, and nobody apparently knew one single *real* thing about him, except that he was a four-pack-per-day chain smoker who had served in the navy during the war. No one was even sure which war anymore, not that it mattered worth a rat fart.

Paul "Sonny" Brickland, fifty, who basically drank himself to death in five months flat once he found out he had bowel cancer. Prior to that he had been a machine operator and farmhand on Lester Collins's soybean spread, living rent-free in a tarpaper-roofed shack on the far end of the acreage, near the water pumps. Paul had joked that when he died, he planned to be so pickled in alcohol that it would take his corpse months to start rotting.

Jason Allan Lowwens, thirty-four, death by misadventure (auto accident), the regional district manager of the biggest Chrysler dealership in Custer County, had been driving red-eye from god knew where on his way back to Lincoln to see his wife; he dozed off at the wheel and plowed his lovingly restored 1935 Ford Woodie into the guts of a power tower that overcooked both him and his ride. Folks who read about the mishap in the *Star-Ledger* had always found it curious and noteworthy that Lowwens was not driving a Chrysler.

Dolores Anne-Marie Whitaker (nee Collins), thirty-two, maternal death due to obstructed labor, whose much-sought and rigorously planned pregnancy ultimately killed both her and her daughter, who was to have been named Cherie Camela. Dolores had insisted on a home birth, and by the time the ambulance reached the farmhouse occupied by her and her husband, Brian, trauma and hemorrhage had taken charge.

Cherie Camela Whitaker, intrapartum death (stillborn).

The three recently deceased people in Williamson yet unknown to either Chief Delaney or the *Star-Ledger*, in order of their demise, were:

Allyson Roberta "Minx" Manx, twenty-two, former Williamson High cheerleading captain, who had been strangled last Wednesday by the love of her life (this week), Cameron "Chip" Jackson, former Williamson High Corsairs fullback. The issues of contention had been threefold: their immediate need for a revenue stream, vague and unfounded issues of sexual fidelity, and the equitable distribution of a dwindling ration of assorted chemical stimulants. Chip boldly protested that his mild interface with the world of crime, so far, was not his fault. It was the sort of argument that could only escalate. Now, he had introduced himself to the "crimes of passion" bracket, and was already upset enough that he'd had to choke Ally with a length of barbed wire to shut her up, and less perturbed that he had manifested a raging erection while killing her. Once he had metabolized his initial panic, he stashed Ally's corpse deep in the Pickton wheat fields. He didn't want to think any more about somehow getting the body closer to the tempting facilities of Kendrick Meats for disposal purposes, but it was Monday already, and he was going to have to do *something*.

Richard "Ramses" Coverdale, fifteen, had decided he had taken the last beating he was ever going to take from his father, over school grades. His first impulse had been to work such overdue patricide using Dad's very own antique Savage/ Fox 20-gauge side-by-side, which Rick knew to be loaded at all times, like all the firearms in the house—that way, so lectured his father, "you'll never shoot yourself with an 'unloaded' gun." Thanks to a worn trigger sear, the damned thing went off as soon as Ricky pulled it (bore-first) from the gun case, atomizing the left side of his head so quickly that he wasn't alive long enough to see the muzzle flash of his own erasure.

Lorena Darling, forty-four, had died at home of a brain aneurysm, completely unexpectedly. One moment she was laughing and joking, smoking some after-dinner weed and forking up great gobs of apple pie with too much cornstarch in it, partaking of giggles with her de facto life partner, Buddy Rawls, with whom she shared a small clapboard house on a five-acre plot that was mostly potato field interrupted by two modest greenhouses. Past inadequate camouflage, the greenhouses were mostly full of marijuana plants. Buddy, his brother Bernardo, Bernardo's girlfriend, Tammy, and a fifth-wheel guru ostensibly named Kersawani had wound up here two years ago after Buddy and Bernardo successfully altered their identities, thereby ducking the military draft. They played guitar, shared campfires, sold kush to most of the delinquents in Williamson, and fancied themselves true Age of Aquarius psychedelic savants . . . which was the problem. Kersawani had insisted that involvement by the Man not despoil the beauty of Lorena's unanticipated death, that she be cleansed and worshipped and honored and duly given back to Mother Earth right here, in private, on the property, according to customs and rituals they could invent themselves, not shoplift out of someone else's life-handbook. So, on that same

Monday, Lorena was laid out on a repurposed door in the living room, barefoot, doused in patchouli and surrounded by wildflowers. She was beginning to stink and Tammy had already mentioned the possibility of calling in an actual adult, for which Bernardo *almost* slapped her, but he knew better. He also knew that harboring a corpse after twenty-four hours hung between major misdemeanor and minor felony; failure to report the death, failure to report the disposition of a body, and possible desecration *at least*.

"That's if we're caught," Buddy argued him down. "It probably ain't legal, but who cares? Is it legal to drive over the speed limit? No, but people do it all the time and what usually happens? *Nada*."

"It's one of ours," Dr. Steckler said unnecessarily.

Sheriff Delaney's boys had strung hazard tape and established a perimeter while Brice Handelmeyer rolled his eyes and moaned about the damage to his store to Olnee Strats, whose wife, Emmalene (a former Husker Queen and still a head-turner on a good day), had also come down to demonstrate something or other; maybe the full power of the local fourth estate. More likely to get a jump on the out-of-town reporters who would soon swarm to Williamson in droves if this was some kind of lost government bird or top-secret space project. She quickly scampered back to the *Star-Ledger* office bearing fresh intel and Olnee's latest rolls of undeveloped negative.

With the help of Delaney's men, the Credit Union had posted a door notice advising temporary closure *due to unforeseen circumstances*. General Manager Tommy Tighe had given his employees the remaining half-day off rather than waste that time explaining the hole in the wall to irate customers. In half an hour, Dill Barrett's pickup would arrive, and by sundown Dill would have fixed up the wall just fine, because he was a good craftsman who knew what he was doing, one of those guys who had an almost Zen relationship with bricks and mortar, with lathe and plaster and raw lumber.

Dr. Steckler had brought a Geiger counter from the hospital, a clunky, halogen-tube warhorse model at least fifteen years old, plus latex gloves and assorted kit. Delaney thought Steckler looked like one of those, what did you call them, character actors, like the guy who always plays the hero's best friend, or the good-hearted buddy who always gets killed ten minutes before the end of the movie. He had dramatic hair and very pale blue eyes. Big, competent, veiny hands. Harsh spectacles.

Steckler thought Joseph Delaney fit right into the mold of the community father figure, twenty pounds over fighting trim but the kind of guy who still starched his uniform blouses. Receding hair but advancing intellect. A "bold baldie." A man quick to counsel and slow to violence.

"This isn't radioactive, is it?" said Delaney.

"No," said Steckler. "Not in the sense you mean. Don't let the clicking make you nervous. This measures any sort of ionizing radiation—alpha, beta, gamma, all down the line. The number of clicks is the number of ionization events detected. See?" He showed the chief the dial. "No giant ants."

Delaney furrowed his brow. Was Steckler funning him? Were they going to have their old country-mouse/city-rat argument again?

"Not to worry," said Steckler. "We're not going to start glowing in the dark or anything. But I want to wipe this thing down and bag some samples for residue, just in case."

"In case of what?"

"Well, we know spacecraft reentering the atmosphere heat up due to friction with the air, three thousand degrees or better. That's usually good enough to sterilize this little capsule or probe or whatever it is."

"Burned off all the decals or serials," said Delaney. "But you're right—this is ours. Just look."

The object resembled a nose cone about two feet in diameter. Shiny, still-warm factory-rolled steel with the kind of rivets you see on jet airplane wings. Contact with oxygen at high speed had burnished the metal and left sooty charcoal-colored streaks. The underside was concave and featured a scorched docking collar (it reminded Delaney of a septic tank join) girded by concentric, tubular metal ribs. Stamped on the outermost rib was MADE IN USA.

"So you think there's a possibility this might have some kinda germ or bug or virus inside?" said Delaney.

"Not likely," said Steckler. "This looks like a detector, not a collector. Like Sputnik Seven. Like those testing sensors for the MIDAS missile early warning satellite program. You ever hear of Thor Agena B, or Thor Ablestar?" He grinned gamely at the chief's incomprehension. "I used to like to watch the launches. The blastoffs."

"In Russia?" Delaney said. "I mean, you did just say 'Sputnik,' right?" The telltale brow lines returned as he squinted, not really suspicious, just . . . careful. The sheriff was no fan of Commies.

"No, I only read about those. They were interesting because several of them were off-world probes. The Venera series. Most of them failed to separate or blew up. But one of them made it all the way to Venus, no foolin'."

Both men were now regarding the capsule with respect, as though it could hear and judge them.

"This may be the most exciting thing that's ever happened around here!" said Olnee Strats, butting in, unable to contain himself.

"Olnee," Delaney said in his best parental tone, "now I don't want you getting people all upset prematurely. Hysteria is the *last* thing we want."

Olnee kept snapping photos, looking vaguely chastised, but nothing could dampen his verve right now.

"We're going to be famous," Dr. Steckler said out of one side of his mouth. He took off his glasses and polished them. It was something to do with his hands to buy a small moment of time, now that he had stopped smoking.

"Or infamous," said Delaney, who did not cotton to any loss of control. His town. His people. His call. "This is gonna be one of those all-day, all-night deals; I can just smell it."

"We can always bring those large-sized coffees back here from Diane's," Steckler ventured.

"Exactly what I was thinking, Doc."

At 4:21 p.m. that afternoon, the late Paul Brickland—"Sonny" to his intimates—opened his eyes and tried to sit up on the stainless steel drawer inside the Williamson General Clinic's morgue, locker #2. He banged his head on the low-clearance vault but felt no pain. His eyes were dull full moons of cataract. His movement was not impeded by the excavation of autopsy, which had left the usual crudely tucked, Y-shaped stitches across his chest. His overall temperature was about thirty-nine degrees, none of it self-generated. Inside the constricted space he heaved his naked body forward to thump his yellowed feet against the barrier of the locker door, just as his neighbor in #3, Dolores Whitaker, began to stir.

Casey Fields, a strawberry-blonde candy striper who had transitioned directly to clinic work after graduation, loitered in the ground-floor corridor waiting for the shift change at 4:30 that would bring intern Kyle Fredericks downstairs. At 4:30, Lenny Rana would clock out of the morgue and soon thereafter, Casey and Kyle could steal some time to get recreational out of the sight of their coworkers. Casey wore the regulation thick-soled white shoes and unflattering white pantyhose to complete her eponymous uniform, but in her case the cotton panel part of the pantyhose had been scissored out to liberate her carefully manicured pubis, also strawberry blonde. A little weed, a little vigorous fornication; it had become a semi-regular break routine for her and Kyle, who was going to be an actual doctor soon, so they would never have to worry about money.

Kyle, Scandinavian of jaw, a gray-eyed wonder with superhero hair, showed up right on time, complete with boner. Casey's hand went straight to his groin for reassurance and she smiled, catlike, almost evilly.

"Lenny's still on the desk," she said, flashing forward to when she might be mounted on the same desk. It wouldn't be the first time.

"I'll hustle him up," said Kyle with a wink, bumping through the swinging doors.

Her insides felt *restless*, a term she loved using. Butterflies in her heart chakra. A silvery, plunging anticipation shot through her stomach.

But by then, Kyle was screaming. Not hollering, but *scream-*

ing, raw-throated and primal. Casey pushed open the doors just as fresh blood pooled forth to besmirch her spotless white shoes. She had unwittingly foretold the future: neither she nor Kyle would ever have to worry about money again.

Dr. Steckler put down the counter phone at Handelmeyer's. "There's some kind of problem at the clinic," he told Sheriff Delaney.

"Go," said Delaney. "Go deal. You've got your samples, right? Take care of business. Nothing else is gonna happen here tonight."

"Thanks for the coffee."

"That's nothing; I'll buy you a real drink when we wrap this up."

Steckler passed Emmalene on his way out. She seemed to bear heavy news; her usually sparkling eyes had gone flat with purpose.

"Sheriff?" she said to the room at large. "Apparently there are army trucks lining up near the Kendrick slaughterhouse, and Lester Collins just called the paper to find out what's going on because he says he saw more army guys on the other side of town, near his soybean farm."

"What the hell . . . ?" Delaney muttered. He turned to the proprietor of the hardware store. "Brice? Lemme have that phone." His deputies were still mugging for Olnee Strats's camera. "Lester, Bob—off your asses and get ready to roll."

Another uniform, Chet Downing (the youngest cop in Williamson), bustled through the push-bar glass doors looking mildly shell-shocked. "Joe?" he said to his superior. "You'd better come have a look at this."

Halfway down Main Street, near the intersection with Grapeseed Road (no stoplight), somebody covered in blood was lurching down the center of the street, weaving as though drunk or wounded. A good quadrant of his head was absent. Flies touched down on macerated brain matter and exposed, splintered bone.

"Holy shit, that's Ricky Coverdale!" bleated Chet, his voice cracking. Ricky had been a freshman the year Chet graduated Williamson High.

Like iron filings to a magnet, onlookers and bystanders gravitated from Handelmeyer's to this new attraction. There were close to twenty citizens hanging around with nothing better to do, much like flies themselves. They filled the air with dry-mouthed fear, astonishment, and easy loathing amid much natter about who to summon or what should be done; Sylvia Perkins was in the middle of unnecessarily saying *call an ambulance* when she barfed all over the corner mailbox. Chicken salad and red wine, from Diane Crispen's diner.

Several hardier locals rushed to steady the blood-drenched, nearly Impressionist apparition in the middle of the street until the late Ricky Coverdale chomped a huge, wet bite out of the nearest helping hand.

More screaming.

Tyler Strong, entrepreneur of the 76 gas station two blocks away, fell on his ass with three fingers missing from his right hand, his voiceless, gape-mouthed reaction very similar to someone who has just witnessed an inexplicable magic trick. Then he found his voice and began to howl, crabbing backward as Ricky bit off the nose of Ace Baldwin, a car customizer and wrench who was also Tyler's best drinking buddy. (It was Ace Baldwin who had restored Jason Lowwens's '35 Woodie for a pretty penny two years back, before that asshole had married it to a power pole and destroyed it beyond reclamation, barbecuing himself in the deal.)

Four gunshots, shakily aimed but nicely grouped, drove Ricky into a rearward stagger and finally eliminated the rest of his head in a puffball of crimson mist. What was left of Ricky collapsed in a moist pile of unrealized youthful potential. The living sprang back to avoid getting nastiness on them. Sheriff Delaney caught up just as Chet fired the kill round from his .357 revolver. He put his hand atop the hot weapon to caution his panicked deputy to put the gun down, now.

Out at the clandestine pot farm, Kersawani proclaimed they had all witnessed a bona fide miracle when the supposedly dead Lorena came back to them. They were all sure she had been devoid of heartbeat, pulse, or breath, but they had all read Poe. Never mind that her formerly bright eyes were now the tint of dirty dishwater, and did not seem to see Buddy directly even as he rushed to be first to embrace her. Her joints cracked loudly. She smelled not dissimilar to badly cured pork. She wrapped her arms around him and gnawed about a pound of live meat directly out of his neck. Kersawani was next. Lorena pulled his voice box right out of his throat and ate it while he dropped to his knees, drowning in his own blood. The organ imploded like a dog toy, gushing fluid. Tammy was yelling incoherently at the top of her lungs while Buddy's brother Bernardo fumbled the shotgun and almost blew off his own foot. The tube was full of deer slugs. Bernardo got the weapon up and fired, point-blank. The slug was about the size of a stack of five nickels, a subsonic round that hit with the force of a speeding train. It blew a hit single—that is, a 45 rpm–sized window—through Lorena's middle in a thundercloud of desiccated tissue. But Lorena kept groping toward Tammy, so Bernardo fired once more. Lorena's head violently detached and shattered a window on its way outside. Her body caved in like a clipped puppet. Bernardo and Tammy ran for the pickup truck, trying desperately to formulate a new life-ethos.

Eighteen-year-old John Pickton, Jr., had decided to take his pony Teabiscuit out for an afternoon tear among the sheaves. Both John Junior and the horse loved to breeze along the rows of wheat at full gallop; to them it was the sensation of earthbound flight, zipping down a half-mile with wheat feathering your arms and legs, then cranking a turn and gobbling up another row faster than a clown could blink. Straight line from the elbow to the bit; cue with the reins and push with the leg so the horse turns around your leg in the desired direction. With practice, pro rodeo was not out of the question; John Junior had not inherited his father's love for the harvest.

There was a woman striding down the wheatrow, toward him.

Correction: there was a naked, redheaded woman with D-cup titties and big nipples and long legs striding toward him, and she did not bridle or flee at his appearance. She kept right on coming, nearer.

Teabiscuit, however, bridled.

John Junior wasted vital final moments still trying to process the naked lady from nowhere. The rearing horse failed to slow her attack. She went right for the forearm portion of the front leg, and as John Junior came unsaddled, only then did he notice that the naked lady was kind of . . . well, dusty and crooked.

Teabiscuit crashed down hard on her right side, a thousand pounds of horseflesh losing against gravity, hurling John Junior two rows over, clean. He knew how to land. He came up flash-fire pissed, and tackled the interloper.

Horses can scream. Pretty soon John Junior was screaming, too.

"Sheriff, I'm telling you, this isn't a disease!" Dr. Steckler was practically shouting into the phone and did not care who overheard. "Or contagious psychosis or a virus or space madness or anything like that. *It's not the capsule.* Hell, for all I know it's cosmic rays or God's will or some hippie shit I don't understand. The capsule is just a jumped-up radio! No germs, no ooze, no nothing!"

"We've got a situation down here," Sheriff Delaney growled back. The incipient alarm in his voice hurt to hear. Both men were snapping at each other because they lived in denial of the void in which no explanation was credible, or even available. Rarely if ever had Delaney actually heard Steckler resort to what both their moms would have called *that kind* of language. "A situation where people are dying. A *medical* situation. Doc, I know you're doing everything you can. I know this is big and frightening. But we can't lose our heads. We—"

"I hear you, Sheriff," Steckler overrode. "Fear gets us nowhere. Fear gets us gut reactions and panic and worse. You're not going to want to hear this, but all the dead people in the morgue just got up and attacked my staff. Even Hattie Brainard. We both heard Emmalene Strats say the military was edging up on the town—"

It was Delaney's turn to interpose: "There is no way in Hell or on God's green earth that Ricky Coverdale was *dead* when he attacked Tyler and Ace. He was fucked up, true, probably out of his mind on LSD or something, but *he wasn't dead already*!" So much for not cussing.

"He's dead now, right?"

"Doc, he doesn't have a head."

"What shape are Tyler and Ace in?"

"Tyler lost some fingers. Chet and Cab bandaged them up. They seem woozy but okay. They really need you to look at them, Doc . . ."

"Watch them," said Steckler. "If they lapse or stop breathing or *anything*, lock them up until I can get there. Avoid contact with them however you can and above all, don't let them bite or draw blood."

"That is not rational."

"Look, Joe—even though it's not a disease, it helps to think of this as rabies, but from what I've seen, incredibly fast-moving. That's another reason the satellite isn't to blame. This is all happening too soon, and if what we're up against was from space, how come we aren't *all* affected? We can figure this out later, but we've got to deal with it *now*."

"Something like, kill the symptoms now, fix the disease later?"

"Exactly."

"So I guess we need another dead person to start moving around?"

"That would help convince us both. I haven't witnessed this actually happening yet. If this is systemic, it'll have a pattern, and what we'd call an incubation period. We've got to know what that is."

Steckler paused to release an explosive sigh. No doubt Delaney could hear the background chatter at the clinic, the voices now surrounding him, demanding he make a decision or take action. Likewise, he could hear nondescript people yelling beyond Delaney's side of the call. The only sideshow this circus was missing so far was a goddamned priest, hollering holies and freaking out his flock.

"Jesus," said Steckler. "I can't believe we're actually talking about this as though we were in our right mind . . ."

"Punch a wall if you have to, but don't vaporlock on me," said Delaney. "The whole town's gonna need us. You go ahead on, just keep doing what you're doing, because you're about to get a bunch of new patients, maybe alive, maybe dead, I don't know and don't want to speculate anymore. But you call through on the radio if you get any flashes of brilliance."

"Yeah—in twelve hours we'll probably be laughing about this."

"In twelve hours I hope to be dead drunk or fast asleep," said Delaney. "Meanwhile, I'm gonna go ask the army what the hell they think they're doing, loitering outside my town."

While they were talking, Ty Strong died from shock and blood loss.

There was one more dead person in Williamson yet unaccounted for.

Hollis Grenier (sixty-seven, grocery store manager, kidney disease) was boxed up and lay in state inside the Chapman & Browning Funeral Home, preparatory to a traditional burial service scheduled for the next day at 11:00 a.m. He began to stir about sundown on the Day of the Satellite.

Fleet Jones, an apprentice in mortuary science who had

moved down from the university in Omaha, heard a commotion in the prep room just as he was locking up for the boss. He found Hollis weaving like a willow in a high wind, barefoot, his Velcroed funeral suit hanging in bum tatters. This was unusual. Fleet knew Hollis was full of embalming fluid, pumped via cannula into his (very uncooperative) carotid artery.

Fleet, his hands trembling, inadvertently addressed the risen cadaver as if it were still a human being. "Mister Grenier . . . ?" It lifted its head to look at him. In life, Hollis had suffered from cervical myelopathy due to "dropped head syndrome."

Then Fleet made his second mistake. He moved to steady Hollis, to perhaps reassure this apparition with a human touch. This was some kind of horrific misunderstanding; things needed to be put to rights.

Hollis's joints made a crackling sound akin to rupturing ice as his dead fingers clawed at his own mouth, splitting the gum-stitches and wire that held it shut. He spat out the cotton batting and gnawed a gob of tissue from Fleet's biceps, right through his shirt.

Fleet committed no further errors. His last received sensation was the stench of formaldehyde.

Dr. Manny Steckler watched the dead baby crawl toward him blindly, mewling, trailing a purple umbilical cord, its toothless mouth champing. Somehow it had gotten out of its jar in Pathology; it had not yet been transferred to the morgue, which was now barricaded with utility furniture, quickly scavenged and repurposed.

Steckler's stomach seemed to drop straight down to Hell and bounce back. A sight such as this could force you to seriously recontemplate your place in the universe, or reconsider the advantages of a quick suicide.

Unavoidably he thought of the Kendrick slaughterhouse. Normally the calmest level of the clinic, the morgue had become a hiding bath, bleeding pit, and mulching chamber all in one as grotesque, mindlessly hungry things dismembered and cannibalized at least three of the clinic's staff, identifiable now only by a head count of who was still standing, outside. Was it technically cannibalization when a clinically dead corpse resurrected and chewed pieces out of you?

He had seen just enough to drive him to the edge of the crazy pit before he ordered the morgue buttoned up. It was carnage in there, a bloodbath of sundered limbs and exposed organs, tendons snapping like rubber bands, human fat greasing the floor. The dead revived, to chow down on the living, who in turn became dead, who in turn . . .

Here, now, crept the embodiment of every revulsion he had felt as a med student, the potential healer repelled by the raw pink animalism of infants, the gut reactions and instinctive hatreds he had tamped back with notions of human compassion and species unity. Doctors were not supposed to dislike children, especially in a place like America, where motherhood was unjustly elevated to godhood. He was relieved to leave the clandestine D&Cs to a younger and more idealistic doctor, Felicia Raine, who was willing to take the heat if anybody ever found out that some of the females of Williamson were not falling gently into their presupposed role as brood mares. Discreet and careful even as the militant feminist in her stirred to wakefulness, Felicia had calibrated her own conscience so as not to make a political issue out of a moral one.

Steckler was more or less alone in the corridor; everyone

else was hanging back, because he was in charge, and nobody could venture a useful theory about what was actually transpiring here.

Having dealt with his phobia—risen above it, in fact—did not mean that a fear so elemental, bullied into dormancy, could not erupt fresh, given the correct stimulae, the old prompts. The thing lolling in the corridor was a pallid, leaking grub and though it was clearly not breathing, it made a wheezing, clotted sound as it dragged itself along the floor. Steckler instantly hated it; wanted to kill it with fire—and *that* was also an instinct, vomited up from a much deeper, more primal level than the usual bilge about how adorable babies were, the easy lies by which the subject is swiftly changed.

That thing was *not* Dolores Whitaker's technically stillborn daughter. *Was not.*

Steckler picked it up by the throat. It thrashed in his grasp like a rattlesnake. Since he had the correct keys, he threw it down the elevator shaft before his staff could bear witness. He heard it hit bottom with a snap, like a ripe maggot bursting open.

Then he heard it moving around again.

On the far side of the morgue barricade, Casey Fields resurrected. Her paramour, Kyle Fredericks, reanimated. And attendant Lenny Rana revived. Half of him, anyway. Casey still felt "restless" inside, but was incapable of codifying the modified vector of this new hunger that was so much more *primal* than sex. In combination with the ambulatory remains of Jason Lowwens, Hattie Brainard, Chuck Greene, Sonny Brickland, and Dolores Whitaker, their group now massed to sufficient heft to breach the doors, which—despite the fact they had been dammed outside all the way to the far wall with office furniture—came free at their weakest point, the inside hinges.

Awaiting them in various corners of the clinic were at least fifteen other patients lacking the simple strength to move from their beds with any speed.

Most of the clinic staff had vacated in naked, directionless dread, once their boss, their Number One, their leader, had proven incapable of further leadership.

Something vital and irredeemable had snapped inside of Dr. Manny Steckler when he encountered the baby in the corridor. Once that snowball begins to roll, best to take cover until the avalanche is spent. He was already in his car, headed out of town at top speed, legal limits be damned.

He was T-boned by a pickup truck being driven recklessly by Bernardo Rawls and his girlfriend, Tammy. Per Buddy's pronouncement, people over-sped the legal limit all the time and usually, nothing happened. *Nada.*

There were no survivors.

Not regular army, thought Sheriff Delaney. *Nope.* The soldiers he could see were all in murky-dark fatigues devoid of company or mission patches, and toting the newer M16s. Just as Indochina had become Vietnam, the coveted "black rifles" had evolved to this A1 variant, which would not become the standard service long gun for another nine months. Delaney had never actually seen one before but knew the mags were supposed to be ten rounds bigger.

He got a closer clue when the chrome-plated bore teased

the nape of his neck, about a quarter-mile past the boundary to Lester Collins's soybean field, where Sonny Brickland had drunk himself to death. He heard the crackle of a radio-comm behind him: "Trespasser in the loop, Captain."

Delaney was divested of his sidearm and escorted by a pair of sentries toward a cluster of three-quarter Jeep trucks and larger, "five-quarter" carriers. A low-light field HQ had been set up in one of these latter. The authority of his badge and his standing as sheriff did not seem to impress his captors overmuch. They herded him with monosyllables and prods, almost like an animal, but more like an enemy, which set off the danger alarms in his flesh like firecrackers.

A flap was lifted and Delaney was presented. "Here's our stray," said the soldier who had proven to be quieter than Delaney, out there in the field. Stealthy sonofabitch. The kid looked about nineteen, eager to be a war dog.

"This fella pokes me one more time, I'm gonna lay him out," said Delaney directly to his chaperone . . . who backed up a step without meaning to.

"Come in, Sheriff Delaney," said a man with captain's bars on a brigade sweater, probably the oldest man here except for Delaney, who mentally chalked the soldier as somewhere in his mid-forties. The man had a pretty dynamic mustache for military issue. One of those guys with perfect gray temples but black hair above, resulting in salt-and-pepper eyebrows. He dismissed the guards and waved Delaney toward the nearest bench in the cramped truck bed. "Sit down." He looked up and made direct eye contact. "Please."

"Please," Delaney repeated. "That courtesy shit only works in an equal environment. You just had me brought here at gunpoint, so don't butter my ass, Captain—?"

"Fletcher." The captain removed his steel-rimmed glasses and massaged the bridge of his nose, exuding a precise balance between harried bureaucrat and hardball centurion—a performance that seemed too calculated for Delaney, as though strictly for his benefit. Whatever decisions were to be enacted here had been made already.

Now the guy would try to "confide" in Delaney. He'd act off-the-record and crack a serpent's smile.

"Sorry," said Fletcher. He cracked the smile. "Long day."

"Don't," said Delaney. "Don't offer me bad coffee or pretend you're my pal. If this was legitimate, I would have been notified. This is my town. People are dying and nobody can explain it. So spare me the spreadable cheese and tell me what the fuck is going on here. Do me that kindness, because that's all I want to know."

"Fair enough." Fletcher stacked some paper, uselessly truing the edges—another corporate cue that it was time for plain talk. "We have experienced a terra incognita event. The entire country, so far as we can tell; possibly the whole world. Not just your town, ah—" (he had to check) "—Williamston."

"Nearest 'Williamston' is in Michigan state," said Delaney dryly.

"Oh. Sorry."

"Stop apologizing. Talk plain or shut up."

"All right. A terra incognita event is something we've never seen or experienced before."

"Yeah—'unknown land.'"

"We had a suborbital snooper drop unexpectedly. A satellite."

"Yeah, I know that, too. I've also got a doctor who says the satellite has nothing to do with what's going on with dead people. Or people who are wounded and die. They get back up and attack."

"Yes, we had reports from California, Boston, New York City, all over. But the satellite crashed in Williamson, Sheriff. Your own newspaper has already posted stories to the wire services. It was exactly the kind of story we needed to explain what was happening, in order to stave off major panic for as long as possible."

A beauty of a headache—the kind caused only by the truth—was settling into the space between Delaney's eyes with the sizzle of a hot bullet casing. "You need a cover story. Deniability for some larger screwup."

Fletcher brought his steepled hands down on his meager desk with a thump—the first honest reaction Delaney had seen. "That's just it, Sheriff. There was no screwup. Our first guess was that it was a biowar spill, an accident from . . . somewhere. Nope—nothing reported yet. No ground zero. It's not from space unless it's a cosmic ray belt that saturated the entire planet at the same time . . ."

Delaney's vision lost focus. "There's no time to investigate and split hairs about what it is or isn't. You've got a bigger and more immediate problem . . . and so do I. Whatever happens, people are going to say it was because a space thing crashed in Williamson and it *isn't true*, and that makes you all happy because now you've got something to blame. Terrific. What *else* are you planning to do for me?"

"We need your cooperation. We've cordoned off the town. Nobody in or out."

"Your men are toting hot weapons," said Delaney, meeting Fletcher's gaze directly.

"We need you to tell the people in Williamson to cope as

best they can while we get a determination from the president." It was a near-classic tied-hands ploy. *I have to wait for orders from my superiors; that's all I can do.*

"Cope," said Delaney, now doubting the meaning of the simplest words. "Cope with their friends and neighbors trying to eat them. And they try to leave, you'll shoot them, plain enough? This is a scared shitless scenario, Captain. *I'm* scared. You'd be scared, too, if you saw what I've seen so far today."

"But containable," said Fletcher.

"Oh, yeah, no big deal at all." Delaney stood up in the narrow space. "I think you and I are done."

The guard just beyond the tailgate brandished his weapon. Fletcher waved off the conflict.

"Sheriff Delaney, my orders are to maintain a sterile cordon."

And *that* brought the face Delaney had wanted to see all along: the humorless mouth, the metallic eyes, all cards on the table, whose dick was biggest.

"Tell your people we're doing the best we can."

Delaney turned back. "Against what? You don't even know. This is all to support a goddamned *story* you just made up."

"Corporal, let the sheriff go back into town, and make sure he's headed in the right direction."

"That's it, huh?" Delaney shot back.

"You said it, not me. We're done." Fletcher nodded, his lips white. He whispered *sorry* one more time, but Delaney could not hear. Then he unracked the receiver for his hot line.

"This is Captain Fletcher." He recited a confirmation code and a few other special numbers. "We are pulling back to the outer marker. We are green, I repeat, green-for-go, for Anubis."

* * *

Sheriff Delaney plodded grimly across the soybean field, looking for his Jeep in the dark. If all else failed, he could tack toward the back-field pole lamps illuminating the grounds around Lester Collins's farmhouse.

The soldiers had returned his pistol but taken all his ammo, and wasn't that a rancid cherry on top of the whole psychotic day?

Delaney had a new job now. Tell anybody who would listen that his whole town had been the victim of a lie. A space thing had crashed and dead people had become ambulatory. Cause plus effect equals falsehood. Because a story, any story, was better than the crimson abyss of uncertainty, even if it wasn't the *entire* story. The alternative was utter chaos, total breakdown. Everything stops, the end.

He thought of all the gentle untruths he had told throughout his whole life, his entire career, in order to keep the peace or avoid a bigger clash.

Dr. Steckler could have told him that the human nervous system requires one-thirtieth of a second to register, and one-tenth of a second to flinch. Nuclear blast waves come in at twice the speed of sound.

Sheriff Delaney lived long enough to see the flash, but the blood in his brain evaporated before he could feel a thing.

Mira Grant is the pseudonym of *New York Times* bestselling author Seanan McGuire, a fact that regularly calls her existence into question but doesn't seem to slow her down much. A resident of the Pacific Northwest, she is more interested in chainsaws, corn fields, and terrible diseases than is strictly healthy. Keep up with her at www.seananmcguire.com, or on Twitter at @seananmcguire. Never follow her into a haunted house. Not because she'll do anything untoward: it's just common sense.

YOU CAN STAY ALL DAY

by Mira Grant

The merry-go-round was still merry-going, painted horses prancing up and down while the calliope played in the background, tinkly and bright and designed to attract children all the way from the parking lot. There was something about the sound of the calliope that seemed to speak to people on a primal level, telling them "the fun is over here," and "come to remember how much you love this sort of thing."

Cassandra was pretty sure it wasn't the music that was attracting the bodies thronging in the zoo's front plaza. It was the motion. The horses were still dancing, and some of them still had riders, people who had become tangled in their safety belts when they fell. So the dead people on the carousel kept flailing, and the dead people who weren't on the carousel kept coming, and—

They were dead. They were all dead, and they wouldn't stay down, and none of this could be happening. None of this could be *real*.

The bite on her arm burned with the deep, slow poison of infection setting in, and nothing was real anymore. Nothing but the sound of the carousel, playing on and on, forever.

Morning at the zoo was always Cassandra's favorite time. Everything was bright and clean and full of possibility. The guests hadn't arrived yet, and so the paths were clean, sparkling in the sunlight, untarnished by chewing gum and wadded-up popcorn boxes.

It was funny. People came to the zoo to goggle at animals they'd never seen outside of books, but it was like they thought that alone was enough to conserve the planet: just paying their admission meant that they could litter, and feed chocolate to the monkeys, and throw rocks at the tigers when they weren't active enough to suit their sugar-fueled fantasies.

Nothing ruined working with animals like the need to work with people at the same time. But in the mornings, ah! In the mornings, before the gates opened, everything was perfect.

Cassandra walked along the elegant footpath carved into the vast swath of green between the gift shop and the timber wolf enclosure—people picnicked here in the summer, enjoying the great outdoors, sometimes taking in an open-air concert from the bandstand on the other side of the carefully maintained field—and smiled to herself, content with her life choices.

One of the other zookeepers strolled across the green up ahead, dressed in khakis like the rest of the staff. The only thing out of place was the thick white bandage wrapped around his left bicep. It was an excellent patch job, and yet . . .

"Michael!"

He stopped at the sound of his name, and turned to watch as she trotted to catch up with him. His face split in a smile when she was halfway there.

"Cassie," he said. "Just the girl I was hoping to see."

"What did you do to yourself this time?" she asked, trying to make the question sound as light as she could. Michael worked with their small predators, the raccoons and otters and opossums. It wasn't outside the realm of possibility that one of them could have bitten him. If he reported it, it would reflect poorly on him, and on the zoo. If he didn't, and it got infected . . .

There were things that could kill or cripple a zoo. An employee failing to report an injury was on the list.

"No," he said, and grimaced sheepishly. "It was my room-mate."

"What?"

"My roommate, Carl. He was weird this morning. Not talking, just sort of wandering aimlessly around the front room. I thought he was hungover again. I figured I'd help him back to bed—but as soon as he realized I was there, he lunged for me and he bit me." Michael shook his head. "Asshole. I'm going to tell him I'm through with this shit when I get home tonight. He's never been late with his share of the rent, but enough's enough, you know?"

"I do," said Cassandra, with another anxious glance at the bandage. "You want me to take over your feedings for the morning?"

"Please. I cleaned it out and wrapped it up as best I could. I did a pretty decent job, if I do say so myself. There's still a chance the smell of blood could get through the gauze, and well . . ."

"We don't need to exacerbate a human bite with a bunch of animal ones, even though the animal bites would be cleaner." Cassandra frowned. "You're sure it's cleaned out? I can take a look, if you want."

"No, really, I'm good. I just wanted to ask about the feedings, and it turned out I didn't need to." Michael's grin seemed out of place on the face of a man who'd just been assaulted. "That's our oracle."

"Ha ha," said Cassandra. "Get to work. I'll do your feedings after I finish mine."

"Yes, ma'am," said Michael, and he resumed his progress across the green, seemingly no worse for wear. Cassandra frowned. It was entirely like him to brush off something as unusual and traumatic as being bitten by his own roommate, and it wasn't her place to get involved. At the same time, the situation wasn't right. People didn't just start *biting*.

"Classic Cassandra," she muttered. "If you can't find a catastrophe, you'll invent one. Get over yourself."

She started walking again, trying to shake the feeling that some of the brightness had gone out of the day. The sky was clear; the sun was shining; one little bit of human weirdness shouldn't have been enough to dampen her enthusiasm. But it was. It always was. Humans were *strange*. Animals made sense.

A tiger would always act like a tiger. It might do things she didn't expect, might bite when she thought it was happy to see her, or scratch when it had no reason to be threatened, but those times were on her, the human: she was the one who'd been trained on how to interact with wild animals, how to read the signs and signals that they offered. There was no class for tigers, to tell them how to deal with the strange, bipedal creatures who locked them in cages and refused to let them out to run. Tigers had to figure everything out on their own, and if they got it wrong sometimes, who could blame them? They didn't know the rules.

People, though . . . . people were supposed to know the rules. People weren't supposed to bite each other, or treat each other like obstacles to be defeated. Michael was a good guy. He cared about the animals he was responsible for, and he didn't slack off when he had duties to attend to. He wasn't like Lauren from the aviary, who smoked behind the lorikeet feeding cage sometimes, and didn't care if the birds were breathing it in. He wasn't like Donald from the African safari exhibit, either, who liked to flirt with female guests, talking to their breasts when he should have been watching to be sure that little kids didn't jab sticks at the giraffes. Michael was a *good* guy.

So why was she so unsettled?

Cassandra walked a little faster. Work would make things better. Work always did.

The big cats were uneasy when Cassandra let herself into the narrow hall that ran back behind their feeding cages. They should have been in the big enclosures by this hour of the morning, sunning themselves on the rocks. Instead, they were pacing back and forth, not even snarling at each other, although her big male lion normally snarled at anything else feline that got close enough for him to smell. Cassandra stopped, the feeling of *wrongness* that had arrived with Michael blossoming into something bigger and brighter.

"What's wrong with you?" she asked.

The big cats, unable to answer her, continued to pace. She walked over to the first cage, where her female tiger, Andi, was prowling. She pressed the palm of her hand against the bars. That should have made Andi stop, made her come over to sniff at Cassandra's fingers, checking them for interesting new smells. Instead, Andi kept pacing, grumbling to herself in the low tones of a truly distressed tiger.

"You're not going to delight many families today if you keep hanging out back here," said Cassandra, trying to cover her concern with a quip. It was a small coping mechanism, but one that had served her well over the years: her therapist said that it was a means of distancing herself from situations she didn't want to be a part of.

It was funny how her therapist never suggested anything better. Surely there were situations that *no one* wanted to be a part of. What were people supposed to do then?

"All right," said Cassandra. "I'll go see what's going on. You stay where you are." She pressed the button that would close the tigers in their feeding cages, keeping them from venturing into the larger enclosure. Then she counted noses.

It was unlikely that she would ever mistake three tigers for four tigers, but it only took once. No matter how much they liked her, no matter how often she fed them, they would still be tigers, and she would still be a human being. They would eat her as soon as look at her if she caught them in the wrong mood, and then they would be put down for the crime of being exactly what nature intended them to be. So she counted noses, not to save herself, but to save them.

Always to save them.

The door to the main tiger enclosure was triple-locked, secured with two keys and a dead bolt. It had always seemed a bit extreme to Cassandra, especially since there was the concern that some zoo visitor—probably a teenager; it was always a teenager, on the news—would climb over the wall and scale the moat in order to try to pet a tiger. The number of locks involved would just keep any zookeeper who saw the incident from getting to the fool in time.

But maybe that, too, was part of the point. All it took was one mauling a decade to keep people out of the enclosures. It could be seen as a necessary sacrifice, letting the animals devour the one for the sake of the many who would be spared.

Even if that was true, Cassandra didn't want the sacrifice to involve her charges. Let some other zoo pay the price. Her tigers had done nothing wrong. They didn't deserve to die as an object lesson.

The day had only gotten prettier while she was inside, and stepping into the tiger enclosure—a place where tourists never got to litter, where snotty little children never got to chase the peacocks and squirrels into the trees, where the air smelled of big cat and fresh grass—made everything else seem trivial and small. She paused to take a deep breath, unbothered by the sharp, animal odor of tiger spoor clinging to the rocks. They had to mark their territory somehow.

The smell of rotting flesh assaulted her nostrils. She coughed, choking on her own breath, and clapped a hand over her nose. It wasn't enough to stop the scent from getting through. Whatever had died here, it had somehow managed to go unnoticed by the groundskeepers long enough to start to truly putrefy, turning the air septic. No wonder the tigers hadn't wanted to be outside. This was bad enough that *she* didn't want to be outside, and her nose was nowhere near as sensitive as theirs.

Hand still clasped over her nose, Cassandra started toward the source of the smell. It seemed to be coming from the moat that encircled the enclosure, keeping the tigers from jumping out. That made a certain amount of sense. Raccoons and opossums could fall down there, and the tigers couldn't get to them. If it had fallen behind a rock or something, that might even explain how it had gone unnoticed by the groundskeepers. They worked hard and knew their jobs, but they were only human.

So was the source of the smell.

Cassandra stopped at the edge of the moat, eyes going wide and hand slowly dropping from her mouth to dangle by her side as shock overwhelmed revulsion. There was a *man* at the bottom of the moat.

He wore the plain white attire of the night groundskeepers, who dressed that way to make themselves visible from a distance. He was shambling in loose, uncoordinated circles, bumping against the walls of the moat and reorienting himself, staggering off in the next direction. He must have been drunk, or under the influence of something less than legal, because he didn't seem to know or care where he was going: he just went, a human pinball, perpetually in motion.

From the way his left arm dangled, Cassandra was willing to bet that it was broken. Maybe he wasn't drunk. Maybe he was just in shock.

"Hey!" she called, cupping her hands around her mouth to make her voice carry farther. "Are you all right down there?"

The man looked up, turning toward the sound of her voice. His face was smeared with long-dried blood. Staring at her, he drew back his lips and snarled before walking into the wall again and again, like he could somehow walk through it to reach her. His gaze never wavered. He didn't blink.

Cassandra stumbled backward, clasping her hands over her mouth again, this time to stop herself from screaming.

She had been a zookeeper for five years. Before that, she had been a biology student. She had worked with animals for her entire adult life. She knew dead when she saw it.

That man was dead.

"Now, Cassandra, be reasonable," said the zoo administrator. He was a smug, oily man who smiled constantly, like a smile would be enough to chase trouble away. "I believe that something has fallen into the moat of the tiger enclosure, and I'm dispatching a maintenance crew to deal with it, but it's not a dead man. It's *certainly* not a dead man who keeps walking around. Did you get enough sleep last night? Is it possible that this is the stress speaking?"

"I always get enough sleep," she said, voice tight. "It's not safe to work with tigers if you're not sleeping. I slept, I ate, I drank water and coffee with breakfast, and I know what I saw. There's a man in the moat. He doesn't blink. He doesn't breathe. He's dead."

"But he's still walking. Cassandra, have you *listened* to yourself? You have to hear how insane this sounds."

Cassandra stiffened. "I'm not insane."

"Then maybe you shouldn't say things that make you sound

like you are." The administrator's walkie-talkie crackled. He grabbed it, depressing the button as he brought it to his mouth. "Well? Is everything taken care of?"

"Dan, we've got a problem." The response was faint, and not just because of the walkie-talkie: the speaker sounded like he was on the verge of passing out. "She was right."

Dan blanched. "What do you mean, she was right?"

"There's a man in the moat."

"A dead man?"

"That's biologically impossible. He's up and walking, if non-responsive to questions. Angela thinks it's Carl from the night crew. She's going to get his shift supervisor. But he doesn't an-swer when we call his name, and he keeps snarling at us when we try to offer down a hook. I don't think it's safe for people to approach him. I think he might get violent."

Dan glared at Cassandra as he asked his next question: "But he's not dead."

"That wouldn't make any sense. Dead men don't walk."

"Roger. Deal with it. I'll order the path shut down. Call me as soon as you know what's going on." Dan put the walkie-talkie aside. "So you were right about the man in the moat. That's an unexpected twist."

"Wait." Cassandra shook her head, staring at him. "You can't be serious."

"About what?"

"About shutting the path to the tiger enclosures. People always get around the barricades. They want to see blood. You have to shut down that whole portion of the zoo. Or wait—we haven't opened yet. Can't we just . . . not open? For a little while?"

"Not open. Are you sure that's what you want to recom-mend?" Dan stood. "I can keep people away from that area. I can protect the innocent eyes of children. But admission fees are what pay your salary and feed your precious cats. Do you really want to risk that?"

"No," admitted Cassandra. "But the man in the moat . . . something's really wrong with him. We shouldn't let anyone in until we know what it is."

"Everything will be fine. Go back to work." Dan walked to the door and opened it, holding it for her in clear invitation. After a moment's pause, Cassandra walked out of his office.

The day seemed less beautiful now, tainted somehow, as if the stranger in her moat had cast a pall over the entire sky. Cassandra walked quickly back toward the tigers, intending to help the rescue crew, and paused when she saw a familiar figure staggering across the grass. Michael was walking surprisingly slowly for a man who had never met a path he didn't want to jog on. He looked sick. Even from a distance, he looked sick.

"Michael?" she called, taking a step in his direction. "Are you all right?"

He turned to fully face her, lips drawing back. Cassandra paused, eyes widening. His eyes . . . they were like the eyes of the man in the moat.

He was her friend. She should help him. She should stay, and she should help him.

She turned, and she ran.

The tigers were still locked in their feeding pens, prowling back and forth and snarling at each other. They were restless. Even for big cats trapped temporarily in small cages, they were restless. It was like they could smell the taint in the air, warning them of trials yet to come.

"Sorry, guys," said Cassandra, stopping in the aisle between cages, well out of the reach of questing paws. The tigers didn't want to hurt her. She was almost certain of that. They still would. She was *absolutely* certain of that.

Humans had intelligence, and thought, and the ability to worry about the future. It made them great at things like "building zoos" and "taking over the world," and it made them terrible at being predators. Humans could plan. Humans could think about consequences. Tigers, though . . .

Tigers existed to hunt, and feed, and make more tigers. They existed for the sake of existence, without needing to care about whether tomorrow was going to come. She envied them sometimes. No one ever told a tiger that it didn't know how to be what it was. No one ever said "you must be mistaken," or implied that there was something wrong with a tiger because it didn't want to spend its time with confusing, contradictory humans.

One of the tigers yawned, showing her a vast array of fine, sharp teeth. Cassandra smiled.

"No, I'm not going to feed you early just because you're locked in the feeding cage," she said. "We'll have you out in the enclosure in no time, and you know the guests get cranky when you spend the whole day asleep and digesting. Be good, and this will all be over soon."

As if to put an immediate lie to her words, someone outside screamed.

Cassandra was running before she realized it. A large metal hook on a pole hung on the wall next to the door, intended to be used to remove snakes from the visitor paths and animal enclosures. She grabbed it without thinking. Something about that scream spoke to the need for weapons, the vital necessity of self-defense. Whatever was happening out there, she didn't want to race into it unarmed.

The smell of decay hit her as soon as she was outside the tiger run. It was thinner than it had been on the edge of the moat. It was stronger at the same time, like it was coming from more than one source. The person screamed again. Cassandra kept running.

The tiger exhibits had their own "island" in the zoo's design, dividing the public-facing portion of a large oval structure between themselves. Cassandra came around the curve of the wall and froze, grasp tightening on the snake hook as her eyes went wide, trying to take in every aspect of the scene.

The man from the moat was no longer in the moat. The security crew dispatched to help him had obviously done so, using their own, larger versions of Cassandra's snake hook. Those big hooks were on the ground, discarded. The security team had bigger things to worry about, like the man who was even now sinking his teeth into the throat of one of their own.

She had been screaming when he first started biting her. She wasn't screaming anymore. Instead, she was dangling limply in his arms while the other security people struggled to pull him away. For a dead man—and he *was* a dead man, he *must* have been a dead man; nothing living could smell so bad, or have skin so sallow and tattered, like he had slid down the side of the moat without so much as lifting his hands to defend himself—he had a remarkably strong grip. It took three security men to finally pull him off her.

He didn't go without a prize. The front of her throat came away with him, clasped firmly between his teeth. As Cassandra watched in horror, the security woman hit the ground, and the man chewed at his prize, still staring mindlessly ahead of himself.

This was not predation. Her tigers were predators, would eat a raccoon or a foolish zoo peacock as soon as they would look at it, but they were *aware* of what they were doing. There was a beautiful intelligence in their eyes, even when their muzzles were wet with blood and their shoulders were hunched in preemptive defense of their prey. Tigers *knew*. They might not understand the morality of their kills, but they *knew*.

This man . . . he didn't *know*. His eyes were blank, filmed over with a scrimshaw veil of decay. His jaws seemed to work automatically, inhaling the scrap of flesh he had ripped from the security woman.

The screaming hadn't stopped. It was just more dismay and anger now, as the security guards who weren't restraining the dead man tried to help their fallen coworker.

Then the man whipped around, faster than should have been possible, moving like he didn't care whether he dislocated his shoulders or broke his arms, and buried his teeth in the neck of the guard who was restraining him.

Then the woman without a throat opened her eyes and lunged for the person closest to her, biting down on their wrist. The screaming resumed, taking on a whole new edge of agony and horror. Cassandra's eyes got wider still. This was wrong. Everything about this was *wrong*, and she couldn't stay here any longer, she couldn't, this was wrong and unnatural and she needed to go, she needed to—

When she turned, Michael was standing right behind her.

He couldn't have been there for long; she had been working with predators for too long to be the kind of person who could be snuck up on. The same smell of putrefaction and decay that she had gotten from the man in the moat was coming off of him. Faint, as yet, but there; undeniably there. His eyes were filmed over, unseeing, unblinking.

"Please don't," she whispered.

He struck.

Everything was a blur after that. Cassandra didn't know how she'd been able to escape; only that she had, because it was like she had blinked and been standing in front of the tiger habitat first aid station, with the door firmly closed behind her and the tigers snarling down the hall, still confined in their feeding pens, growing slowly angrier and angrier. Blood had been sheeting down her arm from the deep bite in her shoulder, painting everything in red. The marks of human teeth were unmistakable.

Even if they hadn't been, the fact that Michael had left one of his crowns behind would have made it impossible to pretend that she had been bitten by anything other than a human being. Gritting her own teeth, she used the tweezers to extract the small piece of white porcelain from her flesh. It was jagged where it had snapped off, and had probably done almost as much damage to Michael as he had to her. But he hadn't seemed to notice. He hadn't seemed to *care*.

He had been gone. Impossible as it was to contemplate, sometime between asking her to take care of his charges and their encounter outside the tiger enclosures, he had died, and kept on walking.

"No," said Cassandra. She grabbed for the hydrogen peroxide bottle and emptied it over the wound. It foamed and bubbled and stung like anything, like it was supposed to, but the feeling of rotten wrongness remained, worming its way down toward the bone. "No, no, no. No."

No amount of denial would heal the wound in her arm, or chase the smell of decay from her arm. Time seemed to jump again, taking her along with it: this time, when the haze cleared, she was applying butterfly clips to the gauze encircling her arm, sealing the bite marks out of sight. They continued to throb. Out of sight was not out of mind.

"No," said Cassandra, somewhat more firmly. She shook her head, trying to prevent another jump. What *was* this?

Think about it logically. Think about it like a biologist. Yes: that was the ticket. Think about it like she was back in class, like the worst that could come from getting the answer wrong was a bad grade.

Michael's roommate had been acting strange this morning. Michael had come to work with a bite from that roommate fresh on his arm. Michael had been behaving normally. Now Michael was acting like the man from the moat, and he had bitten her. Michael smelled of decay.

The man in the moat had smelled of decay when she had found him; her first impression had been that he was dead, yet somehow still standing. He was wearing the uniform of the night groundskeepers. She had seen wounds on him, but they had all been consistent with sliding down the side of the rocky wall between the fence line and the ground. What if nothing had bitten him? What if he'd just . . . fallen? It was always a risk, especially when the staff had to lean over the low retaining wall to retrieve something from the moat's edge. There had been falls before.

The woman, the security guard . . . the man from the moat had bitten her. He had torn her throat out with his teeth, and she had died. Cassandra had no doubt at all that the woman had died. She'd *seen* it. But after dying, she had started moving again, attacking another member of her team. So what if . . .

What if the man in the moat had died, only to come back again as something that wasn't quite human anymore? Something dead and terrible, that looked like a human being but smelled like the grave, and only wanted to . . . what? Feed? Bite?

Pass the . . . curse, infection, whatever it was along?

Cassandra turned to look at the bandage on her own arm. Michael hadn't died. Not like the woman. Michael had been *fine*. Human mouths were filthy things, but a bite wouldn't be enough to kill a healthy man, not under ordinary circumstances. She could feel the hot pulsing buried deep in her flesh, telling her that something was very, very wrong. Whatever had been in him, it was in her now, too. Hurting her. Maybe killing her.

"Okay," she said, as much to hear her own voice as for any other reason. "I need to get out of here." Michael's mistake had been coming to work instead of going to the doctor. Doctors could flush the wound, could make things better. Could *fix* it.

She had long since accepted the fact that one mistake at her job could put her in the ground. But she wasn't going to die like this.

Feeling better now that she had a plan, Cassandra started for the door. She needed to get to the locker room, to retrieve her purse and her car keys. She would tell Dan that it didn't matter whether he closed the zoo today, because she wouldn't be here either way. She would be at the doctor's office, getting the flesh on her arm debrided and patched up, until the hot pulsing from within stopped. Until she wasn't scared anymore.

The tigers paced and muttered in their deep feline voices

as she passed them, expressing their displeasure with the whole situation. Cassandra smiled wanly.

"I need to be sure the dead man isn't in front of your enclosure anymore before I let you out," she said. "If he fell back in, that would only upset you. I'll make sure someone comes to open the gates, I promise."

The tigers didn't speak English, but she had been their handler for years. Most stopped grumbling and just looked at her, staring with their wide amber eyes. They trusted her, as much as one apex predator could trust another.

"I promise," Cassandra said again, and opened the door to the outside.

The smell of decay was like an assault. Behind her, the tigers roared and snarled, protesting this invasion. She couldn't see anyone, but that didn't have to mean anything: not when she could smell them.

The zoo grounds had never seemed so claustrophobic before, so crowded with thick bushes and copses of trees. How many dead people could be lurking in there?

This couldn't be happening. This couldn't be happening. This *couldn't* be *happening*. She would get to the locker room, get her purse, and drive herself to the hospital. Maybe stop long enough to make a few phone calls, to make sure that whatever was going on at the zoo was *only* going on at the zoo. Michael's roommate was confined to their apartment, right? And Michael could have been exposed here, at work, picking up some . . . some novel parasite or tropical disease from one of the animals. Spillover diseases didn't always look the same in people as they did in their original hosts. This could be, could be a flu, or a respiratory illness, or *something*, that behaved in a new, terrifying way when it got into a human be-ing. It could be—

Cassandra crested the hill and froze, getting her first look at the zoo's entry plaza.

They had opened the gates after all. Sometime between her leaving Dan's office and coming to in the back hall of the big cat building, someone had turned on the carousel and opened the gates, letting the public—letting the dead—come to the zoo one last time. Bodies thronged around the admin build-ings, moving with that same odd, graceless hitch that she had seen in Michael, before he had attacked her. Whatever this was, it was spreading with horrific speed. Based on what she'd seen in front of the tiger enclosure, it wasn't unreasonable to think that it was spreading to everyone who was bitten.

Including her. She had been bitten. It was spreading—it had spread—to her.

Maybe that would protect her. If this was a disease, they might not attack someone who had already been infected. There was no sense in taking chances: if she got killed, who would take care of the tigers? They were trapped, penned in their little cages, without even the freedom of their enclosures to enjoy. She needed to make it back to them, now more than ever. But she also needed to see. She *had* to.

Carefully, Cassandra crept closer, sticking to the edges of the underbrush, where she might be ambushed, but she was less likely to be seen. When she came to one of the staff gates in the fence, she opened it and slipped through, relieved to see that the path was clear. These pathways were mostly used to transport things—food, equipment, sick animals—during the day; until the crowds got thick around noon, even the most privacy-loving zookeepers would tend to stick to the public side of the zoo. Maybe she could get to the gates without further incident.

Maybe it wouldn't matter.

The throbbing from her arm was getting worse and worse, reminding her with every step that this was how it had started for Michael. Whatever this was, it spread through the bites. If she didn't get medical help soon, she was going to become like them: dead, but still moving, still standing. Still biting. She was going to become a dangerous predator, something both more than animal and less than human.

The path ended at a slatted gate looking out over the zoo's front plaza. The merry-go-round was running, the painted horses dancing up and down in their eternal slow ballet. Cassandra stopped a few feet back, looking silently at the crowd that pressed around the classic amusement. They swayed and shambled, eyes glazed over and focusing on nothing. The smell that rose from their bodies was thick and undeniable, the smell of death, the smell of things decaying where they stood.

There had been people riding the merry-go-round when . . . whatever had happened here had happened. Some of them were still tangled in their safety belts, dangling from their painted horses, unable to free themselves as they pawed mindlessly at the air. Cassandra's stomach churned, bile rising in the back of her throat.

Soon that will be me, she thought. *Soon I will be one of them.*

What would happen to her tigers then? What would happen to Michael's otters, or Betsy's zebras, or any of the other animals in the zoo? Some of them were already doomed, unable to survive in this ecosystem, but others . . .

She could see the parking lot from her current position.

There were dead, shambling people moving there, too. As she watched, a group of them caught up with a screaming man and drove him to the ground, where he vanished beneath a hail of bodies. This wasn't contained to the zoo. This could never have been contained.

Cassandra turned her back on the scene in the front plaza. She had work to do.

Any disease that hit this hard and spread this exponentially was going to overwhelm the city in a matter of hours: that was just simple math. One was bad; two was worse; four was a disaster. The numbers kept climbing from there, until she reached the point where the dead outnumbered the living, and there was nothing left to do but die.

If she hadn't been bitten, she might have tried to find another way. The big cat house, especially, had hundreds of pounds of raw meat stored in the freezers, just in case, and doors that were designed to stand up to a raging male lion. She could have locked herself inside with her beloved cats. She could have tried to wait it out.

But her arm burned, throbbing with every heartbeat, and she was starting to feel . . . bad. Feverish. Like she wanted nothing more than to lie down for a nap, to close her eyes and let her body finish the transition it was clearly aching to undergo. She needed to act quickly, before she was no longer equipped to act at all.

She began with the herbivores. She opened doors and propped gates, leaving the avenues of escape open for anything that wanted to take them. By the time she made her way to the aviary, there were zebras cropping at the lawn, ears flicking wildly back and forth as they scanned for danger. A kangaroo went bounding away down a side path, all but flying in its haste to get away. If there were dead people lurking in the bushes, they weren't fast enough to catch it.

The birds knew something was wrong. As she opened their cages, they flew away, wings clawing at the air, and were gone. Some of them would make it. Some of them had to make it.

Slowly, almost shambling now, she made her way back to the big cat house. The smell of decay was less noticeable now, maybe because she was adding to it. Maybe because her nose was dying with the rest of her.

There were so many doors she hadn't opened. There were so many cages she hadn't unlocked. But there wasn't time, and she didn't want to endanger her animals. Not in the end. Not when the burning in her arm had become nothing more than a dull and distant throb, like the nerves were giving up.

The tigers stopped their pacing when she came into view, staring at her silently. Cassandra pulled out her keys.

"Try . . . not to eat me, okay?" she rasped, and started down the line of cages. One by one, she unlocked them, leaving them standing open. When she finished with the tigers, she began releasing the lions, the cheetahs, until she was at the end of the hallway with a dozen massive predators between her and freedom. They looked at her. She looked at them.

One by one, they turned and walked away, heading for the open door; heading for freedom. Cassandra followed them until she reached the main door to the tiger enclosure. Her fingers didn't want to cooperate, didn't want to work the key or let her turn the lock. She fought through the numbness, until the bolt clicked open and she stepped through, into the open air on the other side.

The door, unbraced, swung shut and locked itself behind her. Cassandra didn't care.

Stumbling, she walked across the uneven ground to the rock where her big male liked to sun himself during the hottest hours of the day. She sat down. She closed her eyes. In the distance, the merry-go-round played on, a soft counterpart to the slowing tempo of her heart.

Cassandra stayed where she was, and waited for the music to stop.

Brian Keene writes novels, comic books, short fiction, and occasional journalism for money. He is the author of more than forty books, mostly in the horror, crime, and dark fantasy genres. His 2003 novel *The Rising* is often credited (along with Robert Kirkman's *The Walking Dead* comic and Danny Boyle's *28 Days Later* film) with inspiring pop culture's current interest in zombies.

PAGES FROM A NOTE-BOOK FOUND INSIDE A HOUSE IN THE WOODS

by Brian Keene

In hindsight, it was probably a dumb idea, but it didn't seem like it when John was explaining it to us. Robbing a bank was a fool's errand, he said, what with all the security technology they have now. Sticking up a supermarket or store was also stupid—too hard to keep the crowd controlled, too many people shopping with plastic rather than cash, and too many chances of some well-meaning civilian wanting to play hero. John said instead, we should pull a heist at the comic book convention—not that big event in San Diego, but the small, regional con right here in rural central Pennsylvania.

So that's what we did—me, John, Tiny, Phil, and Marko. We went in disguise. Later, if the witnesses described us, they would have said the four perpetrators were two super-heroes, an alien, and a clown. Tiny stayed out in the car, so he didn't wear a costume. We walked up to the registration area, displayed our guns (which the other attendees had mis-taken for props), and took all the cash. The girls behind the counter—their nametags read KAREN and ALICIA—seemed to have trouble believing it was happening. Karen kept saying, over and over, "But this is a comic book convention."

We got a nice haul, and we didn't have to kill anybody.

The killing began soon after, and we weren't the ones who started it.

I'm not a bad guy. Well, okay, maybe I'm a bad guy, but I'm not a bad *man*. I've got a wife and kid—Cherie and Pete Junior. He's only two years old, and folks say he looks like me, but I don't think that's true. He's got his mother's same big, beau-tiful brown eyes. You do what you have to do to provide for your family. Some people go to work at the Harley-Davidson plant. Some work at the paper mill. Others go to an office or some sales job to feed their family. Me? I'm a stickup man. I've never hurt anybody. I'm not some shithead mugger, rob-bing people of whatever's in their wallet. I've only ever stolen from big places—the type of joints that have insurance to fi-nancially protect against people like me.

I miss Cherie and Pete Junior. I hope they're okay. I hope things are different where they are . . . but then I go upstairs and look out the window at all those dead people, and that hope fizzles.

Anyway, robbing the convention was smooth and easy. Things didn't start falling apart until we got outside. We heard police sirens, and I remember thinking it sounded like they were racing in different directions, rather than converging on our location. We heard some ambulance sirens, too. Yes, they sound different. Folks like you probably can't tell the difference, but in my line of work, I need to.

Thinking back on it now, the cops never did roll up on us. That wasn't the problem I mentioned. No. What went wrong was Tiny. We'd been so intent on planning and surveillance and mapping getaway routes, we hadn't bothered to make sure Tiny checked the car. That was his job. His one fucking job. Get us a car with valid tags, registration, and inspection sticker. Make sure the headlights and brake lights worked. Make sure there was absolutely nothing about the car that could get us pulled over by some cop out to make his ticket quota. And Tiny did all of those things, and did them well, because we'd told him to. It never occurred to us we'd have to remind Tiny to gas up the fucking fuel tank as well.

We ran out of gas four blocks away from the Holiday Inn where the convention was taking place, near the outskirts of town. There was lots of cursing and name calling and threats, but in the end, we just sort of accepted our situation with grim resignation. Marko tried to carjack a passing station wagon, but the driver merely gaped at the sight of a clown waving a gun at him, swerved around Marko, and sped away.

John shouldered the backpack with the money and led us down an alley and along some railroad tracks. He cursed Tiny a few more times. Phil echoed him, punctuating John's swearing with some profanity of his own. Marko cursed the driver of the station wagon. I stayed quiet, figuring I'd save my breath in case we had to run. Tiny stayed quiet, too, but I think that's because he was embarrassed and frustrated with himself and trying very hard not to cry in front of us.

We heard more sirens, and at one point, somebody shrieked, but the sound was far away, and had nothing to do with us. More troublesome were the occasional gunshots, echoing from different directions.

"The fuck is going on?" Phil muttered. "That can't be for us."

"Maybe we're at war," Tiny suggested.

We reached an abandoned factory—something that's as common in Pennsylvania as trees or convenience stores—and ditched our costumes. I was grateful to take off the mask. My face was covered in sweat and my glasses kept fogging up while I'd worn it. The area around the factory smelled rancid. I assumed that there must be a dead animal nearby, maybe down on the train tracks. I didn't bring it up with the others, but I noticed Tiny and Phil cringing at the stench. We dropped our disguises into an old fifty-five-gallon drum of waste oil, and debated what to do next.

That was when we saw the first dead guy.

A chain-link fence rattled to our left. We all turned. The fence surrounded the factory's parking lot. The asphalt was cracked and pitted, and limp brown weeds thrust up from the fissures. The fence itself was rusty and sagged in some places. The dead guy slumped against it.

How did we know he was dead?

Well, the best indicator was the fact that his fucking throat had been slit from ear to ear. Blood caked the guy's shirt and pants. The wound wasn't clean and neat. Not the kind of cut a razor would make. This looked more like somebody had been at him with a hacksaw. The cut looked kind of like a smiley face, as if he had a second mouth beneath his chin, and was grinning at us with it. I'd heard rumors that the cartels were moving into our area, and wondered briefly if it was related to that. But then I focused on the more important matter at hand—namely, how the hell the guy was up and walking around, despite his condition.

He stared at us, unblinking. I think his eyes were more unnerving than his injury. It was his eyes that cemented it for me. This guy was dead. Nothing living has eyes like that. Except for maybe a shark.

The fence rattled again as he lurched toward us on wobbly legs. His movements were disjointed. He opened his mouth but no sound came out. I saw something move deep inside his wound. Vocal cords, maybe? I don't know. It bothers me just to think about it.

Surprisingly, we didn't run. I don't know why. I can't speak for the others, but in my case, it just didn't occur to me. I stood there, staring at him the way you slow down to gawk at a car crash, until he was almost upon us. I don't even remember feeling afraid or in danger. Instead, I was noticing things about him—how he smelled (it had been him, rather than a dead animal, that I'd noticed upon our arrival), the color and texture of his skin (like light gray cheesecloth), but mostly those eyes. He was dead, but there was still emotion in them.

Hunger.

Phil pulled his pistol while the rest of us stood gaping.

"Don't come any closer, asshole," he warned.

The dead guy's mouth worked pitifully, lips mashing together, but still no sound came out.

"I mean it," Phil said, stepping closer.

When the dead guy didn't stop, Phil strode up to him and shoved the barrel of his pistol against the man's chest. The dead guy lunged, wrapping his arms around Phil's neck. Shouting, Phil squeezed his trigger. The shot was muffled by the dead man's body. Then Phil fired two more rounds. The dead guy stumbled and jittered as the bullets tore through him. For a second, I thought he'd lose his grip on Phil, but instead, his head darted forward, and he clamped his teeth down on Phil's neck.

Phil screamed. Then the rest of us joined him.

The dead man jerked his head back. A piece of Phil's skin dangled from his mouth. Blood bubbled from the wound, and then sprayed, as if someone had turned on a garden hose inside of Phil. Still shrieking, Phil dropped his gun and beat at his attacker. The dead man chewed his prize and stumbled backward. He grasped at Phil, those dead eyes focused in on the pumping blood. Phil dropped to his knees, hands clasping his wound, trying desperately to staunch the blood flow. He opened his mouth to plead with us and blood bubbled out.

John and Marko opened fire, drilling the dead man. This time, the shots weren't muffled. My ears rang from the sound. Empty shell casings pinged on the dirt and asphalt. The dead guy twitched and stumbled, but then plodded forward again, reaching for Phil. He didn't stop until one of them shot him in the head. Then he dropped, as if a switch had been turned off.

I ran over to Phil and knelt beside him, searching for a pulse, while Marko prodded the attacker with the toe of his shoe. I felt a hand on my shoulder and almost screamed again, but then I realized it was John, crouching down behind me.

"Is he . . . ?"

"I don't know. It's hard to feel anything beneath all this blood."

John clutched Phil's wrist and checked for a pulse there, while I slid my fingers along the uninjured side of his throat.

"Nothing," he reported.

I shook my head.

"We gotta do that CPR shit," Tiny urged. "Maybe we can keep him alive long enough to get him to a hospital."

John stuffed his gun into his waistband, then hissed because the barrel was still hot. He jerked it out again.

"We gotta do something," Tiny repeated.

"He's dead, Tiny," I said. "Nothing we can do."

"We need to get out of here," John said. "I guarantee some-body heard all that shooting."

Marko nodded. "Let's jet."

He and John headed for the train tracks. I hesitated, cast one glance back at Phil's corpse, and then trotted off after them.

"Come on, Tiny," I said. "They're right. Only thing we can do for Phil now is to not get caught."

We had just started down the embankment when Phil got up again. He groaned and shook, and moved like a toddler just learning to walk. For a moment, I wondered if we'd been wrong—maybe he hadn't been dead. But then I noticed two things. His wound had stopped bleeding. And his eyes . . .

This time, it was me who pulled his gun first. Taking a les-son from what had finally dropped the first living dead man, I aimed for Phil's head. The first bullet tore out what was left of his throat. He stumbled forward, moaning. My second shot hit him above the left eye. Part of his brains splattered out behind him, steaming on the asphalt. And with that, Phil died again.

Then we ran, following the railroad tracks into the woods.

By the time we stumbled across this house, we'd picked up quite a following of dead people. They loped along behind us, slowly rotting with each step, shedding body parts and organs as easily as you or I shed our clothes. Luckily, they couldn't run, so we were able to stay ahead of them. The only thing we couldn't outrun was their stench. Not all of them stank, mind you. At least, not the fresh ones. But the ones who had apparently been dead for a few days? They were like walking roadkill. It didn't help matters that it was the height of summer. The heat and humidity only added to the reek. With no breeze blowing, the stink sort of sat in the air like a mist.

Just as it had with Phil and his attacker, the only thing that seemed to work against the dead was damage to their brains. We saw corpses missing arms and legs, disemboweled, or suffering horrific injuries, but they kept on coming. At first, we wasted a lot of bullets trying to pick off our pursuers. Shooting someone in the head, from a distance and with a pistol, looks easy on television, but it's much harder in real life. Worse, the gunshots attracted more of the fuckers. Eventually, we just focused on evading them.

I won't spend time describing the house. If you're reading this, then you already know what it looks like. Just another crumbling farmhouse, abandoned out in the middle of the woods, like so many other rural properties in this part of the country. Unlike that collapsed chicken coop outside, or the barn that's leaning heavily to one side, the house was in surprisingly good shape. No broken windows or holes in the roof. We thought it might be occupied, since the doors were unlocked, but once we got inside and saw the dust and cobwebs for ourselves, we knew it had been a long time since anyone lived here.

We swept old, musty books onto the floor and shoved the dust-laden shelves in front of the windows, and pushed a moldering couch against the front door (after locking the dead bolt). We blocked the kitchen door with the refrigerator, and then barricaded all the other windows on the first floor. Then, for the first time since entering the comic book convention, we had a moment to breathe and collect ourselves. Eventually, the dead found us. We didn't have to see them to know they had arrived. Their smell and sounds gave them away.

Those first few hours were nerve-wracking. Groaning and hissing, the corpses banged on the walls and windows and fumbled at the door, but our fortifications held. After a while, we relaxed enough to explore the rest of the house. Tiny was sent to guard the back door and Marko stood watch in the living room, while John and I took inventory. The electricity was out, but there was plenty of canned food and dry goods in the cupboard, and we found six cases of bottled spring water downstairs, along with two cases of soda. We wouldn't starve right away, and as long as we conserved, we could make the water last a bit.

Oddly, the previous tenants had apparently left in a hurry, leaving their belongings behind. Framed family photographs still hung on the walls, and keepsakes and mementos lined shelves and crannies. All of their clothing still hung in the closets, musty and mildewed, but otherwise in decent shape. The food in the refrigerator had long since rotted (as we discovered when moving it to form the barricade), and the dirty dishes left behind in the sink were almost as revolting as the things outside. They'd even left their guns behind. We found a beautiful wooden gun case on the second floor, with ornate glass doors and a storage shelf beneath. Inside were two deer rifles, a shotgun, and a pistol. John took a rifle, and I kept the shotgun, and we gave the other weapons to Tiny and Marko. I won't lie. Somehow, just holding that shotgun made me feel better about our situation in ways my handgun hadn't.

Unfortunately, that feeling didn't last very long.

Tiny saw the woman first.

We slept in shifts—two of us on guard downstairs while the other two bedded down upstairs. John and I were on watch, sometime around two in the morning. The dead were still clamoring outside. I'd found a jar of instant coffee in the kitchen, and was just about to stir the crystals into a bottle of water, when Tiny started screaming.

John and I both ran upstairs. We nearly collided with Marko, emerging from his bedroom bleary-eyed and confused. Tiny was sitting up on the bed, staring at us with wide-eyed panic, babbling nonsensically. When he finally calmed down, he told us that he'd felt somebody sit down on the bed. He even heard the box spring squeak, as if a weight had been placed on it. When he sat up, he saw a depression on the mattress, as if someone were sitting there—but there was nobody else in the room. Then, the springs squeaked again and the depression disappeared. Footsteps sounded slowly across the floor. As Tiny watched, a woman appeared. She opened the door, glanced back at him with what he called "terrible eyes," and then vanished.

All three of us chalked it up to a bad dream. Tiny insisted it wasn't. He said he couldn't sleep, and offered to switch with me. Tired as I was, I accepted. The guys left my bedroom door open. Marko went back to sleep and John and Tiny headed downstairs. Sighing, I lay down in the bed with my clothes still on. I was so exhausted, I barely remembered to take off my shoes. The pillow, despite its musty odor, felt like heaven.

Then my bedroom door slammed, hard enough to rattle the hinges, and I bolted upright in bed, instantly awake again. I heard Marko curse on the other side of the wall, and John and Tiny shouting queries from below.

I didn't sleep the rest of the night.

Throughout the next day, we were all presented with evidence that what Tiny had seen was, in fact, not a bad dream. Doors and cupboards opened and closed at random. Footsteps echoed throughout the house. Something knocked repeatedly on the coffee table. The spigots on the kitchen sink turned by themselves. We felt like we were being watched—all the time.

On the third day, Marko saw the woman, as well. She appeared at the top of the stairs and vanished about halfway down. He looked at the portraits on the wall and pointed to a woman in several of them, insisting that was her. Tiny confirmed it was the same woman he'd seen, too.

That night, something pushed Marko down the stairs. At least, I'm assuming he was pushed. Marko was a big guy, but despite his formidable size, he was never clumsy. He was on his way to the second floor, intent on looking out the windows and seeing how many dead people were outside. We suspected, judging by their clamor, that reinforcements had arrived, perhaps attracted by the noise from others. I remember watching him ascend. John made some wisecrack, and Marko glanced back at him, his mouth forming a reply, and then *wham*—he flew backward, feet leaving the stairs, and tumbled to the bottom. Like I said, it looked like he was pushed. Marko was never able to verify for us what happened, because he broke his neck in the fall and was dead by the time we reached him.

He got back up a few minutes later, moaning just like the rest of those rotten fucks outside. John put him down again. The sound of the gunshot seemed to stir up the dead. None of us slept. We sat huddled together in the living room, desperately trying to come up with a plan.

By morning, John had decided to go for help. Tiny and I weren't crazy about the plan. We didn't like the idea of being left alone in the house with this . . . well, let's call it what it is. A ghost. And we definitely didn't want to open the door, even for a second, and risk letting the hordes inside. But John, just like always, convinced us. He talked us into it, just like he'd talked us into the heist. He even said he'd leave the money from the heist with us.

The plan was he'd sneak out the front door. Tiny would distract the dead, rattling a window to draw them away from the door. We'd open it only for a second, giving John just enough time to get out. Then we'd bolt it shut again and slide the couch back in place. He figured he could outrun the corpses, and lose them once he got into the woods. Then he'd find help. But, just like it had after the robbery, things quickly went to shit.

We couldn't get the door open. Tiny did a great job of creating a disturbance and distracting the dead, but the damn door wouldn't budge. The dead bolt turned, but when I pulled the doorknob, nothing happened. John tried it next, and then both of us, but no luck. Then, as we watched, the dead bolt slid slowly back into place.

"She doesn't want to let us out," I whispered.

"Fuck that." John raised his voice. "You hear that, bitch? Fuck you and your house."

He dashed upstairs. Tiny and I ran after him. When the windows wouldn't open, John smashed one of them out with the butt of his rifle. Before we could stop him, he clambered out onto the roof and climbed over the side, dangling from the gutter. Then he let go and dropped to the ground. For a few harrowing seconds, we couldn't see him, but then he appeared, weaving and dodging the dead like a football player going for the touchdown.

The opposing team sacked him a few yards later, and howled as they tore him apart.

He was far enough away that it's hard to know for sure, but I think I saw his mouth and eyes moving after they'd eaten the rest of him. And his head is still there, even as I write this. What if the dead are aware? What if part of John is still conscious inside that decapitated head?

The next day, we found all of our water bottles poured out on the kitchen floor.

Tiny and I vowed not to sleep, but I did anyway, slumped against the wall. It was the shotgun blast that woke me up.

I don't know if he killed himself or if the ghost did it for him. At least the blast took off most of his head, so I didn't have to worry about him coming back to eat me.

Now it's just me and the dead. The dead outside and the dead in here with me. I'm beyond scared. Beyond panicked. At this point, I'm just numb. I can't sleep. I'm thirsty.

Cherie and I used to go to the movies a lot, before Pete Junior was born. I remember this one time; we saw a haunted house flick. On the way home, Cherie asked why the people inside the house didn't just leave. It was a good question. But now I know why. They didn't leave because the ghost wouldn't let them. I've tried a couple times since Tiny killed himself, and the ghost won't let me open the door.

The corpses outside are restless. And me?

I'm just sitting here watching the door, waiting to see if it opens by itself.

Chuck Wendig is an American author, comic book writer, screenwriter, and blogger. He's known for his wildly popular online blog, *Terribleminds,* for his *New York Times* bestselling Star Wars: Aftermath series and for his accursed, profane psychic character, Miriam Black.

DEAD RUN

by Chuck Wendig

No one's ever woken my ass up with smelling salts before, so when Billy does it, it hits my nose and hits my brain like a herd of cattle going over the edge of a cliff. My head whips back and the world goes full-tilt boogie for the better part of five seconds.

But it's only my head that moves. My hands? Bound behind me. My feet are fixed beneath me. Takes me a second to figure that out: *I'm tied to a goddamn chair.* Held fast by a generous swaddling of duct tape.

Billy's face roams into view: those scrubby cheeks, that wild hair, that grin that shows off his one cracked canine.

"I got you, brother," is the first thing he says.

I got you, brother.

He says it like it's a good thing. Like he's taking care of me. (Ain't that ironic.)

"Billy, you shit, let me go."

"Maybe soon," he says. "Maybe soon."

He pats my cheek, *pat pat pat*, way a parent condescends to a child.

I think to ask him where we're at, but my eyes adjust quick enough and tell me true: we're at Mom and Pop's cabin up near Lake Wallenpaupack. Cobwebs haunt the corners like ghosts. Everything's got a greasy sheen of dust on it. An Amish hex hangs above the door. One of Grammy's quilts hangs above that old leather couch. Kitchen to my right. Hallway and a pair of bedrooms to my left. All around are windows and beyond the glass is the black of night.

On a nightstand, I see it:

My gun. It's a Smith & Wesson 327. Big grip .357 Magnum with the stubbiest two-inch barrel you've ever seen. Like a thumb that'll pop the brain out the back of your head. I keep that in the truck with me always, just in case. Never know what's out there on the road, from coyotes to carjackers. And now, so much worse.

"Why are we here, Billy?" I ask, struggling.

"You know why, Max. You know why."

"Truck's outside?"

"Truck's outside. Trailer, too."

"Then let me *free*. We gotta go. This isn't a time to fuck around, Billy. Things are bad out there. Something's happening—"

"Something's *happened*."

"Whatever!" I bark, angrier-sounding than I mean. "Let me go."

"I can't do that." He's pacing, now. Back and forth, back and forth, like he wants to wear a rut in the ratty rug on the wooden floor. Every step creaks like the troubled dead. "You know I can't."

"You're high."

"A little. Just pills. It's a good high. I'm thinking straight."

Goddamnit. I try to sand down the bumps in my voice, try to speak calmly—I can't razz him, or he'll just recoil further. "Billy. I came to get you because—because I wanted family to be together in this. We're the last of what we got. Just you and me, now. I saw what was going on out there—not just on the news, Billy, but I saw it on the highway, I saw it in neighborhoods—and I knew I had to come get you." My mother's voice rises up in me like an echo bouncing through a cavern: *Take care of him, he needs you. Care of him, he needs you. Care of him, needs you . . .*

Billy stops. He's got a smile hanging between his cheek-bones but it's not a happy one. A sadness lives there. Or maybe died there. "I know, brother. I know. But I also know what you wanted to do. And I couldn't let you do it. This isn't about them. This is about us."

"We can help people."

"We need to help ourselves."

"Billy, goddamnit!" That's when I lose my cool. I feel heat go to my cheeks. Spit wets my lips. I yell at him. I call him names. I don't mean to. He's weak and confused and never had his shit together and I'm here taking him apart like I'm whit-tling twigs with a hunting knife. Every word hurts him, and I can tell because he flinches like he's taking punches. Finally

I guess he just has enough, because next thing I know, he's pulling out a toolbox from under the side table and drawing a band of duct tape from the roll with a sticky stutter—he wraps it around my head a couple times to shut me up. It only makes me madder, but eventually I'm glad to just hear myself stop yelling. But it leaves me to my thoughts.

And in my thoughts, I think about *them*.

First one I saw was on the road. Girl came running up out of the woods along 80, running right out in front of the truck, arms pinwheeling, dress caught in the wind. My foot jammed the brakes. Hydraulics screamed as the truck lurched to a halt—all the while me praying to whatever god that governs the highways that I wouldn't jackknife my truck. It didn't. She staggered, fell at the shock of seeing my Peterbilt coming at her.

Then something came out of the woods.

I say something, because that's what it was. It was human-shaped. But it damn sure wasn't human. It came slow. One leg hanging limp like a piece of meat it had to drag along instead of use, a sharp bone coming out of its thigh—broken like a broom handle you snapped over one knee.

As it stepped into the light from my truck, I saw that its face was mostly gone. Forehead just a red rotten mess. Scalp ragged. The jaw was still intact, but off-kilter, like it had been set a couple inches too far to one side, and it worked the air with a kind of eager, malevolent hunger. Everything about it was gray. Gray like old meat.

I like to think I got out of that truck, a hero, and saved the day.

But I didn't.

Best I could muster was lying on the horn hard. And the Peterbilt has a good one—sounds like a boat coming in through the fog. It woke the girl up, got her back up and running in the direction she was going.

The thing out there, that dead thing, the horn got its attention.

It turned toward me. That jaw opening wide, too wide, like a snake thinking on swallowing a fat hare whole. Its tongue flipped and flopped.

I hit the gas. Truck like mine doesn't leap when it's kicked—it's not quick to rouse. But it hissed and it lumbered to a hard and certain roll, and the thing ahead of me didn't seem to think twice about it. A pair of hands reached for the truck as the lights swallowed it. Like the fucking thing thought it could catch me or something, like it could just reach up and pluck me out through the glass. It couldn't. The truck rolled over it. The bumper thudded dully against its head. I felt every tire of the truck and the trailer run over the thing's body, *thump, whump, badump*. One after the next.

Looking back in the rearview, I saw it in the hell's glow of the taillights—still moving around even though it had been flattened there like a squirrel. Arms up, reaching for nothing, as if to pull itself up by grabbing hold of the light of the moon.

That thing wasn't human.

And neither was the scared sound that rose up out of me.

Second one I saw, I saw in a Giant Eagle parking lot. There by the shopping carts, one of the dead things was lying across a person—still alive, I think—eating out of the back of the guy's head like it was a soup bowl. Problem is, the dead thing had no bottom. Its torso was gone—all spine and loops of bowels, so as it ate, whatever it ate came back out the bottom. Like it was just making sausage.

The man screamed. I threw up.

I saw more that night. More of *them*.

Saw them out there in the woods along the road. Across the highway. Stumbling across overpasses. I hit a few more with my truck. Didn't stop. Plowed forward. My tires turned them to slop and I kept on keeping on.

That's when I had the plan.

My trucking company has me doing runs for the store, Giant Eagle. Grocery runs. Not refrigerated, no, but stuff from the Emp-Ag food company—Emp-Ag owns a whole lot. A fifth of what you see on shelves probably comes from one of their companies. They own cereal, soup, spices, soda, bottled water. They own organic brands and store brands. They own highfalutin hipster locavore small-batch bullshit and they own the stuff only poor people can buy. They own it all.

And I carry it all.

I don't just carry one thing at a time, either. It's not just a truck full of cereal. It's pallets of everything. Food and water, the two core components of survival since fish walked out of water and grew getaway sticks. Cereal and soda. Beef jerky and lemonade. I got every last bit.

And as the fire sirens went off, and as the radio went dead, I knew this was something big and bad and I knew that maybe one day it would be okay again, but that day wasn't today, and that meant I had to survive whatever this was and whatever was still coming down the pike.

But I don't believe in surviving alone. Being a truck driver, sure, you're alone, but you're part of something. You're a blood cell in the American artery. I move things from Point A to Point B. You want to see the country fall apart, you take out the truckers first. Wanna save the country, you save the truck drivers. We'll keep it all together.

So I said to myself, *you ain't taking me out.*

I thought, *I'm gonna take this show on the road.*

I know the highways. I know the back roads.

I know the towns with good people.

I know who needs help.

The vision bloomed like a flower in my head, made me feel mad and giddy like I was high on something other than my own pants-shitting fear. I'll drive around. I'll give out food and water. Maybe I'll find a town to hunker down in, help the people there. The Peterbilt can get me there. It'll get me through all these suckers. Mow 'em down, one by one.

But first, I thought, I needed my brother.

Billy wakes me up by talking. I didn't even know I fell asleep, but I did—nose whistling as the tape pulls hard at my stubbled cheeks. My chin had dipped to my chest and when I yank my head back pain shoots through my neck just from sitting in a bad position for so long.

"Climate change," he's saying, like I missed the first part of the thought. "Thawing everything out. You get reindeer thawed out and then you get anthrax coming back. Maybe it's anthrax or something like it." He looks at me, then says, "Oh, you're awake," like he knew I was asleep but just kept talking anyway. "I was just saying, it's climate change. We did this to ourselves. Warmed everything up and diseases are rampant."

He comes over, rips part of the tape off my mouth—the flap hangs loose, so when I talk, it flutters like the wing of a moth. My cheeks burn like they've been slapped.

"It's not a disease," I say, wincing. "Diseases don't do this."

"You don't know that. I read things. You never read much."

"I read comic books."

"There's your problem," he says, snapping his fingers. "I read like, *books* books, brother. You know there's a fungus that turns ants into zombies? And wasps that can control roaches by messing with their heads? There's that cat-shit parasite, too. Changes the way you think of things. Makes rats wanna fuck cats. Turns humans into hoarders. We haven't even cracked the case on what microbes and parasites can do."

"Doesn't matter what it is," I say. My voice sounds like I'm humming through a jar of gravel. "You and me aren't going to fix it. But what we can do is help people."

"We help each other. We're family."

"We can help other survivors, too."

"They aren't *family*."

"They don't have to be."

"Yes they do!" he says, hurrying over, his jaw so tight I'm afraid he might crack a tooth. "They do. Mom and Pop said family was everything."

"Dad was a police officer. He knew it was bigger than that."

Billy leans back then. Smug, somehow. Arms folded in front of him all protective. "And where'd that get him, huh?"

It got him dead, Billy. We all know that.

"Fuck you, Billy. You weak-ass piece of shit."

He slaps the tape back across my mouth. "You'll thank me,"

he says. "You'll figure out soon enough that we only need each other."

Pop, he died from being a cop. Not like you think. He didn't get shot or anything. He was on a routine stop on the highway, standing there writing a ticket for someone who had been speeding—and a drunk driver in a brand new Camaro came whipping past. Front end hit his hip, twisted him up like a corkscrew, shattering most of what was inside him. He died there on the road, bleeding out like that thing with its lower half missing.

Mom, well. She went slower. It was her lower half, too, though: colon cancer had been cooking her bowels low and slow for months, years, who even knows how long. We got to talk a good bit because that kind of death is bad in part because it takes so damn long.

Her face was like paper. Her eyes shot through with blood. She held my hand tight, though, with surprising strength, when she talked about Billy.

"He's not like you," she said.

"I know that. But he's fine."

"He's not fine. He doesn't have it together."

"Not yet."

"He shoulda, by now. He's past thirty."

I shrugged and just told her that it seemed people didn't grow up as fast as they used to. An excuse, I knew. In part because Billy was all of our fault. He was hers and Pop's and even mine. He was what he was because somehow, we made him that way. Either through how we treated him or through whatever we had crawling around in our DNA.

"You're the older brother," she said, almost an accusation.

"I know that."

"When I die—"

"We don't know you're going to die," I said at the time even though I *knew* at the time she was. We all knew it. On the simplest level, we all die. That's not a thing you get away from. But her? She was coming up on it faster than most. Driving right toward that cliff and yet there I was pretending it was a road ahead and not a thousand-foot drop.

"I'm dead already, my brain just hasn't caught up. When I die—no protests, now!—when I die, you take care of him. You take care of him! He needs you. You listening? Billy can't do this by himself. *Take care of him.*"

"I will, Mom."

"You better."

"*I will.*"

"You're a good boy, Max."

"You were a good mother." *Were*, I said. Not *are*. There I was, betraying exactly what I didn't want to tell her—made me feel like a right shitty coward saying that to her. I saw her face tighten as it came out of me. It stung her. But whaddya gonna do. I said what I said and I couldn't reel it back in and say it differently. Best I could do was smile.

And I made her that promise.

Take care of Billy.

That's why I went to get him that night.

I didn't give him long to pack. He wanted to take time and put together a whole suitcase, but I said we didn't want to mess around. I'd seen those things in his neighborhood. I heard screams coming from down the block, where those rat-ass condos were, where those hillbillies sell weed and meth. As he packed his shit, I told him the plan. Get in the truck. Drive around. Help people. Like the ice cream man of the fucking apocalypse, I said all manic like. He didn't respond to that so I tried just small talk—

Was he still with that girl, Jasmine?

(No.)

He still have that job at the pawn shop?

(No, and blah blah blah it was their fault for losing him.)

Well, he paying his bills okay?

(Yes, of course, he said too defensively—meaning he wasn't.)

I told him I could get him a job maybe at the trucking company—Billy'd gone and gotten his CDL same as I had, and used to drive a dump truck for the quarry, so he knew how to handle a rig.

He was done, we went out to the truck.

He picked up something off his lawn.

I turned, saw him there with a clay pot that contained a set of dead geraniums. He had it raised above his head.

Then he brought it down on mine.

Next thing I knew, I woke up here in Mom and Pop's cabin.

Billy's eating dry ramen noodles like that's a thing you do. He's not even breaking bits off—he's eating it like it's a fucking biscuit or something. Taking big bites right out of it, *crunch crunch crunch*. He must see the way I'm looking at him because he says, "I saw corn chips but the pallet was in the back." All he would've had to do was move them around, but Billy's always been a lazy fucker. I try to tell him what he is.

"Mphlaby pphhggr," I fail to say behind the tape.

He rolls his eyes, comes over, peels the tape off again.

"You want some?" he asks, holding the ramen package at me. The wrapping crinkles and crunches.

"No. I could use some water, though. Throat's dry as a bone."

He nods, goes and gets me a Coke. "I have one open."

It's warm and fizzy and it burns my throat, but it's something, and I gulp it greedily. I gasp as I finish and pull my face away. "Billy, listen. It's dangerous being here. We're in the middle of nowhere—"

"Exactly. Nothing's gonna find us here."

"You don't know that."

"What's even around? Nothing."

"Nothing? Two campgrounds in five miles. Plus the old Methodist church up past the bend—they got a damn graveyard."

"This is a disease. A disease doesn't affect the already dead." He laughs like I'm the idiot. Like he's the expert at something other than being a bona fide fuck-up.

I steel myself. "Here's what we do, Bill. You and me, we get back in the truck. We forget everything that happened here. We won't stop anywhere. We don't have to help people. Just you and me on the road. Mobile. Ready to go at a moment's notice. Truck cab has a bunk. The trailer is safe, locked up tight. It's like a mobile fortress." It's a lie, in part. I'm not abandoning my mission. I just need him to believe it. If he buys it, I'll knock the teeth out of his mouth and drag him wherever I want him to go—or leave him here in the woods to get eaten by *them*.

He swallows visibly. "You wanna go out *there*?" Billy waves me off. "I hit you too hard, big brother. Knocked some seeds loose in that gourd of yours. Out there is where *they* are. We're safe here. Besides, this is our cabin. Our family's cabin. Remember?" His eyes go foggy as he stares at an unfixed point. He smiles. "Remember coming up here. Bag of marshmallows for the fire outside. Hatfield hot dogs. Pop with his pipe. Mom with her wine. You and me out there, messing around—hah, you remember that time you took pinesap and rubbed it in my hair? Mom had to cut off a whole hank of it—had to shave my head to hide the bald patch!" And now he's laughing, braying like a mule until he's wheezing and damn near crying. His mirth dissolves into something more like maudlin grief before he slumps against the couch arm, staring off at nothing.

I'm about to tell him I remember, and I remember that time he ran off without telling everyone and we were worried all day. I remember the time he almost burned the cabin down with one of Pop's old cigarettes. I remember the time he threw my Walkman into the lake because—I can't even recall why he did it, just that he was mad at me for some stupid shit.

But I don't get to say it.

Because we both hear the sound.

A sharp snap outside. Like a branch breaking clean in half.

He gasps. Then immediately he's saying, "It's nothing. Just a deer."

A shushing shuffle follows. Like feet through leaves. Slow. Deliberate. A hissing susurrus.

He holds a finger to his lips.

"The gun," I hiss.

He mouths one word: *What?*

"*The. Gun.*"

Billy swallows hard, looking around for the revolver—I gesture toward it with my head but he finally sees it on his own. He fumbles for it and holds it in a trembling grip.

Could just be an animal, I think. Maybe he's right. Or maybe it's a survivor. And that creates its own worry, because not every survivor is going to be someone looking for shelter or someone looking to help. You get a disaster like this, more people want to help than hurt—but you always have people who want to take advantage, who want to steal, rob, rape, kill. Then my mind runs away as I start thinking that whatever is really going on, the real danger isn't in what's coming but what's already here.

Silence stretches out like a hangman's rope.

"Billy," I whisper as loud as one can whisper. "Come cut me free."

His answer is again holding a finger to his lips.

I'm about to chastise him—

But I don't get the chance.

The window behind me shatters. Glass clatters at my feet. I can't see what's happening because I'm facing the wrong damn way, but a new shadow enters the room and I hear the gassy, wet gurgle behind me—the pawing, the scraping, the viscera gush, and I see that reflected in Billy's eyes. Eyes struck wide with fear. Gun up. Hands shaking.

I'm screaming at him to shoot, *shoot*—

He pulls the trigger.

Click.

Shit.

He never loaded it.

I don't keep it loaded. Not legal to keep it loaded. I keep the speed-loader under my seat and of course Billy didn't think to look—he's not stupid, but he's high, and he *never checked the damn gun*—

Something grabs at me from behind—rotten, soft hands on my shoulders, and with it comes a smell like you get when you drive past a dead deer on a summer day: sickly sweet, pickled death, rancid as hot puke. I cry out and do all I can do, which is rock hard to the side—

The chair goes down as I slip from the thing's grip. *Bam.*

My shoulder cracks hard against the floor. I crane my neck just so. And it lets me see what's come inside our cabin.

It's a man. Or was. Gray cheeks striated with wine-dark stains. Eyes like fat corks straining against the mooring of their puffy sockets. Fluid leaks from cracked lips and black blood crawls from puckered nose holes. I try to imagine who this man was once: a polo shirt soggy with stains, a pair of cargo shorts ripped and ruined, a set of boat shoes muddy and gory. A camper, maybe. A family man, maybe. Doesn't matter.

Whoever he was isn't who he is now.

That man is gone.

What's left is death and hunger, grotesquely intertwined.

The thing lurches toward me. I don't know what else to do so I shift my hips and the chair judders along the floor—the thing's legs step into the tangle of the chair's legs and then the dead thing comes toppling down—

Right on top of me.

Its mouth is right over me. Shriveled teeth inside gummy sockets. Tongue like a separate thing, like a snake trying to escape its handler.

Then it's gone. A *thudding* sound fills the air and it rolls away. Billy drags it off of me. He gets on top of it and brings a side table with a lamp down onto the thing's head. Then he lifts it up and does it again.

And again.

And again.

Until soon it's all just mess. Like a raccoon hit by a score of cars and trucks. Tires turning it to a pudding of hair and organs and mess.

Billy lets me go. He's upset. Rattled by what just happened. So am I, but I'm keeping it together better.

"We're not safe here," he says, packing up his bag. His voice is shaking. Not even shaking: *vibrating*. "You were right."

"It's okay," I say.

"We do it your way."

"Okay, Billy, okay." I swallow a little pride and I say, "You saved me. I won't forget that."

He offers me a weak, mushy smile. "When Mom died," Billy says, "she told me to take care of you. Said you needed me."

I can't help but laugh. I don't bother telling him she said the same damn thing to me. I just nod and tell him he's right. I do. That's why I came to get him, because I needed him.

"I'll take care of you," he says.

"And I'll take care of you," I say back.

Then on the way out to the truck, I see it. Along the underside of his right forearm—two half-moon injuries. Bite marks. The damn thing bit him. My gorge surges. All the stuff Billy said about diseases and parasites comes back into my head and I look down at the gun in his hand and I think to the speed-loader full of rounds under my seat.

And Mom's voice hits me again:

Take care of him.

Take care of him . . .

. .

310

Jonathan Maberry is a *New York Times* best-selling novelist, five-time Bram Stoker Award winner, and comic book writer. He writes the Joe Ledger thrillers, the Rot & Ruin series, the Nightsiders series, and the Dead of Night series, as well as standalone novels in multiple genres. His YA space travel novel, *Mars One*, is in development for film, as are the Joe Ledger novels and his V-Wars shared-world vampire apocalypse series. He is the editor of many anthologies, including *The X-Files*, *Scary Out There*, *Out of Tune*, and *Aliens: Bug Hunt*. His comic book works include, among others, *Captain America*, the Bram Stoker Award–winning *Bad Blood*, *Rot & Ruin*, the *New York Times* bestselling *Marvel Zombies Return*, and others. A board game version of V-Wars was released in early 2016. He is the founder of the Writers Coffeehouse, and the co-founder of the Liars Club. Prior to becoming a full-time novelist, Jonathan spent twenty-five years as a magazine feature writer, martial arts instructor, and playwright. He was a featured expert on the History Channel documentary *Zombies: A Living History* and a regular expert on the TV series *True Monsters*. He is one third of the very popular and mildly weird *Three Guys with Beards* pop-culture podcast. Jonathan lives in Del Mar, California, with his wife, Sara Jo. www.jonathanmaberry.com

LONE GUNMAN

by Jonathan Maberry

– 1 –

The soldier lay dead.
    Mostly.
But not entirely.
And how like the world that was.
Mostly dead. But not entirely.

– 2 –

He was buried.
    Not under six feet of dirt. There might have been some comfort in that. Some closure. Maybe even a measure of justice.

He wasn't buried like that. Not in a graveyard, either. Certainly not in Arlington, where his dad would have wanted to see him laid to rest. And not in that small cemetery back home in California, where his grandparents lay under the marble and the green cool grass.

The soldier was in some shit-hole of a who-cares town on

the ass-end of Fayette County in Pennsylvania. Not under the ground. Not in a coffin.

He was buried under the dead.

Dozens of them.

Hundreds. A mountain of bodies. Heaped over and around him. Crushing him down, smothering him, killing him.

Not with teeth, though. Not tearing at him with broken fingernails. That was something, at least. Not much. Not a fucking lot. And maybe there was some kind of cosmic joke in all of this. He was certain of that much. A killer of men like him killed by having corpses piled on top of him. A quiet, passive death that had a kind of bullshit poetry attached to it.

However, Sam Imura was not a particularly poetic man. He understood it, appreciated it, but did not want to be written into it. No thanks.

He lay there, thinking about it. Dying. Not caring that this was it, that this was the actual end.

Knowing that thought to be a lie. Rationalization at best. His stoicism trying to give his fears a last handjob. *No, it's okay, it's a good death.*

Except that was total bullshit. There were no good deaths. Not one. He had been a soldier all his life, first in the regular army, then in Special Forces, and then in covert ops with a group called the Department of Military Sciences, and then freelance as top dog of a team of heavily armed problem solvers who ran under the nickname the Boy Scouts. Always a soldier. Pulling triggers since he was a kid. Taking lives so many times and in so many places that Sam had stopped counting. Idiots keep count. Ego-inflated assholes keep count. A lot of his fellow snipers kept count. He didn't. He was never that crazy.

Now he wished he had. He wondered if the number of people he had killed with firearms, edged-weapons, explosives, and his bare hands equaled the number of corpses under which he was buried.

There would be a strange kind of justice in that, too. And poetry. As if all of the people he'd killed were bound to him, and they were all fellow passengers on a black ship sailing to Valhalla. He knew that was a faulty metaphor, but fuck it. He was dying under a mountain of dead ghouls who had been trying to eat him a couple of hours ago. So . . . yeah, fuck poetry and fuck metaphors and fuck everything.

Sam wondered if he was going crazy.

He could build a case for it.

"No . . ."

He heard himself say that. A word. A statement. But even though it had come from him, Sam didn't exactly know what he meant by it. No, he wasn't crazy? No, he wasn't part of some celestial object lesson? No, he wasn't dying?

"No."

He said it again, taking ownership of the word. Owning what it meant.

No.

I'm not dead.

No, I'm not dying.

He thought about those concepts, and rejected them.

"*No*," he growled. And now he understood what he was trying to tell himself and this broken, fucked-up world.

No. I'm not *going* to die.

Not here. Not now. Not like this. No motherfucking way. Fuck that, fuck these goddamn flesh-eating pricks, fuck the universe, fuck poetry two times, fuck God, fuck everything.

Fuck dying.

"No," he said once more, and now he heard *himself* in that word. The soldier, the survivor, the killer.

The dead hadn't killed him, and they had goddamn well tried. The world hadn't killed him, not after all these years. And the day hadn't killed him. He was sure it was nighttime by now, and he wasn't going to let that kill him, either.

And so he tried to move.

Easier said than done. The bodies of the dead had been torn by automatic gunfire as the survivors of the Boy Scouts had fought to help a lady cop, Dez Fox, and some other adults rescue several busloads of kids. They'd all stopped at the Sapphire Foods distribution warehouse to stock up before heading south to a rescue station. The dead had come hunting for their own food and they'd come in waves. Thousands of them. Fox and the Boy Scouts had fought their way out.

Kind of.

Sam had gone down under a wave of them and Gipsy, one of the shooters on his team, had tried to save him, hosing the ghouls with magazine after magazine. The dead fell and Sam had gone down beneath them. No one had come to find him, to dig him out.

He heard the bus engines roar. He heard Gipsy scream, though he didn't know if it was because the hungry bastards got her, or because she failed to save him. Impossible to say. Impossible to know unless he crawled out and looked for her body. Clear enough, though, to reason that she'd seen him fall and thought that he was dead. He should have been, but that wasn't an absolute certainty. He was dressed in Kevlar, with reinforced arm and leg pads, spider-silk gloves, a ballistic combat helmet with unbreakable plastic visor. There was almost no spot for teeth to get him. And, besides, Gipsy's gunfire and Sam's own had layered him with *actual* dead. Or whatever the new adjective was going to be for that. Dead was no longer dead. There was walking and biting dead and there was dead dead.

Sam realized that he was letting his mind drift into trivia. A defense mechanism. A fear mechanism.

"No," he said again. That word was his lifeline and it was his lash, his whip.

No.

He tried to move. Found that his right hand could move almost ten inches. His feet were good, too, but there were bodies across his knees and chest and head. No telling how high the mound was, but they were stacked like Jenga pieces. The weight was oppressive but it hadn't actually crushed the life out of him. Not yet. He'd have to be careful moving so as not to crash the whole stinking mass of them down and really smash the life out of him.

It was a puzzle of physics and engineering, of patience and strategy. Sam had always prided himself on being a thinker rather than a feeler. Snipers were like that. Cold, exacting, precise. Patient.

Except . . .

When he began to move, he felt the mass of bodies move, too. At first he thought it was simple cause and effect, a reaction of limp weight to gravity and shifting support. He paused, and listened. There was no real light, no way to see. He knew that he had been unconscious for a while and so this had to be twilight, or later. Night. In the blackness of the mound he had nothing but his senses of touch and hearing to guide every movement of hand or arm or hip. He could tell when some movement he made caused a body, or a part of a body, to shift.

But then there was a movement up to his right. He had not moved his right arm or shoulder. He hadn't done anything in that quadrant of his position. All of his movements so far had been directed toward creating a space for his legs and hips to move because they were the strongest parts of him and could do more useful work longer than his arms or shoulders. The weight directly over his chest and what rested on his helmet had not moved at all.

Until they did.

There was a shift. No, a twitch. A small movement that was inside the mound. As if something moved. Not because of him.

Because *it* moved.

Oh, Jesus, he thought and for a moment he froze solid, not moving a finger, hardly daring to breathe, as he listened and felt for another twitch.

He waited five minutes. Ten? Time was meaningless.

There.

Again.

Another movement. Up above him. Not close, but not far away, either. How big was the mound? What was the distance? Six feet from his right shoulder? Six and a half feet from his head? Something definitely moved.

A sloppy, heavy movement. Artless, clumsy. But definite. He could hear the rasp of clothing against clothing, the slither-sound of skin brushing against skin. Close. So close. Six feet was nothing. Even with all of the dead limbs and bodies in the way.

Jesus, Jesus, Jesus.

Sam did not believe in Jesus. Or God. Or anything. That didn't matter now. No atheists in foxholes. No atheists buried under mounds of living dead ghouls. There had to be someone up there, in Heaven or Hell or whatever the fuck was there. Some drunk, malicious, amused, vindictive cocksucker who was deliberately screwing with him.

The twitch came again. Stronger, more definite, and . . .

Closer.

Shit. It was coming for him, drawn to him. By breath? By smell? Because of the movements he'd already made? Five feet now? Slithering like a snake through the pile of the dead. Worming its way toward him with maggot slowness and maggot persistence. One of them. Dead, but not dead enough.

Shit. Shit. Shit. Jesus. Shit.

Sam felt his heartbeat like a hammer, like a drum. Too fast, too loud. Could the thing hear it? It was like machine-gun fire. Sweat stung his blind eyes and he could smell the stink of his own fear and it was worse than the reek of rotting flesh, shit, piss, and blood that surrounded him.

Get out. Get Out.

He twisted his hip, trying to use his pelvis as a strut to bear the load of the oppressive bodies. The mass moved and pressed down, sinking into the space created as he turned sideways. Sam pulled his bottom thigh up, using the top one as a shield to allow movement. Physics and engineering, slow and steady wins the race. The sounds he was making were louder than the twitching, rasping noises. No time to stop and listen. He braced his lower knee against something firm. A back. And pushing. The body moved two inches. He pushed again and it moved six more, and suddenly the weight on his hip was tilting toward the space behind the body he'd moved. *Jenga*, he thought. *I'm playing Jenga with a bunch of fucking corpses. The world is totally insane.*

The weight on his helmet and shoulders shifted, too, and Sam pushed backward, fighting for every inch of new space, letting the weight that was on top of him slide forward and into where he'd been.

There was a kind of ripple through the mass of bodies and Sam did pause, afraid he was creating an avalanche. But that wasn't it.

Something was crawling on him. On his shoulder. He could feel the legs of some huge insect walking through the crevices of jumped body parts and then onto his shoulder, moving with the slow patience of a tarantula. Nothing else could be that big. But this was Pennsylvania. Did they have tarantulas out here? He wasn't sure. There were wolf spiders out here, some orb-weavers and black widows, but they were small in comparison to the thing that was crawling toward his face. Out in California there were plenty of those big hair monsters. Not here. Not here.

One slow, questing leg of the spider touched the side of his jaw, in the gap between the plastic visor and the chinstrap. It was soft, probing him, rubbing his skin. Sam gagged and tried to turn away, but there was no room. Then a second fat leg touched him. A third. Walking across his chin toward his panting mouth.

And that's when Sam smelled the thing.

Tarantulas did not have much of a smell. Not unless they were rotting in the desert sun.

This creature stank. It smelled like roadkill. It smelled like . . .

Sam screamed.

He knew, he understood what it was that crawled across his face. Not the fat legs of some great spider but the clawing, grasping fingers of a human hand. That was the slithering sound, the twitching. One of *them* was buried with him. Not dead. Not alive. Rotting and filled with a dreadful vitality, reaching past the bodies, reaching through the darkness toward the smell of meat. Of food.

Clawing at him. He could feel the sharp edges of fingernails now as the fingers pawed at his lips and nose.

Sam screamed and screamed. He kicked out as hard as he could, shoving, pressing, jamming with knees and feet. Hurting, feeling the improbably heavy corpses press him down, as if they, even in their final death, conspired to hold him prisoner until the thing whose hand had found him could bring teeth and tongue and appetite to what it had discovered.

Sam wrestled with inhuman strength, feeling muscles bulge and bruise and strain, feeling explosions of pain in his joints and lower back as he tried to move all of that weight of death. The fingers found the corner of his mouth, curled, hooked, tried to take hold of him and rip.

He dared not bite. The dead were filled with infection, with the damnable diseases that had caused all of this. Maybe he was already infected, he didn't know, but if he bit one of those grub-like fingers it was as sure as a bullet in the brain. Only much slower.

"Fuck you!" he roared and spat the fingers out, turning his head, spitting into the darkness to get rid of any trace of blood or loose flesh. He wanted to vomit but there was no time, no room, no luxury even for that.

And so he went a little crazy.

A lot crazy.

All the way.

– 3 –

When the mountain of dead collapsed, it fell away from him, dozens of corpses collapsing down and then rolling the way he'd come, propelled by his last kicks, by gravity, by luck. Maybe helped along by the same drunk god who wanted more of the Sam Imura show. He found himself tumbling, too, bumping and thumping down the side of the mound, the jolts amplified by the lumpy body armor he wore. Kevlar stopped penetration of bullets but it did not stop the foot-pounds of impact.

He tried to get a hand out before he hit the pavement, managed it, but at the wrong part of his fall. He hit shoulder-first and slapped the asphalt a microsecond later. Pain detonated all through him. Everything seemed to hurt. The goddamn armor itself seemed to hurt.

Sam lay there, gasping, fighting to breathe, staring through the fireworks display in his eyes, trying to see the sky. His feet were above him, one heel hooked over the throat of a teenage girl; the other in a gaping hole that used to be the stomach of a naked fat man. He looked at the dead. Fifty, sixty people at least in the mound. Another hundred scattered around, their bodies torn to pieces by the battle that had happened here. Some clearly crushed by the wheels of those buses. Dead. All of them dead, though not all of them still. A few of the crushed ones tried to pull themselves along even though hips and legs and spines were flattened or torn completely away. A six-year-old kid sat with her back to a chain-link fence. No legs, one hand, no lower jaw. Near her was an Asian woman who looked like she might have been pretty. Nice figure, but her face had been stitched from lower jaw to hairline with eight overlapping bullet holes.

Like that.

Every single one of the bodies around him was a person. Each person had a story, a life, details, specifics. Things that made them people instead of nameless corpses. As he lay there Sam felt the weight of who they had been crushing him down as surely as the mound had done minutes ago. He didn't know any of them, but he was kin to all of them.

He closed his eyes for a moment and tried not to see anything. But they were there, hiding behind his lids as surely as if they were burned onto his retinas.

Then he heard a moan.

A sound from around the curve of the mound. Not a word, not a call for help. A moan. A sound of hunger, a sound of a need so bottomless that no amount of food could ever hope to satisfy it. An impossible and irrational need, too, because why would the dead need to feed? What good would it do them?

He knew what his employers had said about parasites driving the bodies of the victims, about an old Cold War weapon that slipped its leash, about genetically modified larvae in the bloodstream and clustered around the cerebral cortex and motor cortex and blah blah blah. Fuck that. Fuck science. This wasn't science, anyway. Not as he saw it right then, having just crawled out of his own grave. This was so much darker and more twisted than that. Sam didn't know what to call it. Even when he believed in God there was nothing in the Bible or Sunday school that covered this shit. Not even Lazarus or Jesus coming back from the dead. J.C. didn't start chowing down on the Apostles when he rose. So, what was this?

The moan was louder. Coming closer.

Get up, asshole, scolded his inner voice.

"What, can't I just lie here and say fuck it?"

Because you're in shock, genius, and if you don't move now you're going to die.

Sam thought about that. Shock? Yeah. Maybe. Concussion? Almost certainly. Military helmets stopped shrapnel but the stats on traumatic brain injury were staggering. Sam knew a lot of front-line shooters who'd been benched with TBI. Messed up the head, scrambled thoughts, and . . .

A figure lumbered into sight. Not crawling. Walking. One of them. Wearing mechanic's coveralls. Bites on his face and nothing in his eyes but hunger and hate. Walking. Not shuffling or limping. Not even staggering, like some of them did. Walking, sniffing the air, black and bloody drool running over its lips and chin.

Sam's hand immediately slapped his holster, but there was no sidearm. He fumbled for his knife, but that was gone, too.

Shit. Shit. Shit.

He swung his feet off of the mound of dead and immediately felt something like an incendiary device explode in the muscles of his lower back. The pain was instantly intense and he screamed.

The dead mechanic's head snapped toward him, the dead eyes focusing. It snarled, showing blooding, broken teeth. And then it came at him. Fast. Faster than he'd seen with any of them. Or maybe it was that he was slowed down, broken. Usually in the heat of combat the world slowed down and Sam seemed to walk through it, taking his time to do everything right, to see everything, to own the moment. Not now.

With a growl of unbearable hunger, the ghoul flung itself on Sam.

He got a hand up in time to save his skin, chopping at the thing's throat, feeling tissue and cartilage crunch as he struck, feeling it do no good at all except to change the moan into a gurgle. The mechanic's weight crashed down on him, stretching the damaged muscles in Sam's back, ripping a new cry from him, once more smothering him with weight and mass.

Sam kept his hand in place in the ruined throat and looped his other hand over, punching the thing on the side of the head, once, twice, again and again. Breaking bones, shattering the nose, doing no appreciable good. The pain in his lower back was incredible, sickening him even more than the smell of the thing that clawed at him. The creature snapped its teeth together with a hard porcelain *clack*, but Sam kept those teeth away from him. Not far enough away, though.

He braced one foot flat on the floor and used that leg to force his hips and shoulders to turn. It was like grinding broken glass into whatever was wrong with his spine, but he moved, and Sam timed another punch to knock the ghoul over him, letting his hips be the axle of a sloppy wheel. The mechanic went over and down and then Sam was on top of him. He climbed up and dropped a knee onto the creature's chest, pinning it against the place where the asphalt met the slope of corpses. Then Sam grabbed the snapping jaw in one hand and a fistful of hair at the back of the thing's head with the other.

In the movies snapping a neck is nothing. Everyone seemed to be able to do it.

That's the movies.

In the real world, there is muscle and tendon and bone and none of them want to turn that far or that fast. The body isn't designed to die. Not that easily. And Sam was exhausted, hurt, sick, weak.

There was no snap.

What there was . . . was a slow turn of the head. Inch by inch, fighting against the ghoul's efforts to turn back and bite him. Sam pulled and pushed, having to lean forward to get from gravity what his damaged body did not want to provide. The torsion was awful. The monster clawed at him, tearing at his clothes, digging at the Kevlar limb pads.

Even dead, it tried to live.

Then the degree of rotation passed a point. Not a sudden snap, no abrupt release of pressure. More of a slow, sickening, wet grinding noise as vertebrae turned past their stress point, and the point where the brain stem joined the spinal cord became pinched inside those gears. Pinched, compressed, and then ruptured.

The clawing hands flopped away. The body beneath him stopped thrashing. The jaws snapped one last time and then sagged open.

After that Sam had to finish it, to make sure it was a permanent rupture and not a temporary compression. The sounds told him that. And the final release of all internal resistance.

Sam fell back and rolled off and lay side by side with the mechanic, their bodies touching at shoulder, hip, thigh, foot, Sam's fingers still entwined in the hair as if they lay spent after some obscene coupling. One breathed, the other did not.

Overhead the moon peered above the treetops like a peeping Tom.

<h1 style="text-align:center">– 4 –</h1>

The moon was completely above the treetops by the time Sam got up.

His back was a mess. Pulled, strained, torn, or worse, it was impossible to tell. He had a high pain threshold, but this was at his upper limit. And, besides, it was easier to man up and walk it off when there were other soldiers around. He'd seen his old boss, Captain Ledger, brave it out and even crack jokes with a bullet in him.

Alone, though, it's easier to be weaker, smaller, to be more intimate with the pain, and be owned by it.

It took him half an hour to stand. The world tried to do some fancy cartwheels and the vertigo made Sam throw up over and over again until there was nothing left in his belly.

It took another hour to find a gun, a SIG Sauer, and fifteen more minutes to find one magazine for it. Nine rounds. Then he saw a shape lying partly under three of the dead. Male, big, dressed in the same unmarked black combat gear as Sam wore. He tottered over and knelt very slowly and carefully beside the body. He rolled one of the dead over and off so he could see who it was. He knew it had to be one of his Boy Scouts, but it still hurt him to see the face. DeNeille Shoopman, who ran under the combat callsign of Shortstop. Good kid. Hell of a soldier.

Dead, with his throat torn away.

But goddamn it, Shortstop's eyes were open, and they clicked over to look at him. The man he knew—his friend and fellow soldier—did not look at him through those eyes. Nothing did. Not even the soul of a monster. That was one of the horrors of this thing. The eyes are supposed to be the windows of the soul, but when he looked into Shortstop's brown eyes it was like looking through the windows of an empty house.

Shortstop's arms were pinned, and there was a lot of meat and muscle missing from his chest and shoulders. He probably couldn't raise his arms even if he was free. Some of the dead were like that. A lot of them were. They were victims of the thing that had killed them, and although they all reanimated, only a fraction of them were whole enough to rise and hunt.

Sam placed one hand over Shortstop's heart. It wasn't beating, of course, but Sam remembered how brave a heart it had been. Noble, too, if that wasn't a corny thing to think about a guy he'd gotten drunk with and traded dirty jokes with. Shortstop had walked with him through the Valley of the Shadow of Death so many times. It wasn't right to let him lie here, ruined and helpless and hungry, until he rotted into nothing.

"No," said Sam.

He had nine bullets and needed every single one of them if he was going to survive. But he needed one now really bad.

The shot blasted a hole in the night.

Sam sat beside Shortstop for a long time, his hand still there over the quiet heart. He wept for his friend and he wept for the whole goddamn world.

– 5 –

Sam spent the night inside the food distribution warehouse. There were eleven of the ghouls in there. Sam found the section where they stored the lawn care tools. He found two heavy-bladed machetes and went to work.

When he was done he was in so much pain that he couldn't stand it, so he found where they stacked the painkillers. Extra-strength something-or-other. Six of those, and six cans of some shitty local beer. The door was locked and he had the place to himself.

He slept all through the night.

– 6 –

When he woke up he took more painkillers but this time washed them down with some trendy electrolyte water. Then he ate two cans of beef stew he cooked over a camping stove.

More painkillers, more food, more sleep.

The day passed and he didn't die.

The pain diminished by slow degrees.

In the morning he found a set of keys to the office. There was a radio in there, a TV, a phone, and a lockbox with a Glock 26 and four empty magazines, plus three boxes of 9mm hollow points. He nearly wept.

The phone was dead.

Sam turned on the news and listened as he loaded bullets into the magazines for the Glock and the single mag he had for the SIG Sauer.

He heard a familiar voice. The guy who had been here with the lady cop. Skinny blond-haired guy who was a reporter for a ninth-rate cable news service.

"This is Billy Trout reporting live from the apocalypse . . ."

Trout had a lot of news and none of it was good. His convoy of school buses was in Virginia now and creeping along roads clogged by refugees. There were as many fights among the fleeing survivors as there were between the living and the dead.

Typical, he thought. *We've always been our worst enemies.*

At noon Sam felt well enough to travel, though he considered holing up in this place. There was enough food and water here to keep him alive for five years, maybe ten. But that was a sucker's choice. He'd eat his gun before a week was out. Anyone would. Solitude and a lack of reliable intel would push him into a black hole from which he could never crawl out. No, the smart move was to find people.

Step one was finding a vehicle.

This place had trucks.

Lots of trucks.

So he spent four hours using a forklift to load pallets of supplies into a semi. He collected anything that could be used as a weapon and took them, too. If he found people, they would need to be armed. He thought about that, then went and loaded sleeping bags, toilet paper, diapers, and whatever else he thought a group of survivors might need. Sam was a very practical man, and each time he made a smart and thoughtful decision, he could feel himself stepping back from the edge of despair. He was planning for a mission, and that gave him a measure of stability. He had people to find and protect, and that gave him a purpose.

He gassed up at the fuel pump on the far side of the parking lot. A few new ghouls were beginning to wander in through the open fence, but Sam kept clear of them. When he left, he made sure not to crash into any of them. Even a semi could take damage and he had to make this last.

Practical.

Once he reached the crossroads, though, he paused, idling, trying to decide where to go. Following the buses was likely pointless. If they were already heading south, and if Billy Trout was able to broadcast, then they were alive. The last of the Boy Scouts were probably with them.

So he turned right, heading toward the National Armory in Harrisville, north of Pittsburgh. If it was still intact, that would be a great place to build a rescue camp. If it was overrun, then he'd take it back and secure it.

It was a plan.

He drove.

There was nothing on the radio but bad information and hysteria, but there were CDs in the glove compartment. A lot of country and western stuff. He fucking hated country and western, but it was better than listening to his own thoughts. He slipped in a Brad Paisley CD and listened to the man sing about coal miners in Harlan County. Depressing as shit, but it was okay to listen to.

It was late when he reached Evans City, a small town on the ass-end of nowhere. All through the day and into the evening he saw the leavings of the world. Burned towns, burned cars, burned farmhouses, burned bodies. The wheels of the semi crunched over spots where thousands of shell casings littered the road. He saw a lot of the dead. At first they were stragglers, wandering in no particular direction until they heard the truck. Then they walked toward him as he drove, and even though Sam didn't want to hit any of them, there were times where he had no choice. Then he found that by slowing down he could push them out of the way without impact damage to the truck. Some of them fell and he had to set his teeth as the wheels rolled over them, crushing and crunching things that had been people twenty-four hours ago.

He found that by driving along country roads he could avoid a lot of that, so he turned the truck out into the farmlands. He refueled twice, and each time he wasted bullets defending his truck. Sam was an excellent shot, but hoping to get a head shot each time was absurd, and his back was still too sore to do it all with machetes or an axe. The first fuel stop cost him nineteen rounds. The second took thirteen. More than half a box of shells. No good. Those boxes would not last very long at that rate.

As he drove past an old cemetery on the edge of Evans City he spotted smoke rising from up ahead. He passed a car that was smashed into a tree, and then a pickup truck that had been burned to a shell beside an exploded gas pump. That wasn't the source of the smoke, though, because the truck fire had burned itself out.

No, there was a farmhouse nearby and out in front of it was a mound of burning corpses.

Sam pulled the truck to a stop and sat for a while, studying the landscape. The moon was bright enough and he had his headlights on. Nothing moved except a tall, gently twisting column of gray smoke that rose from the pyre.

"Shit," said Sam. He got out of the truck but left the motor running. He stood for a moment to make sure his back wouldn't flare up and that his knees were steady. The SIG was tucked into his shoulder holster and he had the Glock in a two-hand grip as he approached the mound.

It was every bit as high as the one under which he'd been buried. Dozens upon dozens of corpses, burned now to stick figures, their limbs contracted by heat into fetal curls. The withered bones shifted like logs in a dying hearth, sending sparks up to the night, where they vanished against the stars.

Sam turned away and walked over to the house.

He could read a combat scene as well as any experienced soldier, and what he was seeing was a place where a real battle had taken place. There were blood splashes on the ground and on the porch where the dead had been dropped. The blood was blacker even than it should have been in this light, and he could see threadlike worms writhing it in. Sam unclipped a Maglite he'd looted from the warehouse and held it backward in his left hand while resting the pistol across the wrist, the barrel in sync with the beam as he entered the house.

Someone had tried to hold this place, that was clear enough. They'd nailed boards over the windows and moved furniture to act as braces. Many of those boards lay cracked and splintered on the floor amid more shell casings and more blood spatter. He went all the way through to the kitchen and saw more of the same. An attempt to fortify that had failed.

The upstairs was splashed with gore but empty, and the smears on the stairs showed where bodies had been dragged down.

He stepped to the cellar door, which opened off of the living room. He listened for any kind of sound, however small, but there was nothing. Sam went down, saw sawhorses and a door that had been made into a bed. Saw blood. A bloody trowel. Pieces of meat and bone.

Nothing else.

No one else.

He trudged heavily up the stairs and went out onto the porch and stood in the moonlight while he thought this through.

Whoever had been in the house had made a stand, but it was evident they'd lost their battle.

So who built the mound? Who dragged the bodies out? Whose shell casings littered the yard?

He peered at the spent brass. Not military rounds. .30-30s, .22, some 9mm, some shotgun shells. Hunters?

Maybe.

Probably, with a few local police mixed in.

Why come here? Was there a rescue mission here that arrived too late? Or was it a sweep? The armed citizens of this rural town fighting back?

Sam didn't know.

There were dog footprints in the dirt, too. And a lot of boot and shoe prints. A big party. Well-armed, working together. Getting the job done.

Fighting back.

For the first time since coming to Pennsylvania with the Boy Scouts, Sam felt his heart lift. The buses of kids and the lady cop had gotten out. And now someone had organized a resistance. Probably a redneck army, but fuck it. That would do.

He walked around the house to try to read the footprints. The group who had come here had walked off east, across the fields. Going where? Another farm? A town? Anywhere the fight took them or need called them.

"Hooah," he said, using the old Army Ranger word for everything from "fuck you" to "fuck yeah." For now it meant "fuck yeah."

East, he thought, was as good a direction as any. Maybe those hunters were protecting their own. Sam glanced at his truck. Maybe they could use some food and a little professional guidance.

Maybe.

He smiled into the darkness. Probably not a very nice smile. A hunter's smile. A soldier's smile. A killer's smile. Maybe all of those. But it was something only the living could do.

He was still smiling when he climbed back into the cab of his truck, turned around in front of the old house, found the road again, and headed east.

Keith R. A. DeCandido has tackled the wacky world of movie zombies before, when he novelized the first three *Resident Evil* films. Over the course of more than two decades, he has written in dozens of worlds, both others and his own, most recently the Marvel Tales of Asgard trilogy featuring Thor, Sif, and the Warriors Three; the *Orphan Black* reference book *Classified Clone Reports*; the *Stargate SG-1* novel *Kali's Wrath*; an urban fantasy series about a nice Jewish boy from the Bronx who hunts monsters, starting with *A Furnace Sealed*; three serialized novellas in the Super City Cops series; *Mermaid Precinct*, the latest in his fantasy police procedural series; and stories in *Aliens: Bug Hunt, Baker Street Irregulars, A Baker's Dozen of Magic, Joe Ledger: Unstoppable, Limbus, Inc., Book III, TV Gods: Summer Programming, V-Wars: Night Terrors*, and others. Keith is also a professional musician, a second-degree black belt in karate, a veteran podcaster, and a bunch of other things he can't recall due to lack of sleep. Find out less at his cheerfully retro web site at DeCandido.net.

LIVE AND ON THE SCENE

by Keith R. A. DeCandido

T his is a fine, all-American home in Butler, Pennsylvania. A family of four has been murdered, and their bodies appear to have been chewed on. According to a statement by the coroner, it is likely the result of an animal attack. However, this reporter did speak to a witness, Miss Ella Rimer, who tells a different story."

"Yeah, I saw a fella shuffling away from the house. It was pretty strange, I'll tell you, just stumbling along. I tried to get his attention, but he just kept going, you know? Wouldn't even pick his feet up off the floor. Strangest thing. And he seemed to have blood on his face."

"Miss Rimer says that she did mention this person to the police. It's possible that this stranger is the owner of the animal that attacked the victims. More on this story as it develops. This is Harvey Lincoln for WIC-TV news. Back to you in the studio."

Harvey stood impatiently at the phone booth, waiting for the reporter from KDKA to finish using the pay phone. Unlike the phone booths in Pittsburgh, the glass was actually clean, which was typical of the suburbs, and Harvey could see his reflection. Since he was stuck waiting anyhow, he leaned in close to make sure his hair was looking good. He didn't really trust Frank, his not-so-reliable cameraman, to tell him if the Brylcreem had failed in its duty to keep his hair in place.

His reflection was irritatingly blurry, though, and then he recalled that he hadn't put his glasses on.

Just as he placed the plastic frames atop his ears and nose, the Pittsburgh reporter hung up and left. "All yours, fella."

"Thanks."

Harvey dropped a dime into the slot and then dialed the station.

"WIC-TV."

"Hi, Maria, it's Harvey, is Jack available?"

"Oh, hold the phone, Harvey, I'll check."

While he waited for Maria to track down their boss, Jack Olden, Harvey looked at his reflection in the metal change holder of the pay phone, checking his teeth.

"Damnit," he grumbled, noticing that there was a sesame seed embedded between a couple of molars. Back when he started in the news biz, the black-and-white film probably wouldn't have even picked the light-colored seed up, but in color? Frank was going to be on the receiving end of a knuckle sandwich for not telling him about that seed, which he picked out with his carefully manicured fingernails.

"What are you complaining about now, Harvey?" came the voice of the station manager.

"Hi, Jack. Uh, nothing, I just—Did the live feed go okay?"

"It was fine, though I wish you'd *said* you were live."

"I thought you might be using it for other broadcasts."

"You think really highly of yourself, don't you?"

"I think highly of the story, Jack. I mean, heck, we're talking the first multiple homicide in Butler County since the Pillow Killer back in the twenties! In fact, if you want, I can dig into the archives, do a little piece for the weekend about the Pillow Killer—"

"You're not gonna have time."

"Hey, that's not fair. I can—"

"Since when is life fair? Actually, I'm glad you called because believe it or not, there's a second multiple homicide in Butler County since the Pillow Killer."

Harvey swallowed down his complaint. "What?"

"Get over to West Penn and North Chestnut. There's a house on the corner with a bunch of dead bodies."

"You bet."

Hanging up the phone, Harvey yanked the phone booth door open and yelled, "Frank!"

As usual, Frank looked up at Harvey with the look of a deer captivated by oncoming headlights. "What'd I do, man?" he asked defensively.

Harvey decided to table the discussion of his seed-infested teeth. "Nothing we need to worry about right now. We got another crime scene to get to."

"Jesus Christ, another one?"

As he climbed into the passenger side of the white WIC-TV van, Harvey said, "You shouldn't take the name of the Lord in vain."

"I'm standing at my fourth straight multiple homicide scene in the last three days, and that's just in Butler and Armstrong Counties. Scenes like this are occurring in Clarion County, Allegheny County,

and Westmoreland County as well. The county coroner's offices and the city, county, and state police are all standing by their story that these attacks are being made by a wild animal. However, witnesses tell a different story."

"I heard a terrible noise next door, so I ran over to see, and I swear to God almighty above that there was a man in there chawin' on Edna!"

"What do you mean by 'chawin',' Mr. Posey?"

"Just what I said! He was eatin' Edna's arm!"

"Other witnesses at the other crime scenes have made similar reports. Butler City Police Chief Brandon Painter had this to say . . ."

"I don't appreciate these wild stories going around about people eating other people. That kind of talk is irresponsible and doesn't help the good men of my police force when they try to work to solve these horrible crimes. We've never seen anything like this in my thirty years on this job, and solving these crimes is hard enough without people spreading foolishness."

"Despite Chief Painter's confidence, these reports would appear to be far from 'foolishness.' This reporter spoke to an employee of the county coroner's office, who would only speak on condition of anonymity, and he assured me that the attacks on these poor people don't match any known animal—certainly not any animal ever sighted in this state. None of the local zoos have reported any animals to be missing. For WIC-TV, I'm Harvey Lincoln."

As Harvey headed for the conference room for the WIC-TV news crew's morning meeting, he was intercepted by Linda Kamin, whose high heels clacked on the linoleum floor as she strode to block his path.

"You're a louse, you know that?"

Harvey smiled. "I'm a reporter, Linda, we're all louses. You'd wilt under a can of Raid, same as me."

"That was *my* source in the coroner's office! And I told you about it in confidence—*I* was going to use it!"

"Oh, really? When was that going to be, before or after you interviewed the head of the school board? Or covered a sewing circle? Or gave us the inside poop about the PTA?"

Linda pursed her lips. "I'm a reporter *just like you*. And I might have gotten a story on this—God knows everyone else is. And it's not fair of you to steal my source like that!"

"Since when is life fair? Don't we have to get to a meeting?"

"I can tell you one thing for free, mister—I'm assuming any conversation we have is *on* the record. And you pull something like that again, I'll tell everyone what your real last name is."

Harvey swallowed. "You wouldn't."

"Watch me." With that, she entered the conference room.

His face had gotten sweaty all of a sudden, his glasses sliding down his nose. Pushing them back up, he took a deep breath and entered the room.

Staring daggers at Linda, he found a seat between the news director and technical director. He hated sitting next to other reporters—especially right now.

Linda's real last name was Kaminski, but she had no problem with people knowing she was a Polack, she just preferred "Kamin" for being on camera because people sometimes stumbled over her real name.

Harvey's real last name was "Lipshitz," and that was a carefully guarded secret.

Jack came in and said, "All right, boys and girls, we've got a whole new ballgame."

Harvey sat up and the susurrus of noise in the room died.

"We just got verified reports from the North Side Cemetery, Greenlawn, Mt. Royal Cemetery, Kittanning Cemetery, and West View Cemetery here in town of corpses climbing out of their graves."

The silence mutated into laughs.

"Yeah, sure."

"Pull my other leg, why don'tcha?"

"C'mon, Jack, April Fools is in *April*, not—"

"*I'm serious!*"

Harvey actually flinched. He'd been working for WIC for the better part of a decade, and he had never in any of that time heard Jack Olden raise his voice.

"Listen to me, boys and girls, because we're gonna be telling this story *a lot* over the next few days. This isn't a bunch of animals on the loose, and this isn't a serial killer. This is the *dead coming to life.*"

"Seriously, Jack?" one of the reporters asked.

"Do I look like I'm joking?"

"No, you look like you're gonna toss your cookies. So I'm worried."

"You should be." Jack turned to Harvey. "That source you had in the coroner's office—any chance of getting a real statement now that things are going public?"

Glancing nervously at Linda, Harvey said, "Well, maybe. I'll see what I can do."

"Good. We've got instructions coming down from the governor that anyone who dies has to be cremated right away."

That took Harvey aback. "Really?"

"Yeah, really, it's common sense," Jack said.

"Well, yeah, but—I mean, what about the Jews?"

Jack gave him a blank look. "What about them?"

"Um, well, cremation is against the Jewish religion."

Shrugging, Jack said, "If you say so. Who the hell knows what those people do."

Harvey winced. That was why he admonished people for "blasphemy." Keeping Christian camouflage kept him employed.

"All right," Jack started, "assignments . . ."

After the meeting, Harvey practically ran out to his desk, hoping to avoid Linda altogether.

Maria waved at him as he walked toward his desk. "Harvey, you got a call on line four."

"Thanks, doll." He sat at his desk, leaning back in the wooden chair so it creaked, picked up the hook, stabbed the blinking button labeled "4," and said, "Harvey Lincoln."

"I'm sorry, I thought I was calling for Harvey Lipshitz. This is his father."

Immediately, he straightened his back, the very sound of Dad's voice forcing him into good posture. "It's me, Dad. How are you?"

"Still dying inside every time I hear you call yourself by that name."

Whispering so he wouldn't be heard in the bullpen, he replied, "I told you, Dad, they don't hire Jews to be reporters. They certainly don't hire Jews whose names sound like swearing."

"Don't give me that nonsense. I know it's because you're ashamed. Why admit that your parents managed to escape before the Nazis came to Poland? Why let anyone know that I

fought for our country against them and helped liberate Buchen-
wald? Why—"

"Dad, I'm really busy, I—"

"I called because of your mother."

Harvey cut off his long-practiced diatribe about how busy
he was in a desperate attempt to get him off the phone—which,
on this occasion, had the benefit of actually being true—once
Dad mentioned his mother. "What's wrong with Mom?"

"She's dying."

"Is this her really dying or you thinking she's dying because
she coughed once?"

"Don't you mouth off at me, she's having trouble breathing! The oxygen tank isn't helping anymore! I keep calling
Dr. Schiff's office and leaving messages with his secretary, but
she *won't* call me back!"

Sighing, Harvey said, "The doctor's probably very busy,
Dad, he—"

"I know, that's why I'm *worried*!"

"Keep trying to call, okay, Dad? Look, I really do have a lot
of work to do, they're working us pretty hard on a story."

"Is it about all the dead people?"

"Um—"

"It is, isn't it? That's why Dr. Schiff can't give me the time
of day anymore. Look, you be careful, Harvey Lipshitz, I don't
want anything bad to happen to you around all those dead
people."

"They're dead, Dad, what can they do to me?"

*"I'm here with Alvin Jefferson, the caretaker of Mt. Royal Cem-
etery. Mr. Jefferson, can you tell me what you saw today?"*

"I'm swearin' to you, Mr. Lincoln, it was like the devil himself came up from down below and brought his fury upon the Earth. It was straight out of the Book of Revelation, right there in the Bible."

"Um, well, thank you, Mr. Jefferson, but can you be a bit more specific?"

"What's it matter? Death ain't death no more! People crawlin' up from their graves and feedin' on the livin'!"

"Thank you, Mr. Jefferson. For WIC-TV, this is Harvey Lincoln."

It took forever for Harvey to find a working, unoccupied pay phone in Glenshaw, but he eventually did and told Frank to pull the van over.

"Can't we just go back to the station?" Frank's voice was almost whiny. "It's only twenty minutes, man."

"I just want to check in and see if there are any messages from my father."

Frank sighed loudly and pulled the van over.

Harvey hopped out and put a dime in the phone booth before dialing the station. It was much better to check there to see if Dad had called rather than call Dad directly and have to actually *talk* to him.

"WIC-TV."

"Hi, Maria, it's Harvey, any messages?"

"Linda's on the warpath looking for you."

Harvey winced. He was still trying to figure out a way to ask her how to contact her coroner friend that wouldn't end with one of her high heels stabbing him in the eye.

"Also," Maria added, "your father called. He sounded pretty rattled."

"Damnit. Thanks, doll."

With a heavy heart, he pushed down the metal lever and then let go, hearing a dial tone even as his dime rattled to the bottom of the phone. He put another dime in and dialed the phone number for the house he grew up in.

"Hello?"

Harvey hesitated. His father sounded awful. "Dad, it's Harvey."

"Oh, Harvey, thank goodness! Your mother's dying, Harvey, and I keep calling nine-one-one and nobody answers!"

Closing his eyes, Harvey said, "Keep trying, Dad. I'll be there as fast as I can."

He hung up and hopped back into the van. "We're going to Kittanning."

"Say what?" Frank got that deer-in-the-headlights look again. Plus, his mouth hung open, making him look kind of like a fish.

Pointing at the road ahead, Harvey said, "Drive to Kittanning, right now."

"That's an hour away!"

"Then you'd better get moving."

"No way, man, I can't—"

"Drive, Frank, or I tell Jack about the reefer you were smoking when you thought I wasn't looking last week."

"Aw, c'mon, man, that's not fair."

"Since when is life fair? Drive."

Frank put the van into gear and grumbled, "This is a bad scene, man."

By the time they arrived at Kittanning, a town that straddled the Allegheny River, it was dark out.

"Man, this is uncool."

"Will you *please* shut up?" Harvey was about ready to strangle Frank at this point. He should have just gone back to the station and then taken his own car here. But Dad's voice was so anxious. He'd never sounded like that, except when Grandma was dying.

"Shit!"

Startled by Frank's interjection, Harvey looked up to see a man standing right in the middle of Market Street.

Frank swerved to avoid the man—who was just *standing* there—and drove the van straight for a bank's façade.

Harvey was thrown violently forward, his head colliding against the windshield, his ribs smashing into the dashboard.

For a few seconds, he just sat there on the floor in front of the passenger seat, his ears ringing.

Reaching up, he yanked at the door handle, and the van passenger door creaked open with a metallic screech.

His first thought was that he was going to have to fill out a *ton* of paperwork on the damaged van.

Glancing over at the driver's side, he saw that Frank was sitting in the seat, held in by his seat belt. He looked unconscious.

Belatedly realizing that he should have worn his own seat belt, Harvey tried to climb out of the van, and instead fell to the pavement.

Something was getting into his eyes. He rubbed his eyes, and then saw blood on his fingers.

Touching his forehead, it felt slick.

Clambering to his feet, Harvey looked back to see that the same man was just *standing* there in the middle of Market Street.

"Hey!" he cried, stumbling toward the man. "What the hell's *wrong* with you?"

Then he got a good look at the man. His eyes were milky white, his teeth were rotten, and he had a giant hole in his flannel shirt—and also in his chest. In fact, Harvey could see clear through to the other side, bits of gore and shattered bone and muscle dripping inside the hole.

For thirty hours now, he'd been hearing about strange people wandering around and the dead coming to life, and all sorts of other craziness.

But this was his first time face-to-face with it.

He ran.

In pure panic, Harvey didn't pick a direction, but his subconscious must have been working properly because after a minute, he found himself on Sampson Street, running toward the house he grew up in.

Aside from that—that animated corpse, he hadn't seen *anyone* on the street at all.

He wasn't sure what was stranger.

It took him several seconds of fumbling to get the latch to the front gate open—his hands were still slick with his own blood mingled with sweat—but he managed it. The gate squeaked like it always did, and he ran down the cracked pavement of the walkway to the front door.

"Dad?" he said as he yanked open the screen door. It was unlocked, the inner wooden door left open on this warm evening. "You home?"

"Harvey? Harvey, is that you?"

"I'm here, Dad."

His father came out into the foyer from the living room

dressed in his usual around-the-house wear: a white T-shirt, boxer shorts, and leather slippers. Tears were streaking down his cheeks and into his thick mustache. "Harvey, I don't know how much longer your mother will be with us."

He led Harvey into the living room, where Mom was lying on the couch, plastic tube in her nose connected to the oxygen tank, her drawn, wrinkled skin white as a sheet. Her stomach was moving up and down ever so slightly, so she was still alive, but that was the only indication that she was.

Against one wall was the giant wooden credenza with the television inside it, and one of the anchors was on the air. Harvey found himself unable to remember the anchorman's name—he wore his glasses on the air, which Harvey thought was dumb—and he was droning on about how important it was to cremate the bodies of anyone who dies.

"Harvey, what happened to you?"

Only then did Harvey remember that he'd left Frank in the van. "I'm fine, Dad. I mean, no, I'm not fine, but—"

"Sit down, I'll take care of that. Army taught me first aid, might as well use it."

Within minutes, he had out bandages, alcohol, cotton, paper tape, and paper towels. It stung when he rubbed the alcohol on the cut on Harvey's head after he wiped it down.

Once he taped the bandage onto Harvey's forehead, Dad said, "I'll call nine-one-one again."

"Yeah, that's a good idea. Tell them about Frank." He'd explained about what happened on Market Street while Dad dressed the wound.

Dad went over to the phone, and Harvey could hear the ringing after he dialed "1" the second time.

All he heard was ringing.

After the twelfth ring, Dad violently hung the phone up.

Just as he did, the camera cut to Harvey's interview with the cemetery caretaker at Mt. Royal.

"Why don't you wear your glasses on the television like that anchorman does?" Dad asked.

Harvey sighed. "Because I look stupid with the glasses on, Dad. Everyone does. Look, maybe I can go over the hospital, see what—"

Suddenly, Mom's body shook with a tremendous coughing fit.

"Rifka!" Dad cried, and ran over to the couch, kneeling by her side, grabbing her hands with his even as she choked out several watery, ragged coughs.

Helplessly, Harvey just stood there. He wanted to do something for his mother—and something for Frank—but calling 911 was what you were supposed to do. It was why they'd just adopted 911 for emergencies, so you didn't need to know the local precinct number or the hospital number.

But if it wasn't working . . .

Reaching into his pocket for his notebook, he flipped through the pages until he found the number for the emergency room at the Armstrong County hospital over on Route 28.

However, dialing it just got a busy signal.

He tried the Armstrong County Sheriff's Office, but that one just rang and rang like 911 did.

After slamming the phone down even harder than his father had, he started, "Dad, I'm going—"

"Rifka!"

Moving over to the sofa, Harvey saw that his mother had stopped coughing. And also stopped breathing.

Getting to his feet, Dad tugged at Harvey's arm. "You have to save her!"

"What? How?"

"Didn't you learn mouth-to-mouth that time last year?"

"I did a story on it, Dad, I never learned it."

"Why won't you help your mother?"

"Dad, there's nothing I can do! The hospital's line is busy, the cops aren't answering, I don't—"

But his father was now pounding his chest with what little strength he had. "You always hated us, you were always ashamed of us!"

"Dad, that's not fair—"

"That's why you changed your name, because you hate me and you hate that she took my name, and now you're happy she's dead!"

"Dad!" He grabbed his father's arms at the wrist. "Stop it! Listen to me, we have to burn her body."

"What?"

"We have to—"

He pulled away from Harvey's grip. "How *dare* you! How dare you reject your heritage *again* for your stupid job!"

"Dad, for pity's sake, you're not being fair! None of this has anything to do with my job! You've been watching the news, dead people are coming back to life!"

"Only the Lord can do that, and it's the Lord who tells us not to burn a body like it was trash! Get out of my house, you filth! Get *out*!"

"Dad, I—" Harvey cut himself off, and stormed past him, through the kitchen and out the back door to the yard.

As he figured, there was a pile of firewood. Dad used to cut it himself, but then he got too old, so they hired a neighborhood kid to do it.

Harvey may not have known mouth-to-mouth, but he was a Boy Scout years ago, and he knew how to start a fire.

Within minutes, he'd arranged the logs into a shape that he could put Mom's body on, and gotten them ignited.

"What are you doing? Are you trying to burn the house down?"

Turning, he saw Dad standing in the kitchen doorway.

"No, Dad, I told you—we have to burn the body."

"There is no body, you smart-aleck! She's still alive!"

Harvey whirled around to face his father, who had a very smug smile on his face. "What?"

"She's alive!" He stepped aside, and Harvey saw his mother stumbling forward toward the doorway.

His heart beating like a trip-hammer in his chest, Harvey cried out, "Dad, get out of there! Dad!"

"You never cared about us at all, did you, Harvey? No wonder you changed your—"

Then one of Mom's hands clamped down on Dad's shoulder.

"Rifka, what're you—"

And then Mom's mouth levered open and she bit Dad's neck.

Harvey couldn't tell where Dad's strangled screams ended and his own frightened screams began.

He ran to the door, pulling Dad away from Mom's attempted mastication of his neck.

Dad fell to the floor, blood pouring from his neck.

Mom started clawing at Harvey, but Harvey was able to fight her off as easily as he had done with Dad.

Then Harvey grabbed Mom's wrists the same way he'd grabbed Dad's and dragged her out to the backyard, throwing her into the fire.

Strangely, Mom didn't make a sound, didn't struggle, she just stood there, burning. The smell of acrid flesh assaulted Harvey's nostrils as he ran back to the house, grabbing Dad's much heavier body and dragging it out into the yard. Harvey had covered enough murders to know that Dad would never survive the amount of blood he'd lost that was now pooled on the kitchen's linoleum floor.

Mom was still just *standing* there, burning up. It was the strangest thing Harvey had seen. And today, that was up against some fairly stiff competition.

He dropped Dad's body into the fire at Mom's feet, hoping that the Lord would understand why he was violating the proscription against cremation.

Certainly, his father was unlikely to have ever understood.

As their bodies burned, Harvey said, "I just wanted to be a good reporter, Dad. Nobody's gonna say, 'Let's go to Harvey Lipshitz in the field' with a straight face. Lincoln was a great president. Lipshitz is a punch line. I don't know why you couldn't understand that."

After a few minutes, he found himself unable to watch anymore.

He walked around the house to Sampson Street, where he saw more people shuffling along, not picking up their feet, moving at an insanely slow pace.

One of them was Frank.

Without thinking, Harvey ran toward the little twerp, never more glad to see his idiot cameraman than he was now. "Frank, thank goodness! Get your camera, we've got to—"

But Frank hadn't stopped walking. And as soon as he was close enough, he bit down on Harvey's arm.

Harvey screamed in pain as Frank bit into him. He tried to

shake the cameraman off, but Frank wouldn't let go—he was like a dog with a bone.

He tried to pull away, but all he did was stumble backward and fall to the pavement. Frank was on top of him now, straddling him, staring down at him with milky white eyes.

I can't die like this! I can't! It's not fair!

As Frank went for his neck, Harvey's last thought was, *Since when is life fair?*

"The scene in Kittanning is a vicious one this morning, as deputies from the Armstrong County Sheriff's office have managed to capture and burn several bodies before the arrival of the National Guard to take control of the situation. I was able to briefly speak with Sheriff Emmett Nelson, who reiterated the cautions we've all heard during this horrible crisis."

"I know the government's been saying all sorts of things about what caused this, but truly, it doesn't matter where it all came from. What does matter is that everyone should stay in their homes, and if they encounter one of these ghouls, or whatever they are, to try to damage their heads or spines. That seems to kill them. And for God's sake, cremate any dead body you see! Even if it's just lighting a damn match, do something!"

"This reporter was able also to ascertain that two of the bodies that were cremated in Kittanning belonged to WIC-TV employees Harvey Lincoln and Frank DeMartino. We all mourn their loss, and those of all the other citizens who, in essence, lost their lives twice. For WIC-TV, I'm Linda Kamin. Back to you in the studio."

Neal Shusterman is the *New York Times* best-selling author of more than thirty novels for teens, including the Unwind Dystology, the Skinjacker Trilogy, *Scythe*, and *Challenger Deep*, winner of the National Book Award. He has collaborated with his son Brendan Shusterman numerous times—including stories appearing in Shaun Hutchinson's *Violent Ends* story collection and Jonathan Maberry's *Scary Out There* collection, as well as a novella in *UnBound*, a collection of tales in the Unwind world. Brendan also created the illustrations for *Challenger Deep*, and is hard at work on his debut novel. Website: www.storyman.com. Twitter: @NealShusterman. Facebook: facebook.com/nealshusterman.

DEADLINER

by Neal and Brendan Shusterman

Some people called Owen a "profiteer." But there was a much better word for it. "Survivor."

This destabilization of society—this sudden outburst of wandering dead, eating friends and neighbors—was an opportunity for a consummate survivor who could play his cards right.

He'd been a carnie for years before the outbreak. Aside from selling rubes on sucker games, society had no place for him:

he wasn't wanted. He was expected to move on when the carnival did, and he obliged. He didn't like the rubes any more than they liked him. But when the hungry dead took to the streets, he knew this could be his chance to win the big prize. They called the summer of 1967 the summer of love. 1968 had brought the summer of death.

When it had first happened, he'd just finished setting up the circus tent in Savannah, Georgia. That's when they came wandering in. He'd watched men he'd worked with for five years getting eaten alive by the incoming assault—and the carnies with enough connective tissue intact after being bitten joined the forces of the dead with a passion. On that day he saved five people, and the legend about him began to grow.

He'd killed hundreds of them in the streets and neighborhoods of Savannah over the next few weeks. He went from dirty townie to town hero. A son of the pacification. That's what they called it. "The pacification." After six months, the living dead were under control, or so the official reports said. People were advised to travel in groups, always have a weapon, and stay away from dark deserted places. A common-sense practice when your rotting mother might just show up to eat you. We could go back to worrying about the Commies, who, people agreed, were far more of a threat than zombies.

And through it all, the big top still stood. Silent. Waiting. Owen knew it was waiting for him. There would be a new show now. And Owen would be the ringmaster.

"Careful with that truck! And keep your hands away from the windows!" Owen was amazed that he had to warn his workers to be careful with the cargo. He had thought all the people without common sense had been obliterated by this new form of natural selection. But idiots were as resilient as cockroaches.

"We got seventeen," Cristoph, his lead hunter, told him. "Five fit the profile you asked for. One of them you ain't gonna believe."

But after the things he'd seen, Owen could believe anything. The hunter told him who they had. Owen believed it—but only barely.

"A grand each for the normals, five grand for the specials, and twenty for your headliner." The hunter reminded him that there had been ten men on his team when they set out. Now there were seven. "The rest got bit and had to be put down. So you'll give me ten grand each to give to their families."

Owen doubted the money would go to the families of the dead men, but that wasn't his business. He and his investors were willing to pay far more for this delivery than Cristoph was asking—so he only haggled him down a little before shaking hands.

"But you and your men will stay on," Owen insisted as part of the deal. "We'll need sharpshooters. Security. We'll work out a good wage."

Owen had a team of his roughies move the truck to the back of the circus camp. Everyone else gave it a wide berth. Owen looked to the rest of his employees. Their faces didn't look as excited as he'd imagined.

"Don't worry, y'all," he said loudly. "Hell, the lions are more dangerous than what we got in there."

"You're barbaric, Owen."

Owen turned to see Clara, the tightrope walker, watching the whole scene with a look of disgust that could have shriveled Owen in an earlier day. Clara was the best at what she did.

Everyone in his show was. The Savannah Post-Apocalyptum was truly the greatest show on earth—so great that it didn't have to move. The world came to him—not just for the acts but to see Owen himself. Such was his legend. He was a zombie-killing Buffalo Bill. The new-world P. T. Barnum. People longed to rub elbows with the man who saved Savannah. He didn't rub elbows much, but he was happy to take their money.

"Clara, this is the business," he reminded her.

"It's barbaric is what it is. I've never seen anything so inhuman in my whole life."

"What about when they were banging at your door, threatening your life?" said Harry, one of the show's clowns. He'd already gotten his makeup on for the evening's show, and it had already begun to melt off. Owen would have to make a point of scolding him for that. But for now, he was just glad the old rodeo clown had his back. He'd hired him from Texas, and he knew the man had lost a sister and an uncle to the beasts.

"You really want to treat them like us?" said Harry, with a laugh. "Lady, they *ain't us.*"

"They were like us once," muttered Clara. "This is a circus, not a . . . not a . . ."

"Circus?" suggested one of the barkers, and everyone laughed.

"Hey, if people will pay to see it, it's fair game," said the show's juggler—a young man from Philadelphia named Ronnie, who had actually helped Owen take down more than a dozen dead in the first attack. He walked over, juggling half a dozen balls at an ever increasing frequency. Then he gave Clara a seductive grin. "You like my balls? People liked my balls. Said I had great balls. Then I switched to pins." He let the balls fall and pulled out a set of pins, producing them from behind him. All part of his act. "Pins got me a bigger crowd on the midway. Flaming pins got me better tips. Then when the dead rose up, I switched to chainsaws. This is the natural progression. Don't try to fight it." Although he didn't juggle chainsaws to make his point. That was reserved for the show.

Owen could tell Clara understood but wasn't ready to accept. "It's the devil's money, then," she said.

"This is the circus," said Harry. "It's all the devil's money. Just look what you're wearing."

This got a laugh out of a few of the performers, and Owen took this opportunity to change the subject.

"We've got less than an hour till showtime. Business as usual tonight—but tomorrow we go dark for a month. We'll create a whole new show the likes of which has never been seen."

There were grumbles at the prospect of going dark, until everyone found out that they'd still get paid. The group split up—everyone went their separate ways except for Clara, who still looked at the truck. Even closed you could hear the ghastly groans from within. She turned to Owen, and rather than an insult or accusation, she softly said, "I don't think you'll be able to control them."

The simplicity of her statement, and her sincerity, gave Owen a moment's pause.

"Honey, I know them better than I know myself," he told her. "You leave it to me."

The two turned to see Cristoph and a few of his men—all with sidearms like gunslingers, rifles at the ready. They were already talking about taking shifts watching the truck of the living dead.

Clara took a deep breath. "All I know is that you don't take away the net until you're sure you're not going to fall."

Then she stormed off with the perfect gait of a tightrope walker.

Owen brought in professional makeup artists and costumers from Hollywood. "They're terrifying up close," Owen told them. "It's your job to make them look just as terrifying from a distance."

He paid the makeup artists the highest salary in the show. Although the dead were chained and shackled, when your hands are that close to such lethal mouths, it was worth quite a lot of combat pay. Owen wasn't going to begrudge them that.

One of the makeup artists—a young woman whose own perfectly designed face was testimony to her skill—burst out in tears when she saw their headliner. "I can't do this," she told Owen. "I just can't."

"She can't hurt you," Owen reminded the girl. "We have her secured so tightly, she can't even move her head."

But the girl quit anyway.

Owen brought in the best lighting and set designers. He hired special-effects coordinators.

"I want the audience to be three seconds from pissing their pants," he told them. "We want them to forget that there's a fence between them and the dead."

Within just a few short weeks, they had the ultimate act. Word got out and the Post-Apocalyptum, which was already wildly successful, became insanely so. Ticket sales were through the roof, even with prices jacked up beyond anything anyone ought to pay.

Owen's investors—dark-suited men who were either too fat

or too gaunt, and looked a bit like the living dead themselves, were both optimistic and nervous. "This act of yours had better deliver," they told Owen.

He despised that he had to answer to them, but his confidence did not falter. "This is more than a gold mine," he told them. "It's a mint. After opening night, it'll be like printing our own money."

Cristoph, although a standoffish and unpleasant man, turned out to be quite a wrangler of the dead. Yes, he had hunted them up, but more than that, he took care of them. He got rancid meat from the market—because it was the only thing they'd eat other than human flesh. He made sure their chains were loose when they were in the truck, and broke the nose of one of the carnies who was getting his kicks tormenting them. Cristoph had worked as a zookeeper before the outbreak, specializing in venomous snakes, but he was well acquainted with the particular hazards of circus animals. What were the living dead but another deadly animal to control?

"I would like very much for you to be a part of the act," Owen told Cristoph.

"Me? What would I do? I'm not like you; I'm not a showman."

"You wrangle the dead better than anyone. Every animal act needs its tamer. Who better than you?"

Although Cristoph's agreement was reluctant, within days he was owning it like it had been his idea. The man actually cracked a smile as afternoon faded to twilight on opening night.

"You may actually pull this off," he told Owen.

Although Cristoph didn't know it, that vote of confidence changed everything. It gave Owen the nerve he needed to really take the show to the next level.

* * *

An hour before the audience was to be let in, he gathered everyone in the back room, and informed his performers that he was having the safety fence between the audience and the ring taken down.

"Owen, are you sure?" asked Harry, his painted clown smile obscuring his true face, masking the depth of his concern. "I've seen those things . . . how they . . . *operate* . . . up close."

"The danger has to seem real," Owen said. "You've seen Cristoph working with them. He can handle them—and if it starts to go south in any way, he'll have six sharpshooters in plain view, with clear shots."

Owen looked to the back of the room and met Clara's eyes. The volcanic look on her face made him quickly look away.

"This is lunacy!" she shouted. "Doesn't anyone else here see how wrong this is? Hasn't anyone else lost someone to them? Or seen a relative become one?"

"I saw my sister get bitten, and my mother," said Horace, an old clown Owen had hired from a circus in Ohio. "Then they both came after me. It was my neighbor what put 'em down."

"I killed eighteen of 'em," said a young clown named Ralphy. "Used my dad's old truck. Ran 'em right over. These things ain't fast and they ain't smart. But still . . . one bite . . . For my dad it was barely a knick on his finger, but that's all it took. It wasn't long till he was one of them. In the end, I runt him over, too."

The testimonies were sobering, and left everyone in silence, suddenly transported back to their first encounters with the epidemic.

"Yeah, I lost people," said Gloria, an old showgirl who had

become a sort of mentor to the newer girls. "I'll never forget that. But I'm not gonna let that cheat me out of good money. These things nearly ended us. I say we put 'em onstage and prove to the world that the show must go on."

A few "here, here's" and claps were given, and Owen breathed a sigh of relief. No one seemed to agree with Clara, who threw her hands up, in far too much shock at her fellow performers to say anything.

"There are always frightful acts in a circus," said Ronnie, the juggler, as he tossed a few balls in one hand. "Always been that way. A circus is about the shock, and the awe. What's more shocking than the things we most fear, forced to perform for our amusement?"

Standing room only.

The audience couldn't get in fast enough when the doors were opened. They practically crawled over each other to get in, just like the dead. *People need this*, thought Owen. *This is a necessary public service.*

Each performer did their part to make it the best show they'd ever had. The clowns, led by Harry, made the audience laugh louder than Owen had ever heard them laugh. The trapeze acrobats were in perfect form, leaving the crowd with stars in their eyes. The only glitch was the tightrope act. Which was a no-show. Clara had up and left without even as much as a note. Her loss. The girl had walked away from a million-dollar career.

It was all going wonderfully as the evening inched ever closer to Owen's big reveal. It was as though he could hear the electric buzz through the audience, the anticipation of what was to come. And he, being the ringmaster, kept everything in line.

When Ronnie's juggling act had finished, Owen raced out into the ring.

"And now, ladies and gentlemen! The moment you've all been waiting for! We bring you something terrifying that may shock the younger viewers of the audience. Can you hear them? Scrape scrape scraping at your door? Can you smell them? Mouths dripping with the unthinkable? Behold! The most terrifying of all acts ever brought to you on any stage . . . the living dead!"

The crowd gasped in shock as two great doors opened in the back of the tent. The dead shambled out of the darkness, with Larry and Carl, two of the troop's strongmen, holding them at bay with chains. A light came up on Cristoph, whip in one hand. Pistol in the other.

"Now, ladies and gentlemen, don't be alarmed," Owen bellowed to the gasping crowds. "Those chains are tempered steel. And as you can see, they are happy to make your acquaintance!"

The crowd's terror quickly turned into laughter, as they saw that the living dead had been done up to look like clowns; faces painted, costumed. As sinister as they were hysterical. Then the second wave was sent out, held by two more strongmen. These were not dressed as clowns. Their outfits were tattered, of course, but they wore replicas of what they had worn in life.

"In fact," continued Owen. "Some of them you might already be acquainted with."

Now the spotlight began to single out five of the "special" subjects that Cristoph's team had been so lucky to catch. The first subject was hit by the spotlight. The audience began to murmur their both gleeful and horrified surprise even before Owen announced the name of the former senator from South Carolina.

The dead senator put up his limp hands to shield his glazed eyes from the bright light. Then he fixed his attention on a pretty young thing in the audience, and stalked toward her, bent on feasting. The strongmen holding him pretended to drop the chains. The audience screamed. Cristoph snapped his whip and the dead senator fell back away, subdued. All part of the show.

"And to the left—you knew him as the king of late-night talk shows. But he's not doing much talking now!"

The dead talk show host wandered to the left and right. Uttered a moan that eerily sounded like the voice America knew all too well.

Then came the TV housewife who used to share her favorite recipes on TV, but was no longer quite the picky eater she once was.

And the comedian famous for his goofy roles, but none goofier than his final one. They were subdued by Cristoph, and forced to do tricks to the delighted disbelief of the audience. The living dead might be mindless—but they were trainable!

Then the lights dimmed, and a hush fell over the big top.

"And now," Owen said. "I give you the star of our show. The headliner of headliners. A woman who needs no introduction . . ."

The spotlight came on, and there, in a pool of light, wearing a tattered replica of the gold gown she wore to last year's Oscars, was the movie star whose gorgeous face was once the subject of countless billboards. Whose violet eyes captivated millions. Who was Helen of Troy and Cleopatra combined. Now her jaw was slack, and her cheeks sunken. Her once-beautiful face now held the pallor of the grave without a grave to go with it. The audience gasped and groaned and wailed. What was it the juggler had said? Shock and Awe? This crowd was certainly getting their money's worth.

This was Owen's shining moment. In his youth, he had always dreamed of meeting her. What he might say if he did. How he might win her heart. Now he had her. Not in a way he ever expected, but she was here. It's true that all things come to those who wait.

For the other subjects, it was simple tricks, but not for the star of stars. She was better than that. She deserved something special. The men holding her let her chains go slack. Cristoph backed away, and Owen stepped forward.

"Dance for us, Miss Taylor," Owen said. "Dance for us!"

The dead movie star began to move her feet. She shuffled to the left. To the right. Her shoulders rolled. Her arms stayed limp. She was dancing the dance of the dead. And the audience slowly began to applaud, getting louder and louder until it rose into a fever pitch.

"Do you hear that, Miss Taylor? Do you hear it? You are still a star!"

Then she lurched forward with a throaty snarl, only to have one of the strongmen pull back on her chains.

As the cheers rose, Owen lifted his hands in triumph.

Then a sudden groan from behind him caught his attention. At first he thought it was one of the dead, but when he turned, he saw that it was Cristoph. He had dropped his whip, as well as his gun, and was down on one knee, holding his chest. He was pale. Very pale.

Owen hurried to him. "What are you doing? Get up! You have to get up, the act isn't over!"

"H . . . h . . . heart attack," Cristoph gasped.

"No! You can't! Not now!"

"All the . . . the . . . excitement. All the . . . all the."

Cristoph's strength completely left him and he sprawled in the sawdust of the ring, gasping, grimacing, then was silent.

And the dead knew.

They saw that their wrangler—the only one who could truly keep them at bay—was down.

Owen knew what was going to happen a moment before it did, and he was powerless to stop it. Almost as if they had one thought—one mind—the dead pulled on their chains with strength that seemed beyond human. In all the rehearsals in all the weeks leading up to this, they had never shown such strength. They pulled the strongmen at the other ends of their chains to them. The men tried to get away, but there were just too many of the dead. No, they weren't smart. Yes, they moved slowly. But in numbers, the dead can do anything.

The strongmen didn't stand a chance.

When the audience saw the blood—saw the bits of flesh being ripped away—and realized this was not part of the show, they panicked. They began to mob the exits—but the exits were too small, and the crowd too dense.

And the dead, with no one to hold them back, began advancing on the crowd.

"Everyone, please! Please stay calm!"

But no one was listening to Owen anymore.

A rifle shot rang out. One of the dead—the senator—was taken down, but there were still sixteen already climbing over the first row of seats to get to the scrambling audience. A second shot rang out, missed the mark completely, and killed a man in the audience who was in the wrong place at the wrong time.

That's when Cristoph's sharpshooters abandoned their posts and ran, deciding it was every man for himself.

Maybe if he hadn't been so confident, Owen might have armed himself with a gun. But there was no time to think of that now. The shock was all he could focus on. The awe of seeing his life crash and burn.

The dead reached the audience. They feasted. They bit as many as they could. Owen fell to his knees. He watched as more and more people went down, and he knew that this would not end here. This tent would be the vector of a new epidemic. A new outbreak of living death.

Then he heard a groan that was far too close for comfort. He turned to see the movie star standing ten feet from him. She was still shuffling from one foot to another, her tattered gold dress fluttering in the breeze coming in from the exits. The living were gone. The dead littered the stands . . . dozens upon dozens of them—too many to count . . . and they were all beginning to rise.

The movie star gazed at him, her eyes cloudy, but still that shade of violet that made them so captivating. She began to shuffle forward, her head lolling to one side, her hands reaching toward him, her teeth snapping in anticipation.

She was not beautiful anymore, but then all beauty fades. Who was Owen to judge such things? There was the beauty of life, there was the peace of death, and now there was the terrible netherworld between.

Owen stood, dusted off his ringmaster's jacket, and held out his arms. "Shall we dance, Miss Taylor?"

And he let her take him into her cold embrace.